I CAN'T BREATHE!

LIBBY, MONTANA 1958

H. M. Bowker

ISBN: 069222002X
ISBN 13: 9780692220023
Library of Congress Control Number: 2014909002
H. M. Bowker, Shoreline WA

Professional Reviews

Kirkus Review:
In this debut novel, horrific health issues and other troubles plague the Bowman family and other residents of the small mining town of Libby, Montana.

. . . Debut novelist Bowker, a native of a real-life mining town of the same name, notes at the end that "a great deal of truth often comes to life through fiction." She provides heartbreaking tableaux of life in Libby, such as the Hardin children playing with asbestos dust that litters their home. Yet this town's asbestos problem takes a rather surprising back seat to Bowker's engulfing, powerful story of Betty's abuse. These and other competing plot threads occasionally threaten to overwhelm the narrative, but the story gains clarity and momentum . . . and almost always, sadly, has the ring of truth. . . fascinating, ultimately absorbing tale.

A multilayered melodrama with a documentarylike feel.

Foreword Clarion Review:
The compelling and chilling story of corporate and child abuse is one that needs to be told.

H. M. Bowker's mystery novel, *I Can't Breathe! Libby, Montana 1958*, is a tale of child abuse, death, and corporate exploitation of human life . . . Libby is a very small town in northwestern Montana that was the site of one of the worst environmental disasters in US history. The town was dominated for much of the twentieth century by an asbestos mine. The material from the mine infiltrate the entire town, and hundreds, if not thousands, of people got sick from their exposure to the asbestos. Bowker builds on this history to craft a plot that explores both corporate abuse and child abuse. She creates a truly dark world in which there are few heroes . . . a riveting and enlightening plot. And, overall, the novel tells a compelling and chilling story.

DISCLAIMER

This is a work of fiction. Names, characters, businesses, places, events, and incidents are either the products of the author's imagination or used in a fictitious manner. Any resemblance to actual persons, living or dead, or actual events is purely coincidental.

ACKNOWLEDGMENTS

Thank you, Jennifer Hager, for your developmental editing services and your kind and thoughtful encouragement. Jennifer Hager can be found online as an editor in Bainbridge Island, Washington.

Thank you, Greg Smith, my former student at Twin Bridges High School, for your professional advice in regard to psychological character development. I appreciate Greg's dedication to defending the rights of others on a daily basis. Greg can be found online as D. Greg Smith in Seattle, Washington and Bozeman, Montana.

Thank you, Amy Phillips, for your thorough content review, as well as your moral support throughout the creation of this novel. Amy Phillips is an attorney in the Seattle area. More importantly, she is my daughter.

Thank you, everyone, who reports abuse and at least tries to protect children and adults from abuse and neglect. A phone call or a written letter explaining the suspected abuse to someone who can change a person's life from fear and pain to a safe and hopeful situation truly makes our world a better place. Corporate abuse touches every one of us, and those who keep companies honest serve us all.

DEDICATION

I dedicate this book to:

- Claudia and Charlotte, my sisters, and to Everett, Clarence, Melvin, and Duane, my brothers. We shared an unusual, disconnected, and painful family life, with each of us experiencing growing up, as well as adulthood, differently.
- My parents. Everything we experience as children contributes to what we become as adults. The good things make us better; the bad things teach us what not to repeat in our own lives. It is up to each of us to make the right choices for a good life.
- Everyone in Libby who personally experienced illness and death due to asbestos-related causes, including my family members, classmates, neighbors, and friends.
- The *Seattle Post-Intelligencer* and the *Seattle Times* for breaking the news about the environmental disaster the black mountain of asbestos created locally for Libby miners, their families, and the residents, as well as the national and international deaths related to the asbestos ore. Government help eventually resulted from the exposure in the news and other research many writers and environmentalists contributed to exposing what may have been the worst environmental disaster in the United States.
- My immediate family who shared every day with me while I wrote this book. Thank you.

AUTOBIOGRAPHY

H. M. Bowker grew up in Libby, Montana. She attended Carroll College in Helena, Montana, majoring in English and minoring in sociology and education. She taught high school and middle school English and art for seventeen years. Then she earned a master's degree in educational leadership from the University of Montana. She was a secondary principal for six years. In 1989, she completed her PhD in educational leadership at Gonzaga University. She served as superintendent for nine years. Her family includes her husband, Michael, and her children, Kirk, Amy, and Jake. They live near Seattle, Washington.

FOREWORD

*S*he heard the floorboards creak—a warning of the pain to come. Would tonight be the belt cutting into her flesh? The suffocating pillow stopping her breathing until she lost consciousness? Or just the whispers threatening death?

I Can't Breathe! is a mystery novel that takes place in Libby, Montana, in 1958. For the three Bowman sisters, life consisted of hanging on to the lower rungs of hell with no hope and no way out. Their mother, Betty, and the girls protected their dark secret of abuse for years. In the fall of 1958, the Bowman family faced challenges that changed all their lives in a community that held a horrendous, deadly, and massive secret of corporate abuse.

From 1919 until 1993, Libby was the location of the Zonolite Mine, which produced asbestos ore used in hundreds of products that were made throughout the United States and internationally. Asbestos was the miracle product that kept homes and businesses warm in winter; it protected ships, automobiles, and buildings from the devastation of fire. Time and science proved that the ore from the Zonolite Mine also guaranteed death. Sometimes death came through short-term cancer or one of several lung diseases; the painful dying process could take less than a year or in excess of forty years. People breathed its dust into their lungs or ingested it by mouth. Not one death certificate in Libby noted an asbestos-related cause of death through all the years from the 1920s through the 1990s. With no hard statistics made public prior to 1958, the number of deaths from asbestos contaminating human bodies is only a guess. There is no way to accurately document the devastation asbestos caused in Libby or in the many places throughout the world where asbestos from Libby was sold and used as a base ingredient in countless products. Present documentation notes that the death rate in Libby was 80 percent higher per capita than in any other city in the United States. In 2014, over thirty million homes in the United States have Zonolite vermiculite (with asbestos) insulation in their walls and attics. Breathing gets to be serious business when the thought of the needlelike fibers hooking into the lungs becomes a current reality and a threat to a person's life simply by breathing the air in one's home.

A mystery of abuse and death weaved its way into Libby in the late 1950s. Corporate abuse held Libby community members captive as they breathed the poisonous air from the Zonolite Mining Company. The Bowman family hid dark secrets of child abuse. The public school harbored a sexual abuser. And then there were the missing children. Who took the children? Why? What happened to them? The discovery of a child's body in a shallow grave had broader implications than the sheriff could understand, unfolding in a community where death was given in exchange for a paycheck, and where child sexual and physical abuse were as commonplace as the people were willing to allow.

LIBBY, MONTANA, 1957

The Montana Power Company needed to rewire the six-story dry mill, an old, dust-filled building at the Zonolite Mining Company six miles north of Libby. The foreman laid out the plans for the crew to take out the old system of wiring for lighting and other electrical services in the dry mill. They had to encase all the wiring safely in conduit to protect the electrical system from the unusual amount of dust in that six-story building. The dust was so bad in the dry mill that the men cleaning it out on a weekly basis could hardly see their progress.

Eric Bowman had a twofold purpose for wanting to be part of the crew on that assignment. He had heard that Zonolite was the best place to work in the area. Wages were higher than he was making at the power company, and pay was time and a half when overtime was available. The real benefit that made it desirable was health care. No place in the area had health care that came close to equaling Zonolite benefits. He wanted to look the place over with the idea of changing jobs in the future.

The following morning, Eric joined his crew in the power company truck and followed a Zonolite bus up Pipe Creek Road to the mine. He was impressed with the size of the mining operation. From the sixth floor of the building they were wiring, Eric could easily look out and see the huge dark mountain of ore. Not even a blade of grass grew on that huge black mountain. There would be work here for hundreds of years, he thought, based on the size of that mountain. He put on his mask, required by Montana Power, and began removing the old wiring. In less than fifteen minutes, his mask was clogged. He could hardly breathe. His boss insisted that his crew continue wearing masks no matter how badly the dust jammed up their masks. The men were allowed to take off the masks, shake them to clear the dust, and then put them back on. Eric noticed a row of masks hanging on hooks along the walls. Most of the Zonolite workers obviously did not wear their masks. Somehow they managed to get their work done. He reluctantly followed his crew boss's directive; so did the rest of the crew.

As the men worked their way through the building, Eric could not help but notice the unusual amount of dust and powder being swept and shoveled onto metal chutes. Several men on each floor swept dust from the top floor down the six floors. By the time the dust reached the bottom floor, the workers were up to their thighs in powder, trying to get it contained and out of the building. He learned that new mining employees were assigned to this building as their entry-level position. From there, if they seemed to have a strong work ethic and they could take the dusty conditions, they were transferred to other mining areas. Eric was only in the dry mill for less than a week. Even though he worked strictly on wiring, for him the dust was intolerable.

At the end of each day, the power truck, with crew standing on the running boards and hanging on to the ladders to keep from dusting up the inside of the truck, drove around the mining area just to see what it was like. Eric was impressed with the outdoor activity, which had at least thirty workers driving large equipment and moving piles of black and gray waste off to the slag piles. Most of the miners were out of his view, chipping ore out of the tunnels and grooves in the huge mountain, solidly made of vermiculite and tremolite ore, and filling the railroad cars with ore.

On the third day at Zonolite, a messenger from the mining office asked Eric to come with him. Mr. Lovett, the general manager at Zonolite, had sent for Eric specifically.

"You're Eric Bowman, right?"

"Yes, sir. That's my name. And you are?" Eric shook his hand.

"Come on in and have a seat. I'm Laurence Lovett. Just call me Larry." Larry closed the door, handed Eric a cup of coffee, and then asked him a few questions about what had brought him to Libby.

Eric gave him a quick overview of serving in the navy during World War II in both the Atlantic and the Pacific. "I worked in the navy's San Francisco shipyard for ten years after the war. That's where I received training in electrical engineering." He left out the part about his fiancée leaving him for someone else. "I have family here and like the idea of small-town living. My dad lives here. Dewey Bowman. Why are you asking? You can be sure that Montana Power wouldn't send you someone who couldn't take care of your wiring."

"Oh, I'm not a bit worried about that. Not a bit." Larry laughed and shifted around in his chair. "I know Dewey. He owns the music store. Nice place. We bought our son's trumpet from Dewey." Eric had impressed Larry the first time he saw him with the Montana Power crew in Libby. Eric was charming, friendly, and competent. When his boss bragged to Larry about what a find he had just hired, Larry knew he had to steal that man for Zonolite.

"I'll get right to the point, Eric. I need a top-notch electrician here, and I've heard you fit that description. Have you ever thought about taking a management job that challenges you and that really puts your training to work?"

"I like my job at Montana Power. They're fair with me. It's true that I am not in management like I was in the navy—but I think that'll change in time."

"Would you consider working here in a leadership position—now?"

"To tell you the flat-out truth, working in all that dust worries me. I don't breathe that well in the dust building—the dry mill. It's overpowering." Eric figured that would be the end of the offer.

"That's just 'nuisance dust' and it's not dangerous in any way," Larry assured Eric. "I wouldn't let our men work in dangerous conditions. Heck, I wouldn't work here myself if there was a problem. If you take this job, you'll experience very little dust. We need someone to organize and manage a major wiring overhaul, and to keep us lighted and heated in the process. You'd have a leadership position with a crew to help you revamp and update our entire electrical system. Excellent pay, health insurance, and a strong retirement benefit if you work here until you turn sixty—or twenty years. Every job doesn't have that full benefit, but the one I'm offering you does—and I'll put that in writing!" Larry was impressed with Eric, who was at least six feet tall and whose dark hair and strong and handsome facial features looked strikingly like his father's.

"I have to say, that sounds good."

"Think about it, Eric. Let's talk on Friday. I'll take you on a special tour then and you can see just what you'd be doing for our company." Larry Lovett stood up, Eric did too, and the men shook hands. Eric liked him, and he liked the offer. He also had some time to think about it.

The Zonolite Mining Company was the second largest employer of local workers. Zonolite's various asbestos products were sold to construction companies, ship builders, automotive companies, and agricultural products providers. The mine was located six miles north of Libby on Pipe Creek Road. Products from the ore, and the ore itself, were sent on the Great Northern Railway all over the United States and to harbors that shipped the ore to several foreign countries. Over time, the unusual, amazing asbestos made the mine owners rich. Vermiculite asbestos was laid in blankets or shoveled into the walls and attic areas to insulate against cold weather, as well as limit noise. It was reasonably priced and easy to use. Sheets of asbestos protected houses from burning by lining wall areas behind stoves and fireplaces. In commercial buildings and large ships, pipes and electrical wiring had layers of asbestos sealing them for fire protection because asbestos did not burn. Asbestos was added to concrete to make it stronger and paint to make it smoother and more durable.

Libby's city park had large piles of vermiculite asbestos. Kids played and jumped in it, throwing it up in the air, and rolling in it. The track fields and baseball fields contained all the free asbestos Zonolite gave them—and they gave it out generously to the city, the schools, and to any individuals who wanted to haul it away.

Each night that week, Eric had swept off his work clothing and washed everything he had worn that day, and then hung the items on a clothesline in the backyard. He could still see the dust, even after washing and drying the clothing. The company did not have a place for the workers to clean up, so the men shared their head-to-toe dust with their families each day.

That Friday, Eric took the guided tour. Larry guided him through the mining areas and gave him a quick history of the mine, which had opened in 1919. He brought him into the administration building and introduced him to his office—if he chose to take the job—and the part-time secretary he would share with two other people. When Larry told him how much he would make, Eric was silently impressed. *More money and no dust in sight!* The figure was almost twice what he was making at the power company.

"Within the next four months, the company plans to start a new operation that will change how we process the ore. A major part of that change depends on a whole new wiring setup. With your electrical engineering training from the navy, you have just what we need to make this change possible." And again, Larry told him to think it over. "Let me know within the next two weeks—no rush. But the offer may not come again because we want to fill the position as soon as possible. If you can handle management—you know, designing this process and organizing a crew to put it together—your pay will take a huge jump over my last quote." Larry definitely had Eric's attention. Eric wanted to accept the job right then, but he knew that he made better decisions when he took his time to think things out. He also wanted to talk to his dad before he made it final.

"This all sounds excellent, Larry. I'll be getting back to you soon." Eric and Larry shook hands, and Eric joined his crew for the ride back to Libby. His crew foreman was sweeping down the men to limit the dust in the power truck. Eric held up his hands and turned around slowly for the sweeping process. He looked forward to a full body wash and the end of the dusty week at Zonolite. *I think I'll throw these clothes away. They'll never come clean.* Eric reviewed Larry's offer in his mind as he traveled back to Libby through the beautiful forest. The rugged Cabinet Mountains captured Eric's eyes as the sun reflected against the snowy peaks at day's end.

"The dust turned a paradise into the worst of America's killing fields, a name at the top of the list that includes Love Canal, Times Beach, and Woburn. A place now known to be deadlier than all the others on the list put together. Libby." *An Air that Kills* by Andrew Schneider and David McCumber, 2004

.

SUMMER 1958

The Bowman girls ran confidently on the rocky path to the Hardin place, a half-mile from their home. Julie, fourteen, kept the lead most of the time; she paused to hold back branches for her six-year-old sister. She lifted Helen onto her back. Helen gladly took the piggyback ride. Julie looked out for her little sister and warned, "Hang on! We're halfway there!" when Helen waved her arms in the air. She held Helen's knees securely as they ran along the path. The girls were headed for Kelly and Adam Holland's ranch. The four of them were going swimming in Granite Creek.

The hill path ran parallel to Market Road in a densely wooded area behind the few houses along the gravel road. The girls climbed through the fence that surrounded the Hardin place and sat down for a few moments to catch their breath. "You are really fast, Julie! Thanks for the ride." Helen smiled. Julie hugged her. The girls loved getting to go to the Holland place and Granite Creek. They especially felt a sense of freedom in being away from their mother, Betty, whose moods changed arbitrarily from sadness to anger. Julie's bruised thigh made getting up and down difficult, but it didn't affect her running ability.

"Come on!" Helen tugged in an effort to help Julie stand. "Your bruise is darker today." Helen's brown eyes welled up with tears. "Why does Mom do that?"

Julie used Helen's help to get up, hoping Helen would shift her sadness about the bruise to a sense of confidence in helping Julie stand. "Darker means it's getting better. Hey, how did you get so

strong? You are really tough, little sis. Let me see those muscles."
Julie loved Helen so very much and feared for her safety every day.

Helen held up her skinny arm, bent into an "L" shape, and
cupped her muscle with her other hand. "See? I am strong!" She
arched her back and jutted her chin forward with a determined look
on her face. Julie smiled at her, reached over and felt Helen's tiny
bulging muscle with admiration, then tousled her curly hair and
kissed her cheek affectionately.

"Yes, you are strong, sweetie. That's a fine muscle for sure." The
two girls walked across the vacant Hardin ranch to reach Market
Road. They continued on to the Holland ranch and then to the icy-
cold Granite Creek to swim and ride the rapids.

3

THE HARDIN FAMILY, 1956

The Hardin family started getting sick in 1954. They had moved away in 1956 after Alan Hardin lost his job at the mine. He had worked for Zonolite for several years, and he liked his job. The year before the family moved, Alan Hardin had to call in sick often. When he told his supervisor that he thought the dust from the mine was causing his illness, the manager arranged for their company doctor to examine him. According to the doctor, Alan had heart disease, a condition unrelated to his job at the mine. "What about my breathing, Doc? I can't seem to catch a breath. How can it be my heart?" Alan's doctor explained that his diseased heart made him feel weak—too weak to breathe deeply. A few months later, the company let him go for missing too much work. The family moved to Nevada to live with Alan's sister.

An empty house can be an invitation for trouble, but no one seemed to bother that place. The cleanup spot where Alan's wife, Sarah, swept the dust from his work clothes was still covered with layers of powdered asbestos. Nearby were the boys' intricate trails, Popsicle stick bridges, and roads where they ran their toy trucks and cars. The boys built the toy roads and hills with tremolite asbestos. How could they know then that the dust was killing all of them?

Except for the path the children made when they played cowboys and Indians on the hill, or when they crossed Market Road to go to the creek, nothing happened at the empty Hardin place. But that day the girls saw several sets of footprints on the porch steps marked in black tremolite. The fresh footprints belonged to both adults and kids.

"Remember how much fun we had with Tommy and Billy?" Julie asked Helen.

"I don't remember them like you do, Julie. I was just a kid."

Julie and Kelly especially liked playing with Tommy, who was their age and in their class in school. Billy was eight and bossy, which did him little good when playing with the older kids. They ignored his demands nicely and played with him anyway. Julie looked up at the platform in the two large oak trees beside the Hardin house; her memories of playing with Tommy and Billy were as strong as ever.

The boys were good at creating games, and they both rode fast on their horses in the Holland fields. Tommy was able to climb the tree faster than the girls could walk up the rope ladder until the fall of 1955. He gradually gave up trying to move fast and ride hard. Billy slowed down even more than Tommy. During recess at school, Tommy used to swing so high, the chains buckled; he'd bail out and keep running when the bell rang. The last few months of school, he quit pumping up the swing. Julie hadn't seen him bail out for months. The summer of 1956 the family moved to Nevada.

Helen ran over to the rope ladder and climbed up. Julie followed her. "Let's just stay a couple of minutes and then go swim." Helen agreed. Climbing that ladder and sitting on the platform in the trees was sort of a ritual for the girls since the boys had moved away. They patted the ribbons on the tree trunk, then climbed down, crossed Market Road, and headed for the Holland ranch.

4

TOMMY HARDIN

In the spring of 1954, Tommy talked to his folks about putting a tree house in the two big trees by the front porch. The trees were strong and their huge trunks and lower branches were naturally aligned to hold a sizeable structure. Alan Hardin brought home some lumber for the flooring and the steps and several feet of strong rope to make a ladder. The building supplies stayed in a pile in the barn for months, and every time Tommy walked by the beams and the lumber, he wanted that tree house even more. He stepped up with his chores and helped out in more obvious ways to get his dad to notice how good and cooperative he was. Tommy knew his dad wanted to build it, but his dad was often too tired after work at the mine or from fixing up their place to take on the project. *If I do more work around here, Dad will have more time to work on the tree house.* Tommy picked the right moment and used his most persuasive manner.

"Dad, you know that lumber in the barn? I think it wants to be up in those two trees out front." *I won't beg or get pushy. Come on, Dad!* Tommy smiled in his crooked, charming way and waited.

"I get the message, son. I have to say your help around here has been real good. Your mom appreciates it, too. Let's get on it the first weekend school lets out for the summer—that's just a month away. How's that sound?" Tommy's eyes lit up and his smile broadened into a big old grin. He tried to stay calm so his dad wouldn't think he was silly or immature, but he broke his attempt at being calm by giving his dad a big hug.

When the bus let the boys off the last day of school, Tommy and Billy were ready to build a tree house. After work that night, Alan Hardin cut the four-by-fours. On Saturday, Alan and Tommy nailed the floorboards onto the four-by-four frame, creating an eight-by-eight-foot platform. Julie and Kelly were lucky enough to come by, and Mr. Hardin let the girls pound in a few nails just for fun. Julie could see that Tommy was excited. *How are they going to get this floor up in the two trees?* Julie curiously watched the progress and waited to see how the platform was going to end up above ground.

Alan invited a couple of neighbors to help put the platform in the two trees. Julie's dad, Dewey, Tom Holland, and Alan made up the crew. It took the three men about two hours to secure it into the two trees. The men provided the labor and Sarah Hardin supplied the lemonade and cookies. Tommy and Billy were the first kids to climb the rope ladder and try out the floor of the tree house.

Just having the floor in the trees was exciting. The boys could climb up and down, haul some toys up for a different place to play, and see the world from another angle. Julie and Kelly loved climbing up the rope ladder. That platform was a pirate ship, the moon, the Eiffel Tower, the top of a mountain, or any place the children's imaginations took them. Tommy mastered riding his horse up to the rope ladder, grabbing it, and swinging onto it in true hero fashion. Tommy was content for a while with just the platform, but eventually he hoped it would have walls and a roof. Tommy had won a blue ribbon and a red ribbon in the school track meet. He was proud of those ribbons and attached them to a branch above the platform. Over time, he added simple treasures to the branches, giving the place personality. Billy kept a few special toys up there, too. Alan knew the boys were eager for a roof and walls, but he wasn't feeling well enough to get the job underway. By the next summer, Alan was having serious breathing problems—and so was Tommy. Within the next six months, the whole family was sick.

The boys missed school frequently. When they were feeling okay, they were great at creating games, and they rode fast on their horses in the Holland field. Their last year before they moved to Nevada, the boys stopped going to school regularly because they were sick, and their mom was even sicker. Sarah Hardin struggled getting out of bed.

Profits poured into the mining company while the dust captured victims like the Hardin family: quietly, over time. With the ease of a python, those fine particles gently but surely took each victim's breath away. All Sarah and Alan could do was try to take care of each other and their boys while the deadly results of asbestos exposure took its slow, painful course.

One summer day in 1956 before the Hardins moved away, Julie climbed the rope ladder to play with Tommy on her way to Kelly's. Tommy was lying on his back, looking at the cloudless sky. Julie said a quick "hi" and sat down by him.

"This is a good place to take a nap. I'm going to Kelly and Adam's. Can you come?"

"No. I don't think so." Tommy wheezed in air. Each breath was a chore. His throat sounded like he had to strain for any air, and his stomach muscles tightened with each effort. The sound of the air being sucked into Tommy's lungs was so much more than inhaling. Tommy had to beg the air to come into his body, and he seemed close to giving up with each effort.

Julie lay on her back and looked up at the sky. "It's so beautiful up here. Whatcha thinking about, Tommy?" *How did he even get up here?*

"I'm wondering how far up there heaven is and if it's real. Do you believe there's a heaven?"

"Looks like there's a lot of room for it. Sure, I believe in heaven. Might as well."

"It won't be long." Tommy paused to take in air. "I guess I'll know for sure one way or another."

Julie sat up and looked intensely into Tommy's eyes. "Why won't it be long? What do you mean—long until what?"

Tommy looked straight at Julie as though he wasn't sure just what to say. *Will she believe me?* "Doc says I'm dying." Tommy coughed his soft, painful, raspy cough that wheezed its way out of his mouth. He used a damp cloth to wipe his mouth; the cloth had spots of blood on it. "One day I won't get in any air at all, and I'll just stop breathing."

Julie's throat tightened. She didn't know what to say. Ever since she'd met him, Tommy used to run so fast that nobody could catch him. He jumped up on his horse and raced like the wind, always nosing out the other kids. He loved his horse, but he hadn't been riding for quite a while. Julie wanted to tell him that he wasn't dying and not to talk like that. But she didn't say anything. She put her hand on his shoulder to let him know she cared. *He might really be dying. He looks so sick.* Julie could not tell him that he looked like he was ready to die.

"I've been thinkin' about dying for quite a while. Our whole family is sick, and the doctor told Dad he was dying, and that we all have his sickness, even Billy. Mom tries to take care of us, but she's sick, too." Tommy started coughing and wheezing. He had to sit up. Julie helped him, feeling his thinness, like a skeleton barely covered with skin. "I just can't breathe. It hurts to try." He was struggling for air, yet he kept trying to talk.

"When I die, I'm gonna come back to this tree house and lie here looking at the sky. If you think about it, come back here and talk to me. Maybe I'll hear you. If I can talk at all—being dead, you know—if I can talk, I'll tell you what it's like."

Julie put her arms around him when he stopped coughing and patted his back. "I hope you don't die, Tommy." She felt tears come. He used to be so strong and fast. Somehow he withered into weakness and sadness. *It's not fair. It's not right. Kids aren't supposed to die!* Julie couldn't stop her tears and sobbed into his shoulder.

"Will you come back here, Julie? You and Kelly and Adam? Will you come up here and talk to me after I die? It would help me to know you all will be here. I love this place, and I'll miss you guys." Tommy cried softly as he rested his head on her. Even holding his head up took effort he had trouble finding in his weakened condition.

"We will, Tommy. I'll tell Kelly and Adam, and we'll come here and talk to you." Julie attempted to lift the sadness. "You might get well, you know. You could get better."

"Sure. That could happen." Tommy lifted himself from Julie's arms. "You go play. And tell Adam and Kelly what I said. I'm gonna rest for a while." Julie helped Tommy lie down. He turned to his side, wheezing painfully in and out, and she thought he fell asleep. Julie patted his arm and sat beside him crying softly. Before she left, she cupped her hand carefully by his nose and mouth so she could feel his breath. *What if he died right here, right now?* When she was sure he was only sleeping, she climbed down and went to Kelly's house.

5

GRANITE CREEK, JUNE 1958

Julie and Helen crossed Market Road to the Holland ranch on the other side. Clumps of trees here and there along the fence line shaded them on a hot day. Cattle grazed on the west field and horses grabbed and pulled up strands of grass in the other fields. Just past the Holland barn, Granite Creek roared with cold, rushing water melted from the snowpack in the Cabinet Mountain Wilderness. Neighboring farm and ranch kids loved a Sunday afternoon rapid ride and swim. Most kids had a different route to get there. Cutting through the Holland place was a privilege to Julie and Helen because Kelly and Adam were their close friends.

Kelly was watching from her living room window and saw the girls running toward her down the long driveway. She and her younger brother Adam ran out to meet them, and they all headed for the creek. "Hey, it's about time! Let's get wet!" Kelly shouted, whacking her towel.

Julie and Kelly buddied up, talking as fast as they walked. Adam made sure that Helen didn't fall behind as they crossed the uneven, multi-veined streams of water that seeped out from the larger creek bed.

"Let's make a chair for Helen." Julie motioned to Kelly to join their hands and elbows in a square, a position Kelly learned in first aid with 4-H.

"Come here, Helen. I'll boost you up." Adam lifted Helen into their arms, and the four of them crossed over the widest and deepest channels near the creek.

"This is so fun!" Helen loved the ride. She felt safe being able to hang on to both girls as they lifted her across the channels.

Julie and Kelly were almost fourteen and eager to begin high school in the fall. Adam was eleven and Helen would be seven in August. They heard the rushing water, and they knew they were in for a cold, wild ride on the swollen rapids due to the heavy runoff from a long, snowy winter and the late spring thaw. The wildest part of the runoff only lasted a couple of weeks. By late August the rapids were gone and the creek was a mild-mannered stream.

The Cabinet Mountains rose majestically around the valley, still amply covered with snow on the higher peaks. The children were used to the splendor of the beautiful valley with its clear streams and snowcapped mountains. They took Montana's natural beauty for granted. They jumped into the creek and yelled out shivering whoops when the cold water surrounded their bodies. That was their world; they knew it well and made it their playground.

Two large mountains with craggy rocks jutting out rose above them. A sharp eye could see three mountain goats near the top, standing on a narrow ledge. One of the three goats took a position on the highest jutting rock on the narrow ledge, looking like he was king of the mountain. Long-needled pines and cottonwood trees crowded the creek's edge on the high mountainside. Gravel, rocks, and parts of tree trunks hunkered into the edge of the water, sometimes commanding the bank to move back and make more room. Two large trees had fallen long ago. They were gradually falling apart but taking their time shedding bark and branches. Swimmers sat on those trees, stashed their towels near them or under them, and even rested under them to get out of the sun. Up another fifty yards was the beginning of the rapids, accessed fairly easily with shoes on gravel and small rocks.

"Helen, you need to stay near me. Okay?" Helen could swim in the pond, but the main current was not about swimming. During the runoff season, the creek was a nonstop rush of roiling water that could pull a child off balance quickly. Most adults could be overpowered by the current, sucked under the water, and taken to shallower waters downstream without their permission. Julie guarded her sister carefully, and so did other swimmers. Two summers ago a child almost drowned, and the reality of the water's power had not faded among the older swimmers. Rules for safety were ingrained in everyone, especially the most basic rule: we are all responsible for every other person here—no exceptions. The current was exciting but dangerous during the runoff season, and the swimmers had to help one another when any of them faltered or took in water unexpectedly.

At least twelve people of various ages, mostly kids, were already at the swimming area when the Bowman and Holland kids eased their way into the freezing water. After the initial icy shock, Julie let Helen play on the rocks with a couple of kids whose mom was watching them.

"Can Helen play here near you while I make another run?"

"Go ahead, Julie. The girls like to play together. I'll watch her real close."

"Thank you! I won't be long, as you know!" Julie made a rapids run with Kelly. After a second exciting run of the rapids, Julie sat on the island where Helen was making a rock castle. She lined the moat with leaves to keep the water from seeping through the sand and gravel. When Helen went into the water with two other children in a shallow place nearby, Julie moved closer to her just in case she slipped on the mossy rocks.

Julie's long brown hair fell down her back to the sandy bank. She shook it down, wrung out the water, braided it, and tied the braid into its own large knot. She was taller than her older sister, Darlene, and she was also strong from doing so many farm chores. Although she was thin, she was wiry, with toned arms and legs. She wore a loose T-shirt over her bra to hide the large shapely additions to her chest that had arrived gradually during the past year. Although her breasts attracted attention from boys, she was embarrassed by them and dressed in ways to conceal her shape. As she sat in the sun, she made sure her T-shirt draped loosely in front. She also wore the T-shirt to hide the scars on her back—leather strap marks and bruises—and the cigarette burns on her arm. Her cutoff jeans were longer than the other kids' cutoffs to cover the marks on her upper thighs.

Helen ran over to Julie and bumped her shoulders. "Let's go down the rapids! Please?" Helen grabbed Julie's hands and tried to help her stand. "Let's do it! Come on!" Helen's blond curls bounced everywhere as she jumped up and down in anticipation of entering the rapids with her sister. Helen's creamy complexion was dotted with just the right number of freckles, and she had bright brown eyes and a skinny frame.

Julie was as eager as Helen to make the run again, and the two of them climbed to the small ridge where the main channel headed downstream. Kelly and Adam joined them, and so did several other kids. Going down in a group was fun and seemed safer than going down alone. No one had life jackets, but the swimmers looked out for the safety of others as well as they could while practically flying down the rapids to the swimming hole below.

"Are you sure you want to do this? You have to let me hang on to you all the way down."

"Yes! Yes! I'll be safe, I promise." Helen had the courage to tackle those rapids and loved the adventure. Her awareness of the hardships that her two sisters faced at home troubled her. At six years old, she didn't understand why it happened. She was afraid to ask anyone but Julie, and Julie's only answer was "I don't know." Helen had no physical scars except for a bite mark or two, but she sensed that the slaps on her face and the back of her head were happening more often—and becoming more severe. Fear lay just beneath her consciousness, awakening her with bad dreams, especially after one of her sisters had been beaten. At the moment, though, her fears and thoughts of her mother were splashed away with the rushing water she was about to conquer. The creek rapids shouted out, crashing water on rocks. Big city roller coasters could offer no finer rush than that mountain stream.

Julie and Helen waded in against the force of the water until Julie could no longer stand against the rapids. "I've gotcha!" Julie grabbed Helen, who was also already moving. Helen was off her feet, spooned against Julie, and one of Julie's arms had a locked hold around Helen's waist. They gave in to the rushing current as it carried them easily and swiftly down the natural chute. They went feet first, exhilarated, flying down the creek. They laughed and yelled whoops of joy mixed with out-and-out excitement as the water flung them forward. As much as Julie loved the rapids, there was a wistful moment when she wondered if rolling under the fast current and staying there might be better than going home. She had been pulled under before, overpowered by the force of waves. The beauty below was captivating—almost hypnotic and definitely not frightening to her. She had been filled with a sense of peace and calmness that breathed for her and told her that staying below, just rolling along with the water, was all right. Then someone lifted her to the surface, and she returned to reality. Just then, as she longed for the water's lower peace, she remembered that the child in her arms needed her. Escape was not an option.

The new boy, Dan Eagle, reached out and took Helen's hand as she and Julie splashed into the swimming hole. Between Julie and Dan, Helen had support on both sides and did not go underwater on the way out of the rapids. She was giddy and joyful as she gained her footing on the bank.

"Let's do it again! Can we?" Helen was wide-eyed, hyped up, and excited to go again. When Dan released her hand, he looked at Julie with a silly grin, and then he laughed in a goofy way.

"You're pretty brave, kid!" Dan complimented Helen. "Heck, I go down and it takes me a month to do it again!" Helen laughed at him.

"Hey, thanks for helping us, Dan." Julie smiled back at him, caught his eyes briefly, but glanced away and folded her arms across her chest when she saw him looking intently at her wet T-shirt. Boys did that, she knew, but she was uncomfortable with her newly developing shape, and her posture became protective as she hunched her shoulders forward. He glanced away and then back to her face with his silly grin.

"Anytime! Wanna go again? We can take Helen, too." Dan was hoping that Julie would go with him down the rapids. He had come to the Libby area with his adoptive family last month just after school had let out for the summer. Dan was quiet, observant, and had just turned fifteen. He was getting to know the kids in his own shy way. Dan's dad was hired at J. Neils Lumber Company, so Dan was transferring from Polson High School to Libby for his sophomore year.

Julie wanted to go down the rapids with him—maybe hold his hand as many of the rapid riders did. *He's so cute! I want to do this.* "Maybe next time." She cringed at the negative sound in her voice and eagerly repeated herself with a more positive spin. "I mean, yes…really, let's do it next time."

"All right. I take that as a promise!" He gave her his winning smile, and Julie blushed, moving with her sister toward Kelly and Adam.

The four of them left the creek and headed back toward the Holland ranch and horseback riding. They were mostly dry by the time they reached the open field where the horses grazed. Dan watched them walk away. *If she looks back, she likes me. Look back, Julie.* She did! He waved, and she waved back. *She likes me.* Dan couldn't see her blush. She had the same secret thought about him.

Julie and Helen rode horses for a short time and then headed for home. Being late was unacceptable and would mean not getting to swim or ride for a long time. Lateness made their mother very angry. Julie did not want to get home and see her mother waiting for them with their dad's belt striking against her hand.

6

THE BOWMAN HOME

When riled and furious, Betty's grip on Dewey's leather belt and her strong swing left stripped skin that took months to blend back to normal. The decorative metal western buckle welted badly and left deep wounds that held their design in the girls' skin for months. Being late was only one thing that set off Betty's rage. Just about anything could bring up the heat and send her into fits of punching, hair pulling, kicking, or jabbing with any object within her reach. When she became desperate to create pain, Betty found an array of ways to torture her two older children.

When Julie was twelve, she took over most of the meal preparation. She had already been feeding the animals and milking their cow, Smokey, twice a day. Smokey had a bull calf Julie fed, cleaned up after, and loved like crazy. The thirty laying hens, forty capons, and at least fifty new chicks under special heat lamps all yielded enough waste each day to take a grown man an hour to clean up properly. Julie fed them and kept their coop in good condition. Gathering eggs, washing them, and putting them in cartons to take to the grocery store in town took care and time. Helen helped with chores; she helped feed, water, and care for the thirty rabbits, and she scraped manure from the barn floors along with Julie.

The pigs were the messiest—two were adults and the two piglets were like household pets. Julie was a major part of the butchering process as well. Many chickens, rabbits, one bull, and two pigs ended up filling the freezer every year with most of the meat needed for the family. Hunting and fishing provided the rest.

Julie and Darlene filled their hunting tags and fished with their dad each hunting season. Dewey had hunting licenses for all his family. He and the girls hunted for deer, elk, bear, and a variety of birds. Julie played a major part in the hunting, the butchering, and the meal preparation. Tom Holland was right—the farmhand job was too much for a fourteen-year-old. He knew the two older girls hunted, but he didn't realize that they also butchered, cut up and packed meat, made sausage, helped with the garden, canned vegetables and fruits, and cooked the meals.

At fourteen, Julie was essentially a part-time mother to Helen, the cook for the family, and the farmhand. Darlene was grateful to pass on the daily cooking job because she had more than she could handle as well. She was in charge of the garden, cleaning the house, and doing the general baking. With Julie, Helen, and some help from her dad, Darlene planted, weeded, and harvested the large vegetable garden. She also organized the laundry. At sixteen, Darlene was the mother figure to her sisters, making sure they arose in the morning, went to bed on time, and did all that they were supposed to do in between. Their mother usually was too ill or unwilling to cook or help with the chores, and she spent very little time with the children.

Julie was exhausted, exhilarated, and worried when the girls arrived at the back door. Helen slid down her back, and both girls quietly began preparing supper. *Did we make it?* They smiled at each other when they realized that they were probably safe and on time. Helen set the dishes and flatware on the table with almost no noise at all. Making noise was not allowed. Julie peeled potatoes and put them on to boil. She rolled chicken pieces in flour, added garlic salt and pepper, and fried them on a low to medium heat—the quiet way to fry and still get the job done. She shucked corn, and Helen helped remove the corn silk. Darlene brought in green beans from the garden. Julie washed and snapped them, and she had them ready to cook when the time was right. Dinner was under control. *If she sees us now, we should be okay.* Julie often glanced toward her mother's bedroom door, checking to see if her mother was coming. *Will she be sick? Angry? Will she hurt us this time?*

As much as Darlene organized cleaning in the house, there was always a messy look to every room. Betty collected things, storing them throughout the house. Piles of sheet music were stacked near the piano. Musical instruments, both in their individual cases as well as unwrapped, lay out on the piano, the mantle, and other boxes. Magazines and old newspapers were stacked near the furniture in case Betty wanted to read them. Religious pamphlets and books from offbeat faiths filled the lower shelf of the coffee table. A few boxes of glass cups and vases accrued near the kitchen. Fairly wide paths throughout the living room went from the front door to the kitchen and the two younger girls' shared bedroom. Other paths led to the other end of the living room with French doors leading into the master bedroom, the only bathroom, and Darlene's bedroom. Every room had collections of boxes, bags, and other stacks of blankets, sheets, pillows, or any number of collections Betty had hoarded over time. In the middle of the living room, an oval braided rug lay on the hardwood floor. The black and white console television was facing the overstuffed sofa and a matching chair. Two footstools held feet in front of the chair and to one side of the sofa. White crocheted doilies covered the worn and frayed fabric on the arms and the headrests of the chair and the sofa. When Dewey and Betty watched television, Dewey sat in the chair, feet up, with a snack and drink on a small table near him. Betty sprawled out on the sofa, snacks at her fingertips on the coffee table. She laid her feet either on the stool, the coffee table, or bent up on the couch. Television was just about the only thing they agreed on, and after they sent the girls to their rooms at about 8:00 p.m., they watched until 10:00 p.m. or even until the test pattern appeared on a weekend night.

Betty would not part with the piles. She added to them, but seldom removed them, which made the rooms look messy. She seemed to need to see her projects and treasures every day. She had plans to sew, crochet, and complete a few paint-by-number sets she bought, and she read the books, newspapers, and magazines she had collected. She intended to let out the many items of clothing in paper bags and boxes. She kept growing larger, but she never seemed to get out her sewing machine to adjust the seams. Time slipped away from her.

Reality also slipped from her grasp at times. She carried out reasoned dialogues within her mind that encouraged the collecting and helped her protect her treasures from her family. Dewey gave up trying to clear the rooms. If she suspected any item had been taken away or moved without her permission, she became nervous and angry and often made the girls look for hours for whatever she thought was missing. Unfortunately, cobwebs gathered, mice found places to hide, and dust accumulated where cleaning was impossible. Betty's bedroom was worse than the living room, but only Dewey had to deal with that area. Betty's stash of sweet treats in her closet provided ants, other insects, and rodents a home and a place to multiply. She had to be careful to shake insects, their eggs, and waste from her clothing due to the accumulation of bugs and their relatives. She had kept her area clean for a few years, but as her mind drifted, those habits deteriorated. Living with her had become unsanitary and unsafe. She had great plans, but she could not bring herself to accomplish them and still follow the directions she convinced herself that she had to take each day. Her inner messages were persuasive, even demanding, as she instructed herself to discipline her children for their own good.

7

BETTY BOWMAN, 1958

There was no need to check to see if their mother was sleeping. She was not to be disturbed when the door was shut. No exceptions. The girls knew the routines of dinner and chores, and they really had no need to ask their mother anything. Knowledge of what to do and the fear of violent reprisal for interrupting her made it easy to respect her wishes. They just assumed she was not feeling well. There were activities other than sleeping going on some of the time in that bedroom.

When the girls thought she was napping, she might have been. She might also have been eating candy bars from the secret stash that she kept hidden in her closet. Sometimes she hid baked goods, like maple bars or cinnamon rolls dripping with frosting. She could cram most of a cinnamon roll in her mouth at once, hardly leaving room to bring her teeth together to chew it. Gobs of the roll would leak out while she tried to make chunks small enough to go down her throat without choking herself. Her forceful eating habits at times brought on gagging and vomiting. When anyone became aware of her choking, she described those sessions as merely having an upset stomach. Her occasional throwing up in the bathroom drew attention from the girls. They felt sorry for her and wanted to help her in some way. They didn't know that her eating habits and her self-imposed vomiting to lose weight after an eating binge caused those reactions, not the flu or an upset stomach.

Betty spent most of each day alone. When she wasn't eating her hidden treats, she may have been trying out assorted makeup products that she had sent for in the mail, or that she purchased in Spokane when she and Dewey went there for business reasons. She adorned herself with cheap jewelry, applied makeup rather heavily, and talked to herself about acting, singing, modeling, or being a film star. She imagined herself rich, thin, and happy somewhere exotic. When she looked at herself in the mirror, she often saw the beautiful face of the young person she had been, radiant and bright-eyed. Other times, she saw the intrusion of fat, the rolls protruding under her chin and her bulging cheeks. A memory would present itself from her past that she had suppressed over time, reminding her of pain and anguish she had known at the cruel hands of others.

She also spent time crying. She cried because she was lonely, overweight, unhappy with herself and her appearance, or for no reason she could explain. Visions of her dead mother and little brother, Jimmy, haunted her dreams, and her inner dialogues reflected her powerlessness to help them or herself when she was young. She may have cried at times because she knew she was abusing her children. Crying did not seem to change her behavior toward them, and it only occurred after she had exhausted herself by beating one of them relentlessly. She hated the rolls of unwanted fat that imprisoned the shapely woman she had been. She had not wanted to become a mother. When she became pregnant, she felt trapped. After the birth of each child, she dropped deeper into despair, sensing no escape from the unwanted responsibility.

She was stressed continually during the several years the three girls were growing from babies to their present ages. She could not stand hearing her any of her babies cry. She spanked them to make them stop crying, which only escalated the crying and pain while increasing her own anger and frustration. Sometimes she left them unattended for hours while she went for a walk or shopping. When she came home and saw her child lying in an unclean diaper, hungry, or sleeping after a long cry, she felt guilty. The sores and rashes on tender baby skin upset her. She vowed to try again to do better from that point on. She did not do better. Eventually, she gave up feeling guilty, and she quietly wished the girls would die. She preferred that the death be from natural causes, but her mind was sometimes crowded with thoughts of how to make the death take place without getting caught. She repeated the neglect and anger through three children who had not died yet, no matter how many times she had willed death to come to them.

Two of her daughters feared that she wanted to kill them because she screamed her intentions while beating them. Her inner conversations that only she could hear suggested she whisper frightening threats in their ears in the night when she thought they were sleeping. Darlene could pretend to sleep through the messages, which seemed to irritate Betty, forcing her to shake Darlene. Darlene refused to acknowledge that she heard her mother, hoping that Betty would not want to awaken Dewey and let her sleep. Julie, however, woke up more easily and reacted with fear. Betty achieved a sense of satisfaction from watching Julie's eyes grow wide as she grabbed her covers and tried to scream.

One night, Betty didn't want to listen to her inner conversation, but again, as she did many other nights, she went to the girls' room. "I'm going, I'm going!" she told herself in a hushed, forced voice. "Okay, I will." *Why do I keep doing this to Julie? Why can't I just sleep?* Betty seemed unable to stop herself. "Julie? Can you hear me, Julie?" *I'll cover her mouth. By the time she wakes up—if she wakes up at all, I'll have crushed her!* Betty climbed on top of Julie, her weight bearing heavily on Julie's thin body. Julie tried to scream, but only muffled sounds came out. After only a brief struggle, Julie stopped moving. Betty released her, causing Julie to gasp for air.

When Betty had attacked Julie in that manner at other times, Julie stayed as quiet as she could, taking in badly needed air as softly as she could. That night she temporarily lost consciousness. "Are you dead?" Betty stood over her, wondering if Julie had really died. *Yes! I think I did it! I'm free of one girl.* Worry quickly replaced joy. *What if I'm blamed for killing her?* Betty grabbed her, shaking her. Julie drew air into her lungs in gasps, and looked at the figure in the dark that had just tried to kill her.

"Go back to sleep. You were having a bad dream, and I had to make you stop screaming. Be quiet so you don't wake up your sister." Betty smiled and patted Julie's cheek. She felt a sense of joy that she had brought Julie to the brink of death without losing the chance to do it again another night. *That was fantastic! Amazing! I have to plan what to do if she really dies. Where could I hide her?* She went back to her own bedroom and rewarded herself by eating two Butterfingers. She slept soundly through the rest of the night.

Julie felt helpless. *I didn't scream.* Her mother had frightened her again, and if she told her dad it would be her word against her mother's lengthy, detailed story. And afterward, her mother would beat her for telling him. She was convinced that her mother was going to kill her somehow—suffocation, strangling, knifing—it was only a matter of when it would happen. *If I tell, I die. If I don't tell, I die.* Helen, frozen by fear, heard the strange sounds from Julie and her mother. After Betty left the room, Helen quietly crawled in bed with Julie, cuddled up close to her, and felt her sobbing sister's body tremble with fear. She gently patted Julie's back. Julie whispered, "Did I scream?"

Helen cupped her hand around Julie's ear. "No. I heard her come in. You didn't scream." Julie pulled the covers over her head and sobbed. Helen pressed tightly against her sister and cried with her. Knowing their mother might come back at any moment made it hard to sleep. Fear finally gave way to exhaustion. The girls, braced solidly for whatever might hit them, fell into nightmarish sleep.

Having the two older girls take care of Helen was a major positive step in Betty's effort at self-control, but it was not enough to change her feelings about the suffocation of motherhood.

Sometimes the girls heard her carrying on conversations with herself. Betty often sat at her vanity, looked in the mirror, and gave orders. She argued with herself when she took out the belt to use on her children. Those arguments occurred in the privacy of the bedroom most of the time, but there were times when she argued while she was beating one of her children. "You can't make me do this." Or, "Please. Not again. Run, Darlene!" All the while she held fiercely to her daughter's hair, swinging the belt and hitting Darlene mercilessly. "Why did you give me children when you know I can't deal with them?" Or, "Take them! I don't want them!" She was drowning like a weak swimmer in a whirlpool, and she came up for air less frequently as time passed.

Those strange conversations were frightening to hear, and both Darlene and Julie had nightmares due to the physical abuse, as well as the mental anguish of wondering what was wrong with their mother. They also wondered at times what sins they had committed that caused their mother to have fits of violence toward them. The fault was not theirs, but no one told them. A mental illness their mother could not control or understand was to blame. The girls themselves felt guilty at times for making their mother angry. They told themselves that if they had only been more careful, or if they had been quieter, or on time, or better in some way—if only. Then she would love them and not hurt them. Other times they blamed her and feared her. They grew a toughness to protect themselves from her. All three girls slept fully clothed under their pajamas, braced for a "visit" in the night by an armed, out of control woman bent on causing pain. The extra layer of clothing helped ease the blow of whatever object their mother selected to appease her inner demons. There were times when she made them take off all of their clothing before she began beating them. She usually targeted just one at a time to ensure her control over her victim. Darlene's size was inhibiting her attacks. Julie was growing faster than Darlene had grown. She usually attacked Julie when Darlene was outside so the two of them would not gang up on her. She did not know that they never thought of attacking her. Julie and Helen loved her and were submissive to her, hoping somehow to become what she wanted them to be in order to get her to stop hurting them. They wanted her to love them.

Darlene had passed that stage. She did not believe that her mother loved her. She was sure that her mother did not want her, even hated her, and most of the time she accepted her mother's rejection. Darlene was going to find a way to leave home before her mother carried out her threats to kill her. She loved her dad, but he did not protect her. He didn't try to change things at home. He was simply not around enough to help them. Darlene thought he didn't know what Betty was doing to the girls, even though sadness and fear filled the air in their house, affecting the girls' and their mother's behaviors. Darlene could no longer stand the abuse from her mother, and she spent a great deal of time planning a way out.

From her bedroom, Betty sometimes watched the girls when they were working. She peered through the sheer curtains that covered the small windows in the French doors, which divided the master bedroom from the living room. At times she hoped to see them doing something wrong so she could rush out angrily and create havoc. Other times she just watched them. She also observed them doing chores or working in the garden. She spied on them secretly, storing up images to use against them during a future attack. She had a deep and desperate need to cause pain, a need that was buried in her subconscious and developed from her own private history of appalling abuse.

8

BETTY STEWART

HER EARLY YEARS, 1919–1935

When Betty's father died, her mother, Mary, had no income and no home. In the fall of 1919, Mary, Betty, and her little brother, Jim, were living in an abandoned farmhouse in Conrad, Montana, when Charles Stedman, a potential buyer, arrived to look at the place. He rode up on horseback.

Charles didn't knock at the door. The postal clerk had told him that the place was empty and that the people had moved over a year ago. As soon as he entered the house, he saw signs of someone living there: the water bucket, two potatoes on the counter, and a cup. He quietly drew his pistol for protection. The small four-room house took little time to search. When he opened the closet door, he saw Mary huddled quietly with Betty, eight, and Jim, three.

"What's this? Come out of there." He holstered his pistol. "I won't hurt you. Come on now." The three "squatters" came out of the tiny room and stood together before the stranger.

"Please, don't hurt my children. We won't be any trouble. We'll just go." Mary slowly backed her two children and herself toward the door.

Charles could see that the three of them were close to starving. As he looked around the room they were in, he saw no evidence of a "home."

"You don't have to go. Really. I'm going to be leaving. I was just looking over the place." Charles backed away from Mary and her children and walked out the door. When he got to his horse, he looked back at the three desperate people. Mary had an arm around Betty's shoulders, and she was holding Jimmy's hand. He dismounted, took the lunch he had prepared for himself, and walked over to Mary.

"Here. Take this." Mary's eyes told him of their need and their hopelessness. Her hands held the food he gave her as though it were a precious gift.

As soon as Charles rode away, Mary served her children small portions of the bread and cheese. Mary sliced the apple. They took their time with each slice as though they were savoring a special dessert. The large slices of bread could make several meals. They each ate a little and wrapped up most of the food for a later time. *Thank you, Lord, for sending this man to give us this food.* Mary and her children had been sleeping on the floor and living on three or four eggs a day from chickens left behind. With determined digging, Mary found a few potatoes and carrots in the garden. Mary brought water from an almost dried-up creek, gathered berries, and hoped to figure out what to do with her family before winter. But she had no plan and no hope for her children. She didn't expect the three of them to survive.

Charles returned home to his eight children. His wife had died a few months earlier while giving birth to twins, and he was trying to hire someone to help him care for his family. He was interested in buying a bigger place and hiring a live-in housekeeper. He kept thinking about the starving woman and her two children. His house was full with his own children, from babies through seventeen years old. His older kids helped care for the younger ones, but they were not patient or skilled with the babies. Maybe the woman could help with his family if he took in all three of them. If he just fed them they would be better off than the way he saw them living that day. He also had dried meat, lots of flour, a large stock of dry goods, and a garden full of food. He had enough livestock to last several winters.

He and his oldest son Peter harnessed two horses to their wagon. During the ride he imagined what he could say to convince the woman to accept the offer of a home and a job with eight children. When Charles first gave Mary food, he had earned her unwavering trust. He easily convinced Mary to work for him, and her children followed their mother without question. He and his son loaded up the three of them. In Mary's starving condition, she saw no other option. She felt her prayers to God to save her children were answered through the saintly man.

"You can come back anytime you want. For now, you can eat your fill at our place and get a night's sleep in a real bed." Mary and her two children huddled together in the back of the wagon, watching their borrowed home slowly fade into the horizon.

Charles had not prepared his children for the visitors. At first the older children in the already overcrowded house were curious, but not eager to greet three dirty, starving people. They were not sure what to make of their father's generosity. Two other women had tried working for the family, but both of them left after a brief attempt due to the older children's unwillingness to cooperate with them.

Over time, the three older children's reticence to accept Mary and her two children took an unexpected turn. As long as Mary cooked, cleaned, sewed, helped with chores, and waited on them, the children put up with her. Mary did not ask them to help her or give them chores. She was quiet, hardworking, and kind. They took out their hostility on Betty and Jimmy, secretly at first, but more brazenly as time passed. Charles may have saved them from starvation, but he essentially let his older children use all three of their new residents as servants.

After a few months, Charles married Mary, and then he announced their marriage to his children. The older children's anger deepened. As little Betty grew older, she became the target of abuse. Five girls and three boys generated a great deal of laundry, ate a lot of food, and showed very little kindness to the three new members of their family. The oldest boy had his own plan for getting even with his father for adopting three strangers into their family.

Peter and the second oldest boy, Frank, took Betty on long walks to get to know her in many ways. Betty was less than forty-five pounds, and Peter easily lifted her up on his shoulders. He often grabbed her unexpectedly, threw her up around his neck, and took off running to the barn or away from the house where there was a small clump of trees. Peter played with Betty, swung her around, and brought her a small piece of candy now and then. She liked his attention at first. After a couple of fun runs to the trees, he hugged her closely and kissed her cheeks and neck. Betty pulled away from him, but he was strong and forceful. One time he took off with her and he brought Frank along.

Betty didn't want to go and yelled to her mother as Peter ran off with her. Mary heard her, but only waved and kept working on preparing dinner. Betty cried and asked Peter to put her down. He laughed at her and ran faster.

"This is going to be fun! You know that we always have fun, don't we, Betty?" When they reached the trees, he sat on the ground and pulled Betty onto his lap. "Relax. I won't hurt you." Betty calmed down, but she was afraid of Peter and ready to cry.

"Frank, come over here and sit with us." Frank did as Peter told him. "Here, hold Betty's arm for me." As Frank held onto Betty's arm, she began struggling and crying. Peter pulled off Betty's underwear and spread her legs apart. He placed one leg on each side of him and pulled her tight to his chest. Betty kept squirming to get away. Frank helped Peter control her by taking both of her hands and holding them behind Peter. Peter put his hands on Betty's bottom and pulled her close. When she tried to bite him, he slapped her face. "Stop it! If you bite me again, I'll kill you!" He put his hand over her mouth. "Hold still!" Peter used his other hand to explore the private parts of her body. Betty tried to scream, gyrating in any way to free herself, but she couldn't get away.

"Stop it!" Peter yelled at her. "Stop fighting! You'll do what I want or I'll kill you." Betty kept fighting. "I'll kill your brother, do you hear me? I'll kill him! And your mother, damn it. Now stop!" Betty stopped moving. "That's better. See, it doesn't hurt at all if you just hold still."

Peter spit on his fingers and went back between her legs, using one finger at a time to penetrate her body cavities. Tears streamed down her face. She sobbed in pain as he violated her tiny body.

Both Peter and Frank forced Betty to have sexual experiences with them several times a week after that. They both threatened to kill her and her family if she ever told on them. After several weeks of enduring this torture, Betty threatened both boys. She asked them what Charles would do to them if he found out. "If you just leave me alone, I won't tell him. I just want you to stop!" Peter laughed and renewed his threat to kill her and her family.

Betty grew older, hating having to live with those people. Jimmy did not. Jimmy died from an accident in the barn. According to Peter, Jimmy fell from the hayloft into the bull's pen. The bull stepped on him several times, crushing his skull and his chest.

When Peter told Betty about Jimmy dying right after the accident, he added a few details. He described Jimmy's fall as a "push," as in, "Somebody pushed Jimmy, and he fell into the bull's pen." Peter had a strange look of pleasure on his face when he told Betty, "It would be a shame to see your mother end up dead, too. Down the well, maybe?" Later, when Peter told Charles, he left out the "push" word and just said that Jimmy "fell." Betty knew his death was not an accident. No one tried to get Jimmy away from the bull. Two of the children watched him die, heard him crying out for help, and, by their own admission, did nothing to save him. Betty kept hearing Peter's lies in her head. *It was over too fast, Daddy. We couldn't do anything.* Betty also knew that the bull was not prone to get riled up. She had fed him many times herself. Betty believed Peter threw Jimmy in with the bull, then poked or spooked the animal into stomping around. Peter deliberately intended to kill her brother because she threatened to tell on him and Frank. As horrifying as Peter's murdering Jimmy appeared to Betty, she felt that she was also to blame for trying to get Peter to stop torturing her. If she hadn't threatened to tell on him, maybe Jimmy would be alive.

An inner dialogue began within Betty as she tried to work through that situation in her mind. A part of her blamed Peter totally, and a part of her wished that she had remained silent. As the inner dialogue progressed, a solution developed that convinced Betty that she could stop the abuse. She wasn't quite sure how that would happen, but she began exploring several ideas through private conversations with herself. Peter had to be stopped.

Charles, his children, and Mary and Betty gathered in the family cemetery for Jimmy's burial service. A preacher said a few prayers and commented on how sad it was to lose someone so young. Betty looked at each of the family members standing together while Jimmy was being buried. *I hate them. They killed my brother. They'll kill me if I stay here. Even my mother can't protect me. She can't even protect herself.* Betty wanted to make those two boys pay for pushing Jimmy and causing his death. And rape. Over and over. In the darkness when she should be sleeping, she lay awake, waiting for the brute force of being gagged and raped by her stepbrothers. *They deserve to die.*

During the three years that Betty plotted her revenge and escape, she kept up a good cover. She continued working as the maid and being the silent victim of the boys. She fought less, enduring the humiliation in silence. She helped her mother cook, and she added interesting ingredients in some food items. The last year she lived on the farm, she began ever so carefully adding very small amounts of rat poison in Peter's food, without getting it into the other portions. Peter ate like a pig, wolfing down his food. He didn't even taste it. Peter became sick and spent more time in bed and less time torturing Betty. She hated Frank, too, but Frank never bothered her unless Peter was present. Peter was the worst, so he was first to learn how violence breeds contempt. She'd make plans regarding Frank later.

When Peter couldn't get out of bed and needed to have food served in his room, Betty added the white milky substance from a milkweed plant to his milk and soup. "This soup tastes terrible!" Peter knew he had to eat to get better, but he didn't like what he was given. Betty was careful and made sure no one saw her add "flavoring" to Peter's food. Unfortunately for Peter, he died a painful death when Betty fed him his final meal that contained both rat poison and milkweed. As he was dying, unable to sit up or speak, Betty tried to give him another spoonful of soup. He could barely see her as she fed him, but he took as much soup as he could swallow, keeping it down in spite of the severe stomach cramps he was experiencing.

"This is really good, Peter. You must eat to get well." Betty smiled at him. "Here, have some more." She squeezed his cheeks, forcing his weak mouth open, and she gave him more soup. "Just a little more." She lifted his head so the soup could run into his body. "I'm so happy I have this chance to help you, Peter, after all you've done for me." Charles and Mary saw Betty wipe his mouth with a damp cloth and pat his forehead. They commented to one another about how kind she was to take care of Peter. "This soup is so good, Peter," Betty said as she pretended to sip some herself.

Peter's last horrified look at Betty's smiling face demonstrated his shocking awareness of Betty's devotion to him. His eyes grew wide as he attempted to form the words. "You made me sick," but Betty dabbed his mouth with a napkin while he spoke, keeping anyone from hearing him. He was too weak to move his body, talking incoherently. During the night he slipped into a coma, and he passed away before morning. He was buried near Jimmy.

As the family gathered for his burial, Betty again surveyed the faces of the family. Betty did not cry; she held a small cloth near her face to conceal her joy. Anyone could have seen the bitterness in her heart by looking into her angry yet somewhat satisfied eyes. She viewed her mother as helpless and worthless to her. She had told her mother many times that the boys were mean to her and forced her to do things she didn't want to do. But her mother had said that in a few years Betty could be on her own. "So right now, Betty, just put up with it." *Put up with it! Put up with it! How can you tell me to take this, Mother?* Stepfather Charles, she decided, had only brought her family into his for his own gain. The remaining siblings could all die, and Betty wouldn't care. After Peter's grave had been covered and the others had left, Betty lingered. *Jimmy, I got him for you. I may get the others, too. Don't let him push you around in heaven. No worry. He'll never get there.*

Betty tried to stay calm and covert in her anger. Unfortunately for her, she could not hide her hate or her sense of satisfaction when she targeted the other children. Many of the mean things she did to her stepbrothers and stepsisters were not traceable directly to her. When she cut off Constance's braid while she slept, however, Betty was too happy about it—especially when she saw how angry and hurt Constance was. Betty was delighted when Constance held her cutoff braid and screamed uncontrollably.

Charles beat Betty for that. The pattern of deeds over the previous months certainly pointed to Betty as the culprit. She put animal waste in the girls' closet, sprinkled salt in the bed sheets, and was caught stirring a wad of hair pulled from a hairbrush into the gravy one night. Charles decided that Betty could no longer live with them, and he arranged for her to go to an orphanage that was run by a Catholic convent in Great Falls. He took her there without letting her say good-bye to her mother. Betty said nothing the whole trip, but inside her head, her thoughts raced happily. *I am free! An orphanage can't control me. Whatever they do to me won't be as bad as what I have been through. I'll be so good. They'll grow to trust me.* She held an inner conference with herself and promised to be the best child in the orphanage.

Betty was eleven years old. In her short life, she had almost starved to death, been repeatedly raped and tortured, lost her little brother to a horrible death, and lost her mother to a family that hated her. She also planned and carried out the execution of Peter. The orphanage was a chance for Betty to start over. She was true to her promise of being good, and the nuns were happy to have her. She learned to read, write, and do math. She escaped through books whenever she had time. She also had many chores, but no one abused her. Not until she was fourteen.

A priest began using her as his personal maid. He tried to groom her to care for him. She would not be "groomed," so he beat her as he did several of the children. She fought him valiantly, but he beat her more severely for trying to stop his blows. He threatened her, and told Sister Margaret, the head of the order of nuns, that Betty had tried to steal from him. Sister Margaret did not believe him. For three years Betty had been a model child, doing everything she was asked to do. She asked Betty if she had stolen from the priest.

"No, Sister, I did not steal from him." Betty was silent and just lowered her head. *He's lying! Well, I can lie, too!* When the nun lifted her chin, Betty looked into her caring eyes. "Can I trust you?"

"Of course you can trust me, Betty. Tell me the truth." Sister expected to hear a confession of a minimal theft—some change taken from a dresser.

Betty was crying. "He made me do bad things with him." She looked at Sister, and then broke down crying. "He made me touch his—you know—down there. And he said if I told anyone, he would make life so hard for me I'd wish I was dead." Betty put on a dramatic display of uncontrollable sobbing as she told the nun about the priest's abusive behavior toward her.

"Oh, my child! Priests are God's chosen ones. You must be mistaken."

Without hesitation, Betty raised her skirt and showed Sister Margaret bruises on her thighs from Peter's abuse. She lowered her collar and showed her bite marks on her neck. "These scars are proof. I begged him to stop, but he wouldn't. He's a bad man, Sister, and I am afraid of him." *I am never going to be quiet again if someone hurts me!*

The priest admitted he had beaten her, but he denied raping her. He was gone the next day. Betty did not want to play the role of "good girl" anymore. She wanted out. She could read, write, and think for herself. A few days went by, and Betty made an appeal to Sister Margaret to help her get a job so she could live on her own. Sister Margaret did not want Betty creating a problem for the church regarding the priest. She agreed to help Betty. Within a week, she found Betty a job in a restaurant. Until she could save enough money to support herself, Betty lived at the convent and worked in the restaurant washing dishes and eventually waiting tables.

Betty's job worked out well. She liked the work and meeting people. She had several relationships with men and convinced some of them to help her financially. After another year had passed, she was able to rent a small apartment. While working one day, a rather good-looking man named Dewey Bowman sat at one of her tables. She learned that he traded with local farmers for produce and sold it to restaurants, grocery stores, and individuals from his truck. He had found a way to make a reasonable living during those hard times. Betty needed someone who could take care of himself. Dewey's traveling life had to be exciting and fun. He did not seem like someone who would abuse her. He was certainly among the potential candidates for her affection. She had to gain his interest so he would stop in again. Using her most congenial smile, she introduced herself and flirted with him as she took his order. He liked her warm, brown eyes, her long hair, and her friendly way of talking to him. He was lonely. She was beautiful.

9

ERIC AND ZONOLITE

THE ZONOLITE MINING

COMPANY, LIBBY, 1958

That Saturday, Eric went to the music store hoping to see Dewey. When he arrived, Dewey was waiting on a customer. He called out a hello and told him he'd be right with him. When Dewey finished with the customer, Eric decided to lead with his thoughts about working at Zonolite just in case more people came into the store.

"Dad, you know that I worked out at Zonolite this past week doing some wiring. Have you ever been out there?"

"No. Well, I've hunted near there, and I've seen the black mountain of ore from a distance, but I've never been to the mine itself. How did the work go? I've heard some stories about the place."

"Like what?"

"You know. Good things like the pay and days off at Christmas."

"You say 'good stuff.' Any bad stuff?"

"I have heard some bad stuff. Some men get sick workin' there. Too much dust and they end up with lung problems, heart problems, cancer—they end up dead. No one at the company wants to talk about that. Hell, most of the workers don't want to talk about it. Just read the obituaries and see who's doing the dying."

"I was thinking of applying for work out there. They pay better and have health insurance."

"When you were out there did you notice it being dusty?" Dewey looked at Eric squarely in the eyes. "Did you feel like the air was safe to breathe?"

Eric looked at his dad. "I don't like the dust, but the rest of the air—you know—outside, seems like regular air to me."

"Think about this. If you breathe that dust every day you may need that health insurance more than you do now. Money isn't everything."

"They want me to be a manager. The boss said I'd have my own crew and that I wouldn't be in the dust much at all." Eric took the coffee cup Dewey gave him.

"Son, I know that you'll do what you think is best. You've been out there and you probably have better information than I do since my knowledge of the place is based on living here and listening to the old-timers talk about their experiences. Personally, I don't trust the company. The owners could be doing better by the workers and make it safer, but they haven't done it as far as I know. They're making lots of money and using up our people to do it. I even heard that their doctors tell the men they have heart problems when it's clear that the men can't get a full breath of air. But—sick people like to blame others for their problems sometimes. Who knows what's true for sure?

"How are you doing at Montana Power? That's a good company. You handle some scary stuff—electricity is nothing to mess with."

"I like my job, Dad. I work with a good crew, and my crew boss is fair—works hard right along with us. The health insurance was a motivator to look at Zonolite. I was covered with dust just being in the building and on site. My mask was hard to use, clogged with dust. I'll give it some more thought. Being out there for the week made me see that there is more to the story of the mining company work than the great rumors I have been hearing about the place. There's one other thing, Dad. I told you that I got offered a management job, my own office, and a big jump in pay over what I make now. I won't be out in the dust as much as the miners."

"Well, I can see why you're thinkin' about it. That makes a big difference. I still don't trust the company, but if they get some good men like you runnin' it, well, I could change my mind. They must be plannin' a big electrical project. Ya figure?"

"Could be. All that navy training just might pay off. I think I might take the job, Dad."

Dewey puffed on his pipe a couple of times. "You know what you want to do, and I support whatever you decide. I'm just glad you're living here now. You need to come out to the house more."

"I'll do that, Dad." Eric saw customers walking in the door. "You got things to do, so I'll catch you later."

As Eric left the store, he had decided to give the new position serious thought over the weekend and then make a decision within the following week. It wasn't like it was a life-and-death situation. He could always find another job if it didn't work out. How harmful could the nuisance dust be anyway?

10

THE SISTERS AT HOME
SUMMER 1958

Darlene was the "general manager" of the household, and when she came in from gardening, she checked the progress of supper. "Chicken's looking good, Julie. Nice job on being quiet." Both girls smiled. "Helen, why don't you pick some flowers, and I'll get a vase for them. You can put them on the table. Here, take this vase with you." Helen quietly went out the back door with the vase to get a few flowers. Darlene trusted her to pick them out. Helen brought back wild roses; she rinsed them off first with a hose to make sure there were no bugs on them. When she brought them in the kitchen, both Darlene and Julie smiled at her. Many of the rose petals were on the ground near the hose due to the water pressure, but enough remained to add color to the table.

"I baked an apple pie for dessert. You both have supper handled, so how about helping me fold the laundry?" The washer and dryer were part of the kitchen counter system, so she had brought the loads of clean laundry into the girls' bedroom. They closed the door and went to work. Quietly, the girls folded their parents clothing and their own items. They folded the towels and the sheets last. Darlene took a sheet, flapped it up in the air, and both Julie and Helen grabbed onto it. The three of them loved that part and quietly, yet joyfully, lifted each billowing sheet several times before conquering it; they folded each in half, then quarters, and so on, until it submitted itself to a neat rectangle for stacking. There was something about the clean smell of the clothing, the team approach to getting the work done, and the sense of working together at a chore they all could do easily that made the job fun for them. Even a six-year-old could fold towels and washcloths well enough for sister praise. They loved each other. They needed times like that to ease the tension in their lives and to get them through the fearful experiences that they could not control.

The girls were pleased with their accomplishments. Julie was in charge of the animals, but all three girls helped her get the chores done. After milking Smokey, Julie led her to the pasture. Smokey rubbed her nose against Julie's arm or pushed her head against Julie as she ambled toward the pasture. Before leaving her, Julie petted her head, stroked her sides, talked to her, hugged her, and then sent her off for a day in the field. Julie loved the animals under her care, yet Smokey was more to her than an animal. To Julie, that cow was her friend. Julie's affection for the cow was, perhaps, unusual by normal standards, but she benefited from the strange friendship. She had someone to talk to who never judged her.

With all of the attention to cleaning and trying to find some order in the unusual system of sorted piles of stuff at home, a person might understand why the girls looked somewhat rough around the edges. Darlene groomed herself as well as she could. Her long brown hair framed her dark brown eyes and freckled face. She was beautiful. Because she was dating, she wanted her sisters to look reasonable. She taught them to shampoo their hair and comb it nicely, clean their bodies, and wear clean clothing. Darlene and Julie learned from watching women and other girls at school just by being around them. But farm chores were dirty and smelly, and the odor could stay with a person who had the job of cleaning up. Julie had the dirtiest jobs, and she smelled a bit like her animal friends some days when she went to school. Other students had farm chores also, so she was not the only farm-fragrant child.

Both Darlene and Julie paid attention to Helen's grooming, but still there was a look about them of amateurish care, and sometimes there was the smell of the barn underlying their best intentions at cleanliness. They lacked what a mother might provide, but did not know how to or care to do. They wore used clothing purchased in Spokane at secondhand stores on Trent Street during their few trips yearly to visit Dewey's sister and her family in the city. Darlene was gifted at picking out items of clothing that fit the girls and that were attractive on them. Betty hastily selected blouses and skirts of ample size for all three girls. Darlene moved quickly with a more discerning eye and traded some items before the girls were stuck with clothing that they would "grow into" instead of blouses or skirts that fit them at the time. She was able to trade out clothing that her mother had placed on the counter by getting Julie to show their mother a coat or a hat that Betty might like for herself. While Betty tried things on, Darlene substituted several blouses, some skirts, and two pairs of shoes.

Darlene traded duties with Julie so she could choose a few items as well. Darlene accepted or rejected Julie's choices, and Julie didn't argue. The girls generally found several things that they encouraged Betty to try on and buy for herself. When Betty paid, she did not even look at each article of clothing the girls had selected. At twenty-five cents—or at the most, fifty cents—for each clothing item, Betty's attention rested with the items she had chosen for herself.

Darlene had saved money from babysitting, and she bought a few things for herself. She had to do it carefully for fear that her mother would forbid her purchases. She paid for two pairs of ear-rings, two small chains with pendants, and three scarves for her hair before Betty finished trying on the coat. If Betty had caught her making purchases, Darlene was creative enough to make up a story to be able to keep the items. The earrings might have been a gift for Betty. Somehow, Darlene could find a way to keep what she wanted. Darlene also had some desires related to dating that her mother wouldn't permit, yet she was creative and downright sneaky in getting what she wanted most of the time.

Dating her special boyfriend, Dick, was the major joy of her life. Darlene found many ways to date Dick without parental permission. One standby excuse was babysitting. She may or may not have a job sitting for a family. If she had a job, she met Dick afterward. Sometimes she spent the entire evening with Dick at his small house on mill row and lied about having a job. Some nights she crawled out her window late at night, then spent the entire night with Dick. When Dick took her home, he dropped her off near the property so Darlene could go directly to the garden, as though she had arisen early to get her work done. The two lovers had been dating for over ten months; at least half of that time, they had been intimately involved. Darlene was sure that she wanted to marry him. She knew that Dick loved her. She just didn't know how much. He used the words "I love you" sparingly, but he was totally committed to her. He did not like her sneaking out, but he wanted to be with her constantly. He felt guilty about their unapproved meetings, especially because he liked Dewey and had wanted to have an understanding with him before their dating became intense. However, he believed Darlene's explanation of not being able to reason with her mother.

Betty caught Darlene coming in late a few times. She beat Darlene severely, using her humiliating method of making her take off all of her clothing first. On two occasions, she saw hickeys on her body, those pesky little witnesses to sensual sucking. Those beatings were worse. After the beatings, Darlene had extra chores for two weeks. Grounding Darlene successfully would have taken a full-time guard twenty-four hours a day. Betty tried it and thought it worked. Darlene simply did not care what her mother said or how crazy she was. Darlene was intent on being with Dick, even if it killed her—a terrible possibility that had formed in her mother's unhealthy mind many times.

11

DICK O'BRIEN

Darlene first met Dick O'Brien at a party in the fall of 1957. She told her parents that she had taken a babysitting job for the Davis family that could last until midnight or later. She knew she would be sitting with the three children until about 9:30, but she also knew her friends were having a party, and she planned to attend. She went straight to the party after the Davises returned home. The party included high school students, as well as a few graduates or young people who had quit school to work in the mine or the mill. There were also some young married people, not necessarily with their spouses. Refreshments were simple: potato chips, popcorn, and two kegs of beer. The KLCB Radio Station played loudly while some partiers danced, some drank, and some were using other rooms of the house for smaller group interactions that included making out, guys talking about guns or sports, and a few girl groups sharing joys and problems related to boyfriends or husbands.

Dick was getting more beer when Darlene asked him to fill up her glass. "You must be new in town? I don't think I've seen you before."

Dick handed her a full glass. "Yes, I just moved here—got a job at the mill." When he looked into her beautiful brown eyes and saw her broad smile, he was sure he had not seen such a lovely girl, especially one who was flirting with him.

Darlene looked him over. He was very cute with curly dark brown hair. He just looked at her and smiled a big shy grin. They spent the rest of the evening getting acquainted. Darlene told him her impressions of Libby. He told her about North Dakota and the small town of Ruso where he grew up. Although they both talked about how unexciting small towns could be, they both seemed rooted in small town ways. They hunted, fished, worked hard, and drank beer. They both liked to have fun.

"Are you free next Saturday? Maybe we could drive around and you could show me Libby and the area—you know—a tour. What do ya think? Could be fun. Maybe we could take in a movie after." Dick raised his eyebrows, smiled, and leaned near her, hoping for a date. He surprised himself by being so forward. Maybe the beer had given him the courage to ask her out. He did not date often due to his own shyness.

Darlene wanted to go with him. Her mind raced. *I want to date you, really I do. How can I possibly get away for a whole day—and a movie at night? How?* "Sounds like fun. I'll have to check with my parents. Do you have a phone? It's better if I call you."

"You betcha!" Dick found a napkin and a pen and wrote his number down.

Darlene read the number, memorized it, and put the napkin in her pocket.

She had to find a way to get out for the afternoon and evening because she knew that her mother would not let her go. Dick was a boy she wanted to see again. He was nineteen, older than any other boy she had been interested in, and he had his own place—one of the mill row houses. She thought that her dad might be more understanding than her mother. She knew a plan would come to her. She was going to go out with him. Babysitting was a successful excuse for dating sometimes, but claiming to work sitting for other families all day was probably not going to work due to her many chores at home. *I can get Julie to cover my chores. Someone here will let me "work" for a day—or longer. I will make this happen!*

Before she left the party, Darlene talked to a married girlfriend who had a baby and said she needed cover for a future plan. Her friend agreed to be part of it; Darlene told her what she might need to say if her mom called. The first plan was only one of many that Darlene created so she could be with Dick.

During the next few months, they dated when Darlene could come up with creative excuses. There were times when she simply crawled out her window, taking the chance that she would not be discovered. She left notes saying she went for a walk. When she returned, if the note was untouched, she burned it in the fireplace. If her mother found her missing, she faced the angry violence with resignation.

In March 1958, she talked to her dad for the first time about dating Dick once a week. She convinced Dick to go to the store and introduce himself to Dewey. He was not sure he wanted to do that because he was a shy person. But he wanted Darlene to date him, and he didn't want her getting into trouble with her parents because she was sneaking out with him. Darlene had not told Dick about her mother's violence toward her—only that her mother was very hard to get along with. She wanted his love, not his pity. Dick had seen the evidence of the beatings when the two of them were intimate. Darlene was good at covering herself, but lapses in her attentiveness occurred, and Dick saw the scarred areas on her back and legs.

Dick screwed up his courage and went to the store. He started a conversation with Dewey first by complimenting him on the look of the store. Then he told him that he had recently moved to Libby from North Dakota. Dewey knew the town of his birth, Ruso. They shared some North Dakota stories since Dewey, raised in Stanley, had spent quite a bit of time in Minot, and Ruso was not that far away. The conversation moved along well, and Dick decided the time was right to get on a more personal level.

"I met Darlene a few weeks ago and I would like your permission to date her." Dewey thought about probing for details of just when and where Dick had met her, but he decided not to. "I moved to Libby for the job at the mill. Les Ramstad is my mom's cousin, and he told me about the job—helped me get it, actually. I like the Libby area and plan to stay here." Dick surprised himself, talking so much.

"Darlene says you like to hunt. Maybe you could give me some ideas on where to hunt in the fall." *I have to let him talk. I've got to shut up! God, I'm so shaky!*

Dewey liked him. He liked the fact that he came to him and introduced himself. He could also see how nervous he was, perspiring forehead, fidgety hands.

"How does Darlene feel about this situation? She hasn't said much to me about this. Although she did mention that she wanted to see you socially." Dewey wondered if the two of them had been dating already, and he assumed that they had been.

"She told me to talk to you before we got into dating very much more than we already have so she knows it's okay with you. She thought you could talk to her mother about this better than she could." Dewey also liked the way Dick acted about Darlene. He seemed honest and straightforward. Dewey finished putting away some sheet music he had been unwrapping. Dick waited for his answer as he looked through some records. He didn't have a record player, but he enjoyed listening to the radio and he knew the kind of music he liked.

"I'd like you to stop at the house after you get off work tomorrow so you can meet Darlene's mother. I'll let her know that you are coming. Seems like we can work things out based on what I know about you right now." Dick took a deep breath, let it out, and then laughed out loud.

"This wasn't easy." He smiled at Dewey.

"I can see that!" Dewey laughed and gave Dick a soft punch on his upper arm. The two men shared some small talk about hunting and where to find deer. "I can give you the names of a couple of landowners who welcome hunters that know the difference between a deer and a cow. The deer take over the grazing fields that their cattle need, so they like to have some controlled hunting to keep their grass for their tame animals." Dewey shared a story of a run-in he had with a bear during a previous hunting season. The incident was serious at the time, yet the retelling took on humorous parts, considering the wounded bear, according to Dewey, wanted to see just how fast Dewey could run; so the bear charged toward him, roaring. Dewey was able to raise his rifle and get off three rounds, fatally wounding the animal. Then the bear wandered a bit, climbed into a five-forked tree, and Dewey had to use a chain saw to get the bear's body out of the tree. Dewey told the story well after having several previous opportunities to tell it. Dick enjoyed the story and imagined going hunting with Dewey sometime during the next season. When a group of shoppers came into the store, Dick took the moment to say good-bye. Dewey shook Dick's hand, and Dick nodded a thank-you as he left the store.

12

DICK AND THE BOWMAN FAMILY
FEBRUARY–JULY 1958

Dick arrived about 6:30 p.m. Darlene had both of her sisters, under her direct instructions, be quiet, say a brief hello, and then go to their bedroom. The girls not only followed her directions, but they also closed the door, except for a couple of inches, and listened quietly as they peeked through the narrow opening. Julie and Helen both thought the boy was cute, and they giggled quietly as they watched from their room.

Dick was nervous, but polite. Dewey welcomed him in and introduced him to Betty. Darlene invited him to sit on the couch by her. Conversation was pleasant as Dick gave a brief description of his background, his parents, and their home in Ruso, North Dakota. He named his relatives in the Libby area who alerted him to the lumber mill job along with an invitation to stay with them until he could rent a place of his own. Dewey knew Dick's relatives—the Ramstads. They were a Norwegian family whose daughter rented a saxophone from him. Les Ramstad worked at the Zonolite Mine for a while and then went into business for himself. A musician like Dewey, Les played bass guitar in a small band for dances in local bars and clubs. Dewey had played drums in previous years with his own group. Betty played saxophone with them for a while but became unwilling to continue playing due to her self-consciousness regarding her weight gain.

Betty talked in a friendly way to Dick at first, and as the evening progressed, she became almost flirty with him. Darlene's impression was positive; she knew that her parents were going to allow her to date him. Darlene served coffee and warm apple pie. When Betty said that Darlene had baked the pie, Dick smiled. That pie was the best he had tasted since leaving home. He liked Darlene and wanted to date her for more than her good looks and her cooking abilities. He genuinely enjoyed being with her, and he was lonely. No one would notice that he was lonely because he was always cheerful and had an infectious laugh. Fortunately, Dewey and Betty agreed to a dating arrangement because those two young people were perfect for one another. Darlene did not know just how lonely she was until she met Dick. He filled her unhappy, torturous life with security and pleasant, fun company. She laughed with him, and he kept her spirits up when her home life was difficult to endure.

Dick managed to ask to date Darlene, and her parents agreed to a one-night-per-week arrangement. That worked well for a few weeks, but Darlene and Dick wanted more time together, and they gradually increased their dating with and without permission.

Dick and Darlene dated at least one night a week, keeping the required curfew of midnight on Saturdays. They often met for a few hours on Sundays, sometimes with permission and sometimes without. Darlene often pushed her luck by going out other nights and sneaking in late. Sometimes she made it in undetected. Other times she faced severe beatings for being late or sneaking out. The beatings occurred at Betty's convenience, so Dewey was unaware of them. Darlene grew hardened to the treatment her mother used on her, not caring if her mother beat her and not responding to her mother with fear anymore. Darlene was going to get out of that house of pain, and she planned to do whatever it took to make that happen.

13

A NEW ARRANGEMENT

In July 1958, Darlene had something personal she needed to tell Dick. "You know that I love you."

"Yes. I feel the same way about you." *You look so serious. You're not breaking up with me. Don't do that.* Darlene was quiet. Dick was concerned. "Just tell me. Is it your mother? Doesn't she want us to date?"

"There's just no way to say this gently." Darlene tried to look serious, but she was happy beyond belief. *Will you be happy?* "I'm going to have a baby—we're going to have a baby." Darlene looked at Dick, watching for signs of disapproval. *He could walk out right now, just like that.*

Dick shook his head, took Darlene's hand. "You really had me worried there, girl. I thought for a minute that you were breaking up with me."

"No, I definitely don't want to break up with you." Her eyes widened, and then she calmed down. "What do you think about this? What do you want to do?"

"Let's get married! That's what I want to do—right now!" It was hard to tell which of the two of them was more excited. Dick even got down on one knee. "Darlene Bowman, will you marry me?" He held her hand, kissed it, and smiled.

"Yes! Yes, I will." Darlene accepted joyously. She could not fully comprehend just how much that meant to her at the time. She came to terms with that major decision in the quiet hours of the night when it dawned on her that she would never face her mother's violence again once she became Mrs. Dick O'Brien.

The next day Darlene asked her parents if she could invite Dick over for dinner. At that time, she wanted to share their plans to marry and keep the pregnancy information to themselves unless they needed it to finalize the deal. Dick came for dinner. The food was plentiful, simple, and tasty. Conversation was limited but pleasant. After dinner, in the living room, Darlene opened the topic.

"Mother and Dad, we have something important to talk to you about." She gratefully looked at Dick.

"I would like your permission to marry Darlene." Direct and brief, Dick waited to see what their reaction was going to be. Betty was caught off guard, but then became rigid.

"I appreciate your feelings, young love and all, but Darlene is too young; Darlene isn't even through high school yet. No. Absolutely no. She has to finish school at least—then maybe work a year or two to grow up first."

Darlene's throat was dry, and her palms were moist as she prepared to answer her mother. "Mother, I can still finish school, and I promise I will. I love Dick, and I want very much to marry him. He has a good job at the lumber mill, and I'll even graduate with my class."

Dewey was quiet as he usually was while Betty continued building internal steam, boiling controllably, but appearing ready to unleash fury. She controlled herself because Dick was there. Betty did not want to lash out at Darlene in front of anyone, but she was not willing to give her permission for the marriage. *How dare she talk back to me? I'll teach her a lesson when I get her alone!*

"I think that we were too hasty in letting you date at sixteen. You were too young, and now you think that you want to get married? Dick, you need to wait a year or two until Darlene finishes high school. Then you can date her again." *That should take care of this. End of discussion.* "You seem like a nice young man, but Darlene is just too young."

Darlene looked at Dick and moved her eyes as though to say, "Now?" Then she said softly, "I'm pregnant."

Betty sucked in air and choked out, "What did you say?" Her face clouded over, her eyes flashed, and she was getting red, blotchy cheeks.

"I'm going to have a baby." Darlene looked happy about the news. Her sweet, full smile further angered Betty.

Betty struggled to get her weight out of her soft chair and started determinedly for Darlene. "You smug little bitch! You whore!" She grabbed Darlene's long brown hair and ripped furiously. Dick was startled by Betty's violent reaction. He and Dewey intervened as quickly as they could to control Betty while Darlene attempted to retain possession of her hair.

"Stop! Let go!" Darlene was in pain. Betty was out of control and gave the two men a struggle before they could pull her hands away from Darlene's hair. Over three hundred pounds of sheer anger was hard to maneuver. The four of them looked at one another, and then the two men helped Betty sit on the sofa. Dewey broke the awkward moment of silence.

"A wedding would be good—and as soon as possible." Dewey was gasping for air, winded from the struggle. So was Dick. Two sisters were watching, wide-eyed, from the bedroom.

Betty changed from violent to sobbing loudly. "How could you do this to me, to us? How could you shame us! What will others think of us? You tramp!" Violence won control again as Betty attempted to get off the sofa and grab Darlene again. Dewey stepped in front of Darlene and held Betty on the sofa. He was grateful when she decided to stay seated. She surrendered herself to the sofa, and Dewey thought she was going to stay there.

Dewey led Dick and Darlene to the door. "Give her time to settle down. Darlene, come home in an hour. I can't say I'm happy about this. You're too young, Darlene. Dick—I'm disappointed. But we will work something out." Dewey could see Darlene was upset. "You're going to get married, that's a fact. No crying, all right?" Darlene nodded. "Go now. Take an hour." Dewey shut the door behind him and headed back toward Betty, wondering where the rest of the night would lead. Betty's reaction frightened him. Her behavior was not unusual from Darlene's perspective. But Dewey had never seen her act as violently as she had.

Darlene and Dick drove away in Dick's car. When they were out of the yard, Darlene cried softly, and Dick pulled her close to him. Tears seldom came to Darlene's eyes. Dick's gentleness helped her soften and allow her emotions their natural venting. He comforted her as well as he could, and his mind tried to wrap itself around the scene he had witnessed.

"You told me before that your mother was hard to get along with. But I never expected her to act like that. My God, has she done that before?"

"Are you kidding? Yes. She always times it when Dad's not home, so he never sees what she does when she loses control." Darlene was still shaking. "I don't want to ever go back in that house, but I know I have to."

"No you don't!" Dick did not want to take her back to that house in an hour—or ever.

"When she gets mad like that, it's hard to tell what she'll do."

"What do you think she'll do—beat you?"

"That's a given. My biggest fear now is that she'll try to make me lose the baby." Darlene was sure that her mother would release her anger in painful ways, if not tonight, within the next few days,

"I can't let that happen. You really think she's that crazy? I mean—would she do that?"

"Of course she would."

Darlene had borne the beatings in the past in a way that made Julie fear for Darlene's life. When her mother went after her, Darlene became intensely quiet, almost daring her mother to hit her. Betty reacted by hitting her harder, beating her with the buckle end of a western belt so hard that some welts would leave scars for life. Darlene refused to cry. She took the beatings unflinchingly, even when her mother knocked her to the floor and kicked her over and over again. Darlene would bundle herself in the fetal position and brace herself for the blows. Her mother could not break her down.

She damaged her daughter in many ways, but she could not seem to kill her defiant spirit.

When Julie faced the belt and fist, she cried out loudly. She wished that Darlene would cry out because she felt that her mother would stop sooner if she could hear the yelling and know she was being effective in her abuse. Julie had scars also, but yelling seemed to make the abuse shorter. Helen was waiting for her turn. She seldom experienced her mother's wrath; her mother slapped her head or pushed her out of the way. The girls knew that when Helen turned nine or ten, she would be as fair game as her sisters were. Mother spanked the girls when they were little, and she taught them lessons in terrible ways. She pressed a small hand on a hot stove to teach them not to touch it. She cut a tiny finger with a sharp knife to prove it could draw blood. She backhanded or slapped down any speech she considered defiant. As the girls grew older, she used the western buckled belt or whatever came into her hand when she became angry. She had burned Helen to "teach her" about a hot pan; she had bitten her as "a lesson." She almost bit a chunk out of her skinny little arm. But she had not started using the belt on her or kicking her.

Betty made Darlene and Julie take off their clothing and lie naked on the bed before she beat them. She used a belt and a leather razor strap to hit their backs, bottoms, and legs again and again. When they were younger, they gyrated back and forth, causing the strap to hit their arms as well as their backs. Even their heads and legs took on belt stripes when mother was out of control with rage. As they grew older, they both lay still, resigned to humiliation and pain, and the strap did not damage the front of their bodies if they controlled themselves against the belt.

Darlene knew what she had been to her mother in her rages: a target struck over and over to accomplish some inner need to cause pain. She knew her mother's ability to control herself could not last after the revelation of her pregnancy and an impending marriage. Darlene knew that when her mother seemed to fall into the chair, she was only resting to regain her strength to abuse Darlene in a different way. Kicking and punching helped release frustration and cause pain. Biting worked.

In the car, Darlene told Dick, "I'm afraid to go home." She expressed her fear calmly. "Mother could unleash her anger at any time." For the first time, Darlene told another person about her mother's abuse. "Mother has threatened to beat us to death if we ever told anyone. Dad was never home when she lost it, so he had no idea how bad it was. She told both Julie and me that she would kill Helen if either of us told anyone."

Dick pulled over to the side of the road and stopped the car. Darlene's words stunned him. "You are really afraid of her, aren't you?" Dick asked her.

"Yes. I told you I'm afraid that she will somehow cause me to lose our baby."

"How would she do that?"

"Once she sets her mind to do something, she finds ways. She might put something in my food to make me sick, or beat me until I lose it. She wouldn't be above tying me up and trying to give me an abortion," Darlene explained in a quiet, convincing way. "I would never let her tie me up willingly, but she could come up behind me and knock me out." Darlene seemed to visualize the scene as she sat silently. She rested her head on Dick's shoulder.

Dick was silent for a few minutes. He could see that Darlene was telling him the truth. Whether Betty would actually do the things Darlene had feared, he didn't know. But he was not going to take the chance after Betty's fierce attack that he had just witnessed. He held Darlene close to him, taking in the frightening information about his future wife's fears and a mother-in-law out of control. It was overwhelming. After sitting for a while, he was quietly, but firmly resolved to make some sense out of the situation. He started the car and returned to Darlene's house.

When they pulled into the driveway, the lights were still on. Darlene started to scoot out behind him, but he asked her to wait until he came out to get her. "I want to be sure your mother has settled down, Darlene. There's no way I want you to get hurt again."

Dick got out of the car, and then bent back inside. "Besides, I love your hair and don't want any more pulled out tonight!" He chuckled, but the attempt at humor was only to calm Darlene. She smiled. Dick went up to the door, pulled it open, and entered without waiting for someone to let him in. Dewey met him and said it was too early for Darlene to come in, that Betty was still not settled down.

"Where is she?" Dick's voice was calm, yet strong.

"In the kitchen. Better give her more time."

Dick went to the kitchen anyway. "Betty." Dewey followed him, fearful for Betty's reaction.

She turned and looked at him. "What are you doing here?" She drew herself up, doubled up her fists, and seemed to prepare herself for a physical confrontation. Dewey looked at her reaction in disbelief. Would she really use physical force against Dick? Dick was taller and much stronger than Betty. Dewey came into the room and stood by to see what might take place, hoping he could head off any violence between them.

"I came to tell you something very important. Dewey, you need to hear this, too." Dick's voice was strong, calm, and firm. He waited until Betty made eye contact with him. "Betty, if you harm Darlene in any way I will call the police and have you arrested. I know you have beaten her, and Dewey, this has been happening for years when you are at work. Do not"—*I have to stay calm*, he thought. *I can't believe I'm doing this*—"do not hit her, slap her, use a belt on her, or harm her in any way or I will call the police." Dick had control. She was listening. "If I even think you have hurt her, I'll put a story in the paper about how you treat your kids. You want to use physical force? I'll show you physical force if you even scare her, damn it! DO YOU UNDERSTAND?" Dick had never raised his voice in anger like that to anyone.

Betty appeared shocked. No one had ever stood up to her or threatened her like that since her childhood. She had as a child experienced unspeakable abuse, but not as an adult. She cried loudly, yelling, "I never beat her. She's lying! How can she say that about me! She's a slut! A filthy slut! She's a liar!" Dewey looked at

Betty as though she were a stranger. He listened to her slander their daughter in disbelief.

"She didn't have to tell me that you beat her. She has scars all over her body! Strap marks, burns, bruises—even bite marks."

Betty screamed, "Darlene was a bad girl! She had it coming! I tried to raise her right. I never did a thing to her that she didn't deserve. But look what she's done—and what you've done!" Betty seemed to swell with power with her last comment. *He's at fault! I've got him!* Betty became calm. Her voice, no longer with a sob in it, became strong. "Don't you even think of threatening me! You raped my daughter—she's only sixteen years old! I'll call the police and we'll see who they believe!" Betty grabbed the phone.

Dick stood there. "Go ahead! Call them right now." He paused. *What the hell am I saying?* "Where's the phone? I'll get it for you!" Dick saw the phone, grabbed it, and handed it to Betty.

Betty was shaking and confused. "Get out! Get out of here!"

"Call the police." Dick was steady, strong voiced, and under control. "All they have to do is look at her back and they'll see who is lying. You've scarred her for life. Like I told you, I will make sure everyone knows what you've done to your children. I'll write the whole story about how you beat your girls! I'll have the *Western News* print it in the paper for everyone to read. Or I'll write the story myself and pay them to print it. I'll put it in every business and house in town, 'Mother Beats Three Daughters.'"

Betty had stopped yelling and was listening intently to Dick as he threatened to expose her abuse of her children. She looked around the room then settled her gaze on Dewey. "Do something, Dewey! Do something! Don't let him talk to me like that!" she pleaded. Dewey stood watching Betty then Dick. Betty looked at the phone receiver in her hand, pounding it against her hand. Dick looked more at Dewey than Betty.

"Darlene is carrying my baby. I do not want my child or Darlene harmed in this house. Until I know that you will not harm her, she will be with me." Dick started to walk to the door to leave.

Dewey moved to Dick and put his hand on Dick's shoulder. "Nobody is going to hurt her again." Dewey turned to Betty, continuing to hold Dick's shoulder. "Betty, hang up the phone. Now!" Dewey moved from Dick to Betty, taking the phone from her. He set it on the pile of magazines near him.

Just moments before, Betty had been ready to attack Dick physically. Her demeanor changed sharply again. She slid down the wall, crying a wailing, helpless, animal-like cry. "I can never count on you, Dewey. When I need your support, you are never there for me. How can you let him talk like that to me?" Betty was swirling in an emotional turmoil of fear, hate, and anger. She wanted to cause pain to someone, she was afraid to be discovered as the abuser she was, and she was both angry and helpless, no longer controlling any part of the situation.

Dewey bent down to her and tried to lift her, but he could not get her up due to her weight. He moved down to her and said quietly, but firmly, "The last thing you want here is for the police to get involved. We've got a business here, our income, our home. You better just calm down and use some sense here, Betty. You might make Dick look bad, but most likely you'll be the one who ends up in jail. You don't want that, and neither do I."

Betty looked at Dewey, his words shocking her with what the future could hold for her, and she began to cry intensely, wailing and sobbing. After a few moments, she settled down and she pitifully asked Dick not to call the police or tell anyone. "And for cryin' out loud, don't write anything. Just...just...don't tell anybody about this. I'm not well." She had the "poor me" sound in her voice. "I'm sick and sometimes I get upset." She began melting into sobbing gasps in an attempt to elicit sympathy, but none was forthcoming. Dick and Dewey, stunned by the wide range of emotional upheaval that Betty had demonstrated in just a few minutes, looked at one another. Both men wondered what Betty might do next.

Dick and Dewey moved away from Betty to talk to one another. "I will take care of Darlene, Dick. I promise you that I will not allow Betty to hurt her."

"Darlene's not just afraid she'll hurt her. She's afraid she'll try to make her lose this baby."

"She said that?" Dewey's brow furrowed.

"Dewey, she's been beating your girls for years. Yes, Darlene is afraid she'll make her lose the baby—even give her an abortion herself."

"She wouldn't do that!"

"Look at your girls, Dewey. This has been going on for a long time."

"I will make sure she is safe. I'll put a lock on her door at night. I'll check on her during the day."

"I got to hear it from Betty, Dewey. Let's get her to say it—that she won't keep up this abuse. You can't watch her every minute, and she needs to know I mean business."

Dewey and Dick walked back to Betty. "Listen, you need to promise to stop what you're doing or Dick means it. He'll do it. And, really, I don't want you beating the girls anyway!" He looked at her and waited for an answer. Betty was silent, searching within herself for support. A memory flooded her mind of her stepfather beating her severely then taking her away from her mother. As the memory ached within her, she became tearful and quiet.

"I promise I won't hurt Darlene." She sounded sincere, and she believed herself at the time.

"Or Julie or Helen," Dewey added. He wanted the abuse to stop, period.

"Yes, I won't hurt them." Betty's eyes rolled back as her head rested on the back of the sofa.

"And the baby. You won't hurt the baby or its development in any way. I want this baby healthy and happy." Dick was firm. Betty agreed.

Dick saw Dewey's look of genuine concern as he nodded for Dick to get Darlene. He went out to the car and brought Darlene into the house. Darlene saw her mother on the floor near the phone, sobbing and distraught.

"Darlene, your dad and mother have assured me that you will be safe here. Your mother will not hurt you in any way." Dick looked directly at Betty. "Your dad has given his word that she will not hurt you, and he will protect you. Betty has promised that she will not ever hurt you or your sisters again. Both of you tell her that what I have said is true. I'm not leaving Darlene here unless she feels she will be safe. Tell her!"

Betty was quiet. Dewey needed no direction. "Darlene, your mother will not harm you again in any way. Isn't that right, Betty? Tell her that's right."

Betty quietly answered. "I won't hurt you."

"I'm sorry, Darlene." Dewey put his arm around his daughter. "I didn't know about all this or I would have stopped it before now." Darlene looked at her mother who was sobbing and talking to herself. "I'll keep you safe. It's all right. She won't do it again. Betty, tell her. Tell her."

Betty started the sobbing again and said she wouldn't hurt her. She then added that she would help plan a wedding and they could all work things out. "My little girl's going to be a mommy!" The scene was eerie. Betty went from total depression, anger, and hostility to fearful, meek, and submissive, giving her blessing to a future marriage. Darlene wanted to believe she was going to be safe. Her mother was unusually upset, but Darlene had never seen her that submissive. Darlene did not trust her and thought that her change of behavior would probably pass by morning or sometime in the night when her dad was asleep.

Darlene went to her mother's side, and she and Dewey helped her up from the floor. They walked her into the bedroom and helped her lie down. Betty rolled over and fell asleep.

Dick and Darlene held one another. Dewey stood by, and then he shook Dick's hand. Dewey held back tears as he said, "Welcome to the family, son. It's not always like this. Come on in and let's have a drink to toast an upcoming wedding!" Dewey tried to make the best of a bad situation. He had learned that night about the severity of Betty's violence and his own lack of awareness of how horrible her treatment of his daughters had become. He knew Betty disciplined the girls, but he had no idea of the severity of the methods she had used. He had been too busy at the store, staying away from home as much as possible because he did not want to face his failing marriage and his unhappy wife.

Dick stayed awhile just to assure himself that the house would not erupt into chaos again. He loved Darlene and was only beginning to realize how difficult her life was. He had seen her scarred back, but not often; when they were together intimately, it was usually dark and he was not as involved with her back. Darlene had told him that she and her mother did not get along, but Darlene had not talked about the details. She did not want Dick to feel sorry for her. She wanted his love, not his pity. She also wanted out of that house, and she was grateful that she was pregnant—very grateful. She was also happy that Dick wanted to marry her.

Dewey kept a bottle of bourbon around for medicinal purposes. He very seldom drank alcohol, and Betty didn't drink much either. He poured some bourbon into small water glasses for Darlene and Dick, and one for himself. He then made a toast. "To the future. It will be better." They drank and sat together for a few minutes, thoughts racing through their minds. Dewey went into the bedroom and returned with the message that Betty was asleep. Darlene sipped the strong liquid and set it down, leaving most of it in the glass. Dick drank his down, and then drank Darlene's. Dewey took three sips and grimaced to finish off his portion.

Darlene walked Dick outside. When they were on the porch, Darlene put her arms around Dick and wept softly. "Thank you for standing up to her. I love you very much."

Dick held her, caressed her, and touched her head, which ached from her mother's hair pulling earlier. "You need to be sure to let me know if she even threatens you. If she gets away with anything, everything that happened tonight will be lost."

"I'll tell you. I promise. Will I see you tomorrow night? Can you come out about seven? After tonight, I think mom will let us talk about a wedding date. Okay?"

Dick said he would be there and that she should get some sleep so she would feel rested the next day. "I want you to be healthy and happy, you know! Oh, yeah. Your dad's going to put a lock on your bedroom door." Dick affectionately put his hand on her stomach, and then kissed her again. He drove away in a bit of a dust cloud. Even his car seemed grateful to be leaving, wanting some distance between the Bowman house and his rented mill row house in town.

Darlene went in, hugged her dad, and thanked him. She went to her room. Just to be sure that she would not have a surprise visit in the night, she stacked up some boxes in front of her bedroom door. Her door didn't have a lock yet, but the boxes would make lots of noise and wake up her dad. She thought about everything that had happened in the last hour. As she stretched out on her bed, she placed her hands on her tummy, warmly and gently. She smiled. Dick had stood up to her parents. He had told them he would not let anyone hurt either her or the baby. In a few weeks she would be married and living somewhere else. She savored the thought of freedom from pain, abuse, and shame. It took her some time to calm her mind and to set aside the mental images of her mother crumbled on the floor, her dad standing up for her, and her future husband taking such a supportive position on her behalf. He was her prince, her savior, and her lover. He would soon be her husband. Sleep gradually settled over her. That might have been the most important day of her life. That day's events had changed everything—she hoped.

Dick was looking forward to the marriage. He had left home two years ago after his mother divorced his father. He had been on his own, getting work as he could. He was an excellent worker, and he could provide skilled carpenter work after helping his dad throughout his teen years. He did not like living alone, and he loved the idea of marrying Darlene and having a family. As he drove home, he thought about coming home and having someone there. Someone he loved. Someone who was carrying his child. Marrying Darlene would be good for them both. She could sure have a better life with him. He knew that for certain after what he had seen that evening. *Would Dewey be able to keep Betty from harming Darlene?* Dick slept fitfully that night, dreaming of having a beautiful child who was murdered by a witch.

14

TWO SISTERS LISTEN AND HOPE

Julie and Helen were supposed to be asleep. They had been watching from their room together, totally attentive to every word and every move of all four of those people. The two girls climbed into Julie's bed. Helen didn't want to sleep alone, and they were both in a state of confused joy as they held onto each other, saying nothing.

Someone was opening their bedroom door. Their dad had a flashlight and was moving the covers from Julie. He lifted her pajamas and the extra shirt she was wearing. He shined the flashlight on her back and saw the damage the years of belting had created as a witness to her mother's abuse. Julie didn't move. Dewey sat on the bed and sobbed softly. "My God, how could I have been so blind? My children. My God, my children." He held his head in his hands. Julie sat up and put her arms around her dad and cried with him.

"Will she really stop, Dad? Or will she just stop beating Darlene?" Julie's tears glistened on her cheeks.

"Did you hear all this tonight?" Dewey asked. Julie nodded that she had.

"She will stop. I don't want any of you beaten. If she ever lays a hand on you or Helen—or Darlene—you promise me right now that you will tell me. Promise me. I have to work at the store, so you have to be my trusting eyes to keep you girls safe. Promise." Dewey sat rocking Julie in his arms.

"But, Dad, she says she will make it even worse if we tell you."

"Is that why you've never told me about this? You're afraid of her so much that you haven't told me?"

"Dad, did you ever see these cigarette burns on my legs? Or the bite marks and burns here on my arm? We know better than to tell anyone. Yes, we're afraid of her. Really afraid of her. If one of us ever told, she said she would..." Julie stopped, her eyes darting to the door. She acted as though she heard something. Julie looked at her dad, and then she pointed toward the door, fearful that her mother might be standing there, listening, waiting for her chance to teach her not to tell. Julie was shaking and tears were welling in her eyes. Dewey could see her looking toward the door, fearful of someone out there in the dark. Julie cupped her hand near her dad's ear and whispered, "She said she would kill Helen."

"I will never let that happen." Dewey followed Julie's frightened eyes to the doorway. "She's sleeping now. You have to tell me everything—any time she hits you girls—or I can't keep all three of you safe. I have to know that you will tell me. This is what we'll do: if she beats any one of you, or hurts you in any way at all, you tell me that Smokey's sick. Okay? Just that. I'll ask you about her and we'll go check on her together. Then you can talk to me without her hearing you."

"Smokey's sick," Julie said. She became thoughtful and quiet, resting her head on his arm. She repeated it again to be sure she would remember.

"I can't do this alone. Think of your sisters. You need to tell me so I can keep all three of you safe."

"Okay, Dad. I'll do my best." Julie wanted to trust him. There had been many times when she wondered how he could not know what their mother was doing to her and her sisters. How could he miss the sadness and fear that enveloped the house? Didn't he see the burns or the bruises, the blood that sometimes seeped through their clothing where the strap had cut their skin?

Helen could not pretend to be asleep any longer. She joined Julie in hugging their dad. Dewey held them, rocked them, cried with them, and promised them that he would keep them safe, but he told them that he needed them to help him. Julie could not remember ever hoping so much that their lives could change. She believed what had happened that night might be the beginning of a safer future.

None of the three people holding each other so securely knew that just beyond the door frame, someone was standing quietly in the dark, just as Julie had suspected earlier, listening to their words. Betty went quietly back to her bedroom when she thought the conversation was coming to an end. The words that very softly left her lips through a smile were "Smokey's sick." She closed her eyes and her facial expression indicated that she had won a victory, however small it might have been.

Dewey tucked in the girls, kissed them good night, and left them to sleep. When he was out of the room, Julie held Helen, and together they whispered about not having to worry about being hit anymore.

Just before she went to sleep, Helen said quietly, "Do you believe that it's over? Really?"

Julie said, "I want to believe it, but I'm still afraid. We have to be careful and stick together. Promise?"

"I don't think it's over, either. After tonight, it could get worse. I love you and I promise to be careful," Helen said.

"I love you, too, Sis." Julie wanted to sleep. Her mind was restless as she waited for her mother's footsteps to come in the night to watch them sleep, or to make them pay for their sins toward her. Mother might watch Darlene instead. After a few moments in the dark room, Helen broke the silence.

"Do you think Dad can stop her?" Helen asked.

"We'll see. I hope so. Now go to sleep, sweetie," Julie patted Helen's hair and kissed her cheek. "It'll be okay. Now sleep." In her heart, she wanted her dad to be able to end the abuse, but her mind seemed to know that it was not over.

Julie had witnessed Darlene getting beaten for years. There were times when Julie would go into Darlene's room after mother had beaten her to be sure that Darlene had not died. Darlene would turn away from her, but Julie would move close to her just to feel her sister's body heat and reassure herself that Darlene was still living. Julie would ease her body close to Darlene and hold her hand without touching her wounds. Julie needed to feel her breathe. Darlene had not been able to admit it, but she had wanted Julie there. She was grateful that Julie cared enough to be there.

When Betty's abuse began to include Julie, Darlene felt fear expand within her, extending to every part of her being. Her only defense was to reject signs of fear and stoically let her mother beat her. How could she let go of her fear when she had been programmed to believe that her very existence and her sisters' lives depended upon her mother's emotional state? "Strong" to Darlene meant no sound, no tears, and no sign of weakness. Somewhere within Darlene was a strong will to live. She had convinced herself that if she let down her guard, her mother would no longer be content to beat her. She believed her mother would kill her.

15

A NEW DIRECTION

Exhaustion won and both Helen and Julie slept until their dad woke them for chores. Dad was especially kind as he woke them with a cheerful pat on their covers and told them, "It's a beautiful day, girls! Let's get out there and enjoy it!" Helen had stayed in Julie's bed all night. The girls hugged each other and smiled like never before, and a quiet, joyful song slipped out of their mouths as they stepped out on the cold floor.

Julie and Helen quickly dressed in their chores clothes and tackled the work happily. They did their work well and finished early. They both liked to start their day with the animals that seemed eager for the water and feed and ready for the girls to pet them. Smokey was always happy to get milked and not so happy if Julie came late. They all had an understanding about the timeliness of milking Smokey and feeding and watering all the animals. Being late or not doing the chores was unforgivable. Both Helen and Julie knew that they had to take care of the penned animals that had no way of taking care of themselves.

After chores were completed, Julie mixed up pancakes and had them on the table for Helen and Dad. Mother was still in bed. Darlene was sick in the bathroom and did not want to even look at a pancake. It was important to them to get out of the house and involved in gardening before their mother awakened. Dad had not left for the store. There would be time for them to talk and to make sure what happened the night before was not set aside.

When Betty awoke, she went into the kitchen for coffee. Dewey poured her a cup, and he also refilled his cup. "Betty, last night was a real eye-opener for me. I had no idea what was going on here with the girls."

Betty was not willing to be chastised that morning. "You never take a stand and make them mind. You're never home. It's up to me to take care of everything—this house, the animals, the cooking—I do it all with some help from the girls. It's hard to get them to mind me without a firm hand now and then." Betty told him with an angry edge in her voice. Dewey was upset.

"You've beaten them. You've burned them, bitten them. I did not know what you were doing, and that's my fault. But I saw the scars for myself last night. This has to stop, Betty. You not only abused them, but you are still lying about it." Dewey was angry and wanted to beat her himself. His hands were formed into fists, and he felt himself on the verge of punishing her for what she had done. If she at least seemed sad about it or said she was sorry and would stop, he thought he would be less outraged. He would not hit her. He didn't hit anyone or act the part of a bully. He was strong, though. If pushed or threatened, he could handle himself in a fight and come out well. He usually talked his way out of trouble, and he was a gentle person.

His calm and quiet nature may have been part of the reason he did not see the damage happening to his children. Far more was going on in his home, far beyond his comprehension.

"Are you going to start taking care of things around here? You spend twelve hours a day at the store, and sometimes you go back nights. I can't cope with the girls by myself all the time." Betty was not shrinking back as she had the previous night. She was regaining her edge.

"I'll tell you what I'm going to do. I'm going to work, but during the day I'm going to come by from time to time to see what's going on here. I'm going to have other people stop in to check on you. I want you dressed in something other than your nightgown all day. I want you to actually do some work around here instead of making the girls do it all." Dewey just watched her and waited for her response. His strong statements about Betty's behaviors were unusual for him.

"How can you say that I don't work around here? I work hard. And you know I'm not well. I have these sick headaches every day," Betty started to explain. She seemed to rock between anger and helplessness, hoping one or the other would help her hold onto some sort of control, but she was unsure which way to go.

"Do you need to be someplace where you are taken care of twenty-four hours a day? Do you think you need that kind of care? Because I can help with that. What you have been doing to the children is horrible. It's insane." Betty looked at him straight on with abject fear in her eyes. *He wouldn't put me in an institution, would he?* Dewey saw the look, and it strengthened him more than he had experienced for years.

"Get dressed. I'm taking you to the doctor this morning to see what can be done for you. You've been sick too long without any real medical help. Let's take care of you and get you feeling better. You need to smoke less often, eat healthier, and you need to do something besides stay in bed all day. Get some exercise—other than swinging a belt at the girls." Dewey was standing up to her. He surprised himself in his confident remarks, especially the harshness of his last comment about swinging the belt. He was angry and just warming up.

"You can't make me go to the doctor." Betty's tone was forceful, even defiant.

Dewey said that he would call a couple of neighbors to come help him. "I'll tell them you are plumb nuts, out of your mind, and then have them help me haul you off to the doctor. I'll tell them that you beat the children, and I'll show them Julie's scars. I'll call Tom and Lavina to come help me. I can get the Conovers also—and the Gehrings. Your days of beating our children are over. Do you hear me? Over!" Dewey took the cigarette from her hand and snuffed it out.

"You have fifteen minutes to get dressed or you're going like you are. If you don't go willingly, I will make you go. I better see you dressing or I'm calling the neighbors." Dewey went into the bedroom and took out some clothing for her. She followed him into the room. He told her to put them on. "People who see you in the doctor's office will wonder why you're in your bathrobe. Get dressed." When she hesitated, he went to the phone, picked it up, and waited for the operator. "I'll call Tom Holland first. He will help me. I'll have him bring his wife, his hired hand, and anyone else he thinks we need." Dewey waited for the operator to ask for the number. When the operator came on, he started to ask to be connected to the Holland residence.

"No, don't do that!" Betty was shocked. "I'll get dressed right now. Don't call anyone." He let her hang up the phone. Betty put on the clothes he had laid out, combed her hair, and got in the car with Dewey. The drive to town could have been four long, quiet miles with limited conversation, but Dewey broke the silence during the second mile by asking her why she beat the girls. Betty remained silent.

Finally, Betty said quietly, "When did you stop loving me?"

Dewey thought about that for a moment. "I'm not sure that I love you right now. But I'm also not sure that I don't. I know we can't go on like this. I can't have you beating my children. It looks to me like you're trying to kill yourself and the girls, too. Let's see what the doctor has to say."

"I'm lonely. I can't stand being at home all the time. The girls are driving me crazy." Silence followed for a couple of minutes. Her mind was racing. She had to figure out a way to keep from being institutionalized. There were times when she wondered about her sanity, and she had become so depressed that she wanted to take her own life several times. She also had experienced wanting, almost aching, to kill one of her children. She hated Darlene's strong will and feared that Darlene would get the best of her if she tried to kill her. Julie would be a good one, but she needed her to take care of Helen. She thought about killing Helen, but Helen was sweet to her, hugged her more than the other girls. Then she thought about what everyone would think and that she could be caught and end up in prison. She always worried about what others would think if she killed her children. But, she imagined, if she killed herself, everyone would feel bad for her. How could she kill herself if she were in an institution?

Dewey responded, "You know, you could go to work at the store for a few hours every day. You'd be out of the house, you'd have to fix up so you look presentable, and you just might like it."

Betty was quiet. She used to love working in the store. That could be her way to keep her freedom. "Who'd look after the girls?" she asked. "I used to enjoy the store, but I gave it up to take care of the girls. They can't hang around the store. Who would take care of them?"

"Would you want to do that? Work at the store?" Dewey asked, surprised that Betty would even consider the option. "There's a lot to do, you know, keeping the store swept up, counters cleaned up, and, most important, organize the inventory and keep the books straight. And be able to wait on customers—talk to people and encourage business—because that's what I do every day." Dewey glanced at her while he drove.

She knew he was watching her. She had to play it just right or she could miss her chance. "I think I would like to do that. I think I'd be good at it. I used to do it, and I was very good at it. But then, I became so exhausted with the girls and all."

Dewey pulled over to the side of the road by the weigh station, stopped the car, and looked her straight in the eyes. "I can't have you do this and then complain every day about how tired you are and how hard I make you work. You have to suck it up and do the job. If you don't think you are up to it, then don't do it."

"Who would watch the girls?" Betty asked again.

"I can only think of one person right now who would be available and who would really love the girls. My mother," Dewey said. "I know that you two don't get along, but we could try this out for a few weeks and see if she likes it here. If she likes it, and you two get along, then we could move her here into a place of her own. She loves the girls and would be great with them. She likes to cook and could help out with the housework. Since Dad died last year, she's lonely. If it works out, I could set her up in her own place, and she could keep track of the girls after school while you work."

"She hates me, Dewey. You know that's true, and I don't like her, either." Betty was shaking her head. But the thought of staying out of an institution and getting back to the store were both powerful incentives. She could put up with his mother if she could just get a daily break from the house and from, well, from being a mother. Betty hated being a mother and a wife.

"If you can handle a full day at the store, and I set my mom up in her own place, she won't be around much when you are home. She can eat dinner with us, and—"

"Does she have to eat with us? Can't she go to her own place and eat?" Betty whined.

"If she's going to head up the cooking and cleaning, the least we can do is feed her and help keep her from having to buy a lot of food for herself. We'll have to pay her something, and meals could help offset what we'd owe her." Dewey was pretty convincing. He pulled out into the stream of traffic and continued into town to the doctor's office. "It's a lot to think about. Let's just take care of getting you a checkup. One thing at a time."

"I'm feeling better. I really don't need us paying for a doctor visit. Let's go to the store and see what I could start with there. Darlene can take care of the girls today while we look things over." Betty seemed like a new person. She was ready to do something different. "Do you think your mom would move here at her age? She has her friends and her church—her own house in Sandpoint?"

"I don't know, but I could ask her." Dewey was pleased with himself. He had no idea that Betty would want to work in the store again. In fact, when he thought about bringing it up again, he was almost afraid that she would throw a fit if he even mentioned her working. And those two women did not get along. Period. Yet there she was, willing to have his mother move there and take over the house while she worked. One major blowup the night before changed everything.

Dewey drove them to the store. It was going to be a moment he would regret later, perhaps, after being so close to seeing the doctor and then giving in to Betty. But he thought he was solving every-thing. With his mother in the house, he knew that Betty couldn't beat the children. He didn't want to miss out on the opportunity by having Betty change her mind.

On the drive to town, there was some conversation, mainly on Dewey's part. Betty had another conversation going on in her brain. The private dialogue she carried on within her mind that guided her toward violence was flooding her mind with conflicting thoughts. She sensed that the impact of the recent traumatic interactions with Dewey and Dick was a chance to make her own life better. She did not intend to erupt emotionally and react physically as she had in the past. The memories from her childhood were powerful and haunting. She pushed them back, trying to ignore them. She looked straight ahead as the car rolled down the highway toward town. She held an inner dialogue with herself, wondering if she should grab the wheel and steer it into the oncoming logging truck. *Dewey might die. I might live.*

Betty looked at the truck coming closer. One hand reached toward the wheel, but the other hand folded its fingers into the other and rested it on her lap. *Now. Take the wheel now! Dewey can't commit me to an institution if he's dead.*

"No," Betty said firmly.

"No, what?" Dewey was confused by Betty's one word comment to the silence between them. "Are you having second thoughts?"

Betty returned to reality. "Oh, no, I was just thinking. Don't mind me." By now, the logging truck had passed by, but another one would be coming along anytime. That was logging country, and she could find another time if she needed an escape. In fact, she could see a large, overloaded logging truck coming toward them, taking more than its share of the road.

16

THREE SISTERS REVIEW
EVENTS

When their parents drove off, the girls decided to take a break. They had a certain number of rows to get weeded, and some of the vegetables had to be dug up or picked for the week's meals. Julie used a small shovel to loosen potatoes, and Helen picked them up, shaking the dirt back to the ground and then putting the potatoes in a bucket. Darlene was weeding the lettuce and bean rows. A few minutes to take cold drinks of water and eat apples would do them good. With mother out of the house, they could actually sit for a few minutes, knowing that she wasn't watching them. They took an apple each from the tree in the yard, sat in the shade with a water jug, and passed it around.

"We heard Dick last night. Helen and I heard everything." Julie smiled slyly at Darlene.

Darlene tried to act uninterested, but she let a small smile sneak out as she said, "Oh?"

Helen added, "We also heard you talk about getting married. Are you excited about that? And, oh yeah, about having a baby!" Helen was excited.

Darlene still attempted to be mildly interested. "Well, we might be getting married." Julie and Helen couldn't contain their excitement. They set aside their apples and jumped all over Darlene until she told them that she was excited. The three girls laughed as the two younger sisters tickled and taunted Darlene until she was laughing loudly and begging them to stop.

"What did Dick say, Julie?" Darlene asked when the three of them settled down a bit and she could catch her breath.

Julie said, "He was amazing. He told mother that she better not ever hurt you again or he would, what'd he say, Helen? He would call the police and he would beat her himself!"

"That's right!" Helen piped in. "We were scared that Dick was going to be dead right there!"

"But Dad was there," Julie continued explaining, "and Mom just didn't know what to do—or who to hit! He really stood up for you, Darlene. I wish I could marry him, and Helen could marry him, too. Can we all go with you and Dick?"

Darlene laughed and grabbed Julie and Helen at the same time. "That's not the way it works! When two people get married, they go to their own house. Some day you will each get married, and then you will move away from home. I'm older than you, so I'm going first, that's all. Besides, we'll just be living in town. I'll see you sometimes."

Julie said, "I know we couldn't actually marry Dick, but getting out of here would be great! If I was the one getting out of here, I don't think I'd want to come back and take a chance on another beating. I would just want to go and stay gone." Julie looked wistfully off toward the beautiful Cabinet Mountains, wanting to be on the other side of them somehow—away from the fear and pain of that house.

Helen added that she would not want to come back. "Darlene, will you come back? I mean, will you really come see us after you're married? You'll have a baby soon, and you'll be busy. Promise you'll come back sometimes." Helen was noticeably sad, and Julie jumped in, hugging Helen.

"Of course she'll come back! She'll miss all the gardening and butchering and cooking and cleaning! She might miss it all so much that she'll change her mind and just stay home!" Julie tried to laugh, but the girls were thoughtful and the comment made Helen cry. Darlene held her and cried, and Julie was crying the loudest. "I'm sorry, sweetie," Julie said, patting Helen's head. "It's gonna be okay, really. Don't cry." They all knew that Darlene was going away from them, and even though they understood why, they were distraught, feeling sadness, fear, and a deep sense of loss, yet at the same time they were happy for Darlene.

A thought that entered all three of their minds was how long it would be until mother let loose on them. Julie was the most likely to feel pain first since Mother had beaten her many times. Darlene had Dick to help her. When Mother did decide to beat Julie or Helen—and of course, she would in a very short time— could Julie dare tell Dad? What would Mom do to Dad if Julie told him? She still felt that her mother knew all about how Dad was going to find out if she did any cruel things to them. She was listening outside the room. Julie just felt she was there. Mother often listened at doors and then came in the girls' rooms at night and watched them. When they were working outside, she would just show up, looking around sneakily from behind a door or stall to make sure they were doing what they should be doing. Julie would have to tell Dad somehow. A workable plan could not involve Smokey. If Dad ever asked how Smokey was doing, Julie had already decided that she would automatically say, "Just fine, Dad."

The girls went back to the garden and had worked for about five minutes when Darlene yelled, "Let's get our work done fast and then go for a swim while the folks are gone!"

Helen yelled out happily and Julie agreed, laughing and saying, "That's a great plan!" They sped up dramatically, yet they knew they had to do a good job. Julie worked fast, and as she worked, her mind raced along as well. What if her parents came home and they were gone? What would happen to them? She knew that she was going to be the next target. Fear was strong. Years of programming were hard to challenge after only one night of verbal promises that the pain would stop.

When they finished the garden for the day, Darlene was ready to change into her swimwear—cutoff work pants and a T-shirt. "Let's go! Get changed!"

"I want to, but I don't think we should," Julie said. Helen looked at her and knew why she felt that way. "Last night Dad said he would keep Mom from beating us and that we had to tell him if anything happened. I know Mom was outside the door listening. She's going to be looking for a reason to get at us, especially me. Dad made a deal with me, made me promise to tell. I said I would. But I don't think I can. If I told and she hurt Helen, I'd…" Fear felt normal to the girls as they thought about what could happen to them.

"If she goes after anybody, she'll go after me," Darlene said. "Getting pregnant, getting married, and, well…not having me to take care of everything. She doesn't want that to happen. Let's go have some fun at the creek for no longer than an hour. I'll leave a note telling them where we are, and I'll tell them it was my treat to both of you since you all worked so well in the garden. That leaves you free, Julie. And Helen, you're too young for her to enjoy hurting you yet. Come on! Get changed!"

Julie then brought up the unborn child. "If she goes after you, she could hurt the baby."

"Dick won't let her do that. He won't. Now, let's go. We may be back before they return anyway, and they'll never know we were even gone. We're wasting time!" Darlene grabbed them and pushed them toward the house. They all ran the rest of the way to the house and changed clothes.

Shortly after they entered the house, there was a loud knock at the front door. Julie, still dressed in work clothing, answered the door and welcomed Eric, their half brother. He had the day off from Zonolite, and he wanted to talk to his dad. Eric was sixteen years older than Darlene, and the girls thought he was the best looking brother ever. He was nice to them and even took them to a drive-in movie a couple of times when Dewey let him.

"Dad's not home. He and Mother just took off for town. You probably passed them on your way here."

"I just came from Market Road, so I missed them. What are you girls doing today—no, let me guess—working! Aren't you always working?"

"We're just getting ready to go for a swim at the creek. Wanna come?" Julie asked without thinking that he really would go with them.

"Yes, come with us. We're going to hit the rapids before they're gone for the summer," Darlene added in a coaxing way.

"I'm not dressed for it. Besides, I don't want to horn in on your fun."

"Are you kidding? You coming will make it more fun! I still have to get my cutoffs on. I'll get you something of Dad's to wear. He won't care." Darlene grabbed a pair of Dad's "swim" wear by the back door and tossed it to Eric. "While you change, I'll throw some food in a bag so we can snack at the creek. And you can run with us the back way. It'll be good for you!"

"Okay, I'm up for it!" Eric grabbed the pants, used the bathroom to change while the girls finished dressing, and he headed out the back door with the girls. Being an adult half brother left little time to get to know his sisters, and Eric wanted to be part of a family. He had a good job at Zonolite, and he had friends at work, but he needed to have a family and not just live alone in a little rental house. Getting to spend time with his sisters and swimming the rapids were just fine with him!

As Darlene packed up some snacks, her mind was racing. *This could work! We'll use Eric as a reason to be gone if we get back late! He won't care and we won't be in trouble.* Darlene was sure that they really could be back before their parents came home. And even if they couldn't make it back before them, maybe their parents wouldn't care. They had finished their work. Mom actually got into the car and left the house. That in itself was unusual. Eric came by at just the right time, too. Having fun was rare for the girls; being able to include Eric was even more special. The three girls and Eric ran down the hill path together, exchanging for the moment the sisters' fears of their mother for fun with their half brother.

ERIC BOWMAN'S YOUTH

STANLEY, NORTH DAKOTA

Eric Bowman was six years old when the Depression hit the nation. He lived in Stanley, North Dakota, with his mother, Agnes, and his father, Dewey. Dewey worked hard at several jobs, traveled to farms in other communities to buy produce, and sold it all each week for a small profit—enough to feed his family. He helped out at the Baptist Church as a relief minister. He took any odd job he could find, including digging graves. Agnes sewed for a few families, and she took in washing and ironing. The 1920s brought Dewey some meager prosperity. He could see work opportunities and found ways to get hired to do a variety of jobs. Being strong and creative, as well as personable and reliable, gave him an advantage over others less gifted and less ambitious. The Depression taught everyone the harsh reality of poverty. Eric's memories as a six-year-old child were only of how happy he was. He didn't know that his dad had to struggle to keep their small family fed. His parents didn't seem to know that they were poor. They enjoyed their life together in spite of their very small rental home and their limited resources. Dewey's connections with farmers helped him make sure that his family would not starve. Selling produce kept the wolf from the door. If happiness could be the measure of life's blessings, Dewey, Agnes, and Eric had the best life possible. Unfortunately, happiness cannot override the devastation that illness can create.

When Eric was twelve, his mother developed influenza. She suffered for a month, but she became unable to fight for the breath that was too hard to pull into her weakened lungs. When she died, Eric seemed lost. Dewey was unable to communicate with his son, and he had trouble coping with his wife's death himself. When religion did not help him find a way out of his depression, Dewey turned from God. He could not accept that it was "God's will" to take his wife and the mother of his child. He took on more jobs and made longer trips away from home while Eric stayed with Agnes's mother. After a few months, Eric moved his belongings to his grandma's house and believed that his father had pretty much abandoned him. Dewey was gone for weeks at a time. Eric's heart ached with the loss of his mother and the absence of his father. Somehow, Eric had let his father down. It must have been his fault that only his grandmother wanted him. He sometimes woke in the night and wondered if he had caused his mother to die and his dad to leave. He took the crushing blame upon himself.

When Eric was fifteen, Dewey asked him if he wanted to go with him on the road and sell fruit. *He does want me!* He watched his dad's every move as he listened to him describe life on the road.

"You know, if you want to go with me, we could do this job together, maybe make a little more money and move to another town. I'd have more access to other farmers for produce and more customers to sell it to. Whatcha think? Would you want to do that?"

Eric tried to contain his happiness. He had wanted to be with his dad for so long, and now it really could happen. "What about school?"

"You wouldn't have to go to school. You know how to read and cipher right now. I never went to high school and look at me. I've got my own business."

"Grandma's been real good to me. Let me talk to her and see what she says."

"Well, it's your life, kid. You can make the choice."

"Yes, but I want to talk to her. I owe her that."

Dewey shook his head. "Okay. Let's talk tomorrow before I leave for Minot. You could come with me right away—in the morning." Dewey patted him on the back, then left to stay with his own parents for the night.

Eric's grandma was embroidering a pillowcase and rocking easily in her worn-out rocking chair that had been her grandma's years before. Eric sat near her, thinking.

"What's on your mind, dear? You look like you need to say something." She used a gentle tone in her voice, hoping he would talk to her. *Such a quiet boy. If he could just say what's in his heart, he'd be happier.*

Eric looked into his grandma's face. "Dad says I can go on the road with him. Work with him if I want to."

Grandma tried to control her facial expressions. She thought that day might come. "What do you think about that? Is that something you want to do?"

"What do you think, Grandma? Do you think I should? You'd have a lot less to do if you didn't have to cook for me and stuff."

"I'll tell you this right now what I think and we won't ever speak of it again. I have never, ever thought of you as someone I do 'stuff' for. You have never, not ever, been a problem to me. From the moment your mama died, I wanted you with me, here—in my home—your home. I love you as my grandson. You are my family. Always. Is that clear to you?"

"Yes, Grandma." Eric put his arms around her. Tears welled up. No one had told him that he was wanted and loved. Those were not words his family used. He still strongly felt the loss of his mother. With his dad gone most of the time, he had felt his dad didn't want him. He also thought his grandma took him just because he had to be somewhere.

He pulled back from her embrace and looked at her. "What do you think I should do, Grandma?"

"You can do what you want, and I'll love you no matter what. But here's what I think you should do. Stay in school. Graduate from high school. You'll have a better life if you get an education. If you don't do it now, it won't happen. You can get a good job, travel, and do what you want after you graduate. Even work with your dad then."

"What about my dad? What'll I tell him?"

"Your dad made his own choices. He left you with me. It was hard for him losing Agnes. It was hard on all of us. But you don't owe him anything—just be his son and do what's right for you. He'll be fine—has been for almost four years. If you join him, you won't have a home. You'll sleep in that truck most nights. Graduate—it's only two more years. Then, if you still think you want a life on the road with your dad, go do it."

"Thanks, Grandma." Eric walked into his room and sat on his narrow bed. *I want a dad. If I go with him, it could be real good. If I stay with Grandma, he might never ask me again. Goin' places, seein' stuff I never saw...*Eric wanted to go and it seemed like the right thing to do. He needed his dad in his life. Then another thought hit him. *Who'd take care of Grandma?* She had dizzy spells. She fell last month and hurt her right side—almost couldn't get out of her bed for a week. Her life had improved since Eric was there to help her. They had a bigger garden, better food to eat with both of them working. He knew she was getting weaker, depending on him more to take care of the place, get wood, buy groceries. She needed him, but he knew she wouldn't speak of her needs to keep him there.

Eric slept fitfully through the night. In the morning, he knew what he was going to do. Dewey arrived, ready to take Eric with him. He had moved some of his convenient items out of the cab of his truck and into the back, tied in a bag to the railings.

"Good morning." Dewey called out at the door.

"How about some breakfast, Dewey?" Grandma had food cooking on the stove, and the aroma of strong brewed coffee invited him in. Dewey sat down.

"Coffee smells good!" Grandma brought Dewey a cup and a small pitcher of cream. He loved cream in his coffee. Eric joined his dad at the table.

Dewey, holding his cup with both hands, began explaining his plans for Eric to Grandma. "I talked to Eric yesterday about going with me on the road. I could use him to help me load up produce, get it ready to sell, and—you know—pitch in as I need him to build up my business." As Dewey talked, Eric heard his father's practical side. He needed a *worker*.

Grandma asked Dewey where they were going to live.

"We will live on the road, staying in a few places I use. Some camping."

"Will he get any schooling?" Grandma didn't want him to give up school.

"I don't see him needing school. He needs to learn to work and get on in the world. The sooner he gets started, the better."

Grandma put eggs and fried potatoes on their plates. Both of them ate all she gave them and seemed to enjoy every bite. Eric watched his dad. He saw his strong arms, rolled-up sleeves, and hearty appetite. Eric thought about what his dad had said and why he wanted him to go on the road. *He didn't say he wanted me with him, only that he could use my help.* He loved his dad and wanted to be close to him.

"Well, Eric, are you ready? I'd like us to get on the road as soon as we can. It's a long way to Montana, and I have several farms to stop at along the way."

"Dad, I've decided to stay with Grandma." Grandma had her back to Eric, and she raised her eyes upward, took a deep breath, and whispered to herself, *Thank you, Lord.*

Dewey looked at him. "Why? I don't understand. Why would you pass up a chance like this?" He had not prepared himself for Eric's refusal. He'd just assumed Eric would go with him.

"I want to finish high school." Eric swallowed hard. "I don't have long to go, and then, if you still want me along, I could come then." Eric watched his dad. Dewey looked at his coffee, stirring it as his hands trembled. He laid his spoon on the table, took a small sip, and rose from his chair.

"Well. I'd best be going. I hoped you'd come. Maybe later, when you're ready." Dewey left the house and was climbing in his truck when Eric caught up to him.

"Dad, I want you to know that I want to go with you, I really do. But I can't leave Grandma. She's not well—hasn't been for a while."

"She'll get on fine, son." Dewey looked into his son's face. He could see himself there. Eric looked so much like him. He could also see genuine concern.

"Dad, she took me in. She's been both a mom and dad to me with you gone so much. Now she needs me, even though she won't say so herself." *This is so hard.* Eric looked back at his grandma on the porch as she watched the two men by the truck. "Doc told me to keep a close eye on her and that he wasn't sure she'd live much longer than a few more months—maybe a year."

Dewey could see that Eric wanted to go. He could also see the boy was having a hard time doing what he thought was the right thing. "I understand. Really, son, I do. I was thinking of myself, and I can see you're a man who knows what's right, and does it."

"Thanks for understanding, Dad." This family was not one that embraced much, or showed their affection in physical ways. But Eric broke through his shyness and put his arms around his dad hard. "I'll miss you, Dad. Come back and see me, okay?" Tears came, though Eric tried to hold them back.

Dewey awkwardly held Eric in his arms and returned his embrace. When he let go, he climbed into the truck. He didn't want his son to see him cry. "Hey, I'll be back in a couple weeks. You take care of your grandma—I know you will. You're a good boy." Dewey drove out of the yard. His heart was aching. He felt the same sense of loss and emptiness as he did when Agnes passed away. Alone in his truck, he let the tears stream down his face. If Eric could have seen these tears, he would have known more surely that his father loved him.

Eric stood in the yard and watched his father drive away. The flat North Dakota prairie let him look for a long time. Had he lost his dad forever? Did he do the right thing? When he walked back to the house and saw his grandma resting in her chair, holding her handkerchief, and dabbing her eyes, he knew he had made the right choice. She had been there for him when his family fell apart. She was his true and steady family. His dad was his true and distant family.

He decided that he could do life better. He resolved right then to be more responsible in school, at home taking care of things for his grandma, and in his heart. His dad was going to be okay with him or without him, so he had to stop feeling guilty and sad so much of the time. He had to let the loss of his mother stop aching so much. He needed to control the waves of grief that swept over him at times, holding him in sadness and despair.

Eric finished high school in 1941. The nation was at war, and many of his classmates joined the various fighting forces to defend their country from Germany and then Japan. Eric enlisted in the navy. After extensive training, he was assigned as an electrician/ maintenance specialist on a destroyer and served first in the Atlantic, then later in the Pacific. He saw more action than he wanted, and he was grateful when the war ended and he could go home. He stayed with the navy in San Francisco for a few years, using his training as an electrician to repair navy ships. The navy gave him additional training, equivalent to an electrical engineering degree with designing and managing major electrical projects. He liked the work and had seriously considered a career in the navy. He had also fallen in love and was engaged to marry a special girl, but she left him for someone else. A broken heart and the lure of connecting with his father brought him to Montana in 1957. His dad had remarried, made his home in Libby, and Eric wanted to be part of his dad's life in some way. He had three half sisters to get to know, as well as his dad's wife. For those reasons, he was ready for a fresh start.

When the Great Northern Railway let him off on Mineral Avenue in downtown Libby, Eric hefted his duffel bag onto his shoulder and walked a block to the music store. He had written his dad that he was coming, but Betty had hidden the letter. Dewey had no idea the young man in the navy uniform entering his store was his son. A lot of young men came home from the service during those ten years since the war had ended.

"How can I help you?" Dewey extended his hand to the young man in white.

"Hi, Dad. How've you been?" Eric took his hand and shook it.

"Son! Eric? My God, it is you!" Dewey put his arms around his son. "Are you okay, son? Did they send you home in one good strong piece?"

"I'm okay, Dad. Luckier than a lot of them, for sure."

"Just a minute, son." Dewey called home and Betty answered. "Betty, great news! I'm bringing my son home for dinner. He'll need a place to stay for a while, so let's make him welcome." Betty only had time to say okay as Dewey hung up the phone and went back to visiting with Eric.

Eric met his half sisters and stepmother for the first time. All three girls were eager to get to know him. Betty's eagerness took a different direction. Eric was only a few years younger than she was, and he was handsome. When he walked in the house in his naval uniform, she was immediately attracted to him. For the few days he stayed in their home, he loved visiting with the girls and helping them with chores. When Betty attempted to join him on the couch in the middle of the night, he knew he had to find his own place fast.

"What are you doing?" Eric had been sound asleep on the folded-out sofa when Betty tried to sit by him, touching his face.

"I just want to get to know you better. Shhh. You'll wake up the girls." She lifted the covers and tried to move into the bed beside him when he jumped up.

"This isn't gonna happen! You want quiet? Go back to your bed. Now." Eric spoke firmly, quietly, and stood his ground with the covers and sheet somewhat wrapped around him. "You try any funny business with me, and I'll make a racket you won't believe!"

Betty was crushed. There was a time any man would jump at the chance to hold her. "I'm sorry. I just thought you might be lonely and want some company."

"First off, you scared the shit out of me. It's the middle of the night, for Christ's sake. Second, you're my dad's wife. What are you thinkin'? There's no way in hell I'll sleep with my dad's wife! Your kids are on both ends of the house. Dad's in the next room." Eric was blunt, honest, and not one to be intimidated by that woman.

"Let's pretend this never happened. Can we do that?" Betty just walked out of the room and went back to bed.

Eric had his duffel bag packed before breakfast and rode into town with Dewey. *Should I tell him what happened? What if she makes up something?* "Dad, the strangest thing happened last night."

"What was it, son?"

"I'll just say it. Betty woke me up, trying to climb into bed with me." *My God, what's Dad going to think?*

"I know, son. I heard her—and you. Don't worry about it." He was silent for a few minutes. "I appreciate your honesty. That wasn't easy to do—telling me, I mean. You're a good son."

"That's a relief! I didn't know what to do!"

"It's all right. We're okay." Dewey smiled at him. "I'm glad you're here for the long haul, son. We've got a lot of catching up to do."

"I'm going to get set up here in town today. Apply for a few jobs."

"Let's drop me off and you can take my car to look around. Pick me up for lunch."

"Thanks, Dad. I appreciate it." Eric had filled out his first application at the Montana Power Company at 9:00 a.m. When he came in decked out in his uniform, the receptionist gave him the application and then told the company manager about the applicant. The manager came out and talked with Eric for a few minutes. When he learned that Eric had been an electrician with the navy for the past several years and that he was Dewey's son, the manager offered him a job on the spot. Eric accepted.

By 10:00 a.m. he was viewing rentals. The third one he saw suited him. It was a one-bedroom house with a fenced yard and a one-car garage with room for a workbench. After lunch, he and Dewey looked for a used car. With Dewey's gift of bargaining and Eric's military uniform, a deal was finalized for a 1952 Buick, previously owned by a woman who was planning to move in with her family and was no longer going to be driving. Eric had saved his money from his years in the service and was able to pay for the car with cash.

He had a job, a house, a car, and the beginning of a family. Eric watched his dad look over the car and talk to the salesman. Dewey knew the man's name and his two children's names, and he made it seem like they were old friends. The part of the conversation Eric overheard that touched his own heart, though, was Dewey bragging about his son. Dewey's description surprised Eric. Dewey described Eric as a war hero, a great boy who finished high school and took care of his grandma until she died. "I couldn't be prouder of this boy—hey, I mean this man." Eric was glad to hear it, even if it was not said to him. Dewey was a talker with everyone except those he loved the most.

18

DEWEY AND BETTY

FACE CHANGES

JULY 1958

Dewey's mind was running at a rapid pace as he reviewed the events of the previous night. Betty had been on an emotional rollercoaster. One minute she was violent, grabbing Darlene by the hair, and the next minute she was on the floor crying. Moments later, she was ready to kill Dick, threatening to have him arrested for rape, and seconds after that she was begging him to have mercy on her. What a night! And now, he may have found some solutions to problems that he had never imagined he could resolve. He could get Betty working again, take care of his mother, and keep his kids safe. How could everything come together so quickly and work out so well! Betty hated work, hated his mother, and seemed to hate taking care of their daughters. But at that point, Dewey decided to make the best of the situation and see if he could win on all fronts: mother, wife, and especially his children. The guilt he carried was heavy for not paying closer attention to the safety of his children. Did he know and just not want to get into arguments? He knew that he stayed at work late to build his business and to avoid going home. He did not enjoy the silence of his house or the arguments with Betty. He had not taken care of his children in his effort to avoid Betty and a marriage that was not working. He decided he couldn't think about that.

It was possible that he would be able to swing a major change for everyone, and it just might work out.

During the drive, Dewey kept glancing at Betty. She took out her compact, powdered her nose, checked her hair, and seemed happy with the image of herself. When she caught him watching her, she said, "What? What are you looking at?"

"You! You look fine, and it's nice to have you out of the house. We can go by the store and stay for a while, then get a bite of lunch uptown. Okay?" Dewey looked like he was going to get a yes answer.

"We'll see how things go," she said. When she had taken care of the store several years previously, she had the place organized. Musical instruments were placed so people could see them, but not reach them for fear they might mishandle them. She had the sheet music set up in alphabetical order, but within categories—gospel, pop, classical, and so on. She loved the store, but after Helen was born, she was sick much of the time. She could not seem to gather the energy to even get out of bed. She gave up what she loved and ended up hating being home.

"You haven't been to town for a while. Let's drive around, and I'll show you some things that have changed since you worked at the store." Dewey drove her by the lumber mill and showed her the pole yard. It had been half the size four years ago. With new lay-offs, it could be downsized within a year, right back to where it was. He drove her up Shaughnessy Road with its beautiful view of the Cabinet Mountains. He told her that there was going to be a golf course up there. Neither of them had an interest in golf, but the idea of a course in Libby was news to everyone. He drove by the ballpark and showed her the piles of Zonolite that the mine had donated for the care of the park and for entertainment purposes. He told her how the children loved to play in it, making rain out of it by throwing in up in the air and letting it fall all over them.

They were near the store, passing Al's Market where the girls used to run for groceries for Betty when they all lived behind the store. Betty had positive memories of the small apartment. She was glad they moved to Libby. She loved setting up the music store and making it her own creative project. When Dewey parked in front of the store, she lingered a moment to look at it before going in. This will be good, she thought. Whatever mess it was in from not having her there to take care of it for six years she could fix. She did not want medical attention or supervision. She needed control of her life and feared losing it if a doctor discovered how conflicted she was about motherhood, her marriage, and her own mental confusion.

She searched for the inner dialogue that helped her sort out what to do, but the inner echoes were silent, probably wondering why she didn't collide with the logging truck on the way to town. Even though she felt ready to change her life, she counted on being alone in her bedroom much of every day, hiding from making her life better. She was strong, however, and she recognized that working in the store was a way to get her life together. During the private times in her room when memories flooded her from her past, she ached to take revenge against someone, cause pain to someone, and free herself from the pent-up hatred she held inside. She could have saved Jimmy if she had been less defiant. He haunted her dreams with his gentle love, deepening her loss and guilt. She focused her love on him to the degree that she was harming anyone connected to her that she was supposed to love. She couldn't stop beating her children. She couldn't seem to carry out the role of wife or mother without lashing out at Dewey and her daughters. The gnawing ache in her heart was clear to her but distorted to any sane person. Before she could be free of her mental anguish, someone had to die. Darlene was getting away. Maybe Julie? Helen couldn't run very fast, maybe—but she was little, like Jimmy. *I must decide soon.*

19

CROSSING THE HARDIN PLACE

The three sisters and their half brother Eric ran most of the way up the hill along the path to Hollands' where they hurried to the creek to enjoy the hot sun and cold water. They used the usual cut across from the hill to the Market Road, then across to Hollands' long driveway, taking them through the Hardin property. The two years since the Hardin family moved away had not changed the pathway the girls had been using for years before their move. The back fence had a convenient opening that easily allowed them to climb through. The four of them were passing the barn and were almost to the house when Julie remembered Kelly and Adam saying someone had been in the house. As the girls passed the house, Julie could see that there was something different about the house.

The girls took turns telling Eric about the Hardin family—how they played with the boys and that they had moved away a couple of years ago.

"Hey, have the curtains been open like that before? I mean—it looks different, doesn't it?" Julie asked her two sisters. As they came closer to the front of the house, they noticed other obvious differences. They saw a white truck parked in front of the house. Some boxes were on the ground near the side of the house. Were their friends moving back or was some other family moving in? The truck was not the one the Hardin family had when they left for Nevada. That was two years ago. They could have a different one.

"Let's knock and meet the neighbors so they won't think we're trespassing," Darlene said. Helen and Julie were curious to meet the new occupants, and the three of them went up on the porch. Eric just followed their lead. Darlene knocked on the door. The girls hoped that the Hardin family was back. The thought that the boys could be in the house was encouraging for the two younger girls who both tried to see through the opening of the drapes. When no one came to the door, Darlene opened the screen door and knocked loudly on the inner wooden front door.

As Helen looked toward the front window, she thought she saw someone inside, but it was dark in there, and she couldn't see very well. No one came to the door. She nudged Julie to look that way just as the shadowy figure moved away from view. "Did you see anybody?" Julie nodded her head yes.

Julie looked at the pickup truck. "Hardins didn't have a white pickup, but maybe they do now. Look, Helen, the back has a cage or something." Julie and Helen looked at the strange cages lying in the bed of the truck. A metal cage about two feet high, even with the top of the bed of the pickup, took up almost the full length of the truck bed. A few boxes were stacked near the tailgate.

"Shall we call out in case they're in the barn? We might miss them," Julie asked.

Eric watched the girls investigate with interest. "Girls, I'm guessing that someone might be inside but may not want to come out right now. Why don't we go for that rapids ride you talked about? We can check on the way back."

Darlene agreed. "Let's go. If they wanted to see us they'd come out, right? If the Hardins are back, we can welcome them another time. Besides, we just have so much time to swim. Let's get going while we can!" Darlene, Eric, and the girls hurried across Market Road to Hollands' driveway and then on to the creek and the freedom of the current that would carry them away from any worries for a little while.

Inside the Hardin house, two adult figures watched the four visitors leave the yard and run for Market Road.

"There are bound to be curious neighbors, Stephen. These four people won't make a difference. Forget about them," Owen said.

Stephen went out the back door to see how the four neighbors had come in without using the front gate. He had been sitting near the window when the girls came up on the porch. They seemed to appear on the porch out of nowhere. He would have seen them if they had come through the front entrance to the property. It didn't take him long to find the path and the opening in the fence. His first thought was to repair the hole in the fence to keep anyone from coming through that way again. But he could see that the fence was low enough that anyone could climb over it, and he might want to use that path himself sometime. Having it open might be better after all. Later in the day, he decided to see what use the path and the hillside might be for his purposes. He doubted that the four visitors would try to cross the property again that day with the truck in the yard. He also did not want to make any noticeable changes in the place. Blocking a trail was a change that others would notice, not just those four.

When Stephen went back in the house, he saw that Owen had allowed the three children to come out of the bedroom. Stephen made sure that the curtains were closed so no one could see them from the front or side of the house. They were all hungry and helped put out bread, peanut butter and jelly, along with some paper plates. The children were old enough to make their own sandwiches with the girl's help, and they did so quickly. Water was the beverage of choice—their only choice. After they ate, the children went back into the bedroom and were told to stay away from the windows for their own protection. Although the children did as they were told, they felt like prisoners who had no choice and no freedom because they could not see their parents again. The two boys missed their parents more than Sandy, a nine-year-old who really only knew her mother. Her dad had left them four years earlier, and her mother had tried to fill his spot with several boyfriends. Those temporary intruders came and went, making her life dismal at best and sometimes frightening. She had decided that since she had no real options other than being where she was, she would make the most of the situation and help the boys. She did not know of any better place to be. When the two men took her, she went without a struggle. To her, there was nowhere different she could go but with those two men since they were taking her from her hell at home.

The bedroom had some books that they had all read, some cards, a few animal toys, and some color crayons with two filled-up coloring books. Sandy had already colored over several pages. She had read to Davy, five, and Jason, six, the same stories over and over. She read to them again, and the children entertained themselves or napped through the afternoon, waiting for the next transport to somewhere. Somewhere unknown to them or the families they had left behind through no choice of their own.

Sandy looked through the curtains carefully, making sure she didn't move them very much. All she could see was more of the same: trees, grass, some birds, and blue sky. Sandy wanted to play outside. Maybe the men would let her and the boys play behind the house quietly. No one could see them from the road. She went into the kitchen to ask Owen, but he was outside working on the truck. When she looked for Stephen, she found him stretched out on the couch sleeping. She had developed a mistrust of men because of her mother's choice of friends and their treatment of her. One guy was pretty nice most of the time, but when he lost his temper, he would hit whatever moved. Three of them hurt her badly in that interior place of pain. She wondered if the pain would ever go away.

She went back to the boys and played with them until Owen came back into the house. She asked him if they could play quietly just behind the house. She showed him through the window that no one could see them from the road. He took them outside with the understanding that they had to stay out of view of the road or they would be in serious trouble. He sat out with them and watched them play tag and run around in the sunshine. He knew they needed to get some fresh air, and so did he. All the hiding was getting to him, too. A little running around in the sun would help their attitudes for the night's ride to another place and a hand-off to other people. He didn't think he could stand traveling in a horizontal cage covered with a tarp and some boxes as the children had endured. Maybe their next transport would be better.

20

PLAYING AT THE CREEK

Eric was laughing at himself. There he was, a grown man of thirty-four, running off to Granite Creek to play with his half sisters. He enjoyed watching each one of them as they talked and laughed and ran to the creek. Since moving to Libby, he had spent very little time with the young sisters. Dinner invitations were rare, and when they occurred, there was little conversation or interaction with the girls. Eric wanted to be part of the family, and that was a gift to him. The girls had invited him to play.

He put Helen up on his shoulders to give her a rest as they made good time getting through the back of Hollands' ranch to the cold, wild water. The girls talked just about all the way, giving Eric little opportunity to get a word in, but also relieving him of having to lead in small talk. He was a quiet person, not one to waste words. He felt comfortable being himself as he listened to the banter of three girls on a beautiful summer day.

When the four of them reached the swimming area, they all jumped in the cold, bubbly water, splashing, swimming, and diving off the rocks. The continual talking on the part of the girls was really a joy for Eric. As Julie pulled herself out of the pond, Eric noticed how her wet T-shirt stuck to the skin on her back, exposing small ropes of healed skin.

"What happened here, Julie? What's that scar on your back?" He was close to her and lifted her shirt a little higher, exposing more damage from Betty's belt. Julie quickly pulled her shirt down.

Helen spoke up without reservation. "That's where Mommy beat her. She's got lots of scars. So does Darlene."

"It's okay. We can't really talk about it or Mom would get really mad. You know. It could get worse," Julie explained quickly. She was out of the pond and ready to head for the rapids.

"Let's all go together!" Darlene beckoned to the three others as they all climbed out of the swimming hole. Eric was thinking about Julie's fear of talking about her scars. The sight of Julie's lower back was one more piece of evidence that his dad had married a strange and violent woman. He had never felt very comfortable around her. She seemed to flirt with him, which made him even more uncomfortable. As much as he wanted to be close to his father, Betty had a way of keeping him off balance. Betty was quite a bit younger than Dewey, and only a few years older than Eric. He didn't want trouble with his dad, and so he usually stopped in at the store to see him rather than going to the house. Unfortunately, that made it hard for him to get to know the girls.

Darlene took Helen on her lap, and the four of them waded in until the strong water forced them off their feet and downstream. They all grabbed onto one another and went as a group. At the bottom of the run, Eric gained footing first and helped the others to their feet. That was fun! The four of them collapsed on the rocky, sandy area and caught their breath.

"That was some ride! Helen! You are quite the brave one. I was hanging on to all of you to stay alive!" The girls all laughed at him. *These girls are so natural and beautiful. I am so glad I came with them.* As they relaxed in the sunshine, Eric stood up and went over to Darlene.

"Stand up, will you Darlene? I want to see how tall you are." When Darlene stood back to back with Eric, he measured her with his hand and noted that she was about five inches shorter than he was. While she had her back to him, he put his hand on her T-shirt collar and looked down her back. She had many lines of healed flesh from belt lashes.

"Sorry. When I saw Julie's scars, I wondered if you had them, too."

The girls were quiet.

"What the hell is going on at your house anyway? Helen said your mother did this. Is that right?" He watched the girls for some reaction.

"Mother loses her temper sometimes when we don't do what we're supposed to do. She's used a belt on us." Darlene tried to make it seem unimportant.

"Does Dad know about this?"

"He does now! Darlene's getting married and Mama can't hurt her anymore. Dad said so. And Dick said so, too." Julie said it clearly, as much for her to hear as Eric.

"Hey, what's all this about getting married?" Eric switched the topic out of his own curiosity and to keep the girls from crying. He watched the three girls each tell about the future wedding and the hope of no more beatings. He wanted sisters, close family, and now he had them. He was glad to hear that there were promises about no more beatings. He was going to make sure that was true by being more involved with them. He couldn't protect them if he didn't spend more time at their house.

Helen gave the most interesting bit of information. "Darlene's going to have a baby!"

"Well now, I'm going to have to get to know Dick, my soon-to-be brother. Right?" The conversation was lively, and the harshness of violence faded again as joyous talk of a future child, marriage, and changes in the safety of the girls' lives filled their conversation.

"You really want to meet Dick?" Darlene looked Eric squarely in his big brown eyes.

"Of course I do. You know, you have to have my permission to get married, too. How can I say yes if I don't even know the guy?" He flashed her a great big smile, and then he winked at Helen and Julie.

"You're funny! Let's get another rapid ride before we have to get home. Okay?" Darlene held out her hand to assist others in getting up. She had a snarky smile for Eric as he laughed at his joke.

"I'm just kiddin' ya. Tell me about this guy. Does he have a job? What's he look like?" Darlene chatted happily about Dick with Eric, and he watched her eyes brighten. He heard pure joy in her voice as she described Dick. They all headed for the top of the natural chute. Eric held Helen on his lap as the four of them grabbed onto one another and, feet first, enjoyed the exhilarating ride.

21

BETTY AT THE STORE

Betty was excited for the first time in many years. When she told Dewey several years ago that she would never work in the store again, she was positive that she would not see the store until Dewey sold it. There she was, over six years later, entering the place she had shaped by herself so completely, and then quit so abruptly. Not only did she want to enter again, she was ready to display a tirade of terror if anything she had set up had been changed in any way. She knew that she would be rewarded for her mental readiness. After such a long absence, of course things would be different. She was ready to rant, rave, complain, and put down whatever changes Dewey had made. She could fill her empty well of destruction that could later strike her children, with deeply brewed venom of poisonous wrath aimed at Dewey. Someone had to feel it. She had to release it on someone on a regular basis in order to live. Drink water, eat food, and cause pain. Torture was a separate, necessary entity. She had to do it to someone to live and breathe. She didn't know why, but there was a release in punishing another person that created a sensation close to joy. Sometimes the image of her little brother came clearly into her mind. Or memories of her mother giving her over to her torturers so many years ago: "Put up with it," her mother had told her. The more pain she inflicted on others, the less she was haunted by the memories of her depressing childhood.

Dewey unlocked the store and they both went in. Betty was ready, really eager to find fault. She literally burst into the room. The store immediately looked different to her. As she took in the wraparound view of everything, it looked inviting and colorful. Musical instruments covered the walls, and a drum set was suspended from the ceiling with a string of lights accenting its features. Dewey had rigged up lighting in several areas, including the glass counters. He had made the store his own creative venture, and it looked good.

When Betty had first opened the store and ran it for a few years, she did not have the quantity of instruments Dewey had, nor had she thought of displaying them with lighting. Getting the music contract from the public school had helped. Every year students rented or purchased instruments for the marching band. Dewey provided the rentals easily to parents who wanted to save money, but still keep their kids in the band for four years of high school. There were always those parents whose children had to have new instruments. Dewey picked up instruments in Spokane wholesale, noted the retail prices in Spokane music stores, and priced his instruments a bit lower. He knew how to keep local business, and he even had some customers from Kalispell. By lighting up the walls and displaying a variety of instruments, the store had a welcoming, warm look to it that customers liked.

Dewey also had put up guitars, banjos, and two accordions, along with colorful sheet music attached to the walls that set off the instruments. He had put up some colored streamers from one group of instruments to another, and he had cut out quarter notes and half notes that he attached in many places throughout the four walls and on the windows at the front of the store. If a record was scratched, he put a nail in the center hole and put it on the wall along with its cover to add to the interesting designs of music. Everything on the walls and counters proclaimed, "This is a music store!" to anyone who came in. Sales were good, considering the fluctuating economy of the area.

Betty looked around, studied the walls, and waited for her inner explosion to come gushing forth so she could make Dewey feel bad. The explosion did not come. Instead, a feeling of loss and disappointment took hold of her, and she began crying. She loved the store. She had worked hard to make it beautiful and productive.

When she became ill after having Helen, she shut it out of her life. Here was her chance to come back and make it her own again. She was facing a difficult decision. Her mind was not well, and she wasn't sure that she could step into the beautiful place. Dewey was watching her and gave her time to look at everything. He couldn't know her thoughts, but he knew she needed to have space and quiet when she was thinking. In that moment, she was thinking.

"Who decorated this store?" Her back was to Dewey. Her lips were pursed tightly.

"Well, I did, but not all at once. I started with a couple of saxophones. Then over time I added this and that. One of the high school boys thought the drums would look good displayed in a set. He and some of his friends helped me suspend them like that," Dewey explained. "Over time the place changed, nothing big at any one time, but small changes that led to other small changes made it look like this. I've had some people say they come in just to look at the stuff on the walls. Most of the time when people come in, they buy something.

"The band kids keep me busy repairing their instruments, and so I like to take their ideas seriously when they suggest something. The notes everywhere were the students' ideas. I think they add something good to the room. Having their ideas up, I think, helps the business. When you are here for a while and see the kids come in, you'll see what I mean. I let three teachers use the back room for lessons—guitar, piano, and a horn of some kind, clarinet—right now. I don't charge them for the space, and in return they have the students buy their books and supplies here. Give a little, get a lot back. Seems to work." Dewey was rambling on, he knew. He was waiting for some reaction from Betty other than tears.

"The kids are going to love you, Betty. Sometimes they come in with friends to show them what instrument they are going to buy. Right now I have a boy who puts down a dollar a week on a guitar. He comes in to see it about three times week. He brings his girlfriend. She's been paying on it, too, so she can surprise him for his birthday." Dewey needed Betty to know that she could not hurt the business with her anger. She needed to be able to enjoy being there or not take on the job. He left her for a few moments to take care of a customer.

Betty went behind the counter and saw that it was organized and clean. *Damn. This is clean, too. It's all so…beautiful!* She used to keep things clean, too, and Darlene helped her. She thought back to when she and Dewey lived in Sandpoint during the war. The two of them ran a restaurant; or maybe it ran them.

22

SANDPOINT, 1941

From 1941 to 1945, Dewey and Betty Bowman lived in Sandpoint, Idaho, in the upstairs hotel of the street-level restaurant they owned and managed. With Farragut Naval Station a short distance from Sandpoint, Dewey counted confidently on the military personnel to make his business a success. Farragut Naval Base provided the war effort in the Pacific with sailors who spent several months on the base participating in numerous training programs before being shipped out. A steady stream of sailors traveled through Farragut, Sandpoint, and the family café.

The Sandpoint Café was open from 5:00 a.m. until midnight, and both Betty and Dewey worked there, covering for each other for brief rests every day. Both worked peak business hours to keep the business turning a profit. The second floor provided several small rooms that Dewey used as both their home and a hotel. The front three rooms were their home. The other seven rooms were rented out to the public on a nightly, sometimes hourly, basis.

Although there were two or three waitresses and a cook hired for each shift, both Dewey and Betty took turns keeping up with the orders as cooks, bakers, and servers. They each floated through every job, making sure that the service was good and that the food was prepared well and served quickly. They were always busy, and they had more customers than they had ever expected. By providing a menu that was reasonably simple, they could accommodate sailors' desires for hamburgers, steaks, and bacon or ham and egg breakfasts. Homemade pies were always available and were a main attraction for both sailors and the locals. Betty baked pies every morning, and they disappeared throughout the day.

Betty and Dewey were an excellent team as they worked together, complementing each other with hard work and creative meals. He came up with menu ideas, and she made those ideas a reality. Even though the food was simple, their specials for the day drew many orders. Who would have thought that throwing fried potatoes, chunks of ham or bacon, and two eggs together in a "scramble" on the grill would sell? The "scramble" was one of their most popular breakfasts and dinners.

They worked themselves to a frazzle, but they were happy. They were excited about their business, and they were excited about each other. Sometimes they took a wild and crazy hour together during a slow time. They rejuvenated one another and their happiness spread to their staff. They were fun to work with, and the harder they worked, the better the tips for everyone. Their staff was loyal and liked to work with them.

Sandpoint was the place Dewey wanted to be for business reasons, and also because his parents lived there. Dewey's parents, Adam and Julia Bowman, had come out at his urging from North Dakota where they had worked a homestead and where Adam also had worked for the Great Northern Railroad. Dewey wanted to be able to keep track of their needs and help them in their retirement years. He had planned to spend a lot of time with them, but the café and hotel kept him and Betty busy seven days a week. He ran over for an hour during a midafternoon break when the business was slow to help them and to check on Darlene, their little daughter.

Darlene stayed with Julia and Adam while Betty worked, which helped a great deal. Betty preferred working in the restaurant to taking care of Darlene. The longer the hours at work, the better Betty's day went. Taking care of a child was painful for Betty, and Darlene did not like it either. Betty did not have patience for a toddler, and Darlene always seemed to get into trouble. She was too young to understand her mother's moods, but she was just the right age to anger her mother frequently. When Betty started hitting her, Darlene would cry at first, and then just hide from her. That worked for Betty. If she didn't see her, she could relax for a few minutes and have Dewey take her somewhere. Darlene often hid for hours, playing with imaginary friends and managing to find crackers or bread to eat when her mother failed to feed her.

When Betty became pregnant with Julie, she contemplated taking her own life. She did not feel well most of the time and could not work as much at the restaurant as she had worked previously. Because she had not wanted the child, she thought about aborting it. She made herself so sick that she vomited convulsively four times before giving up on that plan. She asked two staff members if they knew anyone who performed abortions. One of them told Dewey. That was how he found out that she was pregnant. At first he was angry. Betty had been upstairs sleeping, which gave him time to think about the turn of events. Part of him was excited about having a baby. He knew, though, that Betty would not be able to work as much. That would affect their business. She made things move along well. Getting mad at her for trying to lose the baby would not resolve anything. He avoided arguments as his main means of settling problems with Betty.

When Betty came downstairs, Dewey asked her if she was feeling okay. "If I didn't know better, I'd say you might be pregnant." He threw that out casually to see if she would tell him. She didn't say anything.

"Let's have a bite of lunch. How about it? What would you like? I'll get it and you have your cup of coffee."

"I am hungry. How about some of that chicken soup? Maybe that'll stay down," she said.

"Okay, coming right up! Oops. That was the wrong thing to say," Dewey teased her while he ladled up two bowls of soup, grabbed some rolls and butter, and served the two of them. "You know, if you were pregnant"—Betty looked at him with an almost angry, questioning look—"that could be fine. I'd like to have another child." Dewey said it, but he was not very convincing.

"You don't want another child and I don't either. You have a son from another marriage, and you weren't too happy when Darlene came along. Don't tell me that you really want another child." Betty stirred her soup a few turns.

"Well, let's say you did get pregnant. You know that we could handle having a baby, and we'd love the hell out of it." Dewey was more convincing that time. "And for the record, I love both my son and my daughter. Another child might just be what we need to make us take it easy. We both spend too much time working."

"Well, I guess we're going to find out if we can handle it. I *am* pregnant, and I feel like I've got the flu. I'm sick every day until dinner, and I'm tired all the time." Betty let down her guard and shed a few tears. "This isn't what we planned, and you know it. We have a great thing going, and now I can't keep up my part. Darlene wears me out. How can I do it again?"

"We'll be okay. We are making good money and we can afford to hire another person to cover part of what you do. Nobody can do it all. You could still take care of the books and payroll, help manage, and keep things moving around here. I like the grill work and can keep that moving along." Dewey had a plan that seemed workable to Betty.

"We could take care of this another way." Betty quietly waited for Dewey's attention.

"What other way?"

"You know. I could have an abortion." Betty said it in an offhand way.

"No. You can't do that. It's not safe. Too many women end up dead—or they wish they were dead after some hack cuts them up. The ones the sailors have talked about around here turned out bad. Don't do that. Have the baby, and if we can't get used to it, we'll give it up for some other family to raise." Dewey had given her a way out of having to raise a second child. She could hang in there and have the baby as long as she didn't have to take care of it.

Dewey figured that once she carried the baby to full term she would love it and not want to give it up. He could get used to another child. The idea appealed to him more every day as Betty began blossoming into a large baby machine. Betty was making it every day as well as she could, working as much as possible, and resting when she had to. She was looking forward every day to having the large growth removed and given away. She could not take on another child. She couldn't handle the one she had without help. Although she didn't care for Dewey's mother, she was grateful that Julia took care of Darlene as much as she did.

On June 25, 1944, Julie was born in the front bedroom of the upstairs hotel-home combination. Betty was not doing well, and the doctor that Dewey called to help with the birth came late and under the influence of alcohol. Julia, Dewey's mother, had already delivered Julie by the time the drunken doctor arrived, and Betty later told Julia how grateful she was that Julia was there. Without her, the baby and Betty probably would not have lived. Julie was not breathing at birth. Her mouth was filled with a chalky substance, and the umbilical cord was wrapped around her neck. Julia removed the cord. She worked Julie's tiny body, breathing into her mouth and massaging her to get her heart to beat.

Julie was a blue-purple color. While Julia was working on her, the late, drunk doctor arrived. He looked at her tiny three-pound motionless body and declared in his shaky voice that the baby would not live. He took Julie briefly from Julia's arms, shook his head back and forth, and then he gave her back to Julia. Julia went back to her routine without looking at the doctor who staggered out of the room and bumped his way down the stairs to the street below.

Betty remained unconscious. Julia blew air into Julie's mouth, continued massaging her chest, used force to rub her all over to get the blood circulating, and she even helped reshape her head. When the baby finally cried, Julia wrapped her tightly in a small sheet and set her aside while she tended to Betty. Julia made sure the afterbirth process was completed and the bleeding under control. When Julia had bathed both of them as well as she could, she and Dewey together took away the mess from under Betty's body and made sure she was resting on clean sheets. She covered Betty with a light blanket on that cool summer morning after the hard night. Betty was too exhausted to awaken for hours. She missed the heroic, tender care that Julia gave her. Julia did, indeed, save Julie's life, and quite likely she saved Betty's life as well. During his brief visit, the doctor did not tend to Betty either. He merely lifted the sheet, glanced at her, and muttered something about rest. Julia's account angered Dewey. She described the doctor's lack of care or interest—being drunk and incapable of helping care for the mother and child. Julia voiced her concern for Betty's life as she described for Dewey the massive loss of blood Betty experienced, as well as the hard labor she barely lived through. Dewey saw the bloody sheets and was furious at the doctor. He was determined to get the doctor and make him do his job. Julia convinced him that the doctor was drunk and wouldn't be any help. Julia gave him the pile of towels and sheets and sent him off to wash them. He needed a job to keep him from getting involved with the doctor. Julia spent the two weeks after Julie's birth tending to both Betty and Julie as they each regained their strength.

Julie loved Grandma Julia in a special way, more than any other person in her youth. Dewey insisted on naming his new daughter after his mother, especially because she had saved the baby's life. She and Julie had a special bond. Julia favored Julie over Darlene because she had breathed life into Julie. Julie loved to visit her as she was growing up, but Darlene spent her time hiding from Julia and Adam, a habit she had learned from avoiding her mother. Julia made clothes for Julie and remodeled her older clothing for Darlene. Darlene didn't like wearing her grandma's old clothes while Julie wore cute new clothes. Julia took them to church where fellow churchgoers gushed over the baby and didn't seem to notice the quiet girl who stood behind her grandma, frowning or looking sad in her made-over dresses.

Julia had opportunities over the years to teach the girls many things. She helped Darlene learn to cook and taught her how to plant and weed a garden. She had Darlene help her can fruits and vegetables, make jellies and jams, cure pork, and preserve deer meat. Julia taught Darlene to make great custard pies out of next to nothing. Vinegar pie and milk pie were two of the girls' favorites. Julia did not use recipes—just a pinch of this and a handful of that combined to make amazing dishes. The Depression taught Julia many things, and cooking with hardly any food to work with was one of her strengths. Darlene liked working with her grandma, cooking and sewing. When Darlene was about seven years old, she gave up hiding from her grandma, learned to trust her, and in time convinced her grandma to help her make nicer looking dresses. Julia agreed and the two of them made some dresses that Darlene loved to wear. That helped mend their relationship. The girls always felt close to their grandma, and they did not understand why their mother did not get along with her.

The truth of that relationship was clear to both women. They intensely disliked one another. Julia believed Betty had trapped her son into marriage. The dates of the wedding and Darlene's birth confirmed that fact for Julia. Julia was convinced that Betty was much too young for Dewey. When Julia first met her, Betty had on makeup and high heels, a short skirt, and a fancy hairdo. She made a quick, narrow-minded judgment, assuming Betty was a "fast, sinful" woman.

When Betty first came to Dewey's parents' home, she saw the small, drab place, austere furniture and surroundings, and decided that she didn't want to spend much time in that sad, poor house. She liked his father, Adam, though. Adam always had a twinkle in his eye and a smile for everyone. He was kind to her and welcomed her to the dinner table. Julia put on a fine dinner, and Betty ate joyfully, especially since she was eating for two. The more Betty talked, the less Julia said. Dewey and Adam seemed to enjoy Betty's communication; she tended to take the spotlight naturally, controlling the conversation and making it about herself. She also selected topics that she thought would interest Dewey's parents, like the large garden and the excellent dinner. Julia decided from the first meeting that she was not going to get along with Betty. It may seem interesting that a few years later Julia saved her life and the life of her second child.

After Julie was born, Betty did not regain her strength for months. She slept most days, and Julia took care of both children. At least three or four nights each week, the children stayed with their grandparents. Betty complained to Dewey when she had to take care of the books, pay the bills, and occasionally help out on a shift when another employee was ill. She complained about some of the employees, having to cover for their mistakes, and about customers. Most of their conversations revolved around Betty feeling sick, unhappy, angry, exhausted, and tired. In time she wore Dewey down and talked him into finding another business that would free her to take care of the children and not have to work. Her plan was to continue with Julia's childcare and sleep as much as she liked. In time she thought that she would feel better. Dewey accommodated her. He bought a machine route, as he called it. He had jukeboxes, slot machines, and punchboards in restaurants and bars throughout northern Idaho and western Montana. Gambling was legal and profitable, and he added several slot machines in key places along his route. He sold the restaurant for an excellent profit and plunged into the new business.

In addition to the new business, Dewey bought a small home. Betty was delighted and loved the house, the yard, and the extra building on the property. She loved fixing up the house, painting the rooms, and traveling around to estate sales for used furniture. She also loved having Julia take care of the children while she drove off to sales and secondhand stores. Sometimes she stayed away all night. Betty enjoyed the freedom to be on her own. There were times when she seriously thought about not returning at all. She had the house looking very good just about the time Dewey wanted to move to Libby.

Betty had herself to blame for his decision to move to Libby, Montana. She had complained about the amount of time he spent on the road with the machine route. From the time he arrived home until he left for the next trip, Betty argued with him. "You're never here" and "I have to do everything" were two comments that she used constantly. Dewey appreciated the way she had fixed up and furnished the house. While talking with his mother one day, he pointed out to her how nice their new place looked and how well Betty had furnished it. Julia could not hold back her own anger and let out the information about how little time Betty was spending with her children and her frequent overnight trips. Julia loved having the girls, but she had not planned on becoming a full-time mother to them. Based on time spent with the girls, Betty was the occasional sitter, having the girls a few hours a week, and Julia was, essentially, their mother. Julia loved the girls and thought that she was the better one of the two women to raise them. She told Dewey that if he wanted her to raise them, she would do it. The girls could move in right away and have a stable home rather than going back to Betty.

Dewey did not like that. He and Betty argued several times over Betty taking advantage of Julia and Adam. When he found the store in Libby for sale with a warehouse behind it, and a partially finished apartment with two bedrooms, he decided to buy it and move the family there. Betty was surprisingly in favor of the move because she would no longer have to hear about how grateful she should be to Julia for her help with the children. Dewey could expand the route farther into Montana, increase their income, and make a nice profit on the house that Betty had made into an attractive home.

In Libby, Betty directed her talents toward the store, making it profitable and attractive. She did not like the small apartment in the back. Dewey fixed it up when he was between trips. Betty complained about trying to take care of the girls while managing the store. Dewey often took the girls to Julia's when his route took him to Idaho. Julia loved having the girls, and Betty loved being alone, making the store into a masterpiece and trying to make the apartment more livable. She also drove around Libby, getting to know the small mill and mining town. She drove into the rural areas looking for the perfect house that would free her from the apartment.

She liked solitude. The longer the girls stayed with Julia, the happier Betty was. When the girls were with her, she tended to eat more than she should. She had not lost the weight she had gained from carrying Darlene. The second pregnancy brought more weight, and her excessive eating with minimal exercise added pounds to her small, five-foot-two-inch frame. The beautiful woman she had been was hiding within the additional 150 pounds she had taken on since Julie was born.

On one of her drives around the Libby area toward Kalispell, she found a house that she believed offered just what her family needed. The house was large. The lot had a barn and plenty of acreage for a garden and pasture for several animals. The best part of the scene was the "For Sale by Owner" sign on the front gate. Dewey was making good money on the route. He could sell the store and buy the house. Betty could finally relax, give up working at the store, and take care of the girls. She wanted a piano. She imagined teaching herself to play a little each day. She could get on a diet, eat right, take care of herself, and exercise.

She knew she needed to change something in her life. She was unhappy and had been for years. Dewey could make her happy by buying that house. The more she fantasized about buying the house, the more she convinced herself that it was the only way she would ever find happiness. She planned to do whatever she needed to do to own the house. She found herself driving up the driveway that took her directly to the front of the house. She knocked, and when no one answered, she boldly looked through the large windows.

The floor pattern was simple. A large living room made up the middle of the house. On one end were French doors, probably leading to a master bedroom. She could see a small bathroom. On the other end of the living room were the kitchen and a bedroom. The large living room had oak flooring stained a medium brown tone and brightly colored braided rag rugs. Betty loved the house. She noticed the double garage. She drove into the backyard and saw a small barn with a large fenced area and a large garden.

That was it. *Dewey will love it. He has to love it!*

Betty convinced Dewey to check out the house and she was right. He did love it. The barn offered the storage area he needed for his jukeboxes, slot machines, and records. An area to raise animals was also appealing. He grew up tending to animals, and he thought it would be good for his children as well.

When Dewey talked to the owner, he learned quite a bit more about the house. The owner needed to move into a care facility, and his son had built the house. His son had made sure to insulate the attic, the walls, and even under the house. He used the Zonolite insulation in the barn to keep the animals warm against Montana's cold winters. The owner also noted that the large garden and the alfalfa fields had vermiculite mixed into the soil to increase the growth of anything he might want to plant.

Dewey made a low offer and the owner accepted. There was no need to sell the store.

23

PLAY ENDS. WORK BEGINS

Swimming that morning was much more of an adventure for the girls because they were supposed to be home. The most exciting part, of course, was Eric deciding to go with them. Eric was having a very good time getting to know his sisters better. As they sat enjoying the sunshine on the rocky beach, their conversation turned to the Hardin house.

Julie asked Darlene if she had seen anyone inside. Darlene thought she had seen someone, but she wasn't sure just what she saw. If someone was there, perhaps they were sleeping or just didn't want any company right then. Julie asked out loud to anyone who might hear, "Hey, did anyone see people at the Hardin place?"

"Where's that?" Dan asked. He didn't know the Hardin family since he was relatively new to the area, but he wanted to get to know Julie better, so he jumped into the conversation.

"It's right across the road from Hollands' driveway. Hardins used to live there, but they left a couple of years ago," Julie explained. "We saw a truck there today and wondered if anybody knew if they came back or sold out." The children speculated a bit about who might be moving there, if anyone. No one had any definite information. The Bowman girls decided not to cut through the property on the way home.

"Let's just take Market Road home," Darlene said. "It's longer, but we won't bother the new people."

"What if we see them outside when we go by?" Helen asked. "Then we could stop and say hi, couldn't we?"

"We could cut through to the hill path at the edge of their property and save ourselves time getting home. The main road is quite a bit longer, and we need to get home pretty soon," Julie added. Darlene thought about it and decided to see what the place looked like. If anyone was around, they could stop and say hello, but if they didn't see anyone, they would go farther down Market Road and cut up the hill at another place to get home more quickly. They had a plan, and they decided to ride the rapids at least two more times, jump into the swimming hole for a few glorious laps, and then head for home.

The rapids were always both wonderful and frightening due to their unrelenting swiftness and strength. Darlene kept track of both of her sisters, and all three of them knew how to ride the fast moving water. Dan jumped up and joined the three girls and Eric as they headed for the top of the rapids. Three other swimmers joined the group.

"Mind if I tag along?" Dan was right by Julie. He put his hand on her back and gave her just a touch of support as they climbed up the gravelly rocky ground to the entry spot. When he touched her, Julie bit her lip slightly, rolled her eyes a bit, and felt ecstatic. *He's touching me!* She stayed composed on the outside, but she was joyously happy on the inside. When they entered the rapids, Darlene put Helen on her lap, and Eric held Darlene's free hand. Dan took Julie's hand, and the two of them were a separate pair facing the rapids and their emotions together.

In moments, Eric, Darlene, and Helen were on their way, well in front of Dan and Julie. Dan moved behind Julie, encircling her waist with his arms. They were laughing, enjoying the moment of togetherness, and surrendering to the gushing water surrounding them. Before they reached the end of the ride, Dan lightly kissed Julie's cheek. *Did he kiss me? Did I imagine it?* The ride was over. All five of them gained solid footing and jumped into the pond for a brief swim.

"That was fun!" Dan winked at Julie. "We'll definitely have to do that again. Ya think?"

"That was really fun, and we should do it again." Julie wanted to go again right then. Darlene had a different idea.

"We have to get home, you two. You'll have to wait for another time."

"Next time!" Dan walked off smiling.

The girls and Eric took one more wild ride down the chute, then swam in the pond, enjoying the cold water and splashing one another. Darlene announced that it was time to go home.

After the girls and Eric dried off and walked toward home, they saw Mrs. Holland hanging out some laundry. The girls yelled out hi to her, and she responded with a warm, happy comment about the creek and the swim. The girls stopped and visited with her briefly.

"This is our brother Eric. We talked him into coming with us."

"My goodness, you look just like Dewey! It's so nice to meet you." Lavina gave him a hug. Eric laughed a bit and hugged her back.

"Nice meeting you. You have a beautiful place here." Eric smiled and looked at the ranch house with admiration. "It looks so well taken care of. Thank you for letting us cross through to the creek."

"You just come any time you want, Eric. We love having the Bowmans come our way. My kids like playing with the girls. When they're not swimming, they're riding horses. You're welcome to ride, too." Lavina liked Eric right off.

"Do you have new neighbors?" Julie was curious.

"I saw a truck there earlier in the day, but I haven't heard if the place had been sold or rented recently." Lavina offered them a drink and some cookies. The girls and Eric thanked her, but explained that they had to get some work done at home and said their good-byes.

When they reached Market Road, the white truck had been moved. The girls could see it partly sticking out of the barn door with the back of the truck out of sight. There was a tall, large man with a stained white T-shirt working on the front wheel. He was changing a tire. He stopped a moment and looked at the girls, then turned away as they were walking on Market Road. He did not look like he wanted to chat. He looked sweaty and frustrated with the pickup truck. The four of them did not stop. They walked at a fairly fast rate down the road. When they passed the house, the man could no longer see them, but they could see part of the backyard. There were three children playing. One boy was on the swing, a bigger girl was pushing him, and another small boy was running around trying to catch a bird or something.

The Bowmans did not stop; they had to get home. But seeing that some new kids were in the neighborhood was good news. Julie thought the girl looked about her age and the two boys were about Helen's age. They knew, though, that those were not the Hardin children. New kids meant new adventures. They would probably see them when school started in another month, and they could get to know them and help them meet everyone else at school. They arrived home all dried off from their haste in walking fast and feeling the warm sunshine along the way. Julie made a quick telephone call to Kelly and told her about seeing the children. Kelly was really excited.

They all dressed and the girls went about their chores so when their parents came home they might not even know that they had been gone. Darlene tore up her note.

"What can I do? I might as well hang around if you think Dad's going to be home soon."

"You could chop wood. We always have wood to chop." Darlene showed Eric the woodpile and the ax. He went to it, happy to be able to pitch in. Julie went out to stack wood for him and to make a special request.

"Eric, thanks for helping us, and for going swimming."

"Hey, I had a lot of fun! Thanks for talking me into going."

"You know how you saw some marks on me—you know—from Mother? I would really appreciate it if you wouldn't say anything to anyone. It looks like it's not going to happen anymore, and if Mom finds out we told you, maybe she'll get mad all over again. Would you please not saying anything?"

"I wouldn't do anything to hurt you girls, Julie. But I plan to check with you to make sure things are all right. And you can tell me anything. I won't say anything to your mother, but you need to tell me if she's back at it. Deal?"

"Deal!" Julie breathed more easily, and the two went back to chopping and piling wood. Julie idolized Eric. He was older, almost like a father, and very kind. She loved her dad, but he just wasn't around much, and he spent time away working or on trips to Spokane to buy things for the store. "It's fun to have you here, you know?" Julie commented somewhat shyly. "We really like it when you come out here. You don't have to chop wood, either."

"I like to help out. I especially like to see you girls. You know that I don't have other family than you all. So, be prepared, kid! You're gonna see me a lot more." He set down the axe and walked over to Julie. He winked at her and then hugged her. "You can't get rid of me now!" Julie was in heaven! The two of them went back to stacking and chopping wood.

Darlene threw their swim clothing into the dryer, hoping to get them dry before their parents came home. To Darlene, that was part of the fun—getting away with something. Eric's presence would keep the day's adventure from being a problem. Darlene loved to push her luck and do what she wanted to do, no matter what her mother demanded she do. She had sneaked out a number of times to date Dick. Most of the time she did not get caught. A few times she paid the price of discovery. To Julie and Helen, it was scary. They had both witnessed their mother's treatment of Darlene about a month ago when she came in after an unapproved date with Dick. Mother made her take off her clothing and lie on the bed for a strapping. Darlene wouldn't cry. Their mother beat her until blood ran from her wounds.

Getting caught was frightening to them. Had they known how late their parents were going to be, they could have taken their time. The fear of violent punishment was present, whether their mother was home yet or not. If she objected to their water adventure, she could vent her anger at any time without warning. Maybe she would be angry that Eric came out and went swimming with the girls. Who knew what she would do. Julie and Helen lived in fear. Darlene pretended not to care, but she understood the dangers to her sisters and herself. She hoped her daring defiance of mother's rules would not create a violent situation or put her sisters in danger because of her "fun" idea. She could take a beating, but she hadn't really thought seriously until then about what might happen to her sisters. She teased them, and often took out her frustrations with her mother on her sisters—especially Julie. She learned abusive tactics from her mother, and she did not hesitate to use them when she was angry with her sisters.

That day was different. That day she realized that she would be leaving her home for good. She would take her clothing, a few personal items, and leave that house forever. Dick was going to marry her, and her life would never be the same. Her sisters had to learn their own survival methods. She hoped that Dick's strength last night made a difference for her sisters' future, but after what she had experienced through her own growing-up years, she doubted that anyone could keep her sisters safe from their mother. She had felt the terror of knowing that she was going to die at her mother's will. Darlene knew that she would always lock her doors and windows at night. She also knew that if she ever came back to that house, it would only be with Dick and when her dad was at home. Darlene waited with anticipation for the day she could walk away and never return.

24

BETTY AT THE STORE

Dewey watched Betty looking intently at the store. He could see that she was not sure what to say. He had changed it quite a bit over the last six years. Betty wanted to be angry, but she could not find anything she saw that she could get upset about. She liked everything. No. She loved the whole bright, happy appearance of the store. She needed that change in her life. She began to realize that she could come back to work and not have to change everything. She could breathe again. Being out of town, not feeling well, and gaining so much weight were all gradually choking the life out of her. The store was her salvation. She wanted to stay and help out immediately, and Dewey thought that would be fine. He showed her the details of the business, where he stored the rental instruments, where the teachers came to give lessons, the list of students who came each day, and the inventory of everything in the store.

"You can stay as long as you want to. I have some instruments to repair and I can do that while you wait on people, if you like. Or I can fix the instruments later. You can just relax and have a cup of coffee. We can close up in a couple of hours and go out to lunch. What do you want to do?" he asked.

"Go ahead and work on the instruments. If someone comes in and I need help, I'll let you know. I would like to get started, and right now is just fine with me. Oh, lunch sounds like a good idea, too!" she responded. He could tell she was happy. It had been a long time since she had been happy. The conversation might have been the longest one they had shared in years or at least since Helen was born. He hoped it was not going to be too much too fast.

Two ladies came in together looking for a specific record. Betty greeted them, and they went to the record section with ease, as if they had shopped there before. One of the ladies picked out the record and took it to the cash register. The price was clear, and the lady paid cash. Betty made change and thanked them for coming in. Easy. Betty felt exhilarated! She made her first sale! Why had she not done it earlier? That whole scene with Dick the night before moved to the side in her mind as working in the store became the most important thing in her life. It consumed her, actually thrilled her. Another customer came in the store and asked for Dewey. She felt she could take care of anything, but she called for Dewey and he came out of the workroom.

"Hello, Dewey. I heard that you take used instruments," the man said in a sad voice.

"Hello, Carl." Dewey reached out and shook Carl's hand warmly. "I haven't seen you for a while. How are you?"

"Oh, okay I guess. Can't complain—don't do no good." Carl smiled and patted his shoulder. "Thought you might be interest in this." Carl opened his banjo case.

"I do take used instruments. You know that. What do you have here? Are you looking to sell it or trade it in on a new one?" Dewey asked him as he picked up the banjo and looked it over.

"Hate to have to do it, but I need to sell it for whatever I can get for it. It's been my favorite banjo. I've had it for three years and really don't want to part with it. I bought it from you. Remember? The tuning keys hold pitch just fine. I was hoping to get thirty dollars for it. What do you think?" Carl took the banjo from Dewey. He put some picks on his fingers, rested his foot on a chair, propped the banjo on his thigh, and began playing. Dewey was impressed.

"Why are you selling it, Carl?" Dewey asked.

"Looks like I'm losing my job at the Zonolite mine. You know, a lot of the men can take that nuisance dust, as they call it. I just can't hardly breathe anymore. The boss moved me to the intake room when I kept missing work. It's the dustiest place out there. I think he did it just to make me quit. Of course, sweeping dust is easier than digging ore. But, well, I need a change. They're gonna give me a change all right, by letting me go. The lumber mill just isn't hiring, and I need to trim where I can, you know." Carl looked down, picked part of another tune, and then stopped. "It's got a good sound. Like I said, you sold it to me, and I've enjoyed playing it."

Dewey went to the front of the store where he found a card and took it down. He handed it to Carl. "Before you give up on that, why don't you go out to the Cedar Creek Inn and apply for this job. They need a musician and a part-time helper. You could fill in for both positions until you find something you like better. If you don't get the job, I'll buy your banjo. But first, why don't you give this a try? You'll need the banjo if you get the job, and, hey—you like to play! This could be fun. The fellow out there at Cedar Creek just put this up a few days ago. Can't hurt to try. You may not like the 'part-time help' part, but playing the banjo will be good, and any work is better than no work right now. Right?"

Carl's face lighted up. He took the card and thanked Dewey. He would have said something, but his eyes were watering. His harsh, painful coughing spasm took over, and he spit blood into a hand-kerchief. "Sorry about this." He packed up his banjo, shook hands with Dewey, nodded at Betty, and left the store. Betty watched him leave. Carl was only one of six others laid off recently. Zonolite often rebounded quickly when it received new orders. J. Neils was having its own recession due to regulations about clear cutting and the closure of logging in a few areas. That adversely affected overall employment for the community. When the logs didn't come in, the mill kept fewer employees on the payroll. Zonolite was always up and down, too, though mainly up. A big construction company or an agricultural group would put in an order for vermiculite and employment would soar. They had a turnover based on men getting sick or retiring early. If a man could last twenty years, he could get a pension. The job paid well, so lots of people wanted to work there. But not too many men lasted more than fifteen years, let alone twenty. The company did not have to spend much on retirement benefits.

"Why didn't you buy that banjo? What a deal! You passed up a beautiful instrument for only thirty dollars. I'll bet he would have taken ten. He looked desperate," Betty said. She seemed angry at Dewey's decision as though it were money lost from her pocket. She also wanted Dewey to know that she was a savvy business woman who could make deals—maybe better than he could—like that one.

"He'll need the banjo to get that job, and he bought it from me three years ago, used, for forty. One of these days, if he has work, he'll buy a new one from me. In the long run, I'll make more helping him out, getting him a job, than if I take the short road to thirty bucks. He'll be happier, stay around, say good things about our store. What goes around comes around." Dewey explained it as good basic business. He enjoyed helping people, and he believed it made a difference in making a business successful. Betty would have taken the banjo without hesitation and offered him five bucks for it. She liked the banjo and knew it would sell. Dewey's explanation helped, though. Dewey went on to explain that Carl had a son in school who rented a trumpet. If Carl couldn't get work, Dewey could lose that rental fee. Worse yet, Carl's son would no longer be in band— not good for the son or Carl. "Here's a case where I would let the boy keep the rental for the rest of the summer, even into fall if Carl doesn't find work," Dewey told her.

"But letting them have the horn free isn't right," Betty said. "You can't make money if you give things away."

"Good will goes a long way. There are thirty-seven other instruments rented right now. Two years ago, I had only fourteen rentals. With the large junior high and high school band program at school and the private lessons, I could easily double that number in a couple of years. When I do a favor that helps a local kid, word gets around. Other parents shop here instead of going to Kalispell or Spokane. Again, we have to give a little to the community. As you get used to the regular customers, you'll get the hang of it. I want to keep a good relationship with the customers and the town. I let the kids paint the windows for Homecoming and Christmas. Yes, I know, it's not professional and it's downright messy. But it makes us part of the downtown and the school community. We sell more records to the kids than any other age group. We need to treat them with care and work with them if we want to stay in business. They can buy elsewhere, even by catalog, if they want to." Dewey wasn't sure Betty would be able to control her temper or stay in a calm state to work in the store. She had lost it with him many times. What if a smart-mouthed kid came in there and lipped off to her? What would she do? He decided he would talk to her about that during lunch after she had eaten, not then. He had a lot in the balance there, and what he said in the next hour might make or break getting life in better shape for Betty, his daughters, and his mother.

Dewey and Betty went to lunch at the Surprise Cafe. Betty had not eaten out for a long time. Dewey ate lunch at different places around town most days instead of driving four miles home. He knew the owners and employees and they knew him. He and Betty were greeted warmly when they came in, and Betty was almost embarrassed when the waitress called her by name and said how nice it was to see her. "Dewey tells us you are so busy with your place out there that you never have time to get to town. You gotta take a break now and then, girl! I'm Sherry. Do you remember me from Girl Scouts?"

Betty thought a moment and then said, "Of course! You were in Darlene's group. My, you have grown up. Are you finished with high school already?" When Betty saw the sad look on the girl's face, she wished she had not brought that up.

"No, I quit school last year. My dad passed away, you know, and my mom needed help. This job is just what we need. Besides, I like working here," Sherry said as she gave Betty and Dewey menus.

Betty didn't know what to say, so she said, "I'm glad you like your job, Sherry. I'm going to be helping out at the store now and then, so I may see you again soon. I'm so sorry about the loss of your father. How is your mother doing?"

"She's doing okay. She's been taking care of kids—started baby-sitting for some families. There wasn't any help from the company, though. Dad worked at Zonolite for eighteen years, but that didn't help us when he died. Anyway, enough about that." Sherry dabbed her eye with the corner of her apron.

"You look over the menu, and I'll be right back. Our soup today is split pea with ham. It's usually good, but not as much today. Don't tell the boss I said so," Sherry said quietly to Betty.

"Thanks for the tip," Betty whispered as part of the conspiracy. Betty and Dewey looked over the menu. Betty was happy. Someone she knew was talking to her. Someone she remembered fondly. She knew she was out of touch with people and the way things worked at the store. She was nervous about coming to work. When Sherry came back, they ordered sandwiches and coffee.

"What happened to Sherry's dad?" Betty asked. Dewey explained that he had lung problems.

"I talked to him a few months before he died. When I saw him at Wood's Hardware Store, he was feeling poorly. You know, coughing that raspy, painful way some miners do. I think the obituary said he died of heart failure. Zonolite won't admit it, but that dust from the mine is bad stuff."

Betty reflected on Sherry's situation. Darlene will be quitting school, too. Lots of girls quit school. She wanted to get the marriage done quickly for all those folks out there who would be counting the months backward from the baby's birth to the marriage. If they hurried, she could say the baby was premature.

Dewey was ready to set out a plan for the future of his family. "Betty, I think it might be good for you to come back on mornings when I come to work. The girls will be in school in another month and Darlene can watch them until then. You could work until noon, sometimes we could have lunch in town, or we could eat at home when I drive you out. You could go from nine to twelve. If you want to stay longer eventually, you could. I'm worried that you might not want to do this at all if you get overtired or worn out by too much at once. What are you thinking? Would afternoons be better?" Dewey was watching her, waiting for signs of something positive from her facial expressions. He had to make himself be quiet so Betty could talk.

Betty sipped her coffee and took her time answering. "I think my coming back to work would be a good thing. I'm excited right now and want to be there all day, to be honest. But you may be right. If I do too much too fast, I might give it up before I really get going again. How about I work two weeks during morning hours and see how things go? We can try it out. Mornings would be best. I could rest in the afternoon if I felt like it, and Darlene could watch the girls." Dewey could see that she was looking forward to working at the store. In fact, he was grateful to see Sherry arrive with the sandwiches because Betty looked like she was just about to cry. Betty looked up at Sherry and smiled a warm, friendly smile. Dewey hadn't seen one of those in years. Quietly, within his own private happy moment, he believed it could work. He also imagined that one day she might smile warmly at him again. His next topic was bound to disappoint her, but he was ready to take his chances.

"I was also thinking that I'd bring my mother from Sandpoint, if she's willing to come, to help out with the wedding preparations, and she can see if this works for her as well." Dewey watched Betty take a bite of her sandwich, chew slowly, and then finally set her sandwich down and use her napkin to dab her mouth.

"That's the hard part. You know we don't get along. When the girls are in school we won't need her enough to make the change worthwhile." Betty did not want Dewey's mother to come. *She won't want to come.*

"Well, we need her now. I could let her know that we could really use her help with the upcoming wedding. On Saturday, I'll take the girls to Sandpoint and we'll get her. I don't have to talk about staying on past the wedding. You can go with us, or stay home and rest. Better yet, you can run the store for the day if you want. Or part of the day—lock up early. It's up to you." Dewey waited for Betty to answer. She dived back into her sandwich and said nothing for a while. She watched Dewey as he left part of his sandwich on his plate.

He saw her looking at it and offered it to her with a glance. She took it and finished it off for him.

"I think I'll run the business. I'd like that. A day by myself would be fun." Betty seemed resolved to her new situation. She had a few days to work with Dewey, and anything that she couldn't handle he could take care of when he returned. She hadn't had a day alone for a long time. She wondered if the haunting visions of her brother would leave her alone. They seemed to ache within her until she had to hurt someone. She was unable to figure out what to do about Dick and his threats. What if she became upset with a customer and did something at the store that hurt business when Dewey was gone? She couldn't let that happen. Besides, the last few hours she seemed more settled. She hadn't been consumed with hurting the girls. All three of them would be gone! She could do it. She decided to drive home for practice. She hadn't driven for quite a while. If she could get home without steering the car into a logging truck, she could make it through Saturday.

25

PEOPLE AT THE HARDIN PLACE

When the Holland family pulled out of their driveway heading for town and grocery shopping, Adam announced that there was a white truck sticking out of the Hardin barn. Mrs. Holland said that when the Bowman girls were going home from the creek, they asked about the Hardin family and said they saw the truck, too. "Mom, do you think we have new neighbors? Did someone buy their place?" Kelly asked. "It sure would be nice to have some more kids in the neighborhood. When Julie called she said they saw three kids in the backyard."

Lavina Holland said that she would ask around to see if anyone knew who might have bought the place or rented it. "Maybe our neighbors know. They seem to keep up with that kind of information. I'll give them a call tonight. Did you see anyone as we drove by the place?"

"There was a man by the truck, but I could only see his backside kneeling down by the tire," Adam said. "When we come back home, we could drive by sort a slowly, and we can get a better look."

"We don't want to be too snoopy with newcomers," their mother said. "Friendly is one thing. Snoopy is another and not very welcoming," she warned. Lavina was a loving mother who required her children to apply the golden rule as the basic standard for behavior. "We don't like it when people we don't know come down our driveway and think they can park in our yard to go to the creek. I don't want you kids going over there or using the hill path through their yard until we know who they are and they say it's okay. Do you understand me?" Both Adam and Kelly agreed.

"Remember when those hunters from Idaho drove in and wanted to hunt in our field because they saw a deer there?" Adam said. "We have horses and some cattle out there all the time, and they wanted to shoot the deer."

"That's what I mean, Adam. Even though we let some local people hunt on part of our land at certain times, we don't want just anyone coming in who might not care about our animals. We don't even know if the Hardins sold the house. Maybe these people are friends of the Hardins and they are just checking on the place for them. Or maybe they bought the place for themselves. Until we know more about them, we need to respect their boundaries just like we want people to respect ours. Your dad will pay them a visit, and then we will know more."

Lavina wanted the children to be patient. With new children in the area, she also knew her children's curiosity was strong and could lead them into trouble. Being a good neighbor was important to her. The ranchers and farmers in the area knew one another and had good rapport; bringing a new neighbor into that group was good for the newcomers and good for the locals as well.

"Once we know them, you both need to do all you can to be friendly and kind to them. It's hard to move to a new place, especially for children starting in a new school and all. You'll get your chance to know them."

Both Kelly and Adam were quiet for a few minutes. Kelly was the first to speak up. "What if they don't even know the Hardins and they just stopped there because the place looked deserted?"

Adam looked open-eyed at Kelly. "You mean they could be stealin' the place like poachers? Wow! What would Dad do if they were poachers, Mom?"

"Where do you get your wild ideas? Now just start thinking about something else, you two! We haven't even met them and you're painting them as outlaws! Is that fair? If you were new in a town, would you want people to think you were poachers before you even met them? Get your imaginations under control and let's see what Dad finds out, okay?" She made eye contact with each child. "Okay?"

Both children answered "okay" and then looked at each other and laughed. They talked softly with one another about how they would help the kids on the bus and in school. It was fun to plan for them, even though they had not even met them yet. Just the idea of having some new friends was exciting to think about. Living four miles out of town limited the number of children they could play with any summer day. They both had lots of chores to do as any farm kids had, but they also had a good amount of playtime. Being near the creek helped bring kids their way, and the creek really was a great place to play. They loved that creek, especially in the runoff season with the rapids. Granite Creek's natural water park was their connection with friends in the summer.

26

A FAMILY TOGETHER

When Dewey and Betty arrived home after Betty's first day at the store, the girls had dinner ready, the house was clean in its unkempt way, and Julie was helping Helen churn butter. The girls had a system that Darlene developed and directed, and when they carried out their duties, it was good. Betty went to the stove, dipped out some potatoes, tasted the gravy, and then told Julie to put dinner on the table. The meatloaf and some fried side pork were the main entrees, with corn on the cob and snap beans added to the usual potatoes and gravy. Jell-O with apples and marshmallows filled out the meal. There was a raisin cake for dessert and hot rolls with dinner.

"Who's doing that chopping?" Dewey walked toward the back door.

"Eric stopped by to see you and decided to wait—and help out while he waited." Darlene did not fill in the rest of the details of Eric's visit.

Dewey stepped out the back door and invited Eric to dinner. "You're just in time to eat, and it looks like you've earned your supper! Come on in." The men laughed, carrying on small talk about the rapids and the swim as they walked in together. Helen and Julie had a place set up for Eric.

Everyone sat down, passed food around the table, and ate in silence for a short time. No one told Julie the food was good except Eric. No one else commented at all, good or bad. They just ate. Darlene grew into the cook without comments as well. Good cooking was expected. Anything that did not measure up was soundly criticized. Both girls learned that "no comment" was the best report they would get.

Dewey broke the silence, as was the usual custom. "Your mother is thinking about working at the store for part of the day for a while. What do you think of that?" The girls were silent, looked at their mother and dad, and waited for more information. If they said the wrong thing in the wrong way, they knew they would pay later.

Darlene spoke up first. "Mom, do you want to do that?" She didn't want to sound too eager, but she was hoping it would work out. Peace in the house during the day. What could be better?

"I'm going to help out your dad for a week or two and see how it goes. I may keep doing it, or not. I'm going to start tomorrow for three hours. If it works out, I may stay for a longer day. We'll see. That means you would have to look after the girls, Darlene. I have to count on you to make sure things get done around here." Betty looked at the girls, seeking what they might be feeling about that. Darlene did not say a word, but she thought to herself that there would be no change in her responsibilities. She already took care of the girls and the place because her mother was in bed all day. Both Julie and Helen were quiet, still looking at their parents' faces to see what might happen next.

Then, out of the blue, Helen blurted out, "We might have some new neighbors at the Hardin house!" The big secret was right out there for everyone to examine.

Eric laughed softly, and he watched with interest as the girls reacted to Helen's information. Helen realized what she had done too late, and her face showed fear. She rolled her eyes back and sighed.

"I took the girls to the creek today for a short swim because they worked so hard in the garden and cleaning the house. They promised to get the chores done and dinner ready when we got home. They did a great job. I'm really proud of them," Darlene explained strongly and confidently, though secretly knowing it could blow up depending upon their mother's reaction.

Eric had to speak up. "I have to admit my part here. When Darlene mentioned going to the creek, I really wanted to go, so I talked them into going—and to taking me—promising that I would make it right with both their parents when you got home." He watched Dewey and Betty. "See? I even chopped some wood! We all went together for a short swim and a few rapid rides. I loved it! Thank you, girls, so much for letting me go with you today. Oh, and please pass the meatloaf. Great stuff. Who cooked this? Julie? Nice job on everything."

Betty was quiet briefly, and then said, "Well, they can't be going to the creek every day while I'm working. You didn't have my permission."

Darlene responded quickly, "Oh, Dad said we could go if we did our work. Right, Dad?"

Dad was caught off guard, yet managed to stay composed. "Oh, yes. Yes. I forgot"—*What am I going to say here?*—"I said they could go sometimes when they did their work and today they did it. Good job, girls." Dewey was looking at Betty, waiting for the scene to break wide open in their faces. He seemed as worried about upsetting her as the girls did.

Betty looked intently at the food. "Pass the potatoes and gravy over here, please." Helen reached for the gravy, and Dewey passed the potatoes. "Helen, what's this about new neighbors?"

Helen had been staring at the scene before her with no thought about the Hardin place after their secret came out. All she could think about was the trouble she might have created for her sisters and herself. She looked at Darlene, who nodded at her and gave her a smile. Helen began explaining what the girls had seen. "When we were cutting through the Hardin place to get to the creek, we were almost past the house when we saw a white pickup in front of the house. Darlene thought we should say hello since we were already in their yard, but nobody answered the door."

Julie added, "It looked like someone was inside, but it was just a shadow I saw from the porch. When we came back from the creek, someone had moved the truck—backed it into the barn halfway. A man was working on the front tire."

Dewey asked the girls if they knew who the man was. They all said they didn't know him. "It would be nice to have someone in that place again. Could be the Hardins sold or rented it and we'll have some new neighbors, or they could be just passing by, checking on it for Alan. Maybe we'll hear something tomorrow at the store. What do you think, Betty?"

Betty was deeply involved with her food, placing large amounts into her mouth. When she heard her name, she looked up from her potatoes. The girls looked away from her face because her mouth was crammed full and overflowing with potatoes and gravy. They gave their full attention to their own plates.

"When did the Hardins move away exactly?" Betty managed to say through a large bite of food. Dewey thought they had left two summers ago.

"Maybe someone will know in town. They used to shop at Al's Market. Al may have heard something."

It dawned on Betty that she was going to be in town the next day, too. "Yes, we might hear something tomorrow." She smiled at the thought, and that smile hit the girls in a special way. They smiled, too. It could happen. It all could get better.

"Girls, clean up while Darlene and I talk about an upcoming wedding." Betty and Darlene went into the living room. Dewey beckoned to Eric to join them. Eric picked up his plate and two others, took them into the kitchen, and then followed his dad into the living room. Dewey lit his pipe and settled into his chair with a cup of coffee at his side. He and Eric were quiet, listening and smoking like they didn't have a worry, not even one. Darlene told her parents that Dick was coming over at 7:00 p.m. and that they could include Dick in planning the wedding.

"It's fine that Dick comes over, but he isn't going to be planning this wedding," Betty said in a calm manner, looking at Darlene and waiting for her comment. Darlene took time to answer, thinking first about what she was going to say. It was her life that soon would be changing for the better. Her comments surprised both her parents.

"Dick is not going to want to plan the wedding. He just may want to help out with costs and setting up chairs. You know—just to support what we plan to do. Let's just help him feel like he's part of planning things."

Betty smiled at Darlene. "Good idea. Let's plan on doing this before summer ends—three weeks from now should be enough time. With this baby on the way, we want to get the wedding over as soon as possible." The two women talked calmly and were able to come up with several ideas without any conflict. Normal conversations did not happen often in the house where one woman controlled everyone else with her emotions, anger, and physical dominance.

Eric thanked everyone for a nice dinner. He went into the kitchen to say good night to the girls. "Let's do this again, girls! That was fun." They agreed. "Maybe your folks will let me take you girls to a movie next week. I'll buy the popcorn." He made the girls feel special, and they hugged him. *I love these girls—Darlene too. I really do have a family.*

"Can we go, Dad? Can we?" Julie spoke up quickly, and Helen was right there hoping for a positive answer.

"Are you sure you want to get mixed up with these two wild kids?" Dewey teased the girls and waited to see if Eric really meant it.

"I absolutely would like to take them. It seems to me there's a Disney picture Friday night. How does that sound, girls?" Both girls responded with happy sounds and hugs for Dad and Eric. "I'll pick you up at seven thirty and dress warm. Even though it's summer, it cools down a lot at night. Bring a blanket, too. And, Darlene, you and Dick can come too if you like."

"Thanks, Eric. I'll see what Dick wants to do." Darlene smiled.

The girls and Dewey walked with Eric to the door, and he was on his way home. Julie and Helen glanced at times from the kitchen as they finished cleaning up following dinner.

Helen whispered to Julie, "Do you really think Mother will stop—you know—hitting?"

"We'll see, Helen." Julie recalled her mother telling her many times in the heat of beating her that she was going to kill her. She also remembered the many whispered messages in the night when her mother told her softly that she was going to die. Julie desperately wanted to believe her mother would no longer hurt them. In her heart she knew that her mother might try to stop, but those weird conversations her mother carried on with herself or invisible people were not going to fade away easily. No, Julie did not believe the beatings were going to stop. If Darlene lived until the wedding, Julie was sure that Helen's life, as well as her own, was going to change for the worse when Darlene moved away.

The girls learned later that night that they were going with their dad to Sandpoint to get their grandma on Saturday. Dewey told them after they went to bed, and they were elated. He said that Darlene wanted to stay home and get her room arranged so there would be room for their grandma. Julie and Helen were excited to get to go with their dad. The three of them had to talk her into coming back with them. Both of the girls knew that their grandma living with them would make it that much harder for their mother to cause them harm. Grandma would help them with the cooking and chores. She was also kind to them and made them nice clothing. Since Grandpa Adam had passed away, she seemed lonely. They could keep her cheered up every day if she lived with them.

That Saturday in Sandpoint, Dewey spent some time talking with his mother alone while the girls worked in their grandma's garden, picking strawberries, peas, and green beans.

"We've got a busy summer since Darlene's getting married and we're doing the wedding at our house."

"Wedding? Darlene's too young to get married."

"Well, she's going to be a mother soon, and the boy she's marrying seems real sincere about it all."

"I can see how I could help out. How does Betty feel about this— you know, my helping out?" Dewey said that he needed her there to help protect the girls. Julia was very upset about the abuse of her grandchildren. "How long has this been going on, Dewey?"

"Too long. It has to stop, and I need you there with the girls to make sure they're safe." Dewey shook his head. "I just didn't see it, or I would have stepped in sooner."

"I know a family that can check on my house and garden. If this doesn't work out, well, you can bring me home." Knowing the rocky relationship she had with Betty, Julia thought that she might be back after a few days.

When the girls brought in the buckets of strawberries and vegetables, Julia told them to rinse them off and put them in the small fruit boxes to take with them to Libby.

"Are you coming back with us, Grandma?" Julie asked. Both she and Helen looked intently at Julia as she took her time answering them.

"Now what would I be doing coming to Libby with you two?" Julia teased; then she laughed and opened her arms. The girls went to her and hugged her.

"We really want you to come and live with us, Grandma. We really do." The girls were sincere as they hugged her, trying not to beg too much. Julia looked around at her home. There had been lonely times there by herself since Adam had passed away. She had all of her things around her, and the freedom to do as she pleased. Was she willing to give it up to move to a place where she knew Betty would not welcome her? The girls would fill her life with joy. Would that joy compensate for her loss of freedom to run her own home?

"Dewey, I'll tell you what I will do. I'll go with you and help at least until after the wedding is over. That might be a month or so. That will be long enough for us to see if the arrangement works and if we can all get along. In the meantime, I'll need to shut down the house and pack some things."

"We can help you. I'll get some boxes from the grocery store and the girls can help you get ready. Girls, you can help your grandma, can't you?" The girls were laughing and dancing with their grandma.

"You know you have to mind me, now, don't you, girls?"

Both Helen and Julie were happy. "We know, Grandma. We will," Julie told her.

Dewey left to get a few boxes, and Julia sent the girls to do some work in the garden so the food would not spoil on the vine. Julia thought that trying out the living arrangement was better than just moving out right away. She needed to know that she had a place to live if she could not get along with Betty. It took the four of them less than three hours to pack up Julia's personal items, close up the house, and head for Libby. Julia sat in the front seat, looking out the window as she left her home. She watched the streets and the buildings in a different way than in the past. She was trying to hold the images in her mind for future reference because she was not sure she would ever pass that way again. Since she had turned eighty, she looked at each day as a gift of life. How many days were left for her? If she could serve in some way to help her family, she felt she should do it. Maybe her worth could be summed up in just a few boxes of items. Tears quietly streamed down her face; she looked away from Dewey and out the window as she traveled closer toward the end of her life.

27

DAN EAGLE

Dan Eagle had been swimming at the creek just about every day since he moved to Libby from Polson in June. He loved to swim, and the other kids welcomed him, especially when they were flying down the rapids and they needed an uplifting hand. Dan had finished ninth grade in Polson and was going to be a sophomore at Libby High School. Although he was half Indian and half Swedish, his birth certificate indicated that he was Native American. His hair was short, styled in the typical crew cut of the day. He loved sports, lived and breathed basketball, and spent a great deal of time keeping in shape. He ran from his home to the creek, which was about four miles east along the Market Road. Running to town from his home, an eight-mile distance, was a standard practice for him. He carried a basketball in a bag on his back so he could shoot hoops at the school-yard. He swam, worked at home on his parents' place, lifted weights, and seemed to have a bottomless well of energy. He spent most of his time alone doing whatever he chose to do.

His parents, Robert and Adele Eagle, were Native Americans with a French Canadian background. They adopted Dan from the Montana Children's Center in Twin Bridges, Montana, when he was six years old. His parents let him do whatever he wanted most of the time. His dad worked in the green chain portion of the lumber mill. The men who worked the green chain pulled the new logs into the mill. They had to have above average strength to get the logs under control and through the bark-shedding process. Rob was considered one of the strongest workers. He was a big man, weighing over 280 pounds with muscular definition all over his body. His thick black hair framed his Native American facial features. When he smiled, which was often, his white teeth glimmered. He was also one of the hardest drinkers. After work he made it a point to head for the Frog Pond Bar to drink with the crew. Adele often met him there, and the two of them would drink for hours, leaving Dan and the other boys on their own.

Dan had serious plans to become a professional basketball player. He intended to go to college on a basketball scholarship. He was not a strong student, but he was sure his basketball skills would take care of getting him into a college.

Dan never knew his biological parents. He was born at the Florence Crittenton Home for Unwed Mothers in Helena, Montana, in 1942. Someone named him Daniel, and after a few days, he was taken to the Montana Children's Center in Twin Bridges, Montana, his home until he was six years old. He tried to remember living at the center, but when he became a teenager he could not recall much at all about his early years. When he was six years old, Dan's most vivid memory was of a woman he did not know taking him on a huge bus to a place he had never been. He held the woman's hand, and she guided him to a window seat on the bus. On his knees with his hands pressed against the window, he looked out at the only home he had known and watched the buildings disappear in the distance. He was afraid, simply afraid, and he sat back in his seat holding again the hand of the woman as the bus took him to a new life with strangers in another part of Montana.

28

THE HARDIN PLACE, JULY 1958

Owen had fallen asleep in the sun or he would not have let the children play outside for as long as he had. When they awakened him with their noise, he told them it was time to go inside. They did as he said without argument, even though they would have loved to stay outside longer. Owen told them to play in the back bedroom with strict instructions to stay away from the windows. He went out to the barn to see how Stephen was coming with the truck.

"Are we leaving tonight?" Owen asked him.

Stephen threw a wrench on the ground. "Doesn't look like this truck is going to make it without a mechanic." Stephen had worked on it all morning.

A black half-ton pickup stopped at the front gate, and Tom Holland got out. He walked across the cattle guard and over to the two men. "Hello, I'm Tom, your neighbor across the way. Looks like you're having some trouble here." Tom held out his hand and Owen took it and shook hands strongly with Tom.

"Yeah, this thing may be on its last legs," Owen said.

Tom bent down by Stephen and looked at the problem. "I think you might need a different wrench for that. I've got one in my truck," Tom offered, and went to his truck. He returned with a larger wrench. "I'll give you a hand, if you like," he said and climbed down on the ground and under the truck. "The key to this repair is having two people do it together. You hold there, yes—right there with that wrench, and I'll turn this end with this wrench," Tom explained.

Stephen took the help, did as Tom directed, and the all-day job was just about completed. It worked. Both men climbed out from under the front end of the truck. "Thank you, Tom. I have to say that I couldn't have done this without your help. You came along just in time." Stephen shook Tom's hand.

"Glad I could help. Are you moving in here?" Tom asked. Stephen looked at Owen who returned the look.

"No, just looking. It's not quite what we need," Owen said.

"We were hoping we were getting some new neighbors. Sorry you aren't planning to stay on," Tom said. "Say hello to the Johnsons for me, will you? I believe they still own it," Tom commented as he walked back to his truck. As Tom stepped into his truck, he saw Stephen come toward him with a quick step and the wrench still clutched in his fist.

"Sure thing," Owen called out. Stephen did not respond. He was striding toward Tom briskly. Tom wasn't sure what to think. Did he need to defend himself? Stephen had yelled out for him to wait, and as Tom turned around, he wasn't sure what might happen. Then Stephen handed him his wrench.

"You just about left this behind." Stephen extended his other hand with the obvious intent of a handshake. "Thanks for the help."

Tom took his wrench, nodded to Stephen, and responded hesitantly to the handshake. He tipped his hat, made a gesture of farewell to Owen, and went out the gate. As he started up the engine, he glanced toward the house and saw a child looking through a small opening in the curtain. He drove down his own driveway, wondering who those men were and why they didn't know the owners' real family name. He mulled over their lack of response to his saying "Johnson" as the owner, except to say "sure thing." Maybe they had never met the Hardins.

Alan Hardin could have sold that property long ago. And maybe that was none of Tom's business. He only knew that the men did not belong on that property. They would soon be gone, and that was a good thing. They needed help. He helped them. That ended it.

Until dinner, that is, when his wife and kids brought up the three children that those men supposedly had at the house.

"Three children? Who said there were three children?" Tom inquired as he passed the bowls of food around the table. Lavina had prepared her usual excellent dinner, and everyone was hungry, willing to pass food, and anxious for the next bowl to reach them. "Where did you hear that they had three children?" Tom asked.

Kelly spoke up first. "Darlene and Julie saw them when they walked home yesterday. Julie called me and told me about the three kids playing in the backyard."

Lavina explained that the three Bowman girls had asked her if she knew about the neighbors because the girls told her that they went through the yard as they always have done over the years, and then they saw the truck in the yard. Adam added, "Darlene knocked on the door and thought she saw someone inside, but nobody answered."

Kelly explained that there were two boys about Helen's age and a girl about Julie's age. "The girls saw the children when they went home from swimming yesterday and told us. We hope that they will start school here and maybe play with us. It would be fun to have some new kids around to play with."

"The Bowman girls are swimming two days in a row? What's this world coming to!"

"Not only the girls, but their half brother, Eric, was with them. Looks just like Dewey," Lavina added.

Then Tom told his family that he had met the men. "I stopped to be neighborly, and I saw one of the two men working on his truck, not doing so well on it, either. I could see he had axle trouble, so I got my wrench out and helped him tighten up the wheelbase. I'd have to say they weren't too friendly, but they both seemed okay with my help. I didn't stay long. But then I was only in the yard out by the barn. As I was leaving, though, I saw a child looking out the front window—sort of peeking through the curtain."

"Should I take them over something to eat, Tom?" Lavina asked.

"Can I go, too?" Kelly said in a quiet, slightly pleading voice. She wanted to meet the girl who might be about her age.

"I'm not sure we should bother these people right now, Livvy. They weren't, well, ready to be neighborly. In fact, they didn't even introduce themselves. Just a handshake," Tom answered.

"Maybe some dinner and a piece of apple pie will sweeten their dispositions. I made plenty of food." Lavina was ready to do the neighborly thing. After dinner, she, Kelly, and Adam each took a food item up their long driveway and across the road to the neighbor's house.

Lavina knocked on the door as the three of them stood with arms full on the porch. The curtains on the front window were closed, but someone peeked through. The Holland family waited for some time. Lavina called out. "I know you are home and probably tired, but you could have some chicken and apple pie if you'll just open the door. My family ate the same dinner and they're doing fine!" Kelly and Adam laughed quietly.

Owen opened the door, and he could immediately smell the chicken and the pie.

"Please feel free to help yourself and share with your folks. Welcome to our neighborhood." Lavina handed Owen the pie.

Owen's directive from Stephen was to send whoever was out there away. The food was just too good to pass up after their long journey. "Thank you, ma'am. We appreciate your hospitality. We aren't in any position to send anything home with you," Owen offered.

"No problem. Just enjoy your dinner and we'll see you around. My name's Lavina and this is Kelly and Adam. Tom was here earlier and thought you might need something to cheer you up after working on your truck. Just take it and we'll pick up the dishes later." Owen made no attempt to introduce himself or offer any information about himself or others who might be in the house. Lavina and the kids said good night. Owen took the food inside.

A man's loud voice was loud enough for the Hollands to hear, "What in the hell are you doing?" as the door shut and cut short most of the sound of their unpleasant conversation. Adam looked over his shoulder at the house and saw a short person looking through the slit in the curtain again. Then the slit became a solid barrier.

"Mom, I saw a kid, a boy I think, look out the window," Adam said.

"Well, that child will get some food for dinner tonight, and you helped him get it. Thank you both for coming with me."

"I think something's wrong there, Mom. Something isn't right with those people. I'm worried about the kids with those two men," Kelly said softly and in a somewhat fearful voice.

"Now let's not make more of this than it is. We'll have time to get to know these people if they stay around here. I don't want you children worrying about them. Just mind your own business, and in time we may become real good friends with them. Who knows?" Lavina had agreed with Kelly's assessment that something was wrong, but she did not want to unduly frighten her children.

When they entered the living room, Tom said, "Well, did you find out anything new about our neighbors?" Each of the three food bearers told Tom what they thought about their welcoming visit. Adam was still focused on seeing a boy at the window, Kelly shared that she didn't like the man and that she was worried about the children, and Lavina said again that in time they will all get to know the neighbors, and then probably laugh at themselves for being concerned at all about them. Tom could see that Lavina was trying to keep the children from being worried, and he agreed with Lavina, encouraging their children not to worry. "They're going to get some good food tonight, and that's the best we can do for them right now. Let's get the chores finished and then off to bed with you two," Tom directed. The chores were mostly done before dinner, so the rest of the job was finished before 7:30 p.m. There was time for one television show if they hurried. *Lassie* started at 8:00 p.m. If they were all ready for bed, and if Dad and Mom weren't too tired, they might get to watch some of it. Kelly and Adam were out the door and on the job, leaving further speculation about the new neighbors for another time.

When Owen brought the food into the house, the children were excited. In spite of the argument between the two men over taking in the food, the children were helpful in taking it to the table and getting out a dish and a spoon for each person. It was real food. They missed real food. They were glad the two men were in a discussion and missed getting in on the initial round of potatoes and chicken. Their cooperation was amazing, organized, and quiet. The food didn't last long. The children saved some for the men, and they went for the pie enthusiastically. They cut it in five pieces and three pieces disappeared in moments. When their portions were devoured, they went into the bedroom and fell on the floor exhausted and happy for the first time in a long time. Finally, their stomachs were full.

"You put yourself out there, Owen. Another person knows what you look like—and their kids. That's four people who know what you look like, and one of them has seen me." Stephen was angry. "We're into something here that could turn bad at any moment. You have to be more careful or you'll ruin this for all of us." Stephen was quiet for a moment. He knew Owen was thinking of the food. "Go eat," he said. "Just go eat."

Owen went for it. No one bothered to clean the fine dust off the table before they set out the food. An observant eye would have seen a small pile of dust that had sifted down from the attic through the loose light fixture above the table. The dust lightly lifted into the air a bit when the dishes of food came in contact with the table. The children had brushed it away with their hands. They had eaten their food with the dust still coating their fingers. When Owen sat down, he brushed the dust to one side, adding dust to his right hand. That was the hand that would bring chicken to his mouth and the hand that bushed the dust into the air they all breathed while they ate. Owen could see that the children had already eaten a fair share of the food. He was ready to devour the rest himself. If Stephen hadn't come into the room, Owen would have eaten it all. The two of them ate in silence, and they finished off the pie as well. When they were done, they looked in on the children. All three of them were asleep on the floor.

"Let's let them rest while we get ready to move out," Stephen said. "We need to load those boxes and cover the truck bed. The kids can crawl in the cages last this time. They know the drill."

"How much time would we get if we get caught at the border with these kids?"

"Don't think about that. Just think about the end result if we don't get them over there. Let's get this load ready," Stephen responded impatiently. "I don't like this any more than you do, but we're here and we're doing it. Let's move!"

It was getting dark. The children put on their coats, took their cloth bags with their only belongings, and did as they were told: they crawled into the long, narrow cage on the bed of the pickup. They hated the cages and the smell of gas from the exhaust. There never seemed to be enough fresh air. They climbed in, moved their cloth bags in a manner to provide a pillow, and heard the cages shut and click. Their blankets held dust from the house. The dust they breathed was from the asbestos-laden insulation in the ceiling and the walls. How many breaths did it take to become infected with a lung disease? For some people, it took only one breath to lodge asbestos into a lung to incubate and develop future disease and death. For others, a lifetime of breathing it could pass unnoticed. A few minutes later, the white truck moved out on Market Road, then turned onto Highway 2 on its way to Libby. Owen drove and Stephen kept the map handy. In Libby, Stephen watched for California Avenue, also named Highway 37. They turned north at that point and drove toward Eureka. They read the sign "Zonolite Mine" along Highway 37. The two men discussed their future opportunities for employment if they decided to come back to the Libby area. With Zonolite and J. Neils, the possibilities for secure employment looked very good to two men with criminal records who often worked temporarily until their backgrounds came to light.

When Stephen and Owen met at the Montana State Prison in Deer Lodge two years earlier, they didn't know they would both be working together transporting children illegally. They weren't close friends, but they tolerated one another, and they both liked to keep to themselves. Few conversations took place between them during that time period, but they each knew the other one planned to go to Missoula after they served their time. Cheap housing put them in a run-down apartment complex in Missoula. Except for passing each other now and then, they seldom spoke to one another until the person who hired them brought them together.

About forty-five minutes later and less than a mile from Eureka, Stephen saw the small highway sign "Airport Road." They turned left toward an airstrip that could accommodate small propeller planes. Off to the left was a six-passenger Cessna. Owen drove across the field to the plane, hoping it was their contact. As they approached, they saw a flashlight blinking four times, stop, then four more times. It was their plane. Owen stopped the truck, and both of the men helped the children crawl out of the cage and onto the ground. Only one of the children had to be awakened, and all three were glad to get out of the cage. They saw the airplane. Owen and Stephen helped the three children climb into the small plane and get strapped in. They talked briefly with the pilot, some papers changed hands, and the pilot asked the men to shine their headlights onto the runway. Owen climbed into the truck and positioned it so the headlights would help light up the airstrip. Stephen had a cigarette while the plane took its position and moved from the ground into the air toward Canada. Another delivery was made. Three children would have much different lives. Stephen didn't want to think about their lives or about the people who were receiving them. The whole business of taking kids from their homes made him wonder how he let himself get involved in the illegal operation. The job made him a kidnapper, a crime that meant real time—or the death penalty. He just wanted to get back to Missoula. He climbed into the truck. Owen drove back out onto Highway 37, and when it intersected with Highway 93, the men turned south toward home. The dark road, lighted only by their headlights that late at night, did not keep Owen and Stephen from watching for a sheriff's car or a highway patrol car. The very few vehicles on the road at that time of night eased their minds after many miles. The two men settled into the rhythm of the ride, letting their fear of going back to prison slip back into the recesses of their minds. Maybe watching for deer and seeing the night animals crossing the highway became the focus of the night, distracting Stephen, at least, from thinking about his involvement in his present illegal activity. Owen stared into the darkness watching for deer, most likely not wanting to think at all.

29

STEPHEN ROARK AND

FATHER FLYNN

MISSOULA, MONTANA, 1956

Stephen Roark had spent seven years in prison in Deer Lodge for robbery. There was no time like prison time for a person who couldn't stand to be in small places. Stephen had been brought up better than to steal from others. His family was a long way from wealthy, but they had food, worked hard, and had good values. When Stephen sat in playing guitar with a band in Missoula one night in 1948, he earned a permanent spot doing what he loved best—making music. Then he met Gina. He did not know that he could love anyone the way he loved that beautiful woman.

Gina introduced him to angel dust and a heavenly hell that took his love of music away from him, replacing it with a love of drugs. He would do anything to keep Gina and to stay high with her. After he lost his ability to keep a job, he stole to keep the two of them supplied with drugs. He accrued a felony record and a prison sentence of ten years. While serving his time, he cooperated and earned parole during his seventh year.

When he was paroled, he took a job as a logger for Cascade Logging Company in Missoula. The work was seasonal, but he saved some money out of each check to get through the winter. He bought a guitar and spent his evenings alone in his apartment strumming old tunes and writing new ones. He did not drink, had no plans to play music professionally, and would not get involved with a woman. His neighbor was Owen Gifford. He talked to him from time to time, but he did not socialize with him. He had known Owen in prison. He even considered him a distant friend—someone who wouldn't knife him from behind. Someone who kept to himself like Stephen did. They left prison separately, but both ended up in Missoula in the same cheap apartment complex set up in advance by the state penal system. Stephen preferred to be alone, and, except for work, stayed at home most of the time. He liked to go to Warden's for lunch every now and then when he went out for groceries. Mostly, he cooked frozen dinners or hamburgers he made himself. His life was simple. Then he met Father Flynn.

Father Tim Flynn had seen him a few times at Warden's ordering his lunch. Always alone. One day he followed Stephen to the apartment complex. Father Flynn matched up his apartment number with the name on his mailbox; he made a few calls to special contacts. After learning that Stephen had spent some hard time in the Montana State Prison, he sensed Stephen was someone who might be able to help him with his unique project.

On a Saturday in March 1957, Father saw Stephen at Warden's and asked him what was good. Stephen saw his collar. "I've seen you here before. What do you usually get?"

"I always get a burger. Thought maybe I'd try something different." *He's observant. That's good.* "What do you recommend?"

"Well, I like the Reuben, but their hamburgers are real good, too." Both men studied the menu. Father Flynn, with the exception of the collar, looked nothing like a priest. His face was old, lined, and craggy as though he used to box for a living and lost most of the time. Father looked over the samples in the glass counters and then ordered the Reuben and salad. His voice was harsh and gravelly, but his manner was pleasant.

Stephen's order came up first, and Stephen took his meal to one of the high tables and perched upon a tall chair. When Father's lunch was ready, he couldn't find a seat due to the usual lunch crowd at Warden's. "Would you mind if I sit at your table?" Father asked him. Stephen gestured in a positive way. "My name is Tim Flynn."

"Have a seat," he said, swallowing a big bite. Stephen could see that there was no other place for anyone to sit. Father Tim Flynn did not overburden Stephen with conversation. The two ate their lunches and enjoyed the food. Both went back to buy dessert.

Over big pieces of apple pie, conversation developed. Stephen asked him if the collar meant that he was a priest, and Father Flynn said he was. The two men talked of the weather, their employment, and that they both liked to fish. Father Flynn invited Stephen to fish with him on the Blackfoot River Sunday afternoon. "I take some students fishing and could use some adults along with the group. We take a bus, so you don't have to drive, and I have gear for everyone— you don't even need a rod." Father Flynn's invitation was simple. Stephen really had nothing to do on Sunday and said he would think about it. "We leave from Templin's Grocery parking lot about three so we can fish during the late afternoon as the sun starts to fade. We'll be back by eight or so. You're welcome to join us. Just show up on time and get on the bus." Father shook his hand, took his dishes to the garbage can, and left Warden's. Stephen decided to go.

The trip was fun. Two parents and another priest came along with Father Flynn and six teenage boys. The adults prepared a dinner of hot dogs, cupcakes, chips, and soda for everyone at about 6:00 p.m. Stephen enjoyed the fishing and the group. The teens were getting help with their fly rods, learning casting techniques and which flies to use. Stephen learned a bit more about casting himself. He was glad he came. Father Flynn talked with him after dinner while cupcakes were disappearing in the general direction of teenage boys. "I'm glad you came, Stephen. We have a fellowship meeting on Wednesday evenings at seven. Please come if you like. You're also welcome to attend Sunday services, but I don't want to overwhelm you and scare you away. I think you would like the fellowship meetings. These parents here, they attend, and other young adults come. You could meet some people, maybe end up with a couple of fishing buddies. Think about it." Father Flynn was not a pushy priest, but he had an uncanny sense about people; he could read Stephen, and he knew he was lonely and troubled.

Over the next few months, Stephen became friends with Father Tim Flynn. They fished the Blackfoot often, and they took a two-day trip to fish the Madison and the Gallatin Rivers near Bozeman. The priest had an ulterior motive in befriending Stephen. He knew about Stephen's prison time, and he was ready to approach Stephen with an unusual proposition. Unfortunately for Stephen, if he decided to help his new friend Father Flynn he might end up in the Deer Lodge State Penitentiary.

30

WEDDING PLANS, JULY 1958

Betty wanted to have the wedding before the end of summer. The sooner, the better, considering there was a baby on the way. Darlene agreed. She was focused on whatever it took to get out of her mother's house. To save money, they decided to have the wedding in their home. To make room, some of the furniture would be put in other rooms or stored in the barn for a few days. Betty and Darlene planned to make a trip to Spokane to buy the dress. Darlene really liked that idea, and she wanted Dewey to go also. He said he would need to run the store. Darlene heard Dick drive up, and she went to the door to meet him.

Darlene explained their ideas so far, and Dick agreed that a home wedding would work well. Dick said that he could help with expenses, and together they could have a nice small wedding. Dick said that his mother wanted to help in any way she could. It did not take them long to make a simple plan. Dewey asked the Baptist minister he knew to perform the ceremony, Betty arranged all the food, and Darlene hoped that her grandmother, Julia, would make her wedding cake. Cleaning the house would take time, but Julie and Helen worked hard, and Julia also helped with cleaning, food preparation, and everything else.

Dick let the group know that his cousin David might be able to be his best man. Betty pointed out that Darlene's half brother Eric could do that, too, if need be. "If David can't make it, I would be honored to have Eric as my best man." Betty backed off that subject by noting that Dick was committed to the marriage by already lining up his best man. Darlene wanted Julie to be her maid of honor and Helen her flower girl.

Darlene was pleased that her mother seemed to be in a positive mood as they laid out plans together. The family planned a guest list, keeping the size of the living room in mind. There was no sense inviting a bunch of people from out of town who probably wouldn't come. Betty had few family members and friends, so her list was small. Dick said his parents would like to invite a few people, but they would also keep their list small. Everyone seemed to have forgotten the horrible scene they had all lived through recently. Just a few nights ago, Betty, in tears, had collapsed on the floor. Dick had laid down the law to his future in-laws. Julie and Helen had watched as Darlene's future husband took on their mother and father and defended Darlene. Julie and Helen watched and listened from another room just as they had several nights ago, only they were also cleaning up the kitchen and the dishes. Anyone looking in on the family would think they were a very happy, loving group of people.

The girls came into the living room after the dishes were done and wondered if they would be allowed to stay in the room. Darlene asked Julie if she would like to be her maid of honor. Julie was excited and embraced her sister. "Yes, of course. I would love to!" Darlene called Helen to her and asked her to be the flower girl. She hugged Darlene, too. The two younger sisters were laughing and crying at the same time.

"Seems like we could use a couple of nice dresses for you girls. I could help out with that, if you would like," Grandma Julia offered. Helen and Julie were thrilled and hugged her.

"That would certainly make it more affordable, Julia," Betty noted.

Betty decided to take Darlene shopping in Spokane for her wedding dress the next week while both of the younger girls stayed with Julia. Betty had already picked up some plain white cards and envelopes to write out invitations by hand. Darlene took charge of writing out the invitations and mailing them within a few days. There was much to be done with a wedding only three weeks away.

Betty said that they would all meet again for more planning. "We have a beginning. We know who is in the wedding party and what dresses we need. We have a date set in three weeks. We will meet again next week to attend to the other details we haven't thought of yet. I think we should ask Eric to come next week. He may have some ideas for us." Dick and Darlene agreed, and then Darlene asked to go for a drive with Dick.

"Okay, but be back in an hour," Betty said. "I guess I don't have to worry about you getting into more trouble than you are in already," she added as they went out the door. The way she said it felt like an insult to the couple. The meeting was a good one. The planning went well. Betty's final comment brought reality back to everyone. She could have said, "Okay, don't be late," but she felt a need to continue to punish and cause pain. Darlene felt the sting as intended. She did not display any negative emotion.

"Thanks, Mom. See you in an hour," Darlene said, smiling broadly, and she and Dick left. Betty was disappointed that her comment was ineffective. Dewey did not pick up on it, and the two girls were still excited about getting to be in the wedding party. Betty decided to go to bed early. She went to the bedroom after saying good night. Once in the room, she headed for her candy bars stash. After she had crammed two Butterfingers and a Hershey Bar into her mouth as fast as she could, she chewed as though she were in ecstasy. Her eyes rolled back. She had one sticky, three-day-old maple bar left that followed the candy into her mouth. When the maple bar was about half gone, she seemed to settle down. She wanted hot coffee to melt the sugar in her mouth, but she did not want to cross the living room to get to the kitchen. She peeked out carefully and saw that the girls were not in sight. The coffee was important to her. When she crossed the living room, Dewey saw the remnants of chocolate on her mouth. He did not say a word about it.

"Well, we have a lot coming up, don't we, Betty?" He commented to her as she passed through to the kitchen.

"Yes, we do. I need a cup of something hot," she said as she went into the kitchen and turned on the burner to heat up the coffee. "Looks like there's enough for two cups. Want one?" she offered.

Dewey was so surprised that he said, "Yes! I'll take you up on that."

Betty took two cups out of the cupboard and caught a glance of herself in the mirror. She saw the chocolate on her mouth and wiped it off. She wondered if Dewey had seen it. She walked directly to his chair. "Did you see something on my mouth?" she demanded.

Dewey looked up at her. "Let me take a look." Betty stood there. "No, I don't see anything there at all," he said. "Why do you ask?" he responded in the most innocent voice he could conjure.

"Well, I had something on my mouth, and I thought that you saw it but didn't tell me." She waited, watched him closely, and then went back to the kitchen to get the coffee.

"Betty, I didn't see anything on your face," Dewey said. "I am happy to see some lipstick on you, though. It brightens up your smile." She gave him the coffee and left the room. He turned on the television and watched a mystery. After it was over, he decided that he was living a mystery. He wasn't sleeping well because he had to make sure Betty didn't get up in the night and harm the children. He normally tended to sleep soundly. He looked in on Julie and Helen; they both were sleeping in their own beds. He knocked on Darlene's door softly. She opened the door, hoping it was not her mother.

"Just checking on you. Are you happy about how things are going?" Dewey decided he needed to be more involved with the girls and the wedding.

"Dad, I think things are going fine. Better than I had hoped."

"Has your mother been treating you okay?"

"Yes. We're okay. And Dad, thank you for everything. I love you."

"Me too. Good night." Dewey winked at her and smiled. "Me too" was as close as he could get to saying "I love you." He had grown up without hearing those words, as had his parents. Words of emotion were internalized but seldom spoken. Dewey loved his daughters as much as any father could. His intent at that point was to protect them day and night. He had to protect them from their own mother. He thought he had them safe, and he hoped that Betty was ready to do her part to make their home happy and safe.

His enemy, however, was not Betty, but the memories that haunted her and the guilt she could not let die. Her inner self-communication that had dominated her sanity for several years was important to her. Sometimes in the night Betty could not sleep. Some minor issue would begin to bother her, and she would wait in silence for a time to create scenarios in her mind with inner analysis of what to do with Julie or Darlene. The result was often violence against one of the girls while Dewey slept.

Dewey no longer slept soundly through the night. Any time Betty left her side of the bed, he was up, too, seeing where she was going. She sensed him watching her, following her, and listening for any unusual sounds. Very seldom was he asleep when she walked in the night throughout the house. But there were still times when he was working at the store or when he slept that the girls were unprotected. Sadly.

31

GRANDMA JULIA

TWO WEEKS OF WEDDING

PLANNING

Darlene, Julie, and Helen had energy to burn as they prepared for each day when their mother was going to be at work all morning. They had at least three hours without her in the house. That meant three hours of not worrying about noise levels or getting in the line of her fiery temper and violent reactions to minor things. They were up without an alarm, out taking care of chores, and preparing breakfast. In addition to their energy levels, they had their Grandma Julia to help them. She was always energetic and quick to assist in any way she could. Julia even moved discretely away from the stove when she saw Betty approach the cooking food. Betty tasted the hash browns, and then she added more salt. She tasted them again, took some slices of bacon, and crunched them into her mouth. Julie had to make extra food regularly because of her mother's "tasting" process. Betty tasted in large bites, and then at the table she said she just wasn't that hungry and sometimes commented on how she couldn't understand why she put on weight the way she did considering how little she ate. She made the rounds of the food before each meal. No one said a word about it, but the rest of the family knew the truth. She was a compulsive eater and a secret feeder when she thought no one was aware.

Dewey was ready for breakfast and poured the coffee for Betty, Julia, and himself. When Betty sat with Dewey, she had only one slice of bacon and a pancake, saying she was too excited to eat. Julia watched Betty's display of a minimal appetite and wanted to point out that she really had already eaten before she came to the table. But she didn't say a word. She wanted the arrangement to work for everyone's sake, including Betty's. Dewey ate heartily, and then Dewey and Betty left for the store. The girls cleared the table and Darlene laid out a plan for the morning. "We're going to get the house cleaned, the chores all done, the butter churned, and then we will play. You all know your jobs, so let's work hard and then go swimming this morning before Mom gets home. She'll never let us go later in the day. Let's go!"

Julia watched the girls put Darlene's plan into action. The girls worked fast and thoroughly, and they finished everything they needed to have done by the time their mother came home. Julia had time to mend items of clothing in between opportunities to help the girls with their work. In addition to cleaning and gardening, Darlene put a bowl of water with short branches of wild roses in it on the kitchen table.

"We're done!" Darlene called to Julie and Helen. "Let's go to the creek!"

"I'll take care of the laundry, girls. You go have some fun." Julia was happy to see them so excited. Julia loved being with the girls, yet she also looked forward to having some quiet time. After living alone for a while, she missed solitude in a house full of people. She also looked forward to their return.

The girls took off for the creek by the hill path and cut down to Market Road before their usual way so they would not walk through the Hardin property. As they neared the place, they looked for signs of the new neighbors. The place looked deserted. The barn doors were shut, no truck was in sight, and the curtains hung partly open in the front window while the other windows had closed curtains. Darlene decided to see if anyone was home. Both Julie and Helen were worried, but Darlene said, "They'll either answer the door or they won't." The girls all walked up the porch steps and Darlene knocked confidently. No one answered. Then they looked in the window, first as a nonchalant peek, then as full-on stares. Darlene turned the front doorknob, but it was locked.

They turned to leave the place, but curiosity gained over courtesy, and they went to the back door. Darlene reached above the doorsill and took down a key. She opened the door, and the three girls went inside, checking every room. No one was there. They locked the house and checked the barn. It was empty. No truck. No men. No kids. Helen made the comment that it looked just like it did before the white truck came. That meant to the girls that those people were not moving there. There would be no new kids to play with or help make friends at school.

On the way to the creek, the girls saw Lavina Holland, and they all waved. When Lavina called out to them, the girls ran over to her. Lavina asked them if they had seen anyone across the way at the Hardins. Julie was the first to respond.

"No one's there. Not in the house or the barn," Julie burst out, excitedly.

"We went in the house and the barn," Darlene said. "It looks just the same. No change. They didn't even leave any garbage behind."

Lavina knew how the girls were able to get into the house. Everyone left a key somewhere, and above the door was the place most people hid it. "Thanks for telling me, girls. Are you off to the creek? How did you ever get out of the house so early?" Lavina was surprised at herself for being so curious, but she knew those girls worked hard, and she also knew that they seldom were able to get away, especially before lunch.

Darlene briefly explained, "Mom went to help dad at the store this morning." She didn't want to say too much, but felt compelled to add, "And we got our work done. We'd appreciate it if you wouldn't say anything to our folks. The weather is too nice to stay home, and we really like to swim. The runoff season is almost over, too, and we want to catch the rapids before they are totally gone."

"Your secret is safe with me. Now go have fun!" Lavina said. The girls took off at a run for the creek. "Some other kids are already there, including mine!" she yelled after them.

The girls were amazed to see that so many kids were already swimming. The Hollands were there, and so was Dan; three kids they didn't know were there visiting with someone. A father of a neighbor was watching his three kids. Last summer, Dewey sent Julie and Darlene to his house to help him with some cement work. The man paid fifty cents per hour per girl to mix and haul cement and carry bricks for several days. Dewey didn't seem to notice just how much work at home the girls had to do. The girls worked hard, and the best part of the job was the money he gave them for their help. Darlene took Julie's money and hid it, knowing their mother would take it if she found it.

Dan noticed the Bowman sisters first, and he and the Holland kids yelled out to them to jump in. Adam had an inner tube, and he threw it in the water, jumping after it, splashing the girls as he wildly kicked his feet and moved into the pool of water. Dan liked those kids and enjoyed watching them get into the icy water slowly at first, and then plunge full bore into the stream. He specifically enjoyed watching Julie. She liked to swim and took long, graceful strokes across the pond, heading for the current.

The kids liked to get into the choppy, fast moving water and let the current carry them the eighty yards or so to where the water crossed over a shallow rocky area. There they could regain control and get out of the current. Darlene grabbed Helen, and the three girls headed for the top of the rapids. Helen jumped on Darlene's lap and off they went. Julie was just about ready to take the wild ride down the current when Dan decided to join her. It would be their second ride together that summer. He held out his hand to her and the two of them swirled downstream rapidly, laughing and bobbing up and down in the water. When they hit the shallow part, they quickly ran to the top of the current to go again. The other kids were there, jumping into the current and swiftly moving along, giggling and laughing. For about twenty minutes, the group made a steady line of current travelers on cool, frothy, and swift water. Then, exhausted, they all dragged themselves onto the small sandy area and soaked up the sunshine.

"We have to go," Darlene ordered. "We can't be late or Mother will find out and be mad." Both Julie and Helen moved quickly down the path with Darlene toward their home. Julie said a quick good-bye to Kelly and Adam, smiled shyly at Dan, and ran down the road. Dan noticed her good-bye look that was just for him. He knew she liked him. He had made some friends since he'd moved to Libby. Those were the kids who lived near him, and all of them lived out of town and rode the bus to school. He felt comfortable with them, and they liked him. One time, Darlene and Julie helped him when he pretended to need help. He made them feel good by thanking them and telling them that they saved his life. He had lost his footing at the top of the current and made a shaky entry—then he called out for help. They both ran to him and took his call seriously. He had hoped that only Julie would attempt the rescue, but Darlene's quickness interrupted his plan.

On the way home, Julie remembered her mother's whispered comment, "How's Smokey?" the day after Dewey had insisted that both Julie and Helen tell him if Betty hurt them or Darlene again. Julie had been fairly sure that her mother was listening at the door when her dad asked for her help. After her mother's whispered comment, Julie knew that her mother had heard her dad's plan to ask about Smokey as a secret way to find out if everything was okay. Even though Betty seemed happy about working at the store, Julie was afraid to let down her guard for a moment. Darlene seemed much more confident in their mother's change of heart and her less frightening actions. She had Dick's protection, as well as her dad's word that he wouldn't let Betty hurt her. Julie still felt that she did not have any protection. Her fear of her mother was greater than her confidence in her dad being able to protect her. Julie wanted to tell Darlene and Helen, but she didn't tell anyone. Fear is a very compelling thing, and Betty had Julie firmly in her control.

The girls made it home in time to put their wet clothing in the dryer. Julie turned on the oven and began making lunch while Helen set the table. Darlene headed for the garden. She pulled some carrots and cut some loose-leaf lettuce for lunch. Julie punched down the bread dough for Darlene, divided it into four pans, and put it in the oven. The girls took their hairbrushes and went in the backyard to brush out their hair. Julie put Helen's hair in braids, and then worked on drying her own hair by flipping it back and forth to get air drying underway. Once it was almost dry, she put it into a ponytail. Darlene tied her hair in rags so it would curl and look great for Dick's visit that evening. Wedding plans were going to continue that night when Dick came over. Julia was amazed at the organization and effort the three girls had demonstrated as she watched them prepare for their parents' return. She had baked cookies for them while they were gone, and they had not touched one. Nothing interfered with their plans to be ready for their mother's return.

The girls heard the car pull into the front driveway, and they ran into the house to get lunch on the table. Helen had already set the table for lunch. Julie had made potato salad the day before, the bread was almost done, and she just had the vegetables to wash and cut up. Leftover roast beef would taste good on homemade bread. Helen and Darlene met their mother at the door. They hoped to get her involved in a conversation so the bread could bake for five more minutes. It worked.

"What did you do today, Mama? You've worked a week already," Helen said politely.

"Well, I did a lot of things. I waited on some customers. Cleaned off the counters. Heard some piano lessons going on in the back room." Betty shared her half-day happily. Then she asked Helen what she did. Even though both Julie and Darlene had prepared her well, they never knew what Helen would say. Mother knew the questions that helped her find out just what she wanted to know.

Helen eagerly responded, "Oh, Mom, you know what we do. What you do is more exciting. Tell me more. Who came in the store? Did you know them? Did you sell lots of stuff?"

Mother was happy to tell Helen and Julie about her morning, and she gave lots of information about the customers. She was excited to talk about herself and her own experiences. Darlene and Julie thought that they might have made it through their secret swim time undetected. The day was young, though. Darlene made a furtive trip from the dryer to her bedroom with the swim clothing. She seemed to make it undetected. Julie took the bread out of the oven, dropped the loaves from the pans, and buttered the tops of the loaves. Dad was unloading some boxes from the car to the garage. Dewey had a way of bringing home the most interesting things. Betty labeled most of it as junk. When he came through the kitchen door, he yelled out, "Hey, anyone hungry? I smell some food!" He had a coffee grinder in his hands and showed it to his mother. "Look at what I found today, Mom. Does it remind you of your old grinder? Look what good shape it's in. All it needs is a glass jar to hold the coffee and some coffee beans." He was proud of his treasure that he had picked up at the city dump. "Betty even likes it. Don't you, Betty?"

"Well, I didn't want it around the store, and I thought that Julia might like it." Betty was making an effort to include Julia in the family. Dewey handed it to his mother, and she smiled.

"Yes, it does look like my old one. I'll clean this up and see if it's sharp enough to grind some good coffee. Thank you. Thank you both." Julia held the grinder, touching the design that had been molded into the metal, thinking of her past, and missing her Adam.

Dewey also mentioned that he had seen Eric, and that he was going to bring folding chairs for the wedding. "I'm glad we have his support. He's going to be a lot of help during the wedding."

Julie and Julia had lunch ready. Julia sliced a fresh loaf of bread as they were taking their seats. As usual, no one said how great the bread smelled or how good the food looked. No one thanked Julie or Julia for cooking. Julie was grateful that no one complained about anything. The family made thickly sliced beef sandwiches, ate their fresh vegetables and potato salad, and devoured most of an apple pie for dessert. Julia's cookies went fast. No one brought up swimming. Betty's appetite was fierce, and because she took time describing her morning to the girls, she had missed her grazing time "tasting" all the food before the family sat down to eat lunch. She seemed nervous, excited, and starved all at the same time. As much as she tried to keep from overloading her plate, she was famished and put about half of the potato salad onto her plate the first time around. Her eyes had a rapid movement to them as she ate feverishly, yet she watched everyone else taking food and eating, passing food and eating. She seemed afraid that she would not get her share as she gulped down food in a frantic, protective manner. At the end of the meal, she was exhausted from her feeding frenzy. The others at the table did not call attention to her ravenous behavior because they knew any comment might send her into a rage or bring on tears. Either way, no one wanted to upset her. She had made it through her first week of working at the store, and that was far more than Dewey had ever expected. Dewey hoped that Dick's threat only one week ago to expose Betty as a child abuser would protect the girls. He was feeling more confident in Betty with each day.

"Girls, we closed up the store for lunch. I've got to go back right away because I know the instrument rental company is coming by with some instruments I sent out to get fixed," Dewey explained.

"I thought you fixed them, Daddy," Helen said.

"I can fix most things, but sometimes I need help. Anyway, I'm going to leave for town. Girls, when Eric brings out the chairs, have him put them along the wall behind the rocking chair. Betty, you did good today. Girls, you should see your mother with the customers. She's doing great." Betty smiled and said that it was pretty busy and that made the morning fly by. "With the wedding only two weeks away, you all have a lot to do to get the house ready—and I'll help, too, of course." Dewey put on his hat.

"Julia, you wanted to meet the new pastor, and if you come with me, I can drop you off for a visit." Dewey and Julia left together. "I'll be back with Julia about three, so girls, take care of things here and

I'll be back here with your grandma in a couple of hours." The two of them left together. Grandma looked back at the girls, worried that they might need her. Darlene hugged her gently. "We'll be fine, Grandma. It's okay now."

32

THE BROOM

The girls began cleaning up the lunch items by clearing the table and kitchen counters. Having their dad take Julia and leave them alone with their mother made Julie and Helen nervous.

"I'm going to take a nap. Eric might come over tonight to talk about the wedding, and I want the living room cleaned up and dusted. Can you girls do that quietly? I mean quietly."

"Yes, Mama," the younger girls answered. Both Julie and Helen looked at Darlene to see her reaction to their mother's comment. Darlene looked happy and confident.

Once she was in her bedroom, Betty went to her candy stash and ate a large Butterfinger. She enjoyed it, jammed her mouth full, closed her eyes in ecstasy, and stuffed it into her mouth until it was gone. She ate a second one just as quickly, hid the wrappers, and then lay down to sleep. An idea came to her softly, then more adamantly, telling her to watch the girls and see if they were busy cleaning. Betty really wanted to sleep but seemed unable to lie down for long. She was committed to finding fault with the girls.

Helen and Julie washed the dishes quietly; there was no way anyone outside that kitchen could hear a sound. Darlene went out the back door to work in the garden. Although she may have been pulling weeds, her mind was racing, wondering how the wedding would turn out. What did her mother have in store for her?

After the kitchen was cleaned up, Julie and Helen worked on straightening up the living room. There always seemed to be papers stacked up, wood chips around the fireplace area, and mother's projects here and there. She had some knitting with several colors of yarn by her chair, a bunch of sheet music around the piano, and several piles of books detailing an unusual religion she had supported financially in a limited way. A mound of clothing she was going to alter took up quite a bit of space. The room looked pretty junky. Julie wasn't sure just how to handle the mess. If she put her mother's things away in a manner that upset her, Julie knew that she was in trouble. But if she didn't straighten up the living room, she would also be in trouble. She had Helen stack up the music in a neat pile on the piano seat. Julie found a paper bag and put the yarn and knitting in it. She set it by her mother's chair. She folded the clothing as best she could and made several neat stacks. Julie emptied the ashtrays, cleaned up the ashes, and swept up the wood chips. Helen was being very quiet. But somehow a noise happened. It wasn't a big noise, but it was a sharp noise caused when the broom handle slipped from the wall and hit the floor. The girls were startled at first, then frightened. They looked at each other, hoping their mother hadn't heard it. Then they both looked at the bedroom door, waiting. Frozen.

Julie was standing near the arched opening to the kitchen when Betty came storming out of the bedroom. "Didn't I tell you to be quiet?" she screamed. "Can't I even have a moment's rest?" Betty swung her fist at Julie, knocking her head against the wall. Julie could see her mother's mouth moving, but she could not hear her. Either the fist or the wall created pressure that caused Julie to lose consciousness. She slipped slowly to the floor. Betty kicked her and told her to get up. "Get up! Get up!" Betty yelled as she continued kicking her. Julie's body formed into the fetal position; she was semiconscious, and sound came to her as though she were in a tunnel as she tried to fend off the blows from Betty's feet. "You are worthless! I work hard and you can't even let me sleep." Betty looked around, searching for something. Her eyes darted strangely around the room. "Where's Darlene?"

Betty looked out the back door and saw Darlene working in the garden. Betty did not want Darlene to see her beating Julie or she might tell Dewey or Dick—or both. Betty tightened her hands onto her ears, covering them. She seemed to be in excruciating pain. Sobbing followed and tears ran down her face. "I can't do this! I can't do this anymore!" Betty didn't hear the knocking at the door.

Helen backed slowly into a corner and slipped down under the piano keyboard, wrapping her arms around her legs. Tears streamed down her cheeks. She was too small to help, too afraid to move.

Betty picked up the broom and hit Julie with the handle over and over, swinging it back and forth as she connected with Julie's head. She tired of the broom and threw it toward the piano, knocking over the music piles that Helen had stacked. "Helen, clean up that music! Now!" Helen hurried to her feet and began stacking music as fast as she could. Mother slapped her head hard, and Helen fell behind the piano bench.

Eric opened the door when he heard Betty's yelling. He said nothing, but took in the scene. Julie was lying on the floor with her knees pulled up, arms holding them. Helen had just fallen behind the piano bench. Betty was unaware that he stood behind her.

"I'm going to try this again. This time I expect it to be quiet! Do you hear me?" Betty stepped over some sheet music and was attempting to kick Julie when Eric grabbed her arm.

"Stop! Enough!" Eric had pushed her away from Julie, and Betty almost lost her balance.

"Wha—what are you doing here?" Betty looked at Eric as if she were seeing someone for the first time. She pulled her arm away from him.

"I brought some chairs from Zonolite on loan for the wedding. When I knocked and nobody answered, I heard screaming. What are you doing? That's a much better question! What's going on here?" Eric bent down to help Julie. He saw her battered face and swelling beginning on her forehead. Helen was sobbing, stuck between the bench legs and the piano. With Eric's help, Julie was trying to get off the floor and over to Helen. As she and Eric lifted Helen, Betty left the room.

Julie and Helen leaned on Eric, thankful that he came into the house when he did and that Betty had stopped her assault on them when he intervened.

"What happened?"

"We were cleaning up for the wedding, you know, and, well, the broom fell and made a noise. I should have been more careful, but the broom slipped along the wall and hit the floor." Julie was terribly upset with herself, taking the blame for upsetting her mother.

"That's it? That's what caused this beating? Did she beat you with the handle?" Eric was trying to sort out the events that created the confusion and violence. He looked at the impressions the broom handle made on Julie's forehead. Blood trickled from her ear.

"Mother was tired and sleeping. I made the noise. It's my fault."

"Your fault? Are you kidding me? It is not your fault!" Eric shook his head in disbelief. "Give me that broom!" Eric threw the broom on the floor. "Was it that loud?"

"No. Maybe. I didn't throw it. I had put it against the wall and it fell." Julie tried to re-create the scene in her mind.

"It doesn't matter how loud it was. You do not deserve to be hit in the head with a broom handle once, twice—or over and over because it fell on the floor. For Christ's sake! No one deserves to be hit like this ever, Julie." Eric was angry, shaking his head, pacing.

"I'm going to bring in the chairs, and then you two are going with me. Do you girls know where the chairs go?" Julie pointed near the kitchen; he went to the truck to get the chairs. He wanted a moment to sort out the horribly abusive scene he had assumed was at an end. He went back to the truck for a second bunch. As he approached the door, he saw Betty talking to the girls. He quietly listened and watched her.

"I know your scheme with your dad, and if he hears about this, next time you will get even worse. Do you hear me? Do you?" Betty shoved Julie off balance, knocking her over. She grabbed Julie's hair and twisted her head back, and smashed her fist into Julie's face. Eric dropped the chairs and tried to intervene as quickly as he could.

"Yes, I promise. I won't say anything. I won't," Julie cried out tearfully, trying to get her voice to cooperate.

Eric's grip on Betty's shoulder forced her to release Julie's hair. Even with Eric holding her, she was able to push Julie, knocking her into the piano bench. "I thought you were gone!" She yelled at Eric.

"I thought you had stopped beating your children!"

"Get out of my house!"

"Julie and Helen, get in the truck, now." Eric went to the girls to help them.

"You can't take my children!"

"I sure as hell can't leave them here. You can tell Dewey that they're at my house." Eric tried to get Helen up from the floor under the keyboard part of the piano where she hid again when Betty came back to the room. He then helped Julie get up. He was supporting both of them, helping them to the door.

"No, please. Just leave them." Betty used her most convincing tone, trying to stay in control and get Eric out of the house without the girls. She knew Dewey and Julia would be home soon, and she needed things to go back to normal. "I promise I won't hurt them anymore. I've just been under some strain these days. Really. I'm fine. I won't hurt them. Tell him, girls. Tell him that you will stay here."

Neither Julie nor Helen said anything. Eric moved them both toward the door and outside into his truck. Betty went back to the bedroom, leaving the two children with Eric to comfort them. There would be no assistance coming from her. Betty knew that the girls would stay at home. They would talk Eric into leaving them at home. She watched them from her bedroom window, peeking through a narrow opening in the curtains. When they were in the truck, Julie put her arms around Helen. The two girls held each other, and Julie made a rocking motion that seemed to gel them into one person. Helen looked up at Julie. Julie's mouth was split and bleeding; her forehead had knots on it that were swelling. The broom handle had left its marks.

Eric made a third and final load with chairs, leaving them on the porch. When he climbed into the truck, he looked at both girls, not knowing what to say. Helen clutched Julie tightly, pulling herself closer and continuing to cry.

"Eric, we appreciate your helping us. We better stay here. Dad will be home soon with Grandma. Darlene's out back in the garden. How about we go get Darlene? Mom promised not to hurt her anymore. She can stay with us until Dad gets back."

"I hate to leave you with your mother as upset as she is."

"That's how she is. She's done for now. She probably won't hit us until after the wedding. Let's get Darlene and stay here. Okay?"

Eric drove the truck back to the garden and talked to Darlene. She assured him that she could take care of them. Darlene told the girls to go into the house, and she thanked Eric for his help. He didn't like it, but he left with the understanding that he was going to talk to Dewey about it.

The girls went into the house. After a few moments, Helen went to the kitchen for a rag. She soaked the rag in cold water and carefully wiped Julie's face. The kicks had resulted in pains in her back, stomach, and sides. Helen helped her into their bedroom and onto her bed.

Julie rolled onto her side, and Helen took the washcloth back to the kitchen, rinsed it out with cold water again, and brought it back to Julie. Helen wiped Julie's forehead softly. Julie took it from her and held it in place upon her forehead. Helen crawled on the bed next to her, trying to comfort her by patting her arm softly and telling her how sorry she was that it had happened. The two of them fell asleep. When Darlene came in, she saw that the living room was not done. She looked in and saw the girls sleeping. "I guess I have to take care of this." She saw the blood and the broom. When she saw the sheet music all over the place, and the piano stool moved, she figured out what had happened. Eric's description of the beating was clear. She quietly went into the bedroom and carefully moved Helen away from Julie's side. Darlene leaned over Julie and saw more closely the results of what a broomstick and a fist can do to a face.

Darlene cleaned up Julie's face gently with a cool washcloth. As she tended to her sister, Julie cried softly. "The broom slipped and fell. That's all. The broom…She'll ruin your wedding if we make her angry." Then she was quiet as tears continued to stream down her face and onto her pillow. Julie looked at Darlene. "I'll miss you, Darlene. I don't think I can do this without you."

Darlene had given up crying about her mother years ago. Even in the heat of her mother's loss of control, Darlene would not cry. She had seen her sister beaten before, and this time was like the others. She cleaned her up, told her she would just get stronger with every beating, and one day she would also get out of that house. Darlene thought her words would be encouraging to Julie. She had toughened herself, and now she had to toughen Julie. Darlene saw weakness when she looked at Julie, who was escaping from the reality of her situation by fading into sleep. To Darlene, Julie was giving in to her mother's will. But Darlene did not know what went on within the secret zones of Julie's private world of dreams. Julie could imagine her grandmother holding her, patting her head. She could escape from the heartache of her mother's violence by imagining herself in another place, another time. She could endure because Helen needed her. She could not give up because she knew that if she did, Helen would probably die a horrible, painful death at her mother's hands.

33

ERIC AT ZONOLITE MINING COMPANY

Eric drove back to work. He had used his lunchtime to deliver the chairs. He wanted to cry for his half sisters. He did not want to leave them with their mother, but he had to figure out what he could do that would not cause more problems for the girls. If Darlene had not assured him that the girls would be okay, he would not have left them in that house with that wild, angry woman. He had to tell Dewey, and he had to pick the right time to do it. He hoped that Julie was right about her not beating the girls until after the wedding. He had noticed that Betty was almost like two people. Sometimes she was friendly and enjoyable. Other times, she was angry, frightening, and, as he had seen that day, dangerous. He had a meeting to get to at the Zonolite that afternoon, and he had to be on time. He would have to sort through what had happened when he talked to Dewey, and it was not going to be that day.

When Dewey and Julia returned to the house, Julie was asleep in her room. Darlene wanted to tell her dad about the beating, but she wanted to have Dick with her for protection. Betty had been busy packing up some of the sheet music in boxes. Betty grabbed Dewey's arm as soon as he entered the house.

"We need to take this music to the store. I'll go with you," Betty told Dewey. "It's always falling over, and we'll need the space for the wedding." Betty picked up two boxes and handed them to Dewey.

"Darlene, you get dinner ready while we're gone. Julie's sick and is not to be disturbed."

"The girls can help you load the boxes," Dewey told Betty as she strained to pick up three full boxes by herself.

"No! No. I'll get them myself. Let's get these to the store now before I change my mind." Dewey picked up the remaining boxes and loaded them into the car, and the two of them left for town. Betty's breath was heaving due to the strain of the heavy load and her inner knowledge of beating Julie. If she could keep Dewey away from the house for a while, she might get away with this violent action. At least she had time to think of her next step to keep Dewey from getting her medical help.

Dewey was curious but compliant with Betty's orders about the sheet music. "What's wrong with Julie? What's she got? A flu bug?"

"I don't know for sure. She was throwing up and hot all over so I sent her to bed. She'll be fine after a good night's sleep. She definitely needs rest, so I want her left alone for a couple of days or 'til her fever's gone." Betty's hands agitated one another, wringing and twisting her shirttail.

After they dropped off the music and locked up the store again, Betty decided she wanted a hamburger and fries. She prolonged their dinner for a couple of hours with several cups of coffee and made-up conversation.

"I've enjoyed spending this time with you, Betty. We get so busy that we just don't take out time for ourselves." On the drive home, Dewey reached over and held Betty's hand. For the first time in years, she let him.

The girls and Julia were in bed when Dewey and Betty came home. "I'll check on Julie." Betty went quietly into the girls' room. Both girls were awake and in Julie's bed. "Listen to me, both of you. One word about what happened today and you will both regret it. Do I make myself clear?" Her tone was icy, threatening, and frightening. The girls nodded, too scared to say a word. Betty left the room and told Dewey that Julie was fine and sleeping. "No need to wake her, Dewey," she told him when he started to go into the girls' room. He paused at the door, wanting to go in, but he didn't want to wake them. "I don't want you to wake them up," she said strongly.

The next day after work, Eric was ready to bring up what he'd witnessed when he delivered the chairs. "Dewey, I took the chairs to your house—"

"Thanks for doing that, and tell your boss we really appreciate the loan of the chairs. How are things going out at the mine? You like the job so far?"

"I can honestly say that I really like what I'm doing, Dad. And I like the people I work with, too. It was a good move, although I have nothing against Montana Power. They said I could come back anytime I wanted. Can't beat that!" Eric was genuinely moved by that offer from his former employer.

"What about the dust?"

"I'm working in the office, so I don't get much of that. Every now and then I go out to do some measuring and inspecting, but I see very little dust during my workday, and my clothes don't get dusty like the miners do every day. That's good."

Eric knew he had to tell Dewey about Betty beating Julie. "Dad, I have something I need to tell you. Can you spare some time right now?" Just as he was going to describe Betty's behavior with the two girls, Betty came out of the back room with some sheet music to file. When she saw Eric and Dewey talking, she made a loud statement that caught Dewey's attention.

"Don't believe a word he says!" Betty stopped, looked dead serious, and waited to see what anyone else might have to say.

"Now just what would he have to say that I shouldn't believe?" Dewey wondered why she was so antagonistic. Eric remained silent, but he looked at her and smiled.

"He's probably lying about me beating on Julie. I was just getting her to do her job, that's all."

"That's interesting," Dewey said, looking at Eric.

"Well, Dad, I saw this broom handle beating Julie's head a few times, boots slamming against her body a few more times. I saw her fall to the floor trying to dodge kicks, and I saw Helen hiding under the piano, crying, scared to death. That's all I saw. Oh, yeah, and Betty was the one gripping the broom handle, swinging away and kicking Julie. That's pretty much it."

Dewey looked at Betty, then at Eric. "Eric and I were talking about his job at the Zonolite mine." Dewey walked toward Betty. "Is that why I couldn't see my daughter last night? Because you beat Julie and didn't want me to see her?"

Betty drew in a deep breath and looked at both men as though she didn't believe them. She left the room.

"Dad, she was like a crazy woman out of her mind. I was just about to tell you when she walked in. I'm scared for the girls."

"I appreciate your telling me, Eric. There's been too little talk and too much beating at our house. We had quite a scene about a week ago, and I told Betty that she can never beat the girls again. She promised she wouldn't. That's why I brought my mother here—to be at the house and protect the girls. Then the one day I take my mother to visit the pastor, Betty tears after Julie. Damn it!" Dewey looked away and shook his head.

"I'm going to come out more often, Dad, and take the girls out sometimes to get them away from her, especially on the weekend when you have the store to run. They are absolutely afraid to say anything about getting beaten. She's got 'em scared to death."

Dewey nodded. "She's been at this while I've been out of the house. I got her to agree to stop. Looks like she can't stop. You comin' out more often is a good idea. The more help I get, the better. I have to get her medical help now for sure, before she kills someone."

Eric paced to the door, then back to Dewey. "Anyway, I'm liking Zonolite. I like the people I work with. They like working there. Oh, and they gave me a lot more money than I expected."

Dewey's attention was focused on his daughters, but he tried to listen to Eric, too. "I really don't know much about the place—only that some people get sick out there."

"All that navy training might pay off after all. I hope to do some work that just might help control the dust problem." Eric paused, and then went to his dad. "Call me if you need help, Dad. I mean that."

"I will, Eric. And let me know how your job goes. If that works out and you clear up the dust out there, you'll make the work better for the men," Dewey said.

"I hope so. Got to go, Dad. Good luck with Betty." Eric patted Dewey on the shoulder. "You got your hands full. And Dad, take care of those girls. They're pretty special. I like having sisters! We just gotta keep 'em safe. You can always bring 'em over to my house—anytime."

"Thanks, Eric. I appreciate you wanting to help the girls. And Eric, I'm glad you'll be coming by the house more often. And thanks for bringing out the chairs." Dewey looked at Eric, wishing he could stay a little longer. "Come by anytime, son."

"I'll see you later." Eric left the store, feeling relieved that he had told Dewey about the broom incident.

Betty came out of the back room after Eric left. Dewey looked at her and was silent, wondering what she might say.

"Okay, I hit her. She was making noise when I was trying to sleep and I told her not to make any noise. How can I sleep if she's making a ruckus and not doing her work?"

"You promised, Betty. You promised. I don't want the girls hit. We are going to make an appointment with the doctor. I'll make it, and I'll make damn sure you get there. I can't have my girls beaten anymore." Dewey was calm, clear, and sincere.

Betty broke down crying. "He was lying. Eric was lying. You know he's tried to get involved with me—groping me, trying to take advantage of me right in your own house." Betty intended to discredit Eric by driving a wedge between him and Dewey any way she could.

"Yes, I heard the whole thing between you two. You trying to climb in his bed, and him threatening to wake everyone up if you didn't leave him alone! You take the cake, Betty."

34

JULIE, DARLENE, AND HELEN

Julie learned a different way to survive in her world of abuse. Like most children, she looked to the bigger areas of importance. Eating, sleeping, and watching for danger were right up there on her list as she moved through each phase of growth. Julie never felt safe for more than short periods of time. Being hurt was not the hard part for her, although it certainly had a way of reinforcing her fears. Waiting to be hit and bracing for oncoming blows or painful jabs for reasons she did not know usually kept her constant attention. She was a watchful child who assessed the moves of others, reacting quietly by fading into the background whenever the action around her brought potential danger her way. When she could sense her mother's need for violence, she would hide Helen, then fade quietly into a silent, careful task that might please her mother and keep her from losing control. Helen seemed to understand her role and would stay quietly hidden for long periods of time.

Betty might yell loudly in an angry tone, "What are you doing?"

Julie would answer, "Oh, Mom, I was just about to bake you some cookies. Do you want peanut butter cookies?" There would be silence from Betty as Julie made minimal noises getting a bowl, a cookie sheet, and refrigerator items in the kitchen, preparing to mix up the cookies.

"Well, keep the noise down. I have a sick headache!"

Another time, Julie might say that she was going to bake a pie or cake; she selected a food her overweight mother could not resist. That was not always successful, but Julie continually tried to keep a low profile for herself and Helen to protect the two of them from being the focus of their mother's attention. She would use other tactics as well, like keeping busy cleaning windows, mopping the floor, or better yet, working in the yard or barn. If her mother believed she was working, she usually escaped physical violence.

There was another facet to Julie's personality, however, that did not keep her safe from harm. When she was outside raking or working with the animals, she loved to sing. Most of the time she was alone or with Helen when she was doing chores, and she could sing loudly, imitating an opera singer or a popular recording star. The joy of music would catch her off guard, and there were times when she would slip into another world of dreams, leaving her vulnerable to her mother's actions.

She imagined herself able to fly so much that she really believed she could. Lying on her back looking up at the clouds, she knew that if she could just get up above the clouds, her life would change forever. When she was nine years old, she wanted so much to lead someone else's life that she felt she could fly into some other realm. She tried to fly off the barn roof several times, and she flew off the house in the winter onto piles of snow many times as well. As she would stretch her arms out and flap them like wings, she thrust herself upward into the air. She was always amazed that her body did not soar upward as she had intended, but became a rock, plunging directly downward. Somewhere in her knowing self, she would fly some day; she just was not sure when that would happen. Although she seldom dwelled on the day-to-day unhappiness she was experiencing, she daydreamed every moment she could without getting into trouble. Unfortunately, she was not always successful in avoiding detection.

Most of the time she could avoid her mother by being very quiet, but the urge to sing some song would work its way up through her throat, and she would have to burst forth with a melody from somewhere—and dancing at least a few whirls accompanied the song. The crack of a hand on the back of her head would bring her back to reality. It could have happened a thousand times before, and yet she would look at her mother with a dazed look and wonder why she had hit her. Her mother would yell something like, "Didn't I tell you I had a sick headache? Now shut up and…" She would grab Julie's hair or push her into a wall, give her some chore to do, and get her involved in work away from her so she could sleep or rest. Julie wondered why she always seemed to have a "sick" headache. Is that different from just a regular headache? She never asked her to explain.

Julie's ability to daydream kept her from constantly focusing on her heartbreaking situation. Having Helen kept her in the real world enough to keep Helen safe, but she often brought Helen into her dreams and imaginative play. Her love of singing and her creative escapes from the reality of her life provided the mental exercises to keep her own sanity. Because she could escape through singing and dancing, she did not seem to harbor anger or hatred toward her mother. In fact, she loved her very much and longed to be in her mother's arms. After a beating, her mother would tell her how disappointed she was that Julie had again deserved a spanking for being noisy. Julie always apologized, nestled into her mother's arms if her mother would hold her, and she loved the closeness, however brief or seldom it was.

Darlene held a grudge, would not apologize for contributing to her mother's violence, and planned in earnest her next opportunity to defy her mother. The two girls were strong in different ways, and neither girl understood why the other behaved as she did when dealing with their mother. Darlene viewed Julie's gentleness as weakness. Julie's ability to fade, protect Helen, take the violence loudly in order to shorten the time of Betty's rage, and to lessen the potential for Betty to move on to Helen were strengths Darlene did not understand. Darlene's toughness, refusal to cry, staunch acceptance of the violence, and lack of remorse seemed to Julie to fuel their mother's anger and make it worse for Darlene. By keeping the focus of the rage upon herself, Darlene may have saved Julie and Helen from beatings. The reverse was also true; Darlene's stubbornness often fueled their mother's rage, which spilled onto Julie. Several times after Betty beat Darlene, she turned on Julie for the release she needed to vent her anger. However, Betty could also take out her pent-up anger on Darlene and then be too exhausted to look for anyone else to torture.

Betty enjoyed the Sears Roebuck catalogs and had several of them around at any given time. All three girls enjoyed looking through the pages, imagining themselves dressed in the stylish clothing and shoes or sleeping in brightly flowered sheets and blankets with wondrous drapes, paintings, and other items they did not have. Darlene and Julie wrote long order forms listing skirts, blouses, shoes, coats, and accessories that they would love to have. As Darlene grew older, she dreamed less with her sisters. Julie and Helen continued spending many stolen moments pouring over catalogs and imagining themselves as beautifully made up with fancy hairdos and great clothing. They mimed being models, draping themselves in the laundry and spinning around in pretend fashion clothing.

Julie wanted to escape and take Helen with her. Darlene told her that someday it would be her turn. When she was dreaming, time seemed unimportant. In reality, when she sensed her mother watching her in the night or stalking her as she milked the cow or cleaned the chicken coop, she could feel her mother's need to beat her. In her defense, she began making up songs about her mother with lyrics that included descriptions of her mother's beauty, singing ability, and other attributes. She hoped that her lurking mother would hear those tributes to her and give up her need to beat her senseless. Julia didn't know that her plan worked well. Sometimes when her mother heard her sing of her beautiful mother, Betty would cry softly and go back to her bedroom feeling loved. Julie loved her mother. She knew in her heart that her mother loved her. She truly believed that her mother was beautiful, sang well, played musical instruments well, and radiated like the sun when she smiled. She felt that her mother became lost at times and forgot not only who Julie was, but also who she herself was. Julie ached for her mother to hold her with tenderness instead of violence.

Helen was an angel waiting to be defiled. Darlene protected her and helped teach her how to contribute to the sisters' team responsibilities. Julie spent more time with Helen, often shielding her from their mother's view. Both sisters predicted that Helen's age would no longer separate her from the unexplainable violent behaviors that their mother exhibited when she entered a deep rage. Julie had designated areas in the barn for Helen to go while Julie tended to the animals. Helen's favorite place was in the back corner of the barn behind a makeshift corral made with bales of hay that Julie had placed there as a barrier. Within that area, Julie provided Helen with kittens or baby rabbits to play with to keep her happily occupied while Julie completed her work.

The small loft was another hiding spot. Helen loved climbing up there. She kept a doll and a few other toys in a niche above the view of anyone who came into the barn. A few times when Betty came out to spy on Julie, Helen saw her leave the back porch. Helen knocked on the wall to let Julie know that their mother was near. The cue helped Julie get a song rolling about her mother's talents and beauty to fend off what could become a violent scene. Or if Julie was already singing to the animals instead of getting her chores done, she could leave her imaginative play and throw herself into her chores. Helen knew that she had to stay hidden and quiet for herself and for Julie. She developed a sense of timing, and she knew that her sisters needed her to do her part to protect herself. She listened keenly and held herself still for long periods of time. She resisted the childish temptation to yell, run, and act out as a normal child might do. She could not be a normal child and survive in that family.

The girls had individual personalities, alert minds, and an understanding of their immediate world that made them survivors. They were different in appearance, hardly resembling sisters. Darlene looked like her mother with dark hair, large brown eyes, full shapely lips, and freckles prominently brought out due to her gardening and other outside work. Unlike her overweight, short mother, Darlene was thin, medium height, and quick. Julie had light brown hair, blue-green eyes, a clear pale complexion, and a wiry, thin body. She and Helen looked more like their dad. Helen had naturally curly blond hair, light skin, and piercing brown eyes that displayed deep sadness and wonder. Anyone who had just met the girls might say, "My, what beautiful girls! How wonderful that all three girls are so lovely and mannerly." At any given moment, if two of the three girls stood without clothing before someone who had that impression, turning slowly, displaying the fullness of their scarred, beaten bodies, that same person might say in anguish, "My God! How could this happen to any child in a civilized world?" Darlene's scars and bruises were many and deep from her neck to her knees. Julie's back, legs, and arms were tracked with belt ridges and scarred with cigarette burns and teeth marks. With the exception of a couple of burns and bite marks, Helen's body was a clean slate ready for violence.

Within the community, no one knew the terror those three children experienced. In 1958 in Libby, Montana, the Bowman girls lived in a normal-looking family with a dark, well-concealed secret. Very few people know what goes on in their neighbors' homes. Privacy is a wonderful thing in many ways, and yet it is the very thing that keeps many people imprisoned in fear and pain within their own homes. Child abuse and spousal abuse have existed since people began living within clans and families. It is not new. However, the human race has evolved in many ways: cures for diseases, magnificent machines, and worldwide communication. We have learned through trial and error to elevate ourselves above evil and embrace good. Why then do neighbors, friends, and even strangers allow children to be beaten, neglected, and even murdered rather than say something or do something to protect them? Privacy could kill the Bowman children.

35

TRIP TO SPOKANE

On Friday evening two weeks before the wedding, Betty gathered the girls and Julia together and announced that they were all leaving for Spokane early the next morning, not just Darlene and Betty. She had decided to take the younger girls, too, and Julia would be important in keeping them together. She wanted them to arrive in Spokane at 10:00 a.m. That meant leaving no later than 6:30 a.m. In order for that to happen, chores needed to be done, a lunch packed, and everyone ready and looking nice for the shopping expedition. That was the day they would buy Darlene's wedding dress, material for the bridesmaid's and flower girl's dresses, and other items for the big occasion. Betty was happy as she organized the plan for the next day. Her attitude infected the others, and everyone was excited about the trip. No one overslept, and the girls had their chores done in record time.

Betty drove more slowly than usual and seemed very apprehensive as she took the twists and turns on the Moyie Springs Canyon Road. That treacherous piece of highway had vertical drops of over 1,500 feet to the Moyie River below. The car was on the inside lane going to Spokane with equally high canyon walls rising several hundred feet toward heaven. Betty went slowly around the curves and made up time on the straighter stretches through Idaho and Washington. The shoppers arrived in Spokane in time for stores to open. The first department store they entered was the Bon Marche.

Darlene was both excited and nervous. She was obviously excited with the wedding coming up. She was nervous about just how much say she was going to have in selecting her wedding dress. Betty jumped into action, looking through the racks of wedding dresses and pulling out a few that had large, flouncy sleeves, long trains, low necklines, and princess-like beads and pearls sewn everywhere. Darlene selected dresses that were more conservative and less expensive, and she settled first on a waltz-length gown with long sleeves and a high-collared neck accented with seed pearls on the bodice. She tried it on and loved it right away. The sleeves puffed slightly at the shoulder, the lace design was lovely, and she looked beautiful in it. Helen and Julie loved it and gushed all over the place telling Darlene how beautiful she looked. Grandma thought it was beautiful also.

Betty insisted that Darlene try the dresses that she had selected. Each dress was full length, trained, low cut neckline, puffy sleeved, and each required long gloves. When she came out the fifth time, Darlene was wearing her first choice.

"This is the one I feel best in, Mom. I think it works well for me." Darlene was using her kind, but firm voice, not wanting to get into an argument, but also not willing to wear a dress she did not want on her wedding day.

"But that one costs half of what these others cost, and it's plain, really, compared with the others. You look like a queen in the other dresses. This is just, well, ordinary. We can dress you up better than this, Darlene." Betty was beginning to get upset, and Julia could see her anger rising. Betty stood up and moved away from the girls, pacing, and getting ready to explode. Julia moved to Betty and gently touched her arm.

"Betty, I remember when you married Dewey. You selected a dress that looked so nice on you. I remember offering to lend you my dress because I thought you might like it. But you decided on the dress you wanted. Your daughter takes after you, I see. She wants to wear her choice. Like mother, like daughter." It worked. Julia helped Betty back out of her anger and accept Darlene's decision.

"Well, this saves time and money, doesn't it? Let's get this paid for and buy material for the other dresses." The group went to J. C. Penny's and selected several yards of satin and some tulle for the dresses, along with two patterns for the gowns. They visited the shoe department and bought simple satin low-heeled shoes for Darlene and Julie, and a pair of white Mary Janes for Helen. The group bought a few other items for the wedding, and at about 3:00 p.m. Betty pulled up to the Davenport Hotel and announced that they were going to eat their meal at the Matador Restaurant. Because the group was early for dinner, they had no problems getting seated.

The girls were amazed as they walked through the beautiful hotel and entered the restaurant. None of them had ever eaten in such an exclusive place. Helen whispered to Julie, "Look, we each have a small tablecloth that is made into a little tent!" Julie wasn't sure what they were, but she thought they might be napkins. Betty told the girls to take the napkins and place them on their laps.

A waiter brought each of them menus. The menus were large with lists of foods that were unfamiliar to the girls. Julia was as shocked as the girls were. Who would be paying for this, she wondered to herself. If Dewey were there, he would be astounded at the prices and that his family was planning to eat there.

Betty said, "I'll order for the girls, Julia. What do you think that you'll have?"

"There are so many choices. Let's see. What are you going to order?" Julia was hoping for Betty's choice to guide her own. She wondered if Betty was joking about the whole thing and planned to get up and walk them all out with some excuse—or no excuse.

"I think the girls would like the Mexican chicken lunch plate. It's still not dinner hours. I'm going to have the chicken marsala lunch plate. Girls, any thoughts about the Mexican chicken?"

The girls were thrilled with the order. They had no idea what a Mexican chicken tasted like, but they were all eager to eat whatever their mother ordered. All three girls were determined to eat every bite, even if it made them sick. They were so excited to be in that restaurant that they were ready to try anything. Darlene was watching her mother for signs of unusual behavior outside of the amazing choice of restaurant her mother had made. Betty was unpredictable.

"I'll have the same as the girls, Betty. That looks good to me." As Julia watched the girls in their excitement, and as she watched Betty in her unusual role, she sat back and enjoyed the view. As extravagant as it was, Betty was being kind to her daughters, giving them a new experience and laughing with them. Betty ordered the meals, water in wine glasses for everyone, and, considering the prices, she ordered reasonably priced entrees. For dessert, she order flaming cherries jubilee. The women and girls laughed together, enjoyed the food and dessert, and took with them the lovely cards provided for each guest. That was an experience with Betty the girls and Julia would remember for a lifetime.

They left Spokane at about 6:00 p.m. and arrived home before 9:30 p.m. The girls were excited to tell their father about the day. They showered him with hugs and interrupted one another over and over as they told of their wonderful day with their mother and Julia in Spokane. Dewey had not seen his daughters so happy. Ever. He began an inward self-congratulatory assessment of his recent decisions. He also was choked up and had to leave the room to keep from crying in front of the women. When he came back into the room a few minutes later, he took stock of how things were going for his family. Betty was working at the store, Julia had moved in with them, and Darlene's upcoming marriage was going to be a happy family event. Somehow the early marriage of his daughter and the truth revealed to him through her future husband had opened his eyes in time to save his family. After the girls became exhausted telling their stories to Dewey, they helped clear out the car and put away the food they had taken with them. Darlene asked her dad if he would like to see her dress. At first he was going to go outside, but then decided to share the moment with Darlene. He was pleased with her choice and happily watched her light up as she explained to him why she loved the dress.

"It's like me, Dad. It has a simple design, it was a reasonable price, and it just doesn't overpower me with fluff and puffy sleeves. I don't think Mom loves it, but she let me buy it."

"I'm glad you like it, Darlene. And it is like you in another way, you know."

"How's that, Dad?"

"It's beautiful." Dewey tried to keep from letting his emotions show, but he choked up and shed a few tears. Darlene put her arms around him. His tears surprised her and touched her heart. She held him tightly, wanting to keep the moment forever. Darlene also shed some tears in spite of her strong will. Dewey embraced her tenderly. He had never told his children he loved them. He had not been brought up to speak such emotional messages. Darlene never felt her father's love more than at that moment.

"I love you, Dad." Darlene spoke her feelings sincerely.

Dewey found words hard to come by. He wanted more than anything to tell Darlene he loved her. All that came out was "Me, too."

For Darlene, that day held two memories: one of each parent that she would hold in her heart for a lifetime. She had a single day of loving memories to slightly soften the many years of abuse, neglect, and loneliness.

Julia made Helen's dress first. It took only two days to complete, a few hours each day. Helen loved it. Julie's dress was next, and it turned out beautifully. Both girls were excited about their dresses. They wore them while Julia took care of fitting each dress perfectly. Betty liked the dresses and was glad that Julia could sew well. Those dresses were truly beautiful.

When Julia had Helen try on her dress for the last time prior to completing it, Julia told her, "If you had wings, you would look just like an angel! Come now, let's look at you in the mirror." Helen's curly blond hair fell onto her shoulders and accented the dress beautifully. Helen was elated with her image. When she put on her new shoes, she was sure that she was as gorgeous as a model in the catalogs she and her sisters looked through when they imagined their future lives as rich and famous actresses.

Julie loved her dress as well. Julia had to redesign the bust line of the pattern to make it fit Julie. Becoming a teenager brought with it many changes, and Julie's body was showing definite signs of curving in all the right places. Unfortunately, she hunched her shoulders to hide her shape and avoid detection and attention from boys. She made a point of wearing a T-shirt that summer over her mother's made-over bra. There she was in the beautiful satin gown that fit her perfectly. As she looked at herself in the mirror, she turned from side to side. Part of her loved it, and part of her feared the lines that displayed her shapely breasts clearly and accurately.

"Grandma, can you hide me better up here?"

"Where, dear? Here? Heavens no, Julie. This is the body God gave you, and this dress shows what a good job He did."

"But, Gram—"

"No buts. You stand up there, put those shoulders where they belong, and be glad you have what you have." Julie lowered her chin and almost began to cry. "I'm so very proud of you, Julie. You need to stand tall and accept the fact that you're a beautiful young woman. Have you started your period yet?"

"Grandma! Shhh. I don't want Mother to find out." Julie said the words very quietly and took Julia into the kitchen so no one could hear her.

"You started and your mother doesn't know?"

"Trust me, Grandma, we don't want to tell her. Wait 'til I'm older and she's worried that I haven't started. She was hard on Darlene, and I just don't want to go into it with her. Please don't say anything to her."

"Okay. You're in charge of that department." The two went back into the living room so Grandma could double-check the hem. "Now, let's look at this dress! Stand right up here." Julie stood on the stool that Grandma had placed there to measure the hem previously. "You are a sight, an absolute sight!" Julie stepped down and viewed her image in the mirror. She stood up straight, and she had to agree that she looked very good in her maid of honor gown. Seeing herself as an attractive young woman was a new experience for her. She really could pass as one of those models in the catalogs.

Julia called Betty to look at the dress, but she did not answer. She may have been sleeping. She may have been looking through the curtains on the French doors to her bedroom, listening to every word that was said. If she were listening, she did not hear Julie's whispered comments to her grandma. Betty may have seen her lovely daughters in their dresses, happy, beautiful, and excited with Julia's work. It was always hard to say what Betty was doing or seeing.

Darlene had a secret arrangement with Julia to pack her personal items and get them out of the house before she left after the wedding and reception. Darlene had been taking one or two articles of clothing with her when she dated Dick and leaving them at his house. She wanted to make sure that everything she wanted to take was gone because she did not trust her mother to keep her things safe. She believed that her mother would destroy anything she left behind.

36

THE WEDDING

As the wedding day arrived, Betty and Dewey were fortunate to have the help of several relatives and friends. Eric provided invaluable assistance in many ways. He helped box up the many piles of Betty's hoarded items and took them out to the barn. That cleared the way for others to decorate the living room, set up chairs, and arrange flowers gathered from everyone in the area. Eric provided trays of cookies from the Libby Bakery. Julia did an outstanding job on the wedding cake. It was beautiful, definitely professional looking, and a work of art. The wedding seemed to bring out the best in everyone. Betty was disoriented at times, forgetful, but seemed to be able to isolate herself when she thought she might lose her temper. No one focused on Betty, and whatever needed done just seemed to happen as it should. Several neighbors brought food for the reception following the wedding. Family and community support made the day a special occasion for Darlene and Dick.

If Betty had wanted to insert anger or fear within the day, she seemed overwhelmed and unsuccessful in getting any negative force underway. There were times throughout the day when she watched with delight her three daughters in their lovely dresses, happily celebrating with everyone. She felt a sense of pride in their beauty and she reached out to them, helping them dress, hugging them, and telling them that they were beautiful. Darlene received her gestures of caring gracefully and with doubts regarding her mother's sincerity. Helen and Julie accepted each gesture as a sign of change, giving them hope for a less violent future.

The Baptist minister kept his remarks brief and recited the appropriate words for the ceremony clearly and in a confident tone. The couple completed their vows in less than twenty minutes. No one had time to get bored, and everyone seemed delighted with the day. When the chairs were cleared away, a few of the more musical relatives, including Dewey, provided some dance music. Dewey had brought drums from the store for the special day. Darlene and Dick danced, and everyone cut in to dance with the couple and give them dollar bills for their honeymoon with each intruding dance partner. Eric sat in on drums when the bride danced with her father. Dewey was an excellent dancer, and Darlene followed his lead. Other family members joined in. Dick danced with Betty, and she gave her best effort to smile, although within her heart she could not forget the harsh words Dick had used toward her when she first learned of his intent to marry her daughter. Dick laughed a bit while dancing with Betty, told her kindly that everything was going to work out fine, and was able to get her to smile at him. Helen danced her own steps in unique ways that added fun and beauty to the day. The girls were delighted when their mother danced with them, all three together, circling around hand-in-hand to the music. Dewey made sure he danced with all three daughters.

The Saturday afternoon event ended about 9:00 p.m. when Darlene and Dick drove away in Dick's car, which was decorated with flowers on the windows painted with yellow and green frosting and a string of beer cans artfully linked together with ropes and securely tied to the rear bumper. Many of the guests followed the car to town and trailed the couple, honking their horns as they drove up and down Mineral Avenue before leaving for their honeymoon night in Coeur d'Alene, Idaho. One night's lodging was their brief honeymoon, a wedding gift from Eric.

Betty was pleased with the way the whole day had unfolded. She credited herself with making sure everything was done well. She decided to look at Darlene's room and knocked in case Julia was there. Julia had stepped outside for a breath of fresh air when Betty discovered that Darlene's clothing and personal items were gone. How could she have taken everything today? She didn't even leave her wedding dress. There were a few boxes stacked up against the far wall, but Julia's name was clearly written on each box. Betty returned to her own room, sat at her mirror, and looked at her image. Her brown hair was styled nicely, her makeup looked lovely considering the long, busy day, and her dress was beautiful.

She knew she was going to miss Darlene, her defiant girl with a spirit her mother could not defeat. Betty began wishing. She wished that she had loved Darlene more, held her more, and played with her more as a child. She wished that she hadn't beaten her so many times. She wished that she could be the one who was leaving the house and going to a place where she could be happy every day. She wished that she could live each day without having memories haunting her, reminding her of her shame and losses, especially in regard to her little brother. She wanted to be free from the past. She could see herself holding Helen, smoothing her hair, and kissing her cheek. She wanted to brush Julie's hair, hold her closely, and tell her that she loved her. Each step toward love she made, the more the memories crowded into her life and depressed her, frustrated her, and caused her to beat her children, even try to kill them. The pain of migraine headaches that would not stop for hours took away her precious sleep. She held her head tightly with both hands to keep it from exploding.

Working was helping. She had to make the memories stop leading her into horrible dreams and violent acts. As she thought about Darlene again, she saw the tears stream down her face. Betty knew that she would miss Darlene. In that moment, she loved her. She hoped that Darlene's absence might keep the memories from forcing Betty to think about hurting her. If only she didn't know where Dick and Darlene were going to be living.

37

ERIC AND ZONOLITE

Eric decided to take the Zonolite position for two reasons. The first was the fact that he was a well-paid manager. He had his own crew and an exciting project to organize. The second reason was harder to define. He believed he could make a difference in the lives of the men who worked there by cleaning up the dust and making it a more comfortable place to work. The Zonolite manager did all he could to make Eric feel welcome and gave him a signing bonus of $2,000 just for taking the job. Getting a man with Eric's electrical training and experience was quite a feat for the company. The project Eric was going to head up for the company had been on hold for over a year because they didn't have a man with the right qualifications who was willing to work in such an isolated area.

Eric resigned from Montana Power with regret. He'd liked it there. His boss told him to come by when he could, that he would take Eric back in a heartbeat. Eric thanked him. Knowing he had a job if the new one didn't work out was a confidence builder.

From his first day at Zonolite, Eric began earning a reputation for being a competent, hard worker who treated those he supervised with respect, and who was a valuable team member on the administration staff. He was excited about the major project, which turned out to be a whole new building for a special product line. The new fireplace liner asbestos product would be produced on site instead of being manufactured elsewhere. His role was to design the electrical needs for the new center. He also had the responsibility to maintain and upgrade power sources and equipment throughout the whole Zonolite operation. Eric thrived on the job, and he threw himself into it, leaving little time for socializing.

During his "free" time in his office, after hours and on weekends, he designed projects to make working conditions better for various areas in the mine and the buildings. The dry mill, for example, had poor ventilation and an inefficient system of cleaning. Eric designed a vacuum system that would suck out the dust and send it to a central place where it could be hauled away and buried. Cleanup would take a third of the time, making it less costly for the company in the long run because only about one-third of the workers would be needed in that area. The initial expense was high. When he shared his plans with his supervisor, Mr. Lovett thanked him for his ideas and took the plans under advisement. Eric felt he was keeping his initial commitment to improve conditions for the workers. Lovett didn't mind Eric's effort to make improvements since he was aware that Eric worked on weekends. He had no intention of sending the designs onward for approval because he knew the company owners were not interested in spending money in any area that did not generate profit. He was sure they would not spend additional funding on frivolous projects involving vacuuming dust or improving ventilator masks that most men didn't use anyway.

The major project for which Eric was hired would begin to take form a few months after he was employed. Eric was excited to be in charge of such a large operation. He spent most of his effort at the new job, loving it and being the best employee any company could want. However, he had fewer opportunities to keep track of his half sisters. He knew that Julia was there all the time, and he also knew Dewey was more vigilant in watching out for the girls. Once school started he felt that the girls were in safe surroundings most of the day and didn't need him to watch over them. He still checked in on the weekends to be sure they were all right—and that they hadn't forgotten him.

He met an attractive young woman at Zonolite who worked as a secretary for Mr. Lovett. She noticed Eric the first day he arrived, and she was definitely interested in getting to know him on a more personal level. Eric liked her. There was no specific company policy against socializing with fellow employees, so the door was open. They went out a few times. Her name was Celia Jensen, and she was tall, shapely, and blue-eyed. Because Eric was so engrossed in his job and his ideas for the company, though, he didn't date her as often as she wanted. She decided to compromise and joined him at times when he was working overtime. Having her assistance was important to Eric since she could get documents for him that would help him plan upgrading the electrical system throughout the whole company.

Having her there with him made overtime more fun for both of them. Although no one ever knew for sure what they were doing, it was possible that the couch in the administration area was used for more than a casual nap. They radiated affection for one another after hours and maintained professional distance during their work-days. Mr. Lovett liked getting the extra work out of both of them, so he was not concerned about them being together after hours. He could see that Eric had been producing quality, serviceable plans, and he was glad to have Eric on staff.

One night, Celia had fallen asleep on the couch. She had left the files unlocked, and Eric needed to get some blueprints for the layout of one of the mineshafts. Because he didn't want to wake her, he helped himself to the files. As he looked through several drawers, he ran across some interesting information from formal studies done by a firm out of Minneapolis. The studies involved the dust and its hazards for the workers. He read extensively while Celia slept.

A 1951 letter from a Dr. Kenneth Smith, the Johns-Manville medical director, recommended that companies place warning labels on all products containing asbestos. In the same file, a man named Dr. Barry Castleman wrote that he had successfully stopped Smith's letter from being sent out in its original form because of the financial impact it could have on the asbestos-producing companies using asbestos in their products. Castleman made sure the letter was "modified," omitting any reference to requiring warning labels. Eric reviewed a study that was done on five of the kinds of asbestos ore being mined at the Zonolite mine. He didn't want to believe what the conclusions of the studies presented. Tremolite asbestos was deadly. "This waste-white, grayish-green, and black ore Zonolite gave out freely to the entire community was deadly when inhaled. Its long needle-like fibers had significant cancer-causing toxicity." It lodged itself in the lungs or stomach linings of anyone who inhaled it or ate products that had it included in the food. It led, basically, to death.

Eric closed the file and sat down to consider what he had read. When he saw Celia awakening, he put the file back where he found it quietly and undetected. He moved to a different file drawer and took out a blueprint file. Celia walked in and put her arms around him while he was reading.

"What's that about?" Celia asked, giving him a gentle hug.

"I'm looking for the main tunnel wiring system. This looks like it could be it. Here, what do you think?"

"Let me see. Yes, this is the main tunnel system. It is the first one Zonolite used in 1919 and some of the wiring is pretty old. In 1919, there was no wiring. That changed in the late 1920s. I think Mr. Lovett looks forward to a complete upgrade of that system, even though miscellaneous wiring additions were installed here and there in past years."

"Good. I'll take this to my office. What do you say about getting out of here and going to dinner at the Caboose? I'm hungry. How about you?" Eric really was hungry, and he was not ready to talk about his discovery of the study with Celia yet. He was haunted by what he had read and needed some fresh air—away from Zonolite.

"Yes, I'm glad you asked. I could eat a horse! Well, not a whole horse, but—you know. Let's do it!" She smiled at him and he kissed her. "You look pensive. Is anything bothering you?" She definitely sensed his somber mood change.

Eric laughed and gave her a hug. "No. I'm fine. This is going to be a bigger job than I thought. But I'm up to the challenge. Let's go to town and get a steak—a beef steak for me and—you wanted horse steak?" He loved teasing her, and she laughed with him. They put away their work, locked up their offices, and went to dinner. Eric wanted to ask Celia about the study, but first he decided to learn more about it himself before he talked to anyone. The information he read about tremolite asbestos was shocking. If the product was really coming from the Zonolite mine, he wanted to know that first before bringing it up at the office. He also wanted to know just how dangerous it was. The study could have been wrong. On the other hand, the study could have been right. He had seen enough evidence of sickness in his brief time in Libby to know something had to be wrong. He had time and opportunity to read more from the office files and to look up information about the ore on his own. There was no rush, he thought. Not unless people are dying. *Are people dying of exposure to the Zonolite mine products? Who else who lived in the area might have information about the mine?* Eric planned to be careful, thorough, and accurate—that would take time.

At dinner, Eric covered his serious concerns. Both of them ate well and then decided that they better get to their respective homes and sleep so the next day's workload wouldn't take away the whole weekend. Eric decided to try Celia's willingness to get involved with his family.

"How would you like to be part of a wild and dangerous crew that plans to take in a drive-in movie Friday night?" He gave her a somewhat silly look.

"Wild and dangerous?" She looked puzzled.

"I plan on taking a couple of women to the Disney movie this Friday, and you are welcome to join us if you like." Eric winked at her. "They are both good-looking and eat a lot of popcorn. When bribed, they will even eat a candy bar or two." He had her curiosity stirred. At first she was apprehensive, but the added popcorn information made her smile.

"Okay. You have my attention. Spill the beans. I thought that I was your preferred date, but I can see I have some competition. Just how good-looking are they? And how old are they?"

"Well, they are unquestionably beautiful. Both are knockouts, really. They amaze me. I don't know any girls quite as delightful and gorgeous as they are. You may prove to be the exception, but I believe you would agree with me." Eric had the biggest smile on his face as he nodded his head up and down. "Yes. They are the cutest girls I've ever dated. This Friday won't be our first date, you know. I've been out with them before—even swimming with them in a wild creek." Eric took a sip of his wine and sat back smiling.

"Now you have more than my attention. You have my genuine curiosity. Who are these two beautiful girls you have been dating?"

"Enough silliness. They are my half sisters. Julie is fourteen and Helen just turned seven. Fortunately, I get to take them to a movie now and then, and they are delightful to take anywhere. They are shy, usually quiet—not wild. I lied about that part! I am enjoying getting to know them." Eric seemed happy and content to Celia as he settled back in his chair and smiled his warmest smile.

"You are full of surprises, my friend." She smiled at him, and then leaned over and kissed him lightly on his cheek. "I'm so proud of you taking an active interest in your sisters. They must love the attention." She paused, and then said, "You know, this just makes me love you more. But if I find out that you really do have a hot date with two women, you are really in trouble!" Both of them enjoyed the laugh.

"Do you want to join us?"

"No. They need you all to themselves. How about stopping by after the movie? We could watch a little TV and spend some time together at my place?" Celia did not want to take anything away from Eric's date with his half sisters.

"Sounds good to me. Very good." Eric patted her hand affectionately. "More wine?"

"No. We have work tomorrow. Let's go."

As they walked out of the Caboose Restaurant, Eric asked as nonchalantly as he could, "Celia, do you think the Zonolite Mining Company is good to its employees? I mean, do you believe the place is a safe place to work?"

Celia looked into Eric's eyes for a long moment. "I have to believe that or I couldn't work there."

Eric opened her car door and kissed her good night. "See you tomorrow."

"Absolutely," she replied, pulling him to her for a longer kiss.

When he took the girls out, he wanted to get a few pictures of them. He looked through his boxes that were still unpacked and found his old camera. *I need a new camera. This thing is not going to do it.* He took a few pictures of the girls when he picked them up, and that made him even more determined to get a better camera. The following Saturday, he drove to Kalispell to see if he could get a better quality camera. He also wanted to add a few items to his wardrobe. He could be accused of wearing the same clothing every day since he had little variety to choose from. Working in the navy was easy on clothing. Now that he was a civilian, he could mix it up a bit and look more professional at work.

He loved the drive along Thompson Lake and through the national forest land between Libby and Kalispell. Getting out on the road was enjoyable for him and he knew he had to watch for deer and elk on the highway—and cattle. That was free-range country. His mind kept wandering back to the dust in the dry mill. Even with the mask that Montana Power required him to use, he couldn't take the dust. How could men work through that every day and not have health problems?

In Kalispell, he went to the camera shop on Main Street. The shop was small and filled with all sorts of pictures of local people experiencing noteworthy events: weddings, birthdays, parties, celebrations, and just being out in nature. Eric looked through the glass display case at some cameras. A few cameras had special lenses and other equipment that helped the photographer take pictures, such as tripods and attachable cords to set off a picture from a distance.

"May I help you? Seems like you are considering a camera." The salesperson was also the owner and the main photographer and creator of the many photos on the shop walls.

"Yes, I'm looking for a good camera. I have a simple Kodak, but I want something of higher quality. What do you suggest?" Eric was looking at a candid wedding photo of several young girls. "I have three sisters that need to be in some good shots like that one."

"That was a fun wedding. I loved that picture and I got special permission to use it here. It's a great shot of the girls—catches their smiles and eyes." He was obviously proud of that picture. "Here are a few that might interest you. This one is great for both close up and distant shots. This Olympus twin lens reflex camera brings even more quality to a picture once you master using it. Any good equipment takes some practice."

As Eric looked through the display case, he saw a small camera, unusually shaped. It was about four inches long and only an inch wide. "Tell me about that camera. Or is it a camera?"

"Oh, that one is used. I had it for taking pictures of documents when I worked for a law office. It's black and white only. Not what you'd want for family photos."

"Documents. Interesting. Can you show me how it works?" Eric's mind was back in the office. As he researched documents, maybe he could take pictures of them to look at more closely at home. He wouldn't have to write out addresses or names to verify them. He'd have the whole body of the letter or research study to look at outside the office.

"It's really simple to operate. You just aim the lens at the document and slide this toward the middle. Hold still and view. Slide. Done. You'd have to use special film for it, but a roll takes about sixty full-page documents."

Eric tried to look like he wanted another camera. "How much is it? If I bought it, I would also get one of these other cameras."

"Well, I could make you a deal here. It's ninety dollars. But if you take one of these, I'll cut that price in half. Honestly, I haven't had anyone even ask about it for a while. Forty-five dollars."

"Can I order the film to be sent to me? And where do I get the film developed?" Eric's interest was firm. He wanted it. He'd have paid the full price for it.

"I have an address for the film and the processing, and you can order it yourself. Or I can take care of that for you and develop the pictures here. The cost is pretty much a tossup when you consider the time factor."

Eric looked like he was trying to decide, but he had already made up his mind. "If I bring the film here for developing, how confidential are you about what you process?"

"Generally, documents tend to be boring, you know." The owner looked curious, wondering perhaps just what type of documents might be filmed.

"I'm tempted to use this for my job, designing various pathways. I wouldn't want others taking my plans." Eric watched his face. The owner's curious expression relaxed.

"What kind of pathways?"

"Oh, you know, riparian pathways. It's a new interest related to national parks." Eric didn't want to use the word "electrical pathways" in regard to the camera purchase. Zonolite was a big company. He felt that he needed to protect his investigative interests until he knew more about the company and its products.

"I will make sure your film is confidential and that no one may pick it up but you. We can plan on a time for pickup that works for you. Just let me know when you are able to get it, and I will have it in your hands only." The owner wished he had held off on quoting the smaller price. But he might not have taken it at all.

"I'll take this one also." Eric picked out a nice Olympic camera with twin lenses and a tripod. "And some film for both cameras."

"Let's see. I have only a couple of rolls for the small camera. Shall I order some more?"

"Yes, at least another roll or two. Do you have three rolls for this one?" Eric asked. He didn't want to say anything about being from Libby—or being from anywhere. Just to be on the safe side. The less personal information he gave about himself, the better.

Eric left the store with enough equipment to start two new careers—a professional photographer and a secret agent. He had planned to take Sunday off, maybe go fishing or spend time with Celia. Something inside his mind kept pushing him to try out that little camera. He had already forgotten most of what he had read in the study and in the letter. He wanted to be able to read it over at his leisure. He also wanted to get into other files—older files. He planned to prepare a history of the mining operation from 1919 to the present. He wanted everything he read to be positive, proving that the ore was truly a miracle product that saved lives through fire-proofing buildings, making plants stronger, keeping houses warm, and in general, saving the world in hundreds of ways. So far he loved his job. The coughing, the sickness in the eyes of some workers, and the many deaths in the area may have been unrelated to the mine. He set out to prove the mine was safe and not responsible for sickness or deaths. Somewhere in his heart, he knew that the evidence was there in the files. Clear evidence. He felt compelled to move forward and find out the truth. He was fearful that he might be discovered. Unfortunately, his fear was not nearly as strong as it should have been. He should have feared that his journey into the Zonolite story could cost him his life.

38

SCHOOL BEGINS, 1958

The wedding took place Labor Day weekend, and school started the following Tuesday. Julie was just beginning high school and Helen was in first grade. Both girls rode the bus, and, even though Julie usually sat with Kelly, on that day she kept Helen with her. Helen was excited and scared. She had never ridden the bus, it was her first day at school, and she was definitely apprehensive. Kelly sat in front of the two girls and talked to both of them. "Helen, are you ready for school?" Kelly asked her.

Helen looked at her, smiled, and answered, "I guess so. Are you?"

Kelly laughed and said, "Of course! I love school. We live so far out of town that I never get to see many kids in the summer. It's fun to go to school. You're going to love it, too!"

Helen smiled and held Julie's hand a little tighter. Julie moved her shoulder softly toward Helen and said, "Tell Kelly who you get for a teacher."

Helen responded with a smile, "Mrs. Anderson." Julie winked at Kelly to get her to react.

Kelly gushed, "Wow! She's great! And she's very nice."

As the bus moved down the highway, Julie and Kelly visited about their upcoming first day of high school. They were worried about scheduling being different from junior high where they stayed with one teacher half of the day. They knew they had to take a class from a different teacher every hour of the day. They hoped to be in some of the same classes. Helen could tell that they were also nervous about school and what was in store for them. When Kelly visited, she was turned toward Julie and the back of the bus. She saw that Dan was sitting near the back, and she waved at him. Julie turned around, and they both said hi to him quietly enough to avoid a reprimand from the bus driver. Kelly said that the two of them should wait for him when the bus stopped and walk with him into school. Julie said she was taking Helen to her classroom, so Kelly could do that on her own. Kelly thought about it. He might not want to do that.

"Wait for him and see," Julie said. "Nobody really wants to do a new thing alone. Would you? I wouldn't. Besides, he played some basketball this summer, so he'll know some kids. You can offer, and if he says no, then don't worry about it." Julie would have liked to walk with him into school. He was cute, and she liked swimming with him at the river. Those rides down the rapids with him were a special memory. Even though she suggested that Kelly walk with him, she knew that she would not have been able to walk with him alone either. She could have done it with Kelly, but not alone.

"We'll see when we get there." Kelly looked back at Dan who was looking out the window. "No, I can't do it." Kelly was definite. "I'll get off and walk to school. If he comes up beside me, then I'll walk with him. Otherwise, I won't." The two girls laughed about their plans. The girls were not very experienced in flirting with boys, and the thought of making the first step was uncomfortable for both of them.

The bus pulled up to the school complex. The high school was to the left, and the elementary school was about a half block from the high school, but within the same green span of grass and sidewalks. Julie and Helen left the bus and headed for the elementary school. Dan stepped off the bus and called out.

"Julie! Wait a minute." He jogged over to Julie and Helen. "You're going the wrong way."

"I'm taking Helen to her classroom. She's starting first grade today!" Helen held her lunch in one hand and a paper bag containing two pencils, a pad of paper, and a box of crayons in the other. She managed to hold Julie's hand along with her lunch box.

"I'll bet you're excited, aren't you, Helen?" Dan smiled at her and gently pulled on her hair. Helen smiled at him. "I was hoping you'd take me to my class, too." He laughed at his joke. "I guess I have to take myself to class. Do you think I'll get lost?" Helen laughed at him.

"You're too big to get lost." Dan laughed at Helen's little joke.

"Okay, I think I can find the way. Julie, how about eating lunch with me today? Will you look for me in the lunchroom?"

"I'll try. You may end up with the basketball boys. Let's see how it goes."

"Okay. I'll see you later. Good luck today, Helen." Dan walked off to the high school.

"School really is fun, even though it can be a little scary at first. Remember, it's not as scary as staying home with mother." Grandma Julia was there, but still…

Helen looked at Julie, and her eyes brightened up. "I'm a little scared, but I want to be at school." She knew that school would be much better than being at home like the year before when her mother slept all day. Helen relaxed. Her grip on Julie's hand eased a bit. "Yes, I can do this." Helen began smiling. She had been worried about school, yet forgetting the alternative could be staying home with her mother. *I really want to do this. School is the only place I want to be today!* Julie continued to tell her that she would get to play with kids at recess on the swings or merry-go-round.

Julie took Helen to Mrs. Anderson's room. Julie had also been Mrs. Anderson's student when she was in first grade, so when Helen came into the room with Julie, Mrs. Anderson greeted Helen with a warm smile. "Hi, Mrs. Anderson. Do you remember me? This is Helen, my sister."

"Of course I remember you, Julie. How nice of you to bring me a new student this morning. And you are Julie's sister. What is your name again?" she asked Helen, bending down closer to her.

"Helen. My name is Helen," she said with a bit of confidence.

Mrs. Anderson said, "Well, I knew you were coming to my class today, and I have a desk just for you. See. It has your name on it."

The teacher guided Helen to a desk near the middle of the room. It already had her name on it, and it had a cup with a pencil and some scissors in it on the corner. "Julie, you can go now because you have to be on time at the high school. Helen can help me pass out these papers." Helen's expression clearly told Julie that she wanted Julie to stay. But Helen smiled, said good-bye to her, and then started placing a paper on each desk. Helen knew that it was a very good place to be.

As Julie left the room, she told Helen, "I'll see you on the bus!" Julie had her own adventure just a couple of buildings away. High school was going to be different, but she was excited. She loved school. To Julie, school was a safe, warm place to be. For the whole school day she was safe from her mother. And now, so was Helen. As she walked toward the high school, she remembered her days in Mrs. Anderson's class. She thought Mrs. Anderson was the most beautiful person she had ever seen. She remembered specifically that she had a wonderful odor. When Mrs. Anderson came by her desk, she could smell her. Julie had wanted to smell that good, just like Mrs. Anderson. She still wanted that. She also wanted to be as kind as Mrs. Anderson. She wanted to live to become a teacher. Mostly, she wanted to live and keep her sister safe.

39

DAN EAGLE AND LIBBY HIGH SCHOOL

Dan Eagle was one of the athletic dreamers. He had moved to Libby from Polson, and he was ready to make himself into an athlete. He was different from other boys in that he was willing to work hard and focus on his goal more fiercely than most other young people ever thought about doing. Mark Ross, also an athletic standout, wanted to play on the team that could win state before he graduated. He loved to watch the team play, and during the summer, he had already played ball on the outside courts with Dan. Mark and Dan were both setting their hopes on becoming basketball stars at Libby High School—and beyond. Their lives were enriched by their dedication to succeed in sports.

Dan quietly entered high school and spent as much time as he could playing basketball. He ran to school most days, even in bad weather. One late September day, the wind did not let up as he ran home after school. The run that time was along Market Road without the hill. Sometimes he took the hill, but that day was cold and dark, so he bypassed the highway and Whiskey Hill, named for the several alcohol-related accidents that had occurred there. September days in Montana were getting dark earlier each day, and Dan wanted to get at least halfway home on his eight-mile trip before dark. With basketball season on his mind, Dan intended to be in top condition before the grueling first two weeks of the season, even though it was two months away. He wanted to be on the Libby varsity his first year, and he did not intend to lose out for lack of effort. He also did not have a car. He rode the bus, met his dad's work schedule at the mill, or ran home.

As he rounded the last major curve on the turn off to his home, he saw the smoke rising from the chimney over the living room, and a second curl from the cook stove pipe sticking out of the roof over the kitchen. With cold weather moving in, the fireplace and the wood stove were doing all they could to heat the whole house. Sometimes the beds required lots of extra blankets, and the family members put on a few layers of clothes in addition to the blankets in order to ward off the cold and get to sleep. Dan slept in clothes on cold nights. His dad's long-sleeved plaid wool shirt with holes in the elbows was the warmest shirt he had, and he wore it just about every night. The house had a middle chunk about twenty feet square with a few leaning additions attached around the edges over a period of several years. The assortment of metal roofs helped keep snow from building up and caving in on the adjoining portions. It could have been a white house at one time. There were chips of white paint left on some of the sections of the house. Two of the additions were natural pine with a few other lumber types thrown in here and there. One addition had been painted brown, but time, wind, and weather had taken most of the paint, leaving pine. The house definitely varied in its appearance of sturdiness depending on the age of the lean-to portions. The yard included a few car bodies, some grouped together and a couple by themselves off in the distance. Two dogs liked the Chevy truck cab and were curled up there as Dan closed in on the back porch. Other items, including buckets, wheels, tires, tin, and dented garbage cans full of treasures covered the grounds. A metal hoop was attached to a pole near a yard light pole about thirty feet from the house. The hoop looked like it had been cut from a bucket. There were no strings hanging from the hoop, yet a ball went through just fine, abruptly and straight down. Gravel had been the surface at one time, but mostly ground-down, hard-packed clay served as the surface.

When he entered his bedroom, Dan removed his school bag, laid it on his cot, and dropped down himself, somewhat sweaty and tired. After sitting for a few moments, he shed his clothing, took a shower, and put on some sweats before heading for the kitchen. His dinner, leftovers from his family's meal two hours earlier, was sitting on the table, somewhat cold but edible. He took two slices of bread from the plastic-wrapped loaf, put the hamburger patty between them, and tore off big bites, chewing ravenously. He finished with his dinner in a few bites, leaving half of it behind. The potatoes with the cold gravy just didn't attract his attention. He scraped off the plate into the food pail of garbage, rinsed off the dish, added it to the pile by the sink, and went to his room to do his homework.

On the way to his room, he looked in on his parents who were in the living room sitting on the worn couch, their feet propped up on the apple crates used for a coffee table. They each had their usual alcoholic drinks from the Jack Daniel's bottle near the end of the couch. His dad also had a few empty beer cans nearby. He liked his whiskey with a beer chaser. They were watching Lucille Ball and Desi Arnaz carrying on a silly discussion about one of Lucy's deceptive adventures on the screen. Dan said, "Good night, you two." His dad waved his hand and made some sound like a grunt. Both sets of his parents' eyes stayed riveted on Lucy. They each carried extra weight, both rounded by overeating, and his mom did not have much strength. Her job was caring for foster children. They had two foster boys, along with Dan, their adopted son. His dad worked at the lumber mill, and due to the hard work he did every day, he stayed strong. He worked on the green chain and guided large logs toward their dissection into various sizes of lumber. Sometimes, he had to move the large logs to align them with the equipment, and it took great strength to keep the logs moving as they should.

When Dan took out his literature book, he had every intention of reading the next day's assignment. He saw his sloppy writing of Julie's name on the inside cover and wished he had the courage to date her. Somehow the comfort of the cot lulled him into relaxation and then sleep. When his mom looked in about a half hour later, she turned out the light. Dan woke up about 4:00 a.m. He realized he had to cram in some homework. The math was hard for him, so he set it aside and read the literature, a short story assignment for sophomore English class. "The Secret Life of Walter Mitty" was a story he could identify with if he had let himself see the analogy between the main character and himself.

Walter Mitty imagined he was a famous doctor, a hotshot attorney, and a daring military pilot—each a superior human being created through Mitty's imagination, providing heroic actions that were only achievable in daydreams. Dan spent much of his dreaming time planning to be a professional athlete. His daydreams told him he would go to college on an athletic scholarship, he would be outstanding, and he would become a professional standout in the sport. Dan liked Walter Mitty, even felt sorry for him. He did not see his own high standards set far above what an orphaned, adopted, half-breed Indian kid could achieve in a white community—or in any community. Somehow, he just knew it would happen. He would be on the varsity in November. As a senior, he would get a college scholarship, and after four years of college he would play professional ball. Basketball was his total focus. He did not seem to focus on academic success; however, it was an important factor in being eligible to play sports, let alone earning scholarships.

Although he finished reading the short story for his English class, he did not get the written assignment finished. Answering the questions following the story seemed like such a bother, but he managed to complete most of them and would probably get a C or D for his effort. He did not get the math assignment done and would pick up another F in that class, as well as a failing grade on the surprise quiz the teacher gave every class. Some surprise. History went well for him with the basketball coach as the teacher. Dan always kept up in that class and had a strong B average. Coach Ross also taught Dan physical education, where Dan had an A average. The other class where he consistently had an A was choir. Dan was quiet, cooperative, and always on time for choir, as were many of the students in

Mrs. Clark's class. He also could flirt with Julie. He'd catch her eye, wink at her, make silly faces, and then watch her shy smile. He knew she liked him, and he hadn't seen her with any other boy. He was sure he had a chance with her, but he just wasn't sure how to move in and get her to go steady with him.

Mrs. Clark was the most popular teacher in school. It was her second year, and she was young and attractive. Her husband was in the US Army, stationed in Germany in some kind of Special Forces unit. No one in Libby had met him yet, but everyone wanted to meet him. Mrs. Clark made his heroic actions part of her classes. Many students were drawn to her classes in choir, and there was competition to be in the ensembles that performed for ratings at winter prep competitions and divisional and state music festivals. Some students took her classes because she graded very high, and they needed the grade to continue in sports or to keep a high academic grade point average to get scholarships. Discipline was pretty lax; students needed to sing, but they could talk other times and not get corrected. Sometimes the students took advantage of her kindness and acted out, but she let most of it go by her. Students could tell when she had had enough because she would either lose her temper or cry. Any other students would drive a teacher over the edge who showed weakness, but her students truly liked her and would usually pull back just before she reached her total breaking point.

Dan liked her because she was always kind to him. She also selected him for the men's quartet, even though he missed the auditions. She set up rehearsals during lunch and after sports practices so the boys in sports would not miss athletic obligations. She went out of her way to recruit boys, and the combinations of male voices made a major positive difference in divisional and state ratings. Getting boys into choir in most schools was not an easy task. Mrs. Clark's special recruiting and her obvious love for music and students brought the boys and girls together for excellent musical results.

All of Mrs. Clark's classes were full. She taught middle school and elementary grades as well. In addition, she had some characteristics that were highly attractive to high school students. Young, beautiful, and talented, Mrs. Clark was tall, well built, yet thin and energetic. She dressed in modern tailored suits. Her dark hair flowed down her back in waves, and her brown eyes lit up with just the right amount of makeup. She had a strong, mellow voice and played the piano professionally. Students performed well under her direction. She held ensemble and solo practices at her small apartment several nights a week and on some weekends. She seemed to care deeply for her students.

During the weeks prior to the winter music festival, Mrs. Clark had the men's octet and quartet practice on Wednesdays at 7:00 p.m., and the three women's ensembles practiced after school two times per week on Tuesdays and Thursdays. The other two evenings were filled with solo practices and mixed ensembles. The groups had several songs that were classy and still enjoyable for the students. The music was difficult, so adjudicators at the music festival would begin their evaluations with positive appreciation. The students' performances had a much higher chance for high ratings with quality music. Some schools showed up with popular songs that had very little chance for an above-average rating. Students from Libby High School were proud of their excellent ratings, and so was the whole town. Being in choir or in an ensemble under Mrs. Clark's direction was very cool.

When Mrs. Clark finished practice with the octet, the quartet sang their two songs about three times each. They worked on some of the hard parts, and then they headed for home. One of the boys asked Dan how he was getting home, and he said the way he always got home. Mrs. Clark heard the comment and asked the boys if they had rides home. They all said they had rides, and that's when Mark said to Dan, "You don't have a ride."

"Don't worry about it," Dan responded, punching Mark in the arm firmly, yet not painfully. Most of the boys lived in town and could easily walk home, but Mrs. Clark told all four boys she would take them home. When they went out to pile into her car, Dan thanked her, said he needed the exercise, and took off running toward home.

While Mrs. Clark was driving the other boys home, the boys talked about Dan. She found out that he lived eight miles out of town and that anytime he stayed after school, he walked the long distance home. She learned that students liked Dan a great deal, and that they respected his basketball skills and his effort to stay fit through extensive exercise—running home from school. One of the boys commented that he pretty much stuck to himself. Mark Ross, the coach's son and baritone in the quartet, said that half the girls in school had a crush on Dan. Dan did not date mainly because he didn't have a car, and his dad's pickup truck was not very attractive for dating, even if his dad would have let him use it. Mark said that any girl he asked out would provide the car just to go out with him— even the senior girls. Dan just didn't ask for anything from anyone.

After Mrs. Clark had let the last boy off at his home, she drove toward the east highway out of town. Dan had arrived at the three-mile marker by the time she saw him running toward home. She pulled up beside him and invited him to get in the car. He thanked her and said that running home was what he always did. She strongly insisted, and since she was his teacher, he complied and got into the car. His breathing eased to normal in a few moments, and Mrs. Clark made polite conversation for the remaining five miles to Dan's house. Even in the dark, the yard light cast enough of a glow for her to see that Dan did not live in a luxurious setting. She left him in the yard and drove back to town imagining how difficult his life was in the unkempt yard and dilapidated house with its many attachments. In that house, she thought, there could not be much money to go around. She did not know that Dan had very few clothes for school. He hand washed them every weekend so he would have clean clothing to start the week. His mom had a washing machine with the old hand wringer on it; she used it when she was feeling well enough. Dan helped her use the machine some Sundays after Mass.

Next week's quartet practice went well, and at the end when the other boys were going out the door, Mrs. Clark asked Dan to stay and work on his part. The other boys left, and Dan prepared to review his music again. She played the notes, and he sang them through as she directed. When Dan put on his jacket, Mrs. Clark opened a Coke for him and one for herself. "Sit a minute, Dan. You did a very good job on your music, and I'll give you a ride home in a few minutes." The only place to sit that wasn't covered with clothing or music was the end of her bed. The bed was also near the door and the most convenient piece of furniture in her cramped apartment—a motel room, really—one big room with a small kitchenette and a small bathroom in the back. Students sat on her bed until it was their turn to practice with her.

Mrs. Clark sat by him and they drank their Cokes. She asked him how school was going and, in particular, about his math class. He said that it wasn't going well. She said that if he would like, she would help him with the assignments and to study for the tests. He said that he had an assignment due the next day, and he took his book out of his gym bag. He showed her the pages and problems he had to do, and she helped him get the assignment done right then. Dan figured that was one less thing he would have to do at home if he got to it at all.

She talked him through the problems and made the problems almost easy to understand. If Mr. Green popped a quiz on the class tomorrow, he thought, I might be able to pass it. Mrs. Clark was really good at math—and at explaining math. When he asked her how she knew math so well, she told him that math was her minor, and that she was certified to teach high school math and related classes. Dan thanked her for the math help and the Coke. When he started to get up to leave, Mrs. Clark put her hand on his knee and told him how proud she was that he did his math. Her hand felt nice to him, but it also felt awkward. He did not get touched much at home unless his dad or mom became angry. Their touches were downright painful at times, especially from his dad when he was drinking more than usual.

When Dan rose to go out the door, Mrs. Clark put on her jacket and told Dan to get in the car so she could drive him home. He said that he really didn't expect her to take him home, but she insisted and it was late. She opened the passenger side, and as Dan started to get into the car, she put her arm on his shoulder and lightly kissed his cheek. "I'm proud of you, Dan. Just let me help you out now and then." As they rode off toward Dan's home, Mrs. Clark chatted about school and music festivals. *Why is she so kind to me?* He touched his cheek where she had kissed him.

The next day was the best math class he had experienced since the year started. The teacher gave a quiz over the previous day's work. Dan passed easily, and his homework was correct. The exchange of papers was an embarrassing way to grade papers for Dan since he usually had many errors for another student to mark. Other students, in front, back, or across the aisle, exchanged papers for grading purposes. They all knew just how badly he did in math. Sometimes, depending on the student, Dan would get some "help" by having answers altered. That day was different, and it felt great. When the teacher saw his work, he asked him a question, and Dan amazingly demonstrated the answer on the board. Dan was inspired to keep up the math and take the help that Mrs. Clark had offered.

After choir class, Dan waited and thanked Mrs. Clark for the help in math. She again offered help and asked him to come to her office after school to get the next day's assignment done. He came in at the end of the day while her last class of students was leaving. She and Dan worked in her office for less than thirty minutes, and Dan had the homework done. He was relieved and seemed to be getting the concepts. He told her that he felt like he was not only getting the work done, but that he also felt like he understood how to do the problems if he had a quiz. Mrs. Clark told him that after he had help for a few weeks, he would be able to handle the work easily and he wouldn't have to worry about his eligibility during basketball season. He thanked her and left to shoot baskets in the gym as he always did every day after school, getting ready for the season to begin.

When he entered the gym, he had to walk through the cheer-leaders' practice area in the lobby. He was popular in spite of his shyness. Dan was at least six feet three inches tall, dark, with short-cropped hair and beautiful dark eyes. His long lashes made girls notice him—and envy him. His skin was light brown and made him look enviously tan all year round. He was in excellent physical shape, muscular yet lean, and into weights as his coach directed. No wonder the cheerleaders whistled when he quickly moved through the lobby of the gym toward shooting practice. He was too shy to flirt openly with girls, but they were not shy toward him. He had Julie's name written in very small letters inside the back cover of his notebook. He had basketball on his brain all the time. Math was also on his brain because he had to pass in order to play basketball. Someday he would ask Julie out. He didn't see her with any other boy, but then, he didn't see her very often. He couldn't worry about girls. Not now.

The coach chided him about being late, even though there was no official practice, and he asked what held him up. Dan told him about the math quiz and Mrs. Clark's help. Dan said he thought he might not be eligible to play if he couldn't keep his math grade at passing. Coach Ross congratulated him on the improvement in math. He was relieved not to have to worry about Dan's grades. Dan eased into the shooting drills and felt his rhythm as he moved across the court dribbling and shooting, dribbling and shooting. For Dan, the world disappeared and only basketball existed for him for two hours. Once the unofficial practice ended, he stayed behind and made shots from a wide range of points on the floor. When the coach turned out the lights, Dan set out on his eight-mile run home. He paced himself, fell into a rhythm similar to shooting, and made it home before eight o'clock.

When Coach Ross saw Mrs. Clark the next day in the teacher's lounge, he asked her about helping Dan with math. She said that Dan seemed to get it easily, so it was not hard to teach him. They had a good chat about Dan. Both were glad to see the math grade rise. Another teacher heard the conversation and was also glad that Mrs. Clark was willing to help Dan in math. When counselor Van Meter heard about Dan getting help in math, he told Dan in the hall that it looked like he might not fail after all. "You might just fool everyone and actually graduate someday, Dan."

Dan did not smile along with Mr. Van Meter. In other conversations, Mr. Van Meter had made it clear that he did not see Dan as college material. One time when Mr. Van Meter was making his annual visit with each student, he asked Dan what he wanted to do after graduation. Dan had told him that he intended to play basketball in college. He told Dan that he should be realistic. College was not going to work out for Dan. Considering the cost and his family's income, Dan would not be able to afford college, and his grades were very low. Mr. Van Meter said that Dan needed good work habits in school so he could get a job at the mill where his dad worked. In reality, Dan knew that his grade point average did not give a strong indication that he could make it in college. Dan just knew he would be in some college playing basketball in the future no matter what his grades "indicated" to Mr. Van Meter. He felt that Mr. Van Meter should encourage his hopes, not put him down. He had no respect for the counselor, and he planned his life without Mr. Van Meter's opinions or guidance.

When quartet practice night rolled around, Dan, again, stayed for math homework help after the other boys left. Mrs. Clark sat next to Dan on the end of her bed as they worked through the several problems in the homework assignment. She had him explain the problems aloud to her so he could answer orally in class with confidence and achieve a passing grade on the quiz. Once the work was done, she set the book and his notebook aside, and she took his hand in hers.

"I am so very proud of you, Dan," she said smiling. "Coach Ross thanked me for helping you so your math doesn't keep you from playing basketball." Dan at first wondered about Mrs. Clark taking his hand in both of hers so gently. Her hands were soft, and she moved them gently around his hand as she talked to him. "I'm also pleased with the quartet and your part in that group. You are the youngest, yet you show leadership the others don't seem to have. You are just more grown up." Dan was, in fact, not more mature than the other boys; he was quieter, though, and withdrawn when silly interacting horseplay came up. He would watch others and smile at their antics, but he stayed on the edge of the action as a noninterfering observer.

Her hand continued a sort of massaging motion in his palm, which felt very good, and then she set his hand back on his lap with her hand remaining underneath his. The position of her hand on his body was awkward for him and somewhat embarrassing because he could feel himself getting hard. This was silly, he thought. She's a teacher and she will never want me in her house if I embarrass myself and she feels me like this. Dan started to get up, but Mrs. Clark moved closer. Her other hand moved up to his cheek, and she gently pulled his face to hers and kissed him softly on the mouth.

He could feel himself trembling. He felt uncomfortable and nervous. Did he do something to make that happen? *Why is she doing this? Is she just being kind and affectionate? Maybe it's just her way.* Nothing about it felt right to him.

The next time she moved her hand on his lap, she placed her hand casually on his hard area. She then pushed her hand firmly onto it, moving her hand rhythmically. Dan awkwardly moved away from her, rose from the bed, and picked up his jacket and books. At first he missed the doorknob, and then he had it within his grasp. He opened the door and was outside, breathing hard and moving as fast as he could, considering his agitated state of mind. He was clumsily trying to jam his books and notebook into his backpack while he frantically ran down the street toward the highway and his home. In a few moments, he felt more organized with his backpack in place. He had managed to jam his books and notebook in his backpack. Then her car lights approached, and she told him to get in the car.

"No, I'm fine. Thanks for the help, but I need to keep in shape. I—I can't take a ride tonight," he said, still running as she followed along in her car. "It's part of my training routine."

"Promise me you'll talk to me tomorrow after school, Dan," she called out to him.

"Okay, I will," he responded in an effort to get her to leave him alone. He feared that someone would see them and know what had happened in her apartment. The night was cold, but Dan's face was hot and flushed. Dan ran on toward home and Mrs. Clark returned to her apartment alone. That run provided Dan some thinking time, but he could come up with no answers. What was she doing, and why was she doing it to him? Why him and not some other student? Where was her husband, the soldier? His thoughts went on as he ran through the night. By the time he arrived home, the only resolve he had come up with is that he better not be alone with her again for his own sake—and for hers. He also thought he must be pretty special for the most popular teacher in school to select him to touch— she touched him as no one ever had before. It was probably just an accident. She may not have even known where her hand was. He thought that he might have just imagined the whole thing.

40

A PLAN FOR BETTY

Dewey told himself that he could get through the wedding and protect his girls. He had little sleep, but he guarded his family throughout the nights, catching naps when he could during the daytime. He had to get Betty under control. The day Betty beat Julie with the broom handle, Dewey called the medical center and asked for an appointment with any available medical doctor as soon as one was available. Fortunately, Dr. Willis was available that afternoon.

As the appointment time was near, Dewey just walked out with a brief comment to Betty: "I'll be back in about an hour." Betty called after him asking where he was going, but Dewey didn't want to lie. He simply called back to her, "I'll be back."

Dr. Willis had little experience with mental illness. He patiently listened to Dewey's concerns about Betty's behaviors. He advised Dewey to get his wife an appointment for a complete physical as the first step. Dr. Willis offered to make calls to Warm Springs Mental Hospital for guidance in helping Betty receive a complete mental health checkup as soon as possible. Dewey asked for any advice on keeping his children safe while the physical and mental health processes.

"Your mother is in the home, and you can be vigilant as well." Dr. Willis did not have any other advice except calling the police if Betty was out of control. "Here is the admittance form for patients and an information guide about Warm Springs Mental Hospital. Read this and then call me. If I think of anything and want to call you, how shall I identify myself in case your wife or other family members answer the phone?"

Dewey thought a moment. "How about this: say 'I have information about Dewey's last order.' Then only speak to me if I'm there, or leave only a brief message to call you back—but don't leave a number." Betty might call any number left for Dewey, and he needed her not to know his plans right now. A direct call back to a doctor or the medical center could arouse her suspicions.

"Based on your concerns about this phone call, I can see you are sincerely worried about your family's safety. Maybe you should take her directly to Warm Springs right now. I can call ahead to have them expect you." Dr. Willis did not want any responsibility for an out-of-control woman killing her child.

"No, I think we're okay. I need to read this information first. It's a big step, and I need to be sure it's the right thing to do." Dewey shook the doctor's hand. "Thanks for seeing me on such short notice."

When Dewey returned to the store, he appeared calmer to Betty. *Maybe I can relax now. He hates to get me upset! Another week and he'll forget about Julie.* "Where'd you go?"

"Just up the street. Here." He handed her two Snickers Bars. Her eyes lit up as she tore open the first one and forgot about Dewey.

Julie literally ran into Dan in the hall on her way to English. He helped her pick up her books and smiled. "Hey, what's the rush?" He saw her cheeks flush with embarrassment.

"I'm sorry. Are you all right?"

"Right now I'm perfect! Here's your book. Here's a better question. Are you all right? What happened to your head?" Dan was genuinely concerned.

"It's no big deal. I tripped and fell. Thank you for helping me."

"I miss seeing you. We sure had fun at the creek going down the rapids. I'll walk you to class." He winked at her, and she blushed some more. "Your hand, too? That was some trip. Are you sure you're okay? You're mouth is swollen and—"

"I'm okay. I love those rapids. How's basketball going? I don't get to the games, but I hear you're doing really well." It was his turn to blush. "I want to go to the games. It's just, well, I have a lot of chores to do."

"I'm gonna save you a seat on the bus in the morning. Sit with me, okay?" He paused by her English class door.

"Helen too?" *I can't believe he's really asking me to sit with him!*

"Of course, Helen too. Don't forget. Promise?"

"Okay. I won't forget." Julie went into the room. Dan watched her and waited. *Look back, Julie. Look back!* Julie turned, looked at Dan, and smiled widely. *Yes! She likes me!*

Since Julie's meeting with the broom handle, she had been depressed and fearful. She had hoped that her dad would protect her. As far as she knew, he didn't even know about it or check on her after it happened. At the quiet dinner table, Julie looked down most of the meal. He dad had said nothing to her or anyone. She ate a bit, but her mouth was sore and limited what she could eat without serious pain. After dinner when Betty went into her bedroom, Dewey stepped into the kitchen and quickly whispered to Julie. "I know. Just trust me."

Tears streamed down her face. *How can I trust him? If mother sees him talking to me, she'll beat me again!* Julie nodded and returned her attention to the dishes in front of her. *As far as I can tell, nothing's changed. Dad's done nothing. He's afraid of her or he would've already done something. She'll kill him, too, and he knows it.*

41

ERIC RESEARCHES ZONOLITE

Eric was the hit of the administration meetings. He was well prepared each meeting with some interesting historical comments that kept the company leaders involved in his research. He also made it clear that his "hobby" was not on company time. He used specific illustrations of the mining operation that showed the original layout and the modifications that time and mining had made. The first electrical work was primitive, yet still in place in a few areas. He planned to remove the old wiring and replace everything with up-to-date coded wiring over a two-year period.

When he made presentations, he was thorough, but not long-winded. Mr. Lovett was impressed with him and enjoyed private conversations with Eric. The men talked about work, yet they were developing a more personal friendship as well. Hunting and fishing were key factors with fall coming on. Eric looked forward to recreational time with his boss, as well as his dad.

The research on his own time kept Eric engrossed in ferreting out key studies, legal challenges regarding unsafe asbestos, and other interesting documents. He had taken several rolls of film and spent countless hours reading the documents at his leisure. Celia was excited that Eric was fitting in so well with her boss. Mr. Lovett asked her about Eric, and she always had pleasant things to say about him. Lovett liked him, yet always kept a keen eye out to be sure his research was not beyond the scope of electricity and simple history. He made it clear to Celia that certain areas of the files were off limits. She promised that Eric did not access any files without her knowledge. She didn't point out that she often dozed off while Eric entered any filing cabinet he chose. She also didn't offer up information about Eric taking pictures of documents. Of course, she never mentioned that Eric sometimes had her keys and worked after hours when she was not even present. Celia trusted Eric and knew he was devoted to his job—more than she liked at times.

Eric was about to ask Celia for her keys for the weekend when she asked him if he would like to go to Spokane with her. She planned to go after work on Friday evening and return late on Sunday. He didn't like to make up excuses, but he definitely didn't want to leave town for the weekend. He had a chance to take some family pictures with his Olympic camera, and he had already set up Saturday morning with Dewey to do it.

"Sorry, Celia. I've already committed to a family thing on Saturday." Eric really liked her and knew the two of them would have fun in Spokane. He just didn't want to pass up time in the office, especially if he could be there alone to check out some files.

"Okay, I gotcha. I'd go some other time, but I haven't seen my aunt in two years, and it's her birthday. I really need to go." Celia was disappointed, but not enough to change her plans. Eric didn't want to ask her for her keys right then. *She might say no if she thinks I want to stay home to work rather than go with her.* He just let it go. Maybe on Friday he would say something. He didn't.

After work that Friday, Celia was gone when Eric stopped by to ask her for her keys. He could work on several things without the keys. He drove to the A&W and ordered a hamburger, fries, and a milkshake to go and returned to work for the evening. The milkshake went down before he made it back to his office. The rest was gone the first fifteen minutes at his desk. After he threw away the mess, he set out the files on the table in his office. The new project fit nicely on the table, along with his notes. He had been working for less than thirty minutes when Mr. Lovett walked in and surprised him with a cup of coffee.

"This is Friday night, for cryin' out loud. Don't you ever go home?" Lovett handed Eric a cup of coffee and took a close look at the work Eric had set out for himself. It could take weeks. Lovett could see that Eric had plenty of work to do.

"I like this project. Look, here's where the old tunnel ran out in 1943. The expansion was important to keep the ore moving, filling the government's orders for shipping insulation." Eric pointed to the diagram of the tunnel.

"And just what does that mean to me, Eric?" Lovett looked at the drawing.

Eric looked him squarely in the eye. "It means that the Zonolite mine made a major contribution to the war effort. And that's a fact!"

Lovett smiled. "Okay. Keep working. Maybe you can write an article on how Zonolite did its part to keep the nation free. Good publicity." Lovett patted him on the back. "Don't stay all weekend, or I'll have to charge you rent!"

"No, I won't. I have family stuff this weekend."

"Say, Eric. I forgot my keys. Do you have a key to the file cabinets? I need to take a file home this weekend." Lovett was testing Eric.

"Sorry, boss. I don't have the keys. The only time I ever get something is through Celia, and she's gone for the weekend." Eric looked and sounded apologetic.

"No problem. Wait! Here they are. Sorry to bother you." Lovett walked to the file cabinets, opened one, and shut it again, taking nothing. "See you Monday!" He walked out and locked the door behind him.

Eric put himself into the groove again, planning the wiring for the new building. For some reason, he stood up and looked out the window. Lovett's car was still there. Eric kept working. Thirty minutes must have passed when Lovett opened the door wide and burst into the room.

"I just got an idea for the new building. Can you put in lights that can work on reduced power some of the time, like at night or on weekends when we really don't need full power? Could save big over time." Lovett had to think fast to come up with something since his goal was to catch Eric getting into a file cabinet.

"That's a good idea. I've already put that in the design. Good thinkin', boss." Eric smiled and went back to his work. Lovett finally left for the night, confident that Eric was not accessing files when Celia was away from the office.

Eric was a bit suspicious of Lovett's in-and-out routine. *He thinks Celia's giving me her keys. Damn. Why didn't he just ask me?* Eric looked outside and saw Lovett's car leaving the parking lot. He was glad he hadn't asked Celia for her keys. If he'd had them, and Lovett asked him to open a file, he would have done it—and Celia could have been in trouble. Eric wouldn't have lied or hidden the keys from him. Maybe he needed to rethink that idea. Maybe he had better be more secretive about reviewing the files in the future. And maybe Lovett had some files that he didn't want Eric, or anyone else for that matter, to find, read, or know about.

Eric wanted to divide his drawing and cut out a portion to move around and see it from another point of view. He didn't have scissors so he went to Celia's desk to borrow hers. When he opened her drawer, he found the scissors in the back of the drawer—right next to her keys to the filing cabinets. He looked around suspiciously. *Would Lovett walk in right now and see me with the keys?* Eric left the keys in the drawer and took the scissors to his office. Less than a half hour later, Lovett returned to the office and found Eric working on the same project, making excellent progress.

"Looks like you're havin' trouble taking the weekend off, too, boss." Eric smiled and just kept on working. Lovett looked at Eric's work, noted his progress, and left again.

"See you Monday!" Lovett called out.

Eric was convinced that the attention from his boss was unusual. Saturday would be a great day to stay away—all day. Family picture time might take some time anyway. He might as well wrap up his work for the night. As he organized the project file, he remembered the one file he had yet to open. The one file Celia had told him contained personal information about employees. She asked him not to open that one. When he returned her scissors, he put them in just as she had them. There were the keys, waiting for him to pick them up.

He looked at them, noted their position, and then took them out of the drawer. He went straight to the cabinet Celia had asked him not to open.

It took him a few attempts to find the right key, and he looked through the file titles. All names of former employees. Three drawers were full of personnel files. In the bottom drawer, there was a fat file clipped together and wrapped with a rubber band taking up quite a bit of space in the back half of the drawer. He lifted it out and carefully removed the rubber band. The first piece of paper was a letter. "Dear Mr. Lovett, Please help us! I know you care. Our whole family is sick, and it has to be because of the dust…" Eric looked at another letter. "My wife is dying and I need this job, sir. Please reconsider. I know I've been sick, and I had to miss work, but I can still do my job. Alan Hardin." There was letter after letter from employees asking to keep their jobs or get medical assistance or retirement benefits.

Eric decided to take the file home. He locked the filing cabinet and put Celia's keys back exactly as he had found them. Eric saw a grocery bag in the coffee room and used it to hold the file for the trip to his house. It was a special file, and he wanted time to read it without worrying about someone walking in.

When Eric got home, he tried to act calm and as normal as possible. He looked around cautiously, worrying that he may have been followed. Having that file was nerve-racking. Once he was inside, he closed his curtains, made himself a cup of coffee and some toast, and then opened the bag and took out the file. He carefully took one letter at a time, making sure he did not mix them up, and read them slowly. Each letter was from a Libby resident. Eric could tell from the return addresses on the envelopes. Some letters were addressed to Larry Lovett; others were just addressed to the Zonolite Mining Company.

After a few letters, he had to stop. Tears came to his eyes. He stopped reading, took out his document camera, and started snapping photos of the pages and envelopes. He was careful not to get the letters out of order, although he could not tell how they were arranged. Certainly not alphabetically. Not by date. He still kept their order just to be safe. He used all of his film taking over one hundred and forty photos. Following each photo, he added the name and address of the writer to a list, along with the date of each letter. He used the Olympus to finish up the last twenty or so letters. Even though the results might not be as clear, at least he could read them without going into the filing cabinet again. Once he had the letters photographed, he returned them to the file folder, placed the rubber band around them, and put them in the paper bag.

When should he return them? He wanted them back in the filing cabinet as soon as possible. Having those letters in his possession would definitely cost him his job—and Celia. He had never used her keys without her permission until that night. It was after 10:00 p.m. The night watchmen would be suspicious if he went to his office that late. He had to wait until the next day. He would go in the morning. For the night, Eric decided to hide the paper bag with the letters inside. If someone broke in, where would the bag be safe? It only mattered if someone broke into his house to get the file. Eric took out several different files and spread them on his table. If anyone did break in, he had a lot of papers to look through. *Where should I hide this?*

The oven. *Men don't cook, right?* Eric had a roasting pan. He folded the bag tightly around the file, placed it in the roasting pan, and stuck it in the oven. *I'm probably worried for nothing. Lovett came back three times. He's definitely watching me. Maybe I'm being watched right now.* Eric decided to lock his car in his small garage. He locked the house while he was putting away the car. For his own peace of mind, he walked around the house looking for any indication of an attempt to enter his house. Nothing.

Once he was inside his house again, Eric locked the doors and windows, and then he went to bed, leaving all sorts of papers strewn across his table for any trespasser to see, just in case. He placed a few pens in locations he would remember. In the morning he would see if anything had been moved. Eric slept fitfully; he woke several times, sure that he had heard someone in the house. He was glad he didn't have to work on Saturday.

Eric took his cameras with him to take pictures of his half sisters, his Dad, and Betty. He had lunch with his family and then spent over two hours taking pictures and visiting with them. He was ready to go home and take a nap after his sleepless night. After he returned home, it didn't take him long to see that his strategically placed pens and pencils had been moved. Papers had been shuffled around and left in a mess. Whoever came in was not concerned about being noticed. Eric decided to ignore the oven. Maybe the papers were there—maybe not. He was not going to give any observer the opportunity to see him look in the oven, whether the intruder was inside or outside his house. He went outside to look for any signs of entry. While he was checking out the bedroom window, he thought he heard the front door open and close. When he stepped around the corner of the house, he saw a man stepping into a car across the street. *Ford coupe. Black. Dice hanging from the mirror. About six feet tall. Dark cowboy hat.*

Eric hoped that the man was the only intruder in his house. He went inside and checked from room to room, looking for other signs of a person being in his house. He took a quick drive around town, looking for—and finding—a deputy. He had met the deputy before, and he asked him for a few minutes of his time. Eric said nothing about the "borrowed file," but he told the deputy about the papers being messed up on his table while he was out. The deputy went with Eric and walked through his house.

"I'll drive by throughout the weekend, Eric. You saw a black Ford coupe?"

"Yes, with those large dice teenagers like hanging on the rearview mirror. The man was about your height and build."

When the deputy left, Eric opened the oven and looked in the roaster pan. The file was there, just as he had left it. Good. *I'm taking it back right now.*

Roaster pan and all, Eric returned the file. As soon as he arrived, Eric took Celia's keys, unlocked the file cabinet, and put the file back where he found it. He locked up the file, put the keys back in her drawer as he had found them, picked up his roaster pan, and locked the door. When Eric opened his trunk and put away the roaster pan, he saw a black Ford coupe on its way into the parking lot. The driver hesitated, turned around quickly, and took off in a cloud of dust. Eric sensed that nothing was going to be the same for him at Zonolite. He was right.

42

MRS. CLARK'S PLAN

Unlike some of the other boys in school, Dan did not experiment with sex. He had never really had a date. He sat with girls at lunch, even walked a few to classes. He liked Julie, but until he ran into her in the hallway, he had not even walked her to class, let alone dated her. His encounter with Mrs. Clark had been a frightening and very exciting experience. He was mixed up about it. He wasn't sure he would sleep, but when he went home, he ate very little, and then fell into a deep, deep sleep until his mother had to shake him awake the next morning. He'd have to wash his sheets after the mess he left from the night of intimate dreams.

He avoided going to choir by getting a pass to see Coach Ross. He had decided he would tell the coach what had taken place with Mrs. Clark and see what the coach thought. Dan respected Mr. Ross. There was just no one else he could talk to about the situation.

When he arrived at Coach Ross's office, the coach was on the phone with some other school's coach discussing changing the basketball schedule. Dan could tell that Coach Ross was not happy about the change in a game. When he hung up the phone, Dan said he had some concerns about Mrs. Clark. Before Dan could explain incident from the previous night, Coach Ross told him that he should be grateful for Mrs. Clark's assistance. Dan said that he really did get some great help with his math.

"You know, you need to be extra cooperative in Mrs. Clark's class. She's gone out of her way to help you, and the results have been really good. Mr. Green says you are getting your math homework done and passing quizzes. By the quarter, you have a chance to actually pass this class—and stay on the team. Now why are you here?" Coach Ross pointed to a chair for Dan to sit down, and Dan had just sat down when the phone rang.

"Hello?" Coach Ross said. After a few moments of listening, Coach Ross held his hand over the receiver. "I've got to take this call, Dan. Why don't you go to class, and I'll talk to you later today. I've got to get another game into our schedule, and I need to get it done before another school gets hold of them first." The coach took a pass from a pile of small forms on the corner of his desk, scratched his signature on the form, and handed it to Dan, sending him back to class. Mrs. Clark's class.

Dan looked worried and said, "I don't mind waiting." But Coach Ross pointed toward the door, gave Dan a reassuring wink, and turned his attention to the telephone.

Dan could go to class with the pass or take a chance on cutting class. He decided to cut class rather than face Mrs. Clark. He filled in the pass to use the library and headed upstairs to work on homework until the end of the period. When the bell rang, he went to math class. Dan was surprised that he could actually look forward to going to that class and be grateful that he missed choir.

When Dan went to shooting practice, he was early and eager to have the ball in his hands. He lined up at the free throw line and began shooting baskets and chasing after his ball until Mark joined him. Dan and Mark took turns taking twenty shots, and then retrieving the ball for one another until the drills began with the arrival of the coach. Coach Ross set up the first drill. Thirty minutes into practice, Coach Ross called Dan aside.

"When I gave you that pass today, where did I tell you to go?" he asked Dan.

"To class," Dan answered, his eyes concentrating on his gym shoelaces.

"Where did you really go?" coach asked.

"Library. I had to finish my math before class, so since I was already out of choir, I used the time to study math." Dan looked at coach for some sign of his buy-in to his creative excuse.

"I don't want you cutting Mrs. Clark's class again. She has helped you more than any other teacher has helped a ball player. She's going to help two other guys on the team with math also. I don't want you treating her rudely. Understand?"

Dan looked at coach and reminded him that he had wanted to talk to him earlier that day.

"We'll talk after practice. Now let's see some shooting." Dan moved back into the drill.

After practice, Dan waited around for coach to finish talking to the others. He knew he needed to tell someone about what happened. He was not sure how to say it. *Mrs. Clark touched me where I was hard. Mrs. Clark kissed me and said she would help me anytime.* The more he ran words of explanation through his head, the less like a problem her actions seemed to him. And the more he wanted out of the gym and onto the road home. What if he was reading more into her actions than she meant to put into them? What if he turned into a laughing stock with the teachers? Dan was confused. He needed out of there.

Coach Ross called to him as he ran out of the gym door beyond hearing distance. Coach continued getting ready to lock up the gym for the night. *I'll see Dan tomorrow if he still wants to talk. Dan is a quiet kid.* Coach Ross had a couple of sets of papers to grade when he arrived home, and he fell asleep in his chair before getting the last set graded. Meanwhile, Dan was in his rhythm running his eight miles home. With the season practices beginning in a few weeks, he knew he would be too busy to spend time with Mrs. Clark, and that might take care of the problem. He let his mind wander to his favorite subject, basketball. As he ran, he saw himself playing the game with great players. His imagination took him through play after play, up and down the court, shot after shot sinking into the net.

Miles faded into the dark, and when he arrived home, he spent some time shooting his basketball into the metal hoop under the yard light. Both dogs ran around his legs, delighted to see him come home. He made just about every shot he put up, even with the dogs guarding his moves.

The two hot dogs looked anything but appetizing sitting on the table. Dan looked into the refrigerator and moved some of the less spoiled food out of the way. He found some cold potatoes and two eggs left in the bowl his mom used to gather eggs from the shed. Dan took out a frying pan, cut up the potatoes and the two hot dogs, and fried them. When they were hot and getting brown, he added the two eggs, stirred them into the cut-up potatoes, and soon had a fried concoction. He added pepper and salt, put two pieces of bread in the toaster, and poured a large glass of milk. In about two minutes, he ate his dinner and headed for his bedroom. The other kids had to share their rooms, but Dan was the oldest and had the small bedroom to himself. He took out his homework with every intention of getting organized for school the next day.

As he was writing the composition for English class, he was sidetracked by his confusion with his music teacher. On a separate piece of paper, he wrote some of his concerns. He wrote down a description of Mrs. Clark's kissing him, promising to help him, and her touching him where he could not help being hard. He sensed her rubbing him, not just touching him. Maybe he was wrong. Maybe she just rested her hand on his lap. He wrote his account of the incident and his questions, put the date on the bottom of the page, and then he taped the paper under the drawer of his bed stand. He completed the composition assignment. He took a stab at the math and was able to do most of the problems thanks to Mrs. Clark's previous help. He completed at least half the assignment correctly, but he ran into problems he could not answer. He was too tired to worry about it and went to bed.

Dan did not cut any classes the next day. When he came to choir class, Mrs. Clark did not ask him for an admit slip to class from the day before. She just went through the music as usual and did not say a word to Dan. Dan left class without incident, relieved that she had said nothing. Maybe she had accidentally touched him after all. Math class, however, brought a different set of problems.

When Dan turned in the incomplete assignment, Mr. Green noticed and asked him why he had not completed the assignment. Maybe if Mr. Green knew that Dan had a fairly difficult schedule compared to other kids he might have been less focused on Dan's success in his class. Dan did not realize that Mr. Green did not want to be the one that kept a top basketball player off the court. He had Dan stay after class to find out why the progress was taking a negative direction. Dan waited after class.

"What's happening, Dan? You had turned this grade around, and now you're back where you were four weeks ago." Mr. Green used a calm, concerned voice. Dan looked at him and tried to manufacture an excuse that Mr. Green would believe.

"I just got lost in the second half of the assignment, Mr. Green." Dan looked at the floor.

"Did Mrs. Clark help you with this?"

"No, I didn't get a chance to work with her. She's pretty busy with groups after school, and I didn't want to bother her." Dan looked up at Mr. Green and waited for his response.

"I'll make you a deal, Dan. You get some tutoring from Mrs. Clark again before Friday, get this assignment done right, and I'll let you make up this quiz to keep you passing. If you don't, you may not be playing in the opening weekend of basketball season."

Dan tried again by saying, "You know she's real busy, sir. Could you help me?"

"Dan, I would, but I have coaching after school for the seventh graders. The best time I have to help you is when you're practicing basketball. If you want to come then, I'll help you. But I don't think you want to do that. Listen, I talked to Mrs. Clark myself. She's more than willing to help you. Now you get yourself down to her office after school and get this work done. No excuses." Mr. Green turned to his grade book, stacked up some papers, and left the room.

Dan decided to go Mrs. Clark's office right after school. She was there alone and saw Dan approaching her open door. "Hi, Dan." She welcomed him into her office. Dan took out his math notebook and together they completed his homework. She explained to him what the assignment was about, and he explained back to her how to do the problems. He felt he was ready for the retake on the quiz. In less than thirty minutes, he left her office and headed for the gym with his math done. She did nothing and said nothing to indicate any inappropriate previous behavior. Dan hoped that she really was just being kind and not sexually interested in him.

When Dan arrived late to practice, coach asked him where he had been. Dan said he was getting help from Mrs. Clark. "That's good, Dan! I'm proud of you! Now get your butt out there and get some shots off." Coach hit him on the back in a congratulatory way as if he were proud of him for some special deed. During drills, Mrs. Clark entered the gym, talked to Coach Ross briefly, and left. Dan wondered what that was about, and he figured his name came up in the conversation since both of them looked at him during the discussion. Dan wondered briefly about the camaraderie between coach and the music teacher then gave up all thought of outside topics and focused totally on basketball. His dad picked him up after practice. Most nights worked out fine for his dad to pick him up or for Dan to meet him at the mill, but not when Dan had music practices at Mrs. Clark's apartment two nights a week.

For the next three weeks, interactions with Dan and all of his teachers went normally. Dan made all classes and was passing math with Mrs. Clark's help for a half hour daily prior to basketball practice. She acted like nothing inappropriate had happened, and Dan became relaxed during practices in her apartment with the rest of the boys.

One cold night, Mrs. Clark insisted on driving all the quartet members home. The temperature had dropped considerably during the day, and it was about fourteen degrees below freezing that evening. Of course, Dan was last to get dropped off. Mrs. Clark chatted about many things on the long way home while Dan listened politely. Mrs. Clark pulled off the main highway onto Market Road. She commented that she learned that the road also went to Dan's home. As she came to the Hardin place, she pulled into the vacated home's driveway and parked just beyond the barn, out of sight from any passing car.

"I just want to talk with you, Dan." Mrs. Clark turned toward Dan. "I think I made you feel uneasy a few weeks ago, and I want to apologize to you. I know that I am older than you, Dan. You just seem older than the other boys, and you act more mature than they do. I am attracted to you. You are very special to me, you know."

Dan did not know what to say. "You're a teacher and you're married," he said softly.

"I know it seems strange to you. But, Dan, I am a woman, and you are a man. I can't help my feelings for you. You are so very special to me." Mrs. Clark moved closer to Dan. "I want you to kiss me, Dan. If it doesn't feel right to you, then I won't ask you to do it again. I need to kiss you, and I need you to at least try it and see how you feel." Mrs. Clark placed her hand on the back of Dan's neck and pulled him gently toward her. Her mouth was ready for his, and he allowed himself to be pulled into a sensuous kiss. While her mouth touched his, she placed her tongue in his mouth gently, teasingly, and sensuously. She moved closer during the kiss, pulled him closer, and put herself into the kiss with her most sensuous effort. That kiss was followed by another gentle, sensuous kiss, and he allowed her to draw his tongue into her mouth. It felt good, very good, and Dan was cooperating fully in kissing her. His heart was pounding wildly and he felt faint.

Mrs. Clark thanked him for his kiss and told Dan that she had been so lonely that she was thinking of quitting her job and moving away. Dan knew the school would miss her and he said that she shouldn't do that. She moved in toward his mouth again. Her left hand was on his neck encouraging him toward her as they kissed. Her right hand moved toward his lap, and when she found his enlarged place, she laid her hand on him and massaged him firmly. He backed off her kiss and said, "I don't think we should do this, Mrs. Clark. It could get us in a lot of trouble."

"Nobody will know if we don't tell. You can keep a secret, Dan. I want to pleasure you. Let me pleasure you now," she said as she used both hands to lower his zipper and probe for his penis. Dan was closer to shock than he had ever been in his life. He felt unable to move, as though his limbs were frozen in place. She took his penis into her hands, and then into her mouth. He was just about catatonic. He felt unable to move and as hard as he had ever been at home just before masturbating caused ejaculation. She sucked stronger on him, moving her mouth up and down on his penis until he felt himself explode in her mouth. Most of it stayed in her mouth and some spilled onto his pants.

She took a tissue from a box of Kleenex on the dashboard. She wiped her face and dabbed at Dan's clothing. She kissed Dan on his neck, his cheek, and then his mouth. He was not as responsive that time, not fully taking in exactly what happened to him. She asked him if he was okay. He said that he needed to go home.

"Are you upset with me?" she asked. "I care so very much for you, Dan. This is such an unusual relationship for us. You cannot imagine how much you have come to mean to me. I truly love you, Dan. I only want to make you happy."

Dan didn't say anything for a few minutes. Then Mrs. Clark cautioned Dan that it was essential that he not say anything about their relationship. "If you tell anyone, you will not be playing basketball anymore." Dan looked intently at her.

"What does basketball have to do with this?" he asked.

"Coach Ross would never believe that I led you into this. You are the one the girls have crushes on. You are the charming one with the great smile. There is no way that anyone would believe that I am responsible for your having sexual involvement with me. You have to promise me that you will say absolutely nothing to anyone about this for your sake. I do not want you hurt when I care so much for you. Will you do that?" Her voice was strong, but convincing. Dan agreed not to say anything to anyone. Mrs. Clark kissed him again and then started up the car to back out. That's when she saw lights from a vehicle entering the Hardin property. She quickly drove forward again and turned off her motor and lights.

"What's the matter?" Dan asked.

"Someone is stopped in front of the gate!" Mrs. Clark was frightened. Her mind was racing. *Who could that be?* The two of them looked through the back window of the car as the lights became brighter. She rolled down her window to listen and heard someone opening a car door. All was quiet. Dan decided to get out of the car and look. As Dan looked around the corner of the barn, he saw someone looking at a right back tire. He watched as the man opened his trunk and took out a spare tire and a jack. Dan explained to Mrs. Clark that they may as well relax for a while since someone has a tire to change.

"You're kidding," she whispered. "Unbelievable." They both waited in silence. The tire changer was also relatively quiet although two swear words came forth during the time the man was trying to remove the tire. All seemed to go well from that point on. The event had to be a reminder to both teacher and student that they both had a great deal to lose if they were discovered together like that. What excuse could they use? Flat tire? Why were they on the property and on the other side of the barn away from the road? Counseling? Was Mrs. Clark helping Dan with personal issues? No matter how Dan played the scenario, he could think of no excuse that would cover their being together at that time and place. Dan decided that he would walk home so that no one would see him with Mrs. Clark.

"Look, I'm going to walk home from here," Dan whispered to her. "You'll be fine. Just wait here until you hear the car start up and drive away. If anyone sees you, at least I won't be with you. If you are discovered you could say you were tired and just wanted a nap—or you just wanted to be alone. There's no way you or I can explain why we are here together." Mrs. Clark agreed. "I know my way through this property, and I can get to the road without being seen." Dan left the car with the door ajar. She could shut it later. He climbed over the fence, went through the trees for at least two hundred yards, and came out on Market Road.

Dan ran into the dark night, lost in whatever thoughts staggered across his confused mind. He was grateful to be out in the cold, glad to see the snow coming, and full of fear about his future. By the time he reached home, he was numb. He looked at the basketball hoop, but he couldn't bring himself to pick up the ball. When he went inside, the leftovers sitting on the table did little to interest his appetite. He wasn't hungry. He looked at the plate of congealed stew. The meat and vegetables might have tasted okay hot, but it looked like someone left it behind after a sickness. He could heat it up. He had to eat, he reasoned with himself. Peanut butter and bread worked for that night.

Mom and Dad were watching television as usual. His brothers were already in bed. When he looked into the living room, his parents were in their usual chairs with feet propped up on the crates and drinks in hand. Dan sat down by his mom for a few minutes. She patted his hand, but she didn't move her eyes from the show she was watching. Dan leaned back to watch the show for a while. Later, he would not remember what show was on, only that he sat by his mom, unable to tell her about his confusion and fear, yet unable to leave her side. When his mom rose from her chair, Dan decided to get some fresh air. He took his ball and shot baskets furiously for some time. Fast thrusts at the hoop became more thoughtful shots. Dribbling helped him gain more control and better, more artful goals. Eventually, he decided that he could go to sleep.

The next day he wondered if he would look any different. Would people look at him and know that he had been given oral sex? He went through the usual process of getting ready for school and catching the morning bus. His mind was in the car with her, reviewing their actions and her words from the night before. She was insistent that he not tell anyone. He wanted to tell Coach Ross. He wanted to tell a priest everything so he could get rid of the feelings pressing against his chest. Was he crazy? Did he dream the whole thing? How could a teacher, a married woman, do that? She was right. No one would believe that she started it. No one would believe that she was even involved in any way. Everyone would think he was lying. He would look like the bad guy and she would be the innocent one. Everyone liked her. Even his parents who adopted him might decide to send him back, if that was even possible. He was on his own, and he was afraid.

43

ANOTHER TRANSPORT, NOVEMBER 1958

Stephen had talked at length to Father Flynn about finding a different vehicle to transport the children. He suggested a camper so the children could sit or lie down comfortably. Perhaps there was a way to have them hide under the beds or in closets if necessary. He could not put them in a cage for an icy winter journey. Father Flynn said he would find a camper before the next trip that would take place in mid-November. Stephen and Owen arranged to be off work for the next Friday to make another secret trip for Father Flynn. Stephen was not sure just why Father Flynn was transporting the children to Canada, but he had come to trust him and decided not to ask questions that seemed to make Father Flynn uncomfortable. Father Flynn would answer only, "Just trust me, Stephen. God guides me, and I need your help to carry out God's work. Really, that is all you need to know."

Father Flynn explained that the next trip would also loop through Libby, go to the Canadian border, and down Highway 93 to Missoula. "Just use the same route and the same stopping place on Market Road out of Libby." Stephen had already decided not to use the house if Father Flynn found a camper. He planned to drive the vehicle into the barn, stay there until he was given the time to leave, and not give anyone a chance to see them.

Stephen and Owen met Father Flynn early Friday morning at a house near Lolo that had been empty for over two years. When the two men saw that they would be transporting five children, they were worried. Neither one of them was especially good with children. On that occasion they had three boys and two girls ages four through nine years old. The youngest child stayed very close to his older sister; he did not want to look at anyone.

As Stephen and Owen helped the children into the camper, Stephen was concerned that the little boy might be ill. He put his hand on the boy's forehead, and he seemed sure that the child had a fever. Father Flynn said that the boy would be all right, that he could not stay behind. Stephen was glad that the boy's sister was there to watch him. Janie put her brother, Sam, on one of the small beds and sat beside him. The other three children found places to sit. There was food in the small refrigerator and the two small cupboards that the children could access as they wanted. Both Stephen and Owen thought the trip would be much better for the children.

They planned a four-hour drive from Missoula to Libby with a couple of stops to be sure the children ate something and used the bathroom. They needed a stop as well. It wouldn't be long before they were passing Kalispell, eighty-nine miles from Libby. On that trip they would park in the barn and avoid attracting attention by using the farmhouse. They were unaware that the property would be in use by a couple of other people.

44

DAN AND MRS. CLARK

Dan's confusion about his first sexual experience haunted him. His first hunting experience occurred when he was nine years old and he shot his first deer. Dan loved the idea of going with his dad anywhere. He hadn't really thought about killing an animal. He loved fishing with him and being able to laugh with him and listen to his stories. On that hunting trip, Dan shot the deer, watched it die, and helped gut it and load it on the truck. In the night, he dreamed that the deer attacked him. He shot the deer several times in his dreams, and it took him a long time to quit thinking and dreaming about that deer stabbing him with antlers. He never told anyone. He especially couldn't tell his dad. His dad would think he was a coward. Over time the fear worked itself out. His current fear, however, was different, and he wasn't sure what to do. He would go through the motions of the day and then do the same the next day. Maybe it would also fade away or at least feel less threatening later.

He went to classes. In choir, he walked in looking down. Mrs. Clark ran class as usual and said nothing to Dan. In math class, Dan had his homework done. Mr. Green made a positive comment about his improved work, and Dan thanked him. Dan planned to get the work done without special help. The previous night was a motivator for Dan to learn math independently. Coach Ross was his usual self in history class, and after Dan completed classes, he headed for the gym and ball practice. He put in two of the best hours he'd had all day. At least on the court he felt at ease. He knew himself there. Whatever happened in the future, he could not let anything stand in the way of basketball. That was his only way to be successful. He didn't want to work at the mill as his only career choice. He was not sure how she could keep him from playing basketball, but discovery might change everything in his life. All the students liked her. The teachers would stick together and support her over him. The counselor would not believe him, even if Dan decided to tell him.

His dad picked him up after practice, a definite relief. Dan could have run home, but Mrs. Clark could also drive the highway after practice looking for him. He didn't think she would do that, but he just couldn't see her that day. He hoped he wouldn't see her the next day either. On the way home he thought about telling his dad. What would his dad's reaction be? The radio was playing and Dan thought for a while about Mrs. Clark. The miles passed by, and the closer to home he came, the more he came to the unshakable conclusion that he could tell no one about what happened. The loss of Dan's reputation would be more than his parents could handle. He was stuck in a problem he could not control, but he had to keep quiet or ruin his life and cause problems for people connected with him.

One school day folded into another for two weeks. Dan managed to do his own homework in math and pull a C average. He missed a couple of quartet practices, but so did other members. Mrs. Clark did not single him out in front of the class or do anything to indicate she had an unusual interest in him. Dan moved through each day with basketball season in full swing and the first game of the season that Friday. All Dan could focus on was the game and his role in playing that game. Dan rode the bus home after school. His mom and dad brought him back for the game. They visited the tavern down the street until game time.

Dan played well. He was always intense during a game, and he earned the team twenty-seven points; eight were at the free throw line. He had four fouls. One of the fouls just about got him thrown out of the game due to the distinct impression that he had intentionally tried to get a fight going. Dan loved to play aggressively; some called it dirty. Coach Ross loved it. Dan would talk trash to the players, getting them off their game and into foul trouble. Once the game was underway, Dan entered a zone that no one could penetrate. Dan's elbows found sanctuary in his opponents' backs, stomachs, and any other body parts he could contact. Dan was strong on the court and had no fear of anything. Some of his shots and rebounds sent him flying into the air. Coming down was often met with pain as he crashed into the bleachers or the brick wall at the end of the court. He did not seem to notice pain, and he played with abandonment of any concern for his personal safety. His roughness sometimes caused another player to sit on the bench due to injuries. He drew fouls often, sending himself to the free throw line. Dan felt that was part of his job. Coach Ross gave him lectures on keeping himself in the game by not fouling out, playing with integrity and good sportsmanship, and taking care not to get injuries due to wild flying moves to get rebounds. Coach also let Dan know subtly that he appreciated his aggressiveness and that it was the main reason he played varsity as a sophomore. Dan knew what coach expected, and Dan met those expectations.

Saturday, Dan slept in until 10:00 a.m. He had a road trip that left at 2:00 p.m., and his folks let him sleep late on those days. When Dan got up, he ate some cereal and toast, did some homework, and dressed for the trip. He ironed his shirt and tie so he would meet dress standards and look good. All players had to wear slacks, shirts, and ties on the road, along with their letter jackets, even if they had not yet earned a letter. During the summer, Dan had worked a couple of part-time jobs to pay for his new jacket. At the end of the season, he believed he would have a letter to sew on the jacket. His dad drove him into town and wished him well. "Keep 'em guessin', son. You got a talent for makin' believers out of them white boys, huh. Just play your game and you'll come out on top." Dan smiled at his dad, picked up his travel bag, and headed for the team bus.

"Thanks, Dad. We'll be back about one in the morning. Can you pick me up?"

"Sure thing," he yelled out the window on his way out of the parking lot. Dan hoped he would remember, but he knew that he probably wouldn't be there. Eight miles gets long after a road trip, but Dan had run it in better weather. Montana was cold in late November, and the area had about a foot of new snow. His parents meant well, but their alcohol habit would lull them to sleep during a late television show or keep them at the bar past closing time. Dan often came home after a late bus trip to find both of them sleeping with the television on test pattern and the usual collection of bottles and cans decorating the room.

Dan had tried drinking a few times, but he really did not like the taste. His younger brother Bill drank whenever he could sneak some from the folks. Dan did not like the headache the next day. He had a goal that did not include drinking or smoking. He was the most reliable member of his household, and his family knew that Dan planned to go to college. They believed he would make it, even if the other boys had no interest at all in furthering their education. If his brothers could quit school right then, they would do so.

Dan was the top scorer of the game. He had a way of totally focusing on the ball. If anyone tried to come between him and the ball in a crucial moment, Dan could become aggressively wild. If the referee had seen him deliberately hit the boy, the ref would have thrown him out of the game. The referee saw several players pushing one another, the boy on the floor, and Dan reaching out his hand to help him stand up. Fans may have thought that was Dan being a good sport, but it was actually Dan trying to stay in the ball game. It worked.

Although Dan's parents did not subscribe to the newspaper, their neighbor always cut out the articles about Dan and gave them to the Eagles. When his folks finished reading the articles, Dan saved them in his second drawer. He had articles on both basketball and track. As a freshman in Polson, Dan placed second at state in two running events and he placed third in the javelin. He also anchored the four-hundred-meter relay. His points made the major difference in his previous school winning the fifth-place state trophy at state. Dan also kept his ribbons and certificates in that same drawer along with the medallions and pins he received from all of his sports and music activities. He was selected for all-state choir, and his quartet

earned a superior rating at the winter festival. He kept those certificates in the drawer and his descriptions of his encounters with Mrs.
Clark taped to the underside of the drawer. Each time they met, he
wrote about what happened and filed it in the large envelope under
the drawer. Inside the drawer represented Dan's track to success.
Under the drawer held his potential failure. Dan seemed to have a
promising future in high school. He could not let anything ruin his
chances for a scholarship.

When the bus rolled in at 1:00 a.m., John Eagle was not there.
Coach Ross had Dan call home, but the operator said that the number was not a working number. The phone had been cut off due to a
few months of unpaid bills. When Dan called, he pretended that he
was talking to his dad. After he hung up the phone, Dan told coach
that his dad would meet him along the road, and he'd see the coach
in school Monday. Coach let him run home, thinking his dad would
meet him along the way. Dad didn't meet him, but someone else met
him at the two-mile marker.

45

ANOTHER MEETING FOR DAN

Mrs. Clark drove up beside Dan and offered him a ride. "Get in, Dan. You played a great game tonight, and I want to give you a ride home." Dan did not want to get in that car, and later when he thought about it, he wondered why he did when he knew she could ruin his life if she chose to do so. "Come on. It's late, and you need to get home."

She chatted about many topics, but focused on his math. "Mr. Green said that you are holding at a C right now. I could help you raise that to a strong B if you will work with me." About a mile from Dan's home, she pulled off on a secluded side road that went to an empty farmhouse. She stopped just off the main highway, yet out of sight of any passing cars. "Dan, I am afraid that I have scared you. I want you to know that I would never do or say anything to hurt you. When I said I could keep you from playing ball, I was just saying that so you wouldn't tell anyone. The fact is, I could get fired for acting on my feelings for you. Please believe me, I would never hurt you. I don't want you to be afraid of me, and I don't want to be afraid that you will tell someone that I have, well, been intimate with you."

Dan was quiet for a few moments. Mrs. Clark found a radio station playing a Frank Sinatra song. She reached for his hand and asked him if he would forgive her for scaring him, and if he understood how concerned she was about her own situation. Although the car was dark, the light from the radio was enough for him to see light reflected in a couple of tears running down her cheek. She seemed genuinely concerned.

"I won't say anything, Mrs. Clark. I just think this could get us both in trouble, and we should stop this before someone finds out or sees us." Dan looked down at her hand holding his. She moved closer to him.

"Dan, I told you that I care very much for you." Mrs. Clark pulled his hand toward her and gently placed it on her breast. She was well endowed, and he felt the softness of her breast as she moved his hand against her body. She slid closer to him on the seat. Dan wanted to touch her breast, and the opportunity was difficult for him to pull away from. She released his hand, but he continued touching her. He outlined the neckline of her blouse with his finger. He cupped his hand on her breast, gently moving his hand to feel the softness of her flesh. She unbuttoned her low cut blouse and he could see the white bra in the dark car by the light of the radio. She unhooked her bra, slid out of her blouse, and sat by him nude from the waist up.

"You touch very well," she said as she put her hand behind his head and pulled him toward her for a sensuous kiss. Dan continued awkwardly holding her breast, and when their kiss ended, she guided his mouth to her breast. Heavy petting continued until the car windows steamed over. Dan had moved from fear to realizing that it was pleasurable. She was his first lover, and it was definitely a moving experience. Although he had never had intercourse, he was more than willing at that point to give it his best effort. His actions indicated that he wanted her, and she knew she had moved past a major barrier with Dan.

Mrs. Clark was cautious not to overwhelm her young protégé by staying too long or going too far. She moved away from him gently, put her bra and blouse back on, and told him she had better take him home. The cool air cleared the windows quickly once they rolled down the front windows. Mrs. Clark stepped out of the car, tucked in her blouse, and then climbed back in. Dan had slid closer to her, and she kissed him.

"What can I call you besides Mrs. Clark?" Dan reached for her breast again, gently.

She moved his hand away and held it. "I'll get you home now, Dan. I think you need to always call me Mrs. Clark so you don't call me by my first name or a nickname in front of others. You are truly wonderful." He had enjoyed the touching and breast contact. He was definitely interested in more sexual action. But Mrs. Clark knew that she had his attention and interest, and she was going to keep that growing for the next encounter. Mrs. Clark drove up to Dan's driveway and stopped to let him out where no one from the house could see her car if, indeed, anyone was looking out the windows at that time of the morning.

"When will I see you again?" Dan asked.

"Bring your math in on Monday, and we can figure out a time then, okay?"

"Okay. Thanks for the ride and for, well…thank you," he said quietly and sincerely. He did not know how to get himself out of the situation. He feared her power to ruin his hopes and dreams, but he also wanted her sexually. *She makes it so easy.* His best bet was for her to get tired of him and concentrate on her husband who would probably be visiting over the holidays.

After she drove away, Dan continued toward the house and entered quietly. His folks had fallen asleep in the living room, lulled away by Montana Red Eye whiskey and Great Falls Select. Dan said nothing. He quietly went to bed. He was tired from a full day of activity and a hard-played game, yet his eyes were wide open for at least an hour while he reviewed the events in Mrs. Clark's car. He wrote the steamy account, dated it, and taped it in his secret stash. Writing the details seemed to relieve the guilt. He finally fell asleep and his mother woke him up in time to get ready for 11:00 a.m. Mass. His mom drove the truck with Dan and his two foster brothers while Dad stayed home to sleep off the flu (bottle flu).

Dan attended Mass just about every Sunday. He went to confession often, and he even served as altar boy about once a month, sometimes more often if needed. That day, though, he merely sat back and let his mind wander from Mrs. Clark to basketball and back again. No one would believe she was to blame. *I didn't fight her off, did I?* The negative results of it getting out in the community would ruin Mrs. Clark if anyone believed him. It would ruin him either way. At one point he was fearful of her, resentful that she put him in that position. After the previous night, though, he had new feelings about her. He did not respect her, but he really did not fear her as much anymore. The fact that she could lose her job put her in a similar position as he felt he was in. She also had a great deal to lose. The situation was different. He wanted her. He knew he would see her at school for more than just tutoring help. He wanted her breasts again. He wanted to touch her everywhere. When he looked down at his lap, he knew he had better start paying attention to the biblical readings and quit dreaming of intimate events or leaving church would be very embarrassing.

46

DAN'S NEW PERSPECTIVE

Dan met with Mrs. Clark in her office after school and worked on his math. After practice, Mrs. Clark wanted to take Dan home. His dad picked him up some days, and it would not work out until quartet practice on Wednesday. They agreed that Wednesday Dan would bring his math homework to quartet practice and they would work after the other boys went home. During basketball practice, Dan thought about the drills and the coming game defenses and offenses. But the evening and the next day found him focused on Mrs. Clark's breasts. He could not wait to see her alone on Wednesday.

After basketball practice, he walked to her apartment with Mark. Mark chatted about sports and the coming game while Dan listened, as usual. Dan seldom spoke, yet he listened well and was included in conversations whether he contributed or not. Practice was hard and finally came to an end. Mrs. Clark thanked the boys for coming. She told Dan to get out his math and they would get the homework done right away so he could get home. He could feel himself getting excited. His breathing was short, he was perspiring, and he was shaky as though he might faint.

When the other boys left, Mrs. Clark locked the door. Dan had his books on his lap, and she helped him with his homework in a businesslike way. It didn't take long to complete the work. She asked Dan if he wanted a Coke. He said that he would like one. When she brought him a bottle of Coke, she sat on the end of the bed and smiled at him.

"Do you want anything else?" she asked. She reached out her hand and touched his shoulder, then his cheek. "Anything at all?" she asked with a smile.

Dan set down the Coke and moved closer to her. "Yes, I do want something else," he said. He kissed her lightly, and she responded strongly. He placed his hand on her breast, and she encouraged his touch. She removed her blouse and bra. After several moments of petting, she removed her skirt. Dan's heart was racing. She was naked in moments and she moved him toward her indicating that she wanted oral sex. When he was hesitant, she told him what to do. He complied cautiously because he had not done that before. She coached him and praised him; she responded enthusiastically to him. There was considerable touching and oral action between them, but there was no penetration. Dan climaxed through her oral manipulation. Surprisingly, their interaction took less than fifteen minutes, and then Mrs. Clark began dressing to give Dan a ride home.

On the way home, Dan watched Mrs. Clark intently as she chatted away. She talked about the coming concert and some of the songs. She described some of the other choirs in the community that would participate in the concert. Dan was not focusing on what she was saying. He kept thinking of her body and how his body was reacting to her every move and touch. When he left the car, she said good night to him as though she were ending a choir class. And then she was driving out of the yard.

During school, Dan waited for choir, went to choir, sat through choir, and watched Mrs. Clark throughout the period. He watched the way she lifted her arms to direct each song and practice each part: first the basses and tenors, then the altos and sopranos. Then she brought in all four parts together. He watched her facial expressions, he listened intently to her voice, and he measured her body in each movement and gesture. He watched the movement of her breasts as her arms directed a rapid movement or a slow movement of the melody. He was transfixed throughout class as he imagined his mouth on various parts of her body. Usually Dan spent a few minutes trying to catch Julie's attention, but not that day. He was engrossed in Mrs. Clark.

After class he asked Mrs. Clark if she would have time after school to help him with his math, and she said she would, just like nothing had ever happened between them. His eyes dropped to her breasts when he asked her for assistance, and she put her hand on his shoulder and directed him toward the door. Her touch on his shoulder sent a chill through him like electricity. He wanted her, and he could hardly wait until after school to meet with her for math help.

Whatever happened in school that day, Dan would not remember. His mind was totally focused on Mrs. Clark. He met her in her office after school with his math book and notebook. She helped him while he stared at her, watching her mouth say words and her eyes look at the book and at him. He moved his hand to her leg. She did not seem to notice him touching her. He moved his hand up her leg, and she put her hand on his. She patted it softly, and then moved it away from her. He wondered how she could be so calm when he was ready to sexually interact with her. She was calm, controlled, unruffled, and acting as though he was just any student, not her lover. He had to learn that control or he would give away their secret by his actions and expressions in front of others.

"I'll see you after quartet practice on Wednesday. Will you be there?" she asked him with a smile. Dan assured her he would be there. "Dan, you were staring at me today during class. You need to act normally or your friends may notice that you are, well, different from your usual self." Dan nodded and gathered his books together. She sent him off to practice. He left, smiling at her. He could wait until Wednesday. He could wait. He smiled all the way to the gym, and he threw himself into practice.

Julie was aware that Dan often tried to get her attention in choir class. She liked his silly grin and wink directed at her. She would smile back, feeling warm inside. But something was changing. Dan did not look her way. He seemed totally engrossed in watching Mrs. Clark direct the choir. He hadn't glanced her way for several classes.

She talked to him briefly after class twice, but he was waiting for Mrs. Clark, and he didn't have time to talk to her. Julie and Dan were not a couple, but they were friends. Summer had shown them that they cared about each other. Still, something was different. Dan had changed. She hadn't seen him with another girl. Only Mrs. Clark. While Dan focused on Mrs. Clark in choir, Julie became focused on Dan. She discovered something. Dan seemed totally fascinated with watching Mrs. Clark.

47

ERIC'S RESEARCH DISCOVERY

Eric had not told Celia about the file of personal letters he had taken, photographed, and returned to the cabinet with the use of her keys, which she had left in her desk. A week had passed since he had borrowed the file and returned it and since someone had entered his house and searched it. He wasn't sure how to involve Celia, or if he should at all. He didn't want to jeopardize her job in any way or her relationship to Mr. Lovett. The personal letters he had photographed astounded him. From the letters he learned about the pain and suffering many employees experienced. He still had more film to develop so he could read all of them. He had also learned more about the company, its history, its products, and where it planned to go in the future from many of the documents.

The letters held requests for assistance, stories of families facing the tragedy of death with little or no resources for medical help. The emotional content had a strong impact on Eric. He researched several individuals through the *Western News* obituary files, which kept him awake nights. He looked up their families in the phone book, found their addresses, and then drove around town and the countryside to see where each one had lived. After a few weekends of touring the town and finding several homes of former Zonolite workers who had given many years of work to the company, Eric decided to find a way to meet some of the family members. He decided to start with Dewey. He would ask him if he knew a few of the deceased workers. Dewey always seemed to know people through the Moose Lodge or the Elks or through the band kids and their families.

Eric was mindful of Mr. Lovett's curiosity and borderline spying on him on the weekends in the office. He sometimes had the feeling that he was being watched or followed. He was careful with the photos of documents and letters, making sure to keep them hidden from any intruder. He had no idea of how many times his home was searched, but he knew of one time for sure, and there were at least three other times when he had strong suspicions that his house had been entered. Had he known that someone had been in his house many times searching through his papers and closets, cupboards, and files, he might have been more concerned about his personal safety.

In November of 1958, Eric made his first visit to gather a more personal perspective about the depth of Zonolite's impact on individual families in the area. He knocked on Marlene Vernell's door at 11:30 a.m. on a Sunday. Marlene had just returned from church. Eric gave her a warm smile when she opened the door, and he asked if she would visit with him about her husband who had passed away three years earlier.

"Why?" Marlene looked straight into Eric's eyes.

"I heard that he worked for Zonolite. So do I." Eric waited silently.

"Would you like a cup of coffee? I just put on a pot. Please have a seat." Marlene moved her hand toward a chair on her porch.

"Yes, I'd love a cup." Eric sat down and waited for her to return with coffee.

"Sugar? Cream?"

"Yes. I'll take both, thank you." Eric dropped two cubes of sugar and a splash of cream into his cup. He watched Marlene settle in with her own cup, using it to warm her hands on the rather cool fall day.

"My husband worked for Zonolite for about eighteen years. Not long enough to get a pension, but the company gave me a check for eighty-five dollars to help with funeral expenses. I guess I shouldn't have been upset. We knew when he started work there that you had to work twenty years to get a pension." Marlene took a sip of her coffee. "I work at the Libby Motel cleaning rooms."

"Did your husband like his job at Zonolite?" Eric asked.

"Once he started, it became a habit. Good pay. He liked the men he worked with." Marlene paused. "I don't know who you are. Tell me about yourself."

Eric smiled. "That's fair. I stop in and drink your coffee. I better tell you who I am!" He laughed, and she laughed, too. "My dad is Dewey Bowman. He owns the music store down by the depot at the end of Mineral Avenue. I was in the navy during the war, then after working in San Francisco for several years for the navy, I decided to move here to be near family. My name is Eric Bowman, and I am pleased to meet you."

"I know Dewey. Been in that store a few times myself. What do you do for Zonolite?"

"I work on the electrical part of the mine. You know, upgrading old wiring and installing new wiring. I was an electrician for the navy, so when I moved here I felt lucky to find a job in my field." Marlene poured Eric another cup of coffee.

"So you're not here because someone from Zonolite sent you?"

"No. I just heard that some of the people that worked there passed on—maybe before their time. Do you think the mine had anything to do with your husband's health?" Eric asked softly.

"You didn't hear this from me. If you ever quote me, I'll call you a liar. Is that clear?" Marlene looked hard at Eric. Her hands gripped her cup nervously.

Eric raised his hands in surrender. "I won't say a word, I promise."

"Every day Jack brought home dust on his clothes, his skin, all over his face and hair. Both of us cleaned the mess every day. That dust killed him." Marlene set down her coffee. She lowered her head and sobbed softly into her napkin. "Asbestos killed him. Breathin' it in every day. It killed him, and if you work there very long, it'll get you, too."

"I'm sorry. I truly am. I'm sorry to make you cry." Eric sat beside her and put his hand on hers. "Would you let me visit with you again sometime?"

"Right now I'm visited out. Maybe some other time, if you don't mind." They both stood up and Eric patted her hand. "I miss him. He died too young."

"Thank you, Marlene, for the coffee. I look forward to seeing you another time."

Marlene put her hand on Eric's arm and pulled him back briefly. "Don't trust anyone out there. Find a job somewhere else while you still have your health. If you try to change anything, they'll fire you for sure. That's what they did to Jack. He tried to tell 'em he was sick from the dust, and they let him go so he couldn't get a pension." Marlene became weak and settled back onto her couch carefully with Eric's help. "You didn't hear this from me. I make quilts. You came here to see about a quilt if anyone asks." Marlene looked up at Eric.

"I got it, Marlene. I'll be back when you're feeling better to see about a quilt for my sisters for Christmas." Eric thanked her and drove home.

Eric wondered why Marlene seemed so fearful of the mining company or being discovered talking about her husband's illness due to the mine. The next Monday at work he learned more about why Marlene was concerned for herself, and for him.

The meeting was supposed to be short and informative. Larry Lovett started out with the usual reports. Then out of the blue, he asked Eric what Marlene Vernell was up to these days.

"Who?" Eric responded with some surprise?

"Vernell—Marlene Vernell. Someone said you were at her house yesterday. How did you get hooked up with her?" All eyes were on Eric. He looked around the table and wondered how the widow of a former, deceased miner could have such an impact on that particular group.

"Oh, Marlene. Well, I'm going to have her make a quilt for my sister and her husband for Christmas. What's the big deal? Is she someone special around here? I almost forgot her name, but you all seem fascinated by her." Eric noticed the group went from somewhat intense interest to a more relaxed attitude.

Larry Lovett looked at the group. "We know Marlene as a bit of a complainer. Let me know if she grabs your ear and talks about how we owe her something. She's a bit crazy. The crazy quilt maker." Others around the table laughed or gave each other looks.

"All she said to me is come back another time and look at designs. She wasn't feeling well, so I didn't stay long. Makes a good cup of coffee, though. How about it, gentlemen? Have you looked over my idea on the new filter system for the new building?"

"We're going to table that for now. Good work on it. Let's get on with the reports." Lovett moved on with the meeting. When it was over, Eric went back to his office and thought about Larry's comments about Marlene, as well as Marlene's fears regarding the company. Eric could have easily tossed off Marlene as a strange woman, based solely on her own comments. But when Eric added Lovett's comments and the group's interest in Marlene to the picture, Marlene's fears seemed much more credible.

Eric stayed away from the office after hours and on weekends for a while. He thought that his own concerns about being followed and his house being searched from time to time were valid. Was he in danger? In his spare time he took a few photographed letters and read them thoughtfully. They were filled with sadness, sickness, and poverty. They were heartbreaking. Then one letter stopped him cold.

Mrs. Hart's letter began with a question: "Just who did you hire to kill my son?" Eric continued, gripping the letter firmly. "When he contacted our senator and blew the whistle on your murderous company, you took care of business by having someone run him off the road and into the river. How many times did you have someone break into his house and search his files? Was burning his house down the only way you could be sure you got his research and his family? I won't let this die."

Eric reread the letter. He poured himself another cup of coffee. He put the papers away safely and went to bed. Sleep was slow to come, and his dreams were filled with house fires, cars run off the road, and trying to get out of a car under water.

Monday after work he looked up "Hart" in the *Western News* obituary files and local news stories with Hart in the title. He found several articles including "Gerald Hart Dies in Car Accident" and "House Fire Takes Lives of Hart Family." The last one he found hit him the hardest: Mrs. Genevieve Hart's obituary. According to the article, her husband and children preceded her in death. She died from complications following a car accident.

Eric had a lot to think about. He decided to take every scrap of paper he had that had anything to do with his research on Zonolite and get it out of his house. He didn't want to burn it, but he could no longer take chances with the company. He didn't want people reading about his family in the obituary column because he tried to take on Zonolite. He decided to write the article on Zonolite's positive participation in World War II, give it to his boss, and get out of the research business for an extended period of time. All the research he did would be for nothing if he ended up dead—or his family suffered for his efforts.

After he left the *Western News* office, he went to the music store. His dad was just getting ready to lock up when Eric came through the front door.

"Dad, I have a favor to ask you."

"Just name it, son. What can I do for you?"

"I need to hide something, a box about twelve by twelve, someplace dry, out of the weather. Any ideas?"

"How about our barn? Stick it up in the loft where Helen plays. Or upstairs here in the store. I know—I have a drum that's had the skin torn. Put the box in the drum, and I'll cover it with another skin. We'll store it with instruments until you find a better place."

"Dad, that could work. I'll be by tomorrow—say after work? Six? I can help with the drum." Eric thanked his dad and warned him not to say a word to anyone. "Dad, I really mean that you can never tell anyone—and you can't let the drum get thrown away or bought."

"Mum's the word. See you tomorrow." The men left for their homes.

The next day after work, Eric stacked the papers in the box. He also put in every picture, negative, and even the ribbon from his typewriter. He left nothing in the oven, his previous secret hiding place. He looked around the front of the music store and waited until no cars were in the area. He put a blanket over the box and hauled it into the back of the store. He was worried that he might be followed. While his dad started the process of sealing the box into the drum, Eric looked out the window often to see if anyone was watching him.

Once the drum was sealed up, Dewey put it in the back with other drums. He gave Eric another box about the same size and covered it with the same blanket. "Take this to your car, Eric. If anyone was watching you put this in your car or take it out, then this will look like the same box."

"Good idea, Dad. Good idea."

"Don't tell me anything about this. I figure the less I know the better for you."

"You know it. Thank you for this. What did you put in the box?"

"A stack of records and a small player. You can take me to lunch someday to pay me back!"

Eric put the box in his car and headed for home. When he arrived, he checked the items that he used to monitor anyone being in his house. Someone had been there—again. He took the box in, set up the record player, and played a stack of four forty-fives. It was nice to have some music, and it was especially nice to know that anyone searching his place would find nothing about Zonolite asbestos or anything related to mining in any part of his house.

He knew he could pursue the cause later and maybe stay alive. It was not the right time to mess with a power beyond his comprehension. His immediate goal was to live until morning. He heard a sound coming from his bedroom. Someone was in there. He took his car keys and headed out the door. Eric drove off around the block, came up the alley behind his house, and saw the black Ford. Eric turned off his lights and backed into a neighbor's driveway.

A big man in a cowboy hat started up the Ford and, without turning on his lights, slowly moved down the alley and out on the street. Eric decided to follow the car from a distance and see where his housebreaker lived. When the Ford turned left on the next street, Eric took the parallel alley. Eric stayed back and was able to keep out of sight for several blocks. The Ford took Highway 37 across the bridge and made a sharp turn left onto the narrow road along the Kootenai River. Eric didn't cross the bridge. He watched the car headlights take the windy river road, stop, turn around, and wind back toward the bridge. Eric drove home quickly and locked himself in his house.

48

THE HARDIN PLACE

Dan had not been alone with Mrs. Clark for a while because basketball season took his time after school. He had games every weekend. His dad had said he would pick him up after his out-of-town game on Friday night, but, as usual, he forgot. Dan was running home when Mrs. Clark picked him up at the three-mile marker.

"Hey, good-looking! Want a ride?" Miss Clark called out to him.

Dan smiled and said, "Sure!" It was cold and three miles was far enough for him that night. Mrs. Clark had the radio on with Elvis Presley singing "Heartbreak Hotel." Ice had formed on Dan's nose and lashes. When they reached Whiskey Hill, Mrs. Clark turned onto Market Road. After a mile she pulled into the Hardin place and parked on the hillside of the barn, out of sight of the road. She turned off the lights, but left the car running to keep the heat and radio going.

"I've missed you so much! It's about time we get a few minutes together," she said as she moved toward him, wiping moisture from his previously icy face. She kissed him and moved closer. "Why don't you take off your jacket? It's cold, and the heater will warm you up faster with it off." Dan took off his jacket; then he put his arms around Mrs. Clark.

"Are you sure you want to park here? Remember last time we stopped here?"

"I thought about it and decided that we just had bad luck. Who would have a flat tire exactly where we parked? What a fluke. It won't

277

happen again in a million years, and it is an out-of-the-way place to be." Mrs. Clark began getting her coat off.

"Did you hear about our game tonight?" Dan asked.

"Of course! Nice going, Dan! High point man! You are so talented. You sing, you play, you kiss, you…you know." She unbuttoned her blouse. The two made out for a bit, and then they heard something. Mrs. Clark turned off the radio and the engine. They heard a vehicle shifting gears. Then it seemed to rattle over the cattle guard and into the yard. The next sound they heard was a door opening and slamming, and then the barn door opened. The vehicle drove inside and someone closed the barn doors. Mrs. Clark rapidly grabbed her blouse. The sound of the barn door shutting was followed by the sound of the inside bar being put into place.

Stephen saw the fresh tire tracks in the snow that went to the far side of the barn. He could see that a vehicle had made the tire tracks by pulling forward and backing into the shadow of the barn. Once Owen closed the barn door from the inside, he went out the back door with his flashlight to check for any vehicle that may be on the premises. As he came quietly around the back of the barn, he saw the car and read the license plate: 56-321. It was easy to remember. The car was steamed up. Evidently some heavy breathing had been going on. He thought that some teenagers might be enjoying some private time off the main road.

Dan grabbed his coat and put it on. "I'm going to check this out. Wait here." Dan quietly opened the car door while Mrs. Clark scrambled to get dressed. Dan walked around the corner of the barn. Stephen backed out of the way, avoiding Dan's path. When Dan returned, he told Mrs. Clark, "Some vehicle pulled into the barn. I can see the fresh tire tracks in the snow. I'm walking out and then going home on my own. You drive out of here and head to town. See you tomorrow."

"But, Dan, the snow—"

"I run all year round. It's nothing. Now, get out of here as quietly as you can before someone sees you." Dan eased the door almost closed and left.

Stephen saw the boy get out of the car and heard bits of the conversation. The car light allowed him to see that the girl was naked and trying to put on her clothing. He watched the boy leave the car, and then Stephen moved behind the barn to the other side so he could see the person better, and so he could be sure that he was leaving the premises and not trying to go into the barn. He was moving quickly and had reached the cattle guard by the time Stephen could really size up the boy. Steven thought that he was about fourteen or fifteen, tall and thin, and noticed the rhythm he established when he began his run down Market Road. He appeared to be athletic, someone who was used to running.

Mrs. Clark was frightened. She did not want to be discovered. When she had checked the place out, she had asked Kelly if anyone lived there. Kelly had told her that the Hardins had moved two years ago and that no one was living here. After her first stop there when the flat tire situation occurred she had another talk with Kelly. Kelly was sure that no one lived there. Who could be in the barn? She did as Dan had told her, pulled out of the parking place and began crossing the cattle guard when she realized that Dan had left the door open and it cracked against the fence post, swinging with the rattle of the metal bars. She got out of the car and shut the door. She felt the small dent in the door.

Stephen saw her. She was not a teenager. That was a woman. Stephen wondered what she was doing making out with that young boy. Mrs. Clark left the property, turned toward town on Market Road, and headed for town. Her mind was racing with the fear of the unknown. Who could have entered that barn? The more she reflected on it, the less she worried. Whoever drove in there did not want to be seen. If they heard her car, they would have run out to look. Nobody came out that she saw. It was a trade-off, she thought. She was feeling safe again. No one would discover her secret love affair with the delightful student she had groomed so well to give her pleasure. The events of the evening became an exciting adventure to her. She wanted to pick up Dan and continue where they had left off. No, she needed to be home if anything came up regarding the incident. Her best alibi was to watch a television show, write some music, and have her lights on and her car parked at home in case anyone might be looking. The deputy often drove around the streets at night. She parked at home, went into her small apartment, and poured herself a glass of wine. After she drank the first sip, she smiled at herself in the mirror. She felt like she had it all: a job she liked, the sex she craved, and excitement.

When Stephen returned to the camper, he wrote down the license number and a brief description of the car. Whoever the woman was, she did not belong on the property. She drove out with her lights off so she wouldn't be seen, and she headed in the opposite direction as the teenager. Whatever her story, she did not look in the barn to see who had driven inside. She was also a trespasser. Stephen did not believe that his group would be discovered before they left in the morning.

49

NEIGHBORLY ANALYSIS

Stephen was tired, but he wrote more notes when he went back to the camper before he fell asleep. He knew it was important to make sure the operation he was a part of did not get compromised by some fluke or chance meeting with strangers. Someone parking in an abandoned area after dark in that rural area was not unusual. However, the age difference between the two people he saw, the steaminess of the car, and the potential criminal activity that may have been going on intrigued him. In addition to writing down the license number and a brief description of the car, he also described the boy and the woman. He would decide what to do about it in the morning. The men and their precious cargo of children slept through the night. Morning found them waking up in the dark barn, hungry and anxious to see the light of day. After Stephen opened the barn door and then the camper door, he counted the four children who were awake. Janie said that her brother was still sleeping. Stephen looked at the boy's peaceful face and decided to let him sleep. He wanted to see if the boy still felt feverish. When he put a hand on the boy's forehead, he knew there was no fever. In fact, there was no life. The boy was cold and stiff. He must have passed away a few hours ago to be that cold and stiff.

Stephen told the children to let the boy sleep. He told Owen that he needed some help, so Owen gave up fixing a bite to eat and went outside the camper and the barn with him.

"We have a problem, Owen," Stephen said.

"What's wrong?" Owen asked. "Seems like this trip is our best so far."

"It's the boy. He's dead." Stephen said it softly. Owen looked at him in disbelief.

"I think we're going to have to bury him here. We can't take a dead body along. He's stiff now, probably been dead for several hours. I'm going to dig a grave out there beyond the fence while you watch the children." Stephen took a shovel and headed for the hole in the fence where the Bowman children had crossed to Market Road.

The ground was hard, so digging was slow work. Stephen worked for an hour before he had a shallow grave deep enough to cover the boy. He also rounded up some rocks to lie on top of the dirt. He had the children go into the barn area, and he took Janie into the camper and explained to her that her brother had passed away. Janie did not believe him at first, but when she felt him and tried to wake him, she knew that he was dead. Janie sobbed deeply. Stephen explained that they would have to leave him behind. Stephen took her to the gravesite and asked her if she wanted to be with Stephen when he buried her brother. She said that she did. Stephen wrapped the boy in the sheet that he was lying on and carried his body to the gravesite. As the girl and Stephen walked to the fence, then through the fence, Tom Holland was making a turn from out of his driveway onto Market Road. He saw the child with a man who was carrying something substantial with a cloth hanging down. The man and the girl climbed through the fence, and then walked up the hill.

On his way to town, Tom stopped at the Bowmans' to talk to Dewey about what he had seen. He knew that Dewey ran the store on Saturday, but it was still early, and he thought he would be home. Dewey was at the window when Tom drove into the driveway. Because Betty was sleeping, Dewey went out to meet him.

"Good morning, Tom. What brings you over on a Saturday morning? Want a cup of coffee?" Dewey asked.

"Good morning, Dewey. I'll take you up on that coffee," Tom said. The men went into the kitchen where Dewey poured them both coffee and had some homemade rolls and butter for Tom. "These look good," Tom said as he generously buttered a roll. "I appreciate the coffee and roll, Dewey, but I've come about a curious situation."

"What's up, Tom?" Dewey was wondering how he could help the rancher.

"I'll start with last summer. You know that the Hardin place has been empty for some time. I think they moved about two years ago," Tom said.

"That's right, I remember the Hardins. He got real sick and lost his job—just couldn't seem to find work," Dewey noted. "Zonolite claimed another victim if you ask me."

"Well, in July two men in a white pickup stayed there for a couple of days. I helped them fix the truck. Lavina and the kids took them over some food. They had three children with them. As I recall, your girls saw the children playing in the backyard and told my kids about it."

"I remember hearing about that now that you mention it," Dewey said.

"This morning as I was heading for town I saw an open barn and a young girl. One of the same two men that I saw in the summer was carrying something out through the back of the fence and up the hill. The girl went through the fence with him. There were some other kids watching them from the barn door. I'm pretty sure that they didn't see me, but I know what I saw, and I'm damned curious about what they were taking through the fence."

"What do you want to do?" Dewey asked.

"I want you to come with me and see what's going on at that place. Are you willing to do that? And, Dewey, I think you should take your handgun," Tom said. "I'll drive back home and get mine also. I didn't like the looks of the guys the first time I saw them, and I don't want to go there unarmed."

Dewey took a long drink of coffee. He tamped his pipe down and responded, "I'm with you, Tom. Do we want to call the sheriff's office? Shall I call my son to come along? Eric's in town. He won't be working today. Just what are we going to get into over there?"

"I think the two of us can handle it, but call Eric. One more of us can't hurt."

Dewey called Eric. "Can you meet us at the Hollands' place? Good."

Dewey downed his coffee and went to his gun cabinet. He took out his holster and strapped on his .45 caliber pistol. He put on a warm jacket and hat and stepped out the back door to tell Julie he was going over to the neighbors. "Be quiet, now, while I'm gone so your mother can sleep." Julie saw the gun at his hip.

"What's going on, Dad?" she asked.

"I'll tell you when I get back," he answered. "Don't worry. I'm with Tom and we may do some target shooting. Take care of your sister."

Dewey and Tom drove off in Tom's truck. They drove the half mile saying very little. As they reached the Holland turnoff, they both looked at the Hardin place very closely. It seemed deserted. Tom drove to his house, went in, and buckled on his pistol. He told his wife that he was with Dewey and would see her later. He drove down his driveway, and when he was about fifty yards from Market Road, he saw the barn doors swing open and a camper drive out. A man shut the doors behind the camper and climbed into the front seat. The camper crossed the cattle guard and headed toward Libby. Tom had pulled over near some trees to avoid being seen just as Eric arrived, parked his car, and joined the others in Tom's truck. Dewey and Tom watched the camper continue down Market Road. Tom decided to follow the camper and get its license number if he could without being seen. Dewey found a pencil in the glove compartment and a newspaper on the seat. He was ready to write down the number if they got close enough to see it. When the camper left Market Road to cross over to Highway 2, Tom pulled up fairly close to the camper but not close enough to read the plate.

"Tom, take a chance and close in on that camper so I can get the license number." Dewey wrote a description of the camper. He noted out loud as he wrote, "White, rack on top, tire on the back, about twenty feet long. Montana plate with a four something—that's

Missoula County. Got it! 4-807!" The camper took off faster than campers usually do, and Tom turned around and went back to the Hardin place.

"Maybe I'm just nutty, Dewey. Let's go see what might have been carried up that hill before we go getting ourselves into some serious shit. Okay?" Tom commented and Eric agreed.

"Sounds like a good plan to me." Dewey sat back and thought for a minute. "You know, with the camper gone, it will be a lot safer for us to look around. If we see anything we want to tell a sheriff's deputy, that camper will either stop in Libby or be along the road and easy for them to find."

Tom pulled into the Hardin place and parked by the barn. The three of them looked in the barn and the house. No one was there. Eric noticed a shovel in the barn that looked like it had been used recently. He decided to take it with them when they went up the hill. The men could easily follow the path of the two people who had crawled through the fence. Their trail was clear due to a recent snow. After about a five-minute walk, they saw where someone had placed rocks on fresh dirt.

"Do we want to dig this up? Or call the sheriff?" Tom asked Dewey.

"I think we could be messing with a grave here, and we might mess up evidence. If it's a dog, I can live with a deputy laughing at me. If it's a body, I would rather the law handle it," Dewey explained.

"You're right, Dewey. Let's go over to my house and call the sheriff."

The men went to Tom's house. Lavina made some coffee for Dewey, Eric, and Tom while Tom called the sheriff's office. Tom gave a brief account of the situation and asked for a deputy to come by and take a look. After he hung up the phone, Tom said that a deputy would be there shortly because they had a man out on another call who was just about done. He had been at the Gopher Inn.

"You never know what the deputy might have to do at that place!" Dewey laughed. Dewey and the Hollands brought Eric up to speed on the events that had taken place at the Hardin place during the summer. The deputy drove up after only fifteen minutes. Tom, Eric and Dewey drove over to the Hardin place again with the deputy and showed him where they had seen the disturbed ground. The deputy took the shovel and slid away some rocks. He made some progress through the soil, and it didn't take long before he saw the blanket. He pulled back part of it and saw the arm of a child. The deputy called for a backup crew to complete the investigation and asked Eric, Tom and Dewey to write out statements. He called the highway patrol and gave a description of the camper that was heading out of Libby. Tom bent down by the body and moved the blanket enough to see the boy's face. Both Dewey and the deputy also looked at the child's face. The sheet had kept the dirt from the angelic expression of innocence on a young, beautiful boy.

"My God," Tom said. "Who could hurt a child like this? Who could do this?" Dewey saw how hard it was for Tom. Eric thought he was going to be ill. Dewey stepped closer and saw that the boy's eyes were partly open with a vacant look that pierced his heart. He was at first appalled to think that anyone could hurt a child like that. Then he remembered his own children. Hadn't he been absent while his wife beat Darlene and Julie? In his effort to avoid an unhappy marriage, he was not there to protect his children from abuse. His heart ached for the child lying there innocently lifeless instead of running freely, playing, and going to school. Then in his imagination, he saw the face of the child with the light curled hair bordering it change to Helen's face. Just for a moment, the reality hit hard of what could happen to his children at the hands of his wife. Eric reached over and supported Dewey's arm, moving him back from the grave. Dewey resolved at that moment that he would never allow anyone to harm his children again.

Eric helped his dad as he backed away from the grave. Dewey looked at Eric. "That could be Helen or Julie."

"No, Dad. We can never let that happen. Never."

The deputy went back to the barn and swung open the double doors. When he came out, he looked around the barn. On the side away from the road, the deputy saw the tracks of another vehicle, possibly a car that had been parked there recently. With the recent snowfall, he estimated that the car was there between 9:00 and 11:00 p.m. The deputy thought that the vehicle more than likely had a connection with the camper. A set of large footprints had come from the passenger side of the car and left the property turning right, but when the car vacated the property, it turned left. There were also footprints behind the barn and around the other side toward the road. Someone had been walking around the barn, and, based on the depth of the snow in the tracks, that may have happened about the same time as the person left the property in the car. The deputy asked Tom, Eric, and Dewey to make one direct path out of the property, and to back straight out to leave the property so they would disturb the crime scene as little as possible. The men complied and went back to Tom's house to write out their statements. The deputy reviewed what he needed to do: he had already called the office and arranged for a team to investigate the grounds and the burial site. He also called the coroner and the highway patrol. That was it. He sat down on the porch steps and smoked a cigarette while he waited. In a way, he was glad that the incident was happening on a Saturday morning instead of in the middle of the night. It would be easier to get a solid team out there. No one had been murdered or had mysteriously died in Libby for a long time. There were hunting accidents and fights among family members, tribal members, cowboys, loggers, miners, and spouses. Not during his ten years as a deputy had he found a situation like that one. He couldn't say it was murder for sure, but a young boy in a shallow grave just didn't seem right.

Stephen pulled into the Texaco station for gas. Owen filled the tank while Stephen made a call.

"An unusual thing happened last night," Stephen said as he told Father Flynn about the car and its occupants. Stephen gave him the car's license number and the descriptions of the two occupants. He also gave him his impression of what the two were doing in the steamy car.

"A woman at least twenty-five or thirty had a young boy in that steamy car. I saw her puttin' her clothes back on, and when she was leaving, she banged her car door on the fence going out. When she got out to shut the door, I saw her plain. She was definitely a woman, closer to thirty. That boy couldn't be more than fifteen. That ain't right." Stephen paused.

"Is there more?"

"That's the easy part. Here's the bad news. Our sick little boy died sometime in the night."

"No. God no." Father Flynn breathed hard in disbelief.

"Yes, he did, Father. We buried him on the hill behind the place." There was a brief silence, and then Stephen continued. "I'm done, Father. We'll get these kids to the plane, but then I'm on my own." Stephen said that someone may have seen them driving out of the Hardin place. Father thanked him for calling and wished him well. Stephen asked him to leave his money in an envelope in his apartment mail slot if he could. "I don't know when or how I'm coming home, but if I get there, I'd appreciate the pay for this job. I'll be clearing out as fast as I can, and I'll need that cash to travel."

"I told you this is important work we're doing, Stephen." Father Flynn tried to calm Stephen down and keep him from quitting.

"I'm done. I'm not going to prison again." He hung up. Five minutes later the men and the four children were on the road to Eureka.

On Monday, Father Flynn made a phone call to a friend who worked in the department of vehicle licensing. He asked his friend to run the license plate number and let him know who owned the car, the address, and any other information available regarding that number. He made a few more calls to Libby contacts and had them make some inquiries to find out more about the car's owner. When he was satisfied that he had the name and occupation of the owner of the car, he decided to take some action from a distance using the US Post Office. When his friend called back confirming the description of the woman, Father Flynn put together three letters. One was addressed to the superintendent of Libby Public Schools, and the second one was addressed to the Lincoln County sheriff. He decided to take care of the abusive situation as quickly as the mail could make it from Missoula to Libby. His message was simple: "A teacher, Mrs. Clark, is sexually abusing at least one of your male students. Don't sweep this under the table. I'll be watching how you handle this." He addressed one copy of the letter to the sheriff and one copy to the superintendent of Libby Schools. He had one letter left to write.

"Dear Mrs. Clark, you may have noticed that you are being watched by your supervisor, as well as the Lincoln County sheriff's department. Your dirty little secret is out. Shame on you for sexually preying on innocent children. If you are still teaching and living in Libby in thirty days, I will send the story to the *Western News* and a few other newspapers in the area. I will be watching you wherever you go, and if I ever hear of you grooming any student for your pleasure again, I will expose you. You will never teach again. I won't rule out helping you serve some prison time for rape of a child." Father Flynn reviewed his masterpiece. He mailed it to Mrs. Clark a week after he sent the first two letters.

50

LETTERS

Superintendent of Schools Carl Cole noticed a letter marked "personal." *Probably some parent with a complaint.* He set it aside as he continued preparing his report for the board meeting the following evening. His secretary came in and told him that the sheriff was waiting to see him.

Carl Cole went out to greet him personally. "Hello, Sheriff. What brings you to school? Come on into my office. Coffee?"

"Yes, I'll take a cup with a couple of sugars, thanks." Sheriff Marty Burns went in and sat down. He saw the "personal" letter on the desk.

"How can I help you?"

"Well, you can start by opening that letter right there. I'll wait until you read it. I have one also. It may or may not be the same. Let's see."

Carl took a letter opener and slit the envelope. He took out the letter and read its brief contents: "A teacher, Mrs. Clark, is sexually abusing at least one of your male students. Don't sweep this under the table. I'll be watching how you handle this."

"You got one like this?" He handed Sheriff Burns his letter, and the sheriff took a letter out of his jacket pocket and handed it to the superintendent.

"The same. Unsigned. I usually throw out unsigned mail. But now that I see there are two letters, and the serious content—well, it makes me think that might not be a good idea. How about this teacher? Could this be true?" The sheriff settled back in his chair while Carl took a drink of his coffee.

"She's quite the teacher. Students like her. She's the music teacher."

"Does she ever meet with students outside the school day?"

"Yes, she does. She has practices at her house most evenings. She meets with students before and after school, and I think she has weekend sessions, especially around music festival time. The students like her and she puts on good concerts. But I never really thought about her doing anything like this. Who thinks of a woman doing something like this?"

"Well, again, could it be true? She has kids at her house after hours unsupervised how many nights a week?"

"She gives piano lessons, voice lessons, and she has kids over preparing for music festivals—quartets, trios—all that stuff, probably every night of the week. I'd hate to confront her with something like this if she didn't do it."

"It's always tough. If she didn't do anything wrong, it's a shame to bring it up to her because she'll feel bad, and she'll wonder who's talking about her. But if she is doing it, she could be ruining some boy's life. I mean, how young is the boy or boys we're talking about here?"

"Doesn't say. She teaches piano to all ages. She has music for grades one through twelve. Could be ages six through eighteen based on who she teaches."

"Carl, I have an idea. Let's sit on this for a few days. I'll keep an eye on her apartment for any late night activity, and you watch her here at school. Stop in on some classes and watch the students as much as you watch her. See if you get any suspicions. What do you think?"

"Good approach. We can get together next week and see if we have any suspicions or serious reasons to talk with her about this. That late night activity comment?"

"Yeah?"

"It doesn't have to be dark to abuse a child, you know. Private, maybe, but she could be doing this any time of the day when she's not in class. You might want to watch who's coming and going, and who's alone with her. I'll keep a watch on her office traffic for the same private possibilities," Carl offered.

"The letter says that we have someone watching how we handle this. Maybe someone will step forward during the week and give us some specific information," said the sheriff. "Having our patrol car going by her place might give the letter writer an idea that we are doing something." The sheriff thanked Carl for the coffee and left the office.

51

COMMITMENT. BUT TO WHAT?

Dan was in another world. He knew he was loved and he had a sexual connection with someone for the first time in his life. Not only did someone love him, but that someone was Mrs. Clark. Everyone loved her and wanted to be connected to her in some way. Dan was connected in such a personal way that he could hardly comprehend what was going on in his mind and heart. Now they also had an adventure to share. Who was in the barn? They would both speculate, but they could only talk to each other about it for fear of discovery. Why would he be in Mrs. Clark's car beside the Hardin barn in the dark of night? He was euphoric, elated, and happy for what seemed to him the first time in his life. During choir class he tried to keep from watching her every move, but he mostly watched her, listened to her, and waited for the moments after school when she would help him with his math.

During those tutoring sessions, he wanted to touch her in many ways. She was cool, in control, and not available for any serious or obvious touching. She explained to Dan that if anyone walked in, they must be appropriate. Taking any kind of chance would not be wise for either of them. Dan understood, but he could not keep his hand from her body when it was out of sight. She did not protest when she knew the touch could not be seen. Paying attention was also difficult, but the math was getting done regularly, and Dan's average in the class was up to a C+. Everyone in Dan's world was praising Mrs. Clark for her dedication to students and her specific help in Dan's case. Dan's overall grade point average was getting better, and his goal of becoming a college athlete was becoming more possible.

Winter came in full force to the whole state of Montana. Dan very seldom ran home due to the weather. He had someone with a car who was often eager to take him home after some closeness and touching in her apartment. One cold Tuesday, Dan's dad had stayed home with the flu and he needed a ride home after practice. He did not think about lining that up ahead of time because it simply slipped his mind. After practice he went to Mrs. Clark's apartment. When he knocked on the door, he waited a little longer than usual for her to acknowledge the knock, and then he knocked again. She came to the door and opened it slightly. When she saw Dan, she was surprised.

"Dan, what are you doing here today? It's Tuesday," she said.

"Dad's home sick, and I was wondering if you could give me a lift home tonight." Dan never asked for anything, but knowing how much that woman loved him, he stepped out of his nonintrusive manner and asked her for a favor.

"You know, Dan, I would, but I have someone here that I'm working with. If you want to get started on your way home, I could meet you in about thirty minutes," she said. She seemed to be searching hard for words, as though she was making a big excuse—or maybe she wasn't feeling well. Her hair was a little messed up. Maybe she had been sleeping. He could smell her. He loved her smell, especially when they were intimate. She smelled just like that.

"Okay, that's fine. I wouldn't ask except that tonight is pretty cold," Dan answered and left the small cement porch. He smiled at her in his boyish, silly way, and she smiled back warmly.

"I'll be along as soon as I finish here," she said reassuringly, and she shut the door.

Dan took off on a slow, rhythmic run toward home, knowing she would be along soon. He wondered who was at her apartment, and he thought it could be a piano or voice student. Maybe she was doing some tutoring. Maybe some man was there. Maybe she was making love to him. That could be why she smelled like, well, sex. *Would she really become intimately involved with someone now that she was with me?* He wanted to run back and see for himself. He turned around and started back to her place. Then he changed his mind. He would ask her when she picked him up. After all, he could trust her, couldn't he? She said that she loved him and she was taking risks to be with him. Few cars were on the road as he ran along the highway. About thirty minutes later, Mrs. Clark drove up beside him, and Dan quickly got in the car. Even though he was making good time, he was very cold and glad to get into the warm car. She apologized for his having to walk, but she said she had a voice lesson and she had to finish it because she had canceled the last one.

"Who was the lesson with?" Dan asked.

"Just someone in the community. No one you would know. She works hard, though, and I think she's coming along well." Mrs. Clark asked Dan some questions about basketball and the upcoming games for the weekend. Dan answered briefly. Then she chatted about a variety of topics as she usually did. She never seemed to run out of things to say. As they approached the one-mile-from-home place where she had turned off in the past, Dan was surprised that she didn't turn off the highway but continued to his home.

When she pulled into the driveway, Dan moved close to her and kissed her. He placed his hand on her breast, and she responded sensually to his kiss. However, she gently pulled back and said that she couldn't stay, and it was late for him as well. Dan thanked her for the ride, and she said she was glad to see him if only briefly.

"Remember," she said softly, "tomorrow night is quartet practice again. I'm counting on seeing you and working on math after singing practice. Right?"

"I'll be there," Dan said. "Thanks for the ride home." She drove out of the yard and headed to her home wishing Dan didn't live so far out of town.

Dan's life fell into a comfortable rhythm: basketball, quartet practice, school, and Wednesdays with Mrs. Clark. She made a special point of declaring Wednesday evenings as her time with him.

She built her music lessons around those times, she told Dan, so no one would interfere with their special time together. She also made it clear that she did not want him to come any other days unless it was arranged in advance. She did not want anyone to discover their secret. Dan felt confident that she loved and cared for him. The school year moved along fine. Basketball occupied most of Dan's mental and physical activity. When basketball ended, track season followed. Sports would continue to dominate Dan's life because he was destined to be the best long-distance runner in the league. Dan had success in sports and success in love. He was, indeed, a happy man.

One day during class, Dan noticed that Joey, a new boy who had moved there from Thompson Falls, was being uncooperative. When Mrs. Clark asked him to quiet down, he made a rude comment to her. Some kids laughed, but Dan told him to shut up or get out. Dan's tone was strong. Joey, a small boy with blond hair and blue eyes, jumped up and shook his fist at Dan and said menacingly, "Just who's gonna make me!" Dan rose from his chair, picked Joey up by his belt and sweatshirt, and took him to the door. Once there, he opened the door, and threw Joey into the hall. The other kids were laughing because Joey really did look funny wailing his arms and legs around while Dan, much bigger than he, easily lifted him and took him out of the room. Mrs. Clark told Dan to take it easy, that Joey was new and needed help fitting in. Dan said that he was helping him adjust. The kids all laughed again. After class, Joey came back in and told Mrs. Clark that she should have kicked Dan out of class. She explained to Joey that he needed to cooperate in class.

"The other students will not tolerate your antics, Joey. If you want to stay in class, you need to quit mouthing off. Dan isn't the only one who will put you out into the hall." Mrs. Clark was pleased that Dan took care of Joey, but she told Dan that he needed to take it easy on Joey.

Joey looked at Mrs. Clark as though she had betrayed him. "You are a lot more fun during my piano lessons than you are in class," Joey said angrily.

"Piano lessons are different. In class I have over sixty kids to deal with. You simply cannot be mouthy and rude in class," Mrs. Clark explained. "I need you to give me your cooperation in class, and I know you can do that. You are a very talented young man, Joey." Joey walked away from her and out the door to his next class. Dan left, too, smiling at Mrs. Clark as he left the classroom. He felt like he displayed his love for her in a way he had not done before. The other kids, of course, thought the whole scene was funny. Dan heard about it from several kids, and he laughed with them at Joey's expense. Joey, on the other hand, heard about it in a negative way from others who teased him about how funny he looked with arms and legs flailing as he "flew" from the classroom. He went to the counselor's office and tried to get out of the class, but Mr. Van Meter would not let him transfer to another class.

Joey was more cooperative in choir after that day, and he seemed to try to fit in with the other kids. He had the same problems any new student could have when the other students all know each other. Because he was cute, though, the girls took to him quickly, and he had friends within a few weeks. He and Dan became friends also since Joey admired him due to his basketball fame. Joey wanted to play and planned to go out for the junior varsity the next school year. Joey became Dan's shadow and most devoted fan. Dan sort of enjoyed the attention, and he was kind to Joey.

Quartet practice was soon to end with the state music festival being held in May. Dan would need to find another reason to spend Wednesdays with Mrs. Clark. One Tuesday night, Dan was still shooting hoops in the schoolyard. He was trying to come up with a creative plan when Joey grabbed him.

"Hey, man, what's up?" Joey asked, not really expecting an answer. He grabbed the ball from Dan and put up a shot that hit the backboard and plunged into the hoop.

"Nothing. What are you up to?" Dan answered, retrieving the ball.

"I'm getting my stuff ready for the festival. I've got this song to play. It's not going that well," Joey noted.

"Why not? Who's your teacher?" Dan asked.

"Mrs. Clark. I have to be there in a few minutes."

"She's good. You'll do fine," Dan said, trying to encourage Joey.

"Yeah, well, you don't know everything about her, now do you?" Joey said as he rolled his eyes and acted like she was somehow at fault for his disappointment in his festival music.

"What's to know? She's a music teacher. Big deal. You have to practice. Are you doing that?" Dan asked.

"I go over there on Tuesday nights for my lessons. Some of the time we practice. Some of the time we don't." Joey looked down at his feet, then grabbed the ball from Dan and put up another shot. That time he missed and had to run after the ball.

Dan was curious. "What else do you do besides practice?" He tried to sound casual, but he really was interested in Joey's comments.

"I can't say. I shouldn't have brought it up. She just don't always spend the time on the lesson, so when I go home, I really don't know that much more than when I came. I should practice more on my own." Joey passed the ball to Dan.

"So what does she do? Eat dinner? Clean her place? Feed her cat? What?" Dan pushed Joey as he went in for a lay-up. Swish. Joey went for the ball. Joey held the ball, looked at Dan with a serious expression, and stayed silent for a few moments.

"It's hard to say. Really hard. I gotta go," Joey said as he picked up his music book and ran off the playground.

Dan could feel something welling up within his chest. His head felt light, like he was going to faint or be sick. He could read Joey. The way Joey tried not to tell was as revealing as if he had said it. Mrs. Clark was doing more than teaching him piano Tuesdays at four o'clock. He remembered the night he had asked her for a ride home. She had someone. She smelled like sex. He should have turned around. He was stupid enough to believe that she was in love with him. She didn't touch him that night, not like she usually did because she had already satisfied herself with Joey. Maybe Joey meant something else. Dan had to know for sure. He decided to go to her apartment and listen for himself.

It was getting dark, and he needed to head home anyway. Anyone seeing Dan running would not have given it a thought. Dan was always running. Seeing him or any other high school student around Mrs. Clark's place was not unusual, either. Dan went up to the front of her house and heard the piano playing within. He sat on the porch. If she came to the door, he would say he just wanted to ask her a question. He had to think of something so he would be ready. He could ask her about the state music festival. What he had to wear? What time would they leave? Who was driving or were they taking a bus? He could ask her anything like that. He was ready. He listened and tried to look through the curtain. There was a small opening in the curtain. He could see Joey at the piano with Mrs. Clark. Joey was playing. Mrs. Clark played a short passage. Joey played some more. Then he saw her hand move onto Joey's back. She was stroking his back. Then she touched his neck. He saw her facing Joey's ear, and then she licked it.

Dan was frozen at the window. He wanted to run, but he had to stay to see if there was more. He watched her take Joey's head in her hands and turn him toward her. She kissed him. Dan could see one of her hands on the side of his head. Where was the other one? In his lap? She stood up, took his hand, and led him out of Dan's sight. Dan knew the bed was right by the window. He stood still, straining to hear any sounds within that apartment.

He heard Joey say, "I don't think we should do this."

He heard Mrs. Clark say, "You know this feels really good, now doesn't it?"

Joey said, "Please don't."

Dan thought he heard Joey crying. It could have been moaning, but it sounded more like crying.

Dan did not need to hear anything else. He quietly backed off the porch and began his run toward home. Running was a natural process for his body and his mind. When he ran, he had time to think. He had been on a natural high for weeks, thinking Mrs. Clark was in love with him and that they had a special secret that they both needed to keep to protect each other. They were a team, in love, and planning a future together. Well, Dan had a plan in his mind that he had yet to share with Mrs. Clark. The first mile had gone by and Dan was out of town on the highway. Knowing she was teaching Joey her secrets did not really change Dan's position. He thought about exposing her, but still, no one would believe him, even if Joey were willing to tell on her. He let the night air take him for a couple of miles without thinking of her. He needed a plan. He had started writing about their affair and had added to it a few times. He would revisit his notes and fill in for the many times he had been too tired to do so. He would add what he saw on that night. He may never share this personal diary with anyone, but he would have the facts on paper to refresh his memory if she ever turned on him. She could do that. She could hurt him badly, keep him out of college, get him thrown out of school. She had lied to him, telling him that he was her only love. Not even her husband meant as much to her as he did. Seven miles were accomplished when he realized that she could make a terrible difference in his future if he made mistakes. Running cleared his mind. At that moment, he needed to think, really think.

He thought about Joey. What could he do about him? If Joey found out that Dan knew his secret, what would happen? He wanted to help Joey, but he couldn't tell him what he had heard that night. If Joey decided to tell him about Mrs. Clark, he could listen and advise him to do what? Tell? No. Quit seeing her? No. Joey hadn't told him yet, so he had to drop that from his mind. "Don't take on a problem that hasn't occurred." Dan would cross that bridge when he had to. He already had enough to handle.

Only one more mile and he would be home. He would see Mrs. Clark less often. He would have to help his dad. He could come up with a job that needed to be done at home. He could clean up the place. It was the typical junkyard with old car bodies and junk piled everywhere. He could tell her that he had to work at home. His dad needed him. Cleaning up the yard would keep his mind away from town and trouble. What a dump. The thought came to him that, since she had Joey, she might welcome his absence and his having to be elsewhere. He couldn't blow his cover right yet. He would write his notes, keep up outward appearances, and stay away as much as he could. If he had to see her, he would use her, not love her. Two could play that game. She had a lot to lose. If she did get exposed, she would lose her job, her reputation, her husband, and maybe her license to teach school. He did not want to be the one to expose her because he would be exposed as well. He did not want to be part of the gossip mill in Libby High School or the whole town of Libby for that matter. And Julie. How could he have forgotten about Julie all that time? She would never want him if she knew about Mrs. Clark. He decided to throw himself into basketball and track. He would get so good at sports that his talent would carry him through any trouble Mrs. Clark might try to make for him.

He arrived home and looked around at the yard that he planned to turn into an organized place for his parents. Maybe they'd notice him if he did more for them. He was hungry and tired. He made himself some dinner, showered, and went to bed. That night he slept deeply, dreaming of basketball. In the morning, he awoke in a positive mood, knowing he had a plan for the day, the year, and the rest of his life. That plan did not include sex with Mrs. Clark.

52

THE DROP

Stephen and Owen drove through Libby, turned on Highway 37, and headed out of town. When they had crossed the Kootenai River, Owen broke the silence. "What are we going to do?"

Stephen was in deep thought. Finally, he said, "Let's get these kids to the airport right away, and then let's park this camper somewhere. Maybe we'll fit on that airplane. They may have a larger one this time with five kids—well, four kids. They thought they were getting five kids. What did we get ourselves into?" Stephen was not in a good mood. He drove as fast as the camper would allow, trying to get to the airport to send those kids off to Canada. He also thought of walking across the Canadian border. It was only about five miles from the airport. That might be a bad decision in that chilly weather, especially since there was little chance that the child's body would be found until spring. Maybe it would never be found. Worst-case scenario, it may have already been discovered, and he wanted no part of going back to prison. He would prepare for the worst.

The forty-five-minute trip was uneventful. When they arrived at the airstrip, a plane was there. The men helped the children get into the airplane. The pilot asked, "Aren't there supposed to be five children?"

"No, there are only four kids. Do you have room for one more passenger?" Stephen asked.

The pilot looked at Stephen and then at the children crammed into the seats. "What's your best guess on that one?" Maybe the fifth child could have been squeezed in somehow, but not a full-sized adult.

Owen closed the airplane door and walked back to the camper.

"Owen, I'm not going to go with the camper. If you want it, you take it on your own."

"What? Well, I'm not going to get stuck with it. Do you think we're going to get stopped?" Owen was both confused and angry with Stephen.

"I'm not taking a chance. That body may not be found for years, but it might already be found. I am not going back to prison. If you want to drive it home, you can. If you want to park it somewhere, be my guest. I don't care what you do with it. I'm done right here. I'll catch a ride or take a bus, but I'm not going to go anywhere in that camper. I hope you'll respect that and make whatever decision you want for yourself. If you want to stick with me, you can, but we might both be safer going our separate ways back to Missoula." Stephen was clear. Owen could see his thinking, even though he felt he was being overcautious. He decided he would park the camper out of sight from the airstrip and the road and leave it there.

"All right. I think you're overreacting, but I'll park this thing, and I'll see you in Missoula." The plane took off. When the two men parted company, they decided that if they were picked up by anybody—a car or a lawman—they would make up independent stories that involved only themselves to keep from implicating one another. They made a halfhearted wager about who would make it home first, and then parted ways. Highway 93 was their best bet in getting a ride. In Montana's unpredictable weather, just about any trucker would pick up a hitchhiker for at least a short ride. Owen gave Stephen a head start by taking care of the camper, and after he had hidden it in the trees, he figured Stephen had a fifteen-minute head start on him. About five minutes after Stephen reached Highway 93, a trucker picked him up. Owen took a few minutes to wipe down the motor home and then walked out to the highway, hoping for good luck. He was on the highway for ten minutes when a Lincoln County sheriff's car pulled up to him and offered him a ride.

Owen had not had time to concoct a good, believable story, and there was his first opportunity to use it, ready or not. The deputy, riding alone, pulled to a stop by Owen and yelled across the car, "What brings you out here on a cold Saturday morning?"

"Good morning! Just out getting some exercise." Owen smiled at the deputy and made gestures indicating his large outer measurements around the middle. "As you can see, I need it!" Owen laughed nervously.

"Get in. It's cold out here. I'll give you a lift," the deputy offered with a smile.

"Thanks anyway, sir, but I promised myself I'd do this. I'm on my third day of walking, and I want to torture another five pounds off by Friday."

"Suit yourself. I wish you luck! Say, while you've been walking, have you seen a white pickup with a camper on it go by?"

"No, I haven't. Frankly, there hasn't been anyone along here while I've been out," Owen responded. Stephen's instincts were right on target, Owen thought to himself. He hoped the deputy would move on without further questions because his heart was pounding and he felt sick inside.

"Enjoy your exercise!" Deputy Sheriff Gerald Jacobson nodded and gave a departing hand signal, then pulled away, driving off slowly down the highway toward Eureka. He watched the exerciser in his mirror continue at a jogging pace. Saturday morning was slow as usual, and he liked the shift. He could take it easy, watch out for deer and elk crossing the road, and not have to worry about catching speeders until after lunch. He drove through Eureka and continued down Highway 93. He received a second radio broadcast about the camper with two men heading out of Libby in any direction. He hadn't seen a camper, but he had just started his shift and he would watch diligently for one. The all-points bulletin gave a brief description of the two men. Gerald radioed dispatch and asked again for the descriptions of the two men.

"Okay, Gerald," the dispatch operator responded, "I'll read it to you nice and slow!"

"Now don't get cute with me, Sally! Just read it again. Over." Gerald liked Sally, but she could be a pain sometimes.

"Two men approximately forty years old. One has light brown hair, full beard, large features, six feet tall, and over two hundred seventy pounds. The other man has dark hair, dark mustache and sideburns, between six feet and six feet two inches. Weighs one hundred eighty to one hundred ninety pounds. The second man was wearing jeans and a dark green long-sleeved shirt with rolled-up sleeves."

"Thanks, Sally. Was there any clothing description for the overweight fellow?"

"No detail on the first one. A witness never saw the second guy get out of the truck."

"So all the Libby sheriff's department wants from us is to watch for a pickup-camper combination? What's the deal?" Gerald asked.

"I'll check it out and call you back. What else do I have to do on a nice Saturday morning? Over and out."

Gerald pulled into his usual coffee stop in Eureka and got a cup to go. By the time he strapped into his seat belt, dispatch was calling him back. He hated the new regulations about having to wear seat belts. He'd been working for years and never needed it before.

"Hello, Sally."

"Okay, Gerald, I got the story. Seems two guys transported some children through Libby a couple of months ago. Last night they were back with some more kids. One of the children ended up buried near Market Road about four miles east of Libby. A white, older model pickup with a camper on the bed pulled out of a deserted farmhouse area heading toward Libby. There's a Missoula County plate—got it right here. The sheriff wants us watching for a white pickup with a white camper on the back, the two men, or anything that might help them track these guys. The sheriff thinks that they might have at least three or four children with them.

"I got an exerciser guy out here that fits the description of one of the men you described. Over two hundred seventy—more like three hundred pounds—six feet tall, light brown hair...but I didn't see a camper anywhere. The guy said he was trying to lose weight—hey, he should! And maybe that's his whole story. I'm going to go back and see how he's progressing. Are these guys supposed to be armed?" Gerald asked.

"No word on that. But in a camper and in Montana, well—isn't everybody armed?" Sally quipped back at him and laughed. "Shall I call for some backup for you? The closest patrol car is just north of Rexburg not far from you. Over."

"Yeah, let's do it right. Send him my way, and I'll give him about fifteen minutes to reach the airstrip just north of Eureka. That's right about where I met up with this guy. He ought to be no more than a couple of miles from the airstrip walking toward Eureka. Tell the deputy that I'll come from the other direction, and I'll meet him before we stop the guy. Over." Gerald drove north, going back toward the walking man who just might be part of something interesting. If he was, then maybe the other man was nearby. He parked just north of Eureka and waited for backup, drinking his coffee and noting that the five-mile walk would be good for that fellow, whether he was the perpetrator or just a man in pursuit of exercise.

Owen was moving faster than he usually walked, but not so much to lose weight. He was nervous about the deputy, and he wanted to be anywhere but on that road. When a car came along, he actively put out his thumb to catch a ride. At that point, he would go wherever the driver was going, even to Canada, to get off the road. His luck was good. A station wagon pulled up in response to his thumb. The gentleman driving was the car's only occupant. He was at least seventy-five years old, and he reached across the car to unroll the passenger window.

"Need a ride, mister? I'm headin' to Invermere, actually."

"Thank you!" Invermere, British Columbia, was not where Owen had ever even thought of going, but the fear of that deputy returning changed his mind. Owen threw his bag in the backseat and climbed in the front. "I appreciate your assistance. I have a friend I hope to work for up north, and I could use a ride," Owen explained. He didn't want to get into a bunch of made-up stories he might not remember.

"I'm going to see my daughter and her family. Haven't been there for a long time. In fact, I could use some help driving if you feel like helping out an old man," the generous driver offered.

"Thank you. I would be glad to help out." Owen was sincere in his offer and grateful to be moving away from a potential meeting with a deputy sheriff in Eureka. As they reached Highway 93 and the old man turned left toward Canada, Owen could see in the distance a sheriff's department car approaching, signaling a left turn as it approached Highway 37. Owen would have been on that road if he hadn't taken that ride. Considering the lack of traffic the day offered, Owen felt the patrolman just might be looking for him. He rested his head beside the doorframe and scrunched down to be less visible. The border was only a short drive, and getting into Canada involved showing identification. Eldon James was a charmer. When the border patrol officer asked him where they were going, he joyfully explained that they were visiting his daughter after several years while showing the officer his identification. As he looked across Eldon at the passenger, Owen smiled and waved, saying nothing. No problem. The officer waved them through the checkpoint without asking Owen for his identification. Owen began to relax as the Canadian border got smaller in the rearview mirror.

Gerald drove toward the airstrip as he watched for the man he had chatted with briefly, as well as the deputy sheriff's car coming from Rexburg. The two county sheriff cars met at the airstrip. Neither deputy had seen anyone walking. The men leaned against their cars and compared notes.

"I probably should have taken the guy into Eureka, but I really had no reason to make him get in the car," Gerald explained to Brad Wiess. Gerald and Brad had worked in pairs several times ticketing speeders in the area. They took turns catching the fast ones and bet each other on who could ticket the driver with the highest rate of speed.

Brad looked around. "Maybe this airstrip has a part to play in this case." Brad walked over to the lean-to under which a few ranchers who flew in and out of the airstrip parked their cars while they were gone. He went over to the small hangar that held four small propeller planes. There were no windows, but Brad took the key out of its well-known hiding place above the hangar door and opened the padlock. He and Gerald looked inside at the four planes parked and anchored to the ground for security reasons. "I'd like to learn to fly," Brad said as he admired a blue Cessna. "Can't be that hard."

Gerald agreed. "Flying isn't the hard part. Just taking off and landing can mess you up. Making a mistake is harder to live through when you're a few thousand feet in the air. But I agree it would be fun." Gerald walked out of the hangar and around the back of it. Just as he was ready to come around the front side of the hangar, he looked off into the trees. "Brad, lock that door up and take a walk with me," he called out loudly. Brad joined him and the two of them walked through some high grass to a grove of trees about 150 feet from the hangar. They saw a white pickup with a camper on the back. The doors were locked, and the way it was parked looked like someone was trying to hide it. To avoid messing up potential evidence, the men returned to their cars and called the Lincoln County Sheriff's Office. Gerald made the call, but both men would share in the responsibility of writing up the discovery, if it, indeed, turned out to be the camper in question. Gerald also told them the license number, which began with a "four" for Missoula County, so a trace could take place while a team from the sheriff's office began their trek to the airstrip. Just in case there was a connection between the man on the road and the case, Gerald also filled in the sheriff's office about the brief encounter he had with a "walker" on Highway 37, and that he may have been picked up going in any direction. Maybe south, but most likely to Canada based on the minimal traffic Gerald had seen that morning.

"Looks like some folks are going to be giving up the rest of their weekend," Brad said.

"We might end up in that predicament ourselves, Brad. I was hoping to take my kids out skiing tomorrow. We'll see how that plays out. Thanks for coming. I don't know where our man might have gone. He must have gotten a ride. Hell, maybe he's sleeping in the motor home." Gerald decided to keep an eye on the camper until someone arrived. He also decided to call the border checkpoint and alert them to anyone who might fit the description of either of the two men. Timing was in Owen's favor. His ride had taken him through the checkpoint about a half hour before the call. The border patrolman told Gerald that he had only seen a few vehicles that morning passing through either way, and so far he hadn't noticed anyone who looked suspicious.

"The last car through here had two men heading for Invermere, but they seemed okay. One was clearly over eighty years old. The two appeared to be together, heading for a family visit. I'll keep a look out for your men, Gerald," the border patrolman said as he hung up.

Gerald had wanted to ask about the other man, but the border patrolman left the line before he had a chance. Finding the camper changed things. Gerald was worried that he had let a criminal get by him. Brad had walked out to the highway to be able to guide the sheriff's team to the camper. Gerald had time to think about the man, what he looked like, how he acted. After the sheriff's team came and went, he would ask around in Eureka if anyone knew someone who fit the walker's description. In that moment, he thought that the man and the camper were connected.

The Lincoln County sheriff was interested in the coroner's findings on the cause of death of the child his deputy had uncovered. He had also examined the body and could find no immediate physical cause of death. The boy did not appear to have been strangled or suffocated, beaten or traumatized with any object. The coroner, Dr. Sellick, saw no signs of sexual violation. He did, however, find physical violence that appeared to have occurred over a period of time since the child was born. The child showed evidence of several broken bones and scars from beatings. Dr. Sellick called in another doctor for consultation. Between the two of them, they concurred that, in spite of the extensive physical abuse, the cause of death was from natural causes. The boy appeared to have had a fever for several hours before he passed away. He died as a result of spinal meningitis, a relatively unknown disease that was hard to detect.

Sheriff Marty Burns looked at the coroner's report and sighed. "Well, boys, it doesn't look like murder, but we definitely have an unlawful burial, a neglected and abused child who might have had a doctor if he had been with his family. We also need to find two men I damn well want to talk to. Kidnapping is still on the table. Let's see if we can put this together before we get more help than we want from who knows where. The press will make this a big deal if we let ourselves get off track. All contact with the press goes through me. Period. That's our protocol. Any questions? Good. Now let's get to work." Marty sent forensics people to Eureka, he assigned deputies to trace the pickup and camper owner, and he sent a deputy to take any additional information from the three witnesses, Tom, Dewey, and Eric. He reviewed Dr. Sellick's report. "A sick child isn't as newsworthy as a murdered child," he muttered aloud to himself. Once the coroner's information about natural causes got out there, the press would look for another angle to catch readers or some other story.

Marty had a meeting with some reporters an hour later. He didn't like talking about cases for two main reasons. The first reason was his lack of experience with putting statements together that kept the press happy and himself out of trouble. In that town, the usual crimes did not involve in-depth investigation. Marty was a quiet man, and he feared that big-time journalists would get him to say more than he wanted to say, or they would take down his quotes and make him look stupid. The second reason was personal, too. Finding a child buried in a shallow grave was heartbreaking to him. Who could leave a child that way? Not only could he come off sounding like a tongue-tied idiot who couldn't speak very well, but he could just get choked up and cry. That wouldn't do at all. His staff would not support weakness in him. He could lose the next election if he showed that kind of weakness. He went into his office, and in the hour he had before the *Spokesman Review* reporter and the KXLY television crew arrived, he made copies of a carefully prepared statement to read to them. He would give them copies so they would have an accurate reference in their possession when finalizing their stories. He had a good start from his late night efforts since he couldn't seem to get to sleep until he had a complete outline and a strong first draft. That morning when he arrived at work at 5:00 a.m. he edited it again, reviewed the case file, and even practiced reading it in front of the bathroom mirror. He was as ready as he could be.

Stephen's truck driver made a straight run to Missoula with one gas stop, putting Stephen into town in time for a late lunch. He walked the mile and a half distance to his apartment from the Orange Street exit and let himself inside. He picked up the money Father had dropped into his mail slot. He took less than thirty minutes to pack his belongings and box up some items he wanted to keep. He called his aunt and asked her if she would pick up anything she wanted in his apartment and store the few boxes stacked in his living room. He told her he would be out of town and giving up the apartment. She feared the worst, but she asked no questions and agreed to store the boxes. She wished him well and asked him to keep in touch with her. He said he would, but he knew that the chances of his getting back that way in the near future were not good.

He withdrew his money from the bank by cashing a check at Templin's Grocery Store for the small balance. He did not need to close the account. With only a few dollars in the account, the small fee would eventually take the minimal balance to zero and the bank would close it. He had the money from Father Flynn, his $280 from his checking account, and a lot of territory to cover that day before he slept for the night. He had no idea where that would be. He decided to hit the freeway going west, get to Spokane if he could, and then go west to Seattle or Portland, south to California, and farther south to Mexico. North was too cold for sleeping outside. He'd take a bus if he had to, but he wanted to hitchhike to make his money last as long as possible.

53

INVESTIGATION OF THE CHILD'S DEATH

The child's death and surrounding circumstances engulfed the town of Libby and Eureka. Dewey and Tom had additional interviews with the sheriff. Tom had even more time than he wanted conversing with deputies, the sheriff, and reporters since he had seen both men and talked with them on a previous visit. Tom did not mention Lavina and her children taking them food because he wanted to keep his family out of the papers and off television. That suited Lavina just fine. Libby was not normally a center of news activity. The usual mill and mine closures brought minimal attention. Bear sightings on the elementary school's playground, winter storms, and a few lost and found hunters made minor headlines in the *Spokesman Review* from time to time when they had little else to report. Other than that, Libby was a quiet place with very little action. The situation changed that for everyone for the moment.

The sheriff decided to check out the hillside again where the body was found to see if there were any other bodies buried there. He kept his investigation as quiet as he could, and after thoroughly checking out the area with another deputy and a dog, he found one additional grave of a few kittens buried for at least four years. Since the Hardin place was deserted, he spent as much time as he wanted there. The extra set of tire tracks had him confused. Someone had parked a car by the barn; the tires and tracks were clearly visible coming and going. He had taken pictures of the tracks. They came from the north and went out the same way—so did the pickup tracks. Once the vehicles entered the Market Road, their tracks were mixed into the rest of the traffic. There was a trail of someone walking—no, running over the cattle guard and south. Who was the runner? Why east and not toward town? Those were fresh tracks, too. Most likely the car came on the property and parked on the side of the barn where it couldn't be seen from the road. The owners had moved away and left a perfect place for someone to hide undetected late at night. Whoever parked there could have been with the camper or could have been anyone—maybe lovers seeking a hiding place. Teenagers? Adults? A child killer? The sheriff would discreetly check tire tracks in parking lots around town to see if he could match the distinct pattern he found in the snow. His deputies could help and so could the Montana highway patrol. There was a unique mark in the tread of the right front tire. If the owner didn't have a blowout or change tires, and if the snow kept falling as usual, it was likely that he would find that tire. Snapshots took some time, but he thought those tire tracks could identify the car.

The unusual news about the body of the child being discovered in rural Libby, Montana, was a brief major blip on the news that faded nationally when the child's death proved to be from natural causes. Because kidnapping was a possibility, the Federal Bureau of Investigation was involved, but the remoteness of Libby was a factor in no one from the FBI personally arriving on the site yet. Lincoln County Sheriff Burns, however, was not letting the investigation slip away from his department until he had to let it go. When he learned that two deputies found the camper and that a man who claimed to be exercising disappeared somewhere in the area, he decided to pursue the possibility that the "walker" caught a ride to Canada. He drove to the border station himself to question the border patrol officers. Even though Owen had wiped off the steering wheel and some surfaces in the camper, the forensics officer was able to get several sets of prints from the camper. The inside surfaces of both door handles contained full and partial prints of three or four fingers clear enough to produce an identification. The system was slow to trace those prints, but within three days, Stephen and Owen were identified, and their pictures from the state penitentiary in Deer Lodge arrived on the sheriff's desk.

Sheriff Burns decided to call various news organizations and share those pictures with them in an effort to gain their assistance in finding the men. He notified everyone who had come the first time when the news broke about the unmarked grave and the dead child. Having prints, definite identification, and pictures was sufficient to bring the *Great Falls Tribune*, the *Missoulian*, the *Spokesman Review* from Spokane, and representatives from two of the three Spokane television stations. The sheriff meticulously outlined and then wrote a detailed statement, which covered his own professional opinions, the forensic report, and the coroner's report. Being reelected was his second priority. Finding those men and resolving why the child had been buried in a shallow grave was his first. His report included a description of the pickup truck and camper and Tom and Dewey's information regarding the number of children involved. He included the likelihood of it being the second transport of children, perhaps to Canada, by two men with prison records.

Due to Libby's location, at least three hours from Spokane and Missoula and even farther from Great Falls, the news conference time was set for 4:00 p.m. That provided reporters time to prepare their stories, get pictures developed or edit video, and provide the public with the full, updated story by the next day. Sheriff Burns presented information clearly and again had prepared copies of his statement of facts and photos of the two suspects ready for each news source. He was hoping to present a positive image of himself as a confident representative of local law enforcement giving a thorough public accounting of his investigation. As a result of his openness, he received a positive reward. Both newspapers and television news portrayed him favorably. He selfishly wanted to look good in the press, but he also knew his public request to help find the two suspects had a much better chance of success if he looked like he knew what he was doing.

Sheriff Burns did not mind the drive to the Canadian border. He wanted to interview the officer who was on duty the day those men may have crossed into Canada, and he had an appointment with that officer at 9:00 a.m. He missed much of the hubbub from the early local coffee groups, but he wanted to solve the case. He had also hoped that the advance notice to the border patrolman might get him thinking about who went through that day, making the trip a positive one.

Northwestern Montana was buzzing with news of the dead child. Libby residents could not believe something like that could happen in their town. Market Road was busy near the Holland ranch; drivers went by, pausing by the old Hardin place. Several adventurers crawled through the fence behind the house to see where the grave had been discovered. At least three of those were reporters for out-of-state news organizations, one of which had a distant connection to the *Inquirer*. The Hollands had inquisitive visitors until they closed their fence and posted a "No Trespassing" sign on the gate. Their friends were welcome to call, but the uninvited needed to go elsewhere for their information.

The music store experienced a higher volume of trade due to Dewey's role as witness. Betty was enjoying telling the story, taking on a personal angle that kept her listeners' attention. She included the girls seeing other children at first, and then she intimated that she was the one who saw the children, met the strangers, and took them food. Dewey overheard her telling her version to some customers. He lingered to see just how much she was embellishing the story. She looked up and met his gaze. He shook his head slightly while he continued with the repair of an instrument. He had experienced her imagination at work many times, and he wanted to walk over and correct the story for the customers. His mother was watching his children. Betty was working daily, and making Betty tell the truth about the incident was not as important to him as having the other parts of his life work smoothly.

Betty loved being at the store, interacting with the customers, and getting away from the house often. A few weeks ago when she first went back to working at the store, she was not sure she could handle it. But she coped well. The wedding was a success. Julia was staying clear of her, yet helping out in many ways. Betty did not have to do laundry or the dishes, cook, or clean. Life was good. "Fun" was an even better descriptive choice. She was having fun.

The attention the Holland kids and Julie received at school had come and gone rather quickly. Julie and Kelly enjoyed sharing their limited information and having other students pay attention to them at first, but they tired of it quickly and were glad to refer questioners to the newspaper accounts. The basketball team doing well captured the students' interests, and although the adults were still talking about the news, they were also into sports. The news regarding the dead child became lost in free throw shots and two-pointers. The child's identity had not been discovered, the men who buried him had not been found, and the reason for their being at the Hardin place was still unknown. No local children were missing. Sheriff Burns seemed to be headed for reelection, promising to keep crime under control and bring perpetrators to justice.

On another front, Owen had arrived in Missoula. He stopped at Templin's Grocery Store for some bread and a few other items, and he was drawn to the newspaper headlines as he paid for his groceries. He picked up the *Missoulian* and saw his picture, along with Stephen's, on the front page. He added the paper to his groceries and left the store. The picture showed him with long hair and a beard. He had left his beard and most of his hair in Canada, so he didn't look at all like the picture in the paper. When he reached his apartment, he made something to eat and then went to see Father Flynn. Father had also seen the newspapers and heard news accounts on television. When he saw Owen at the door, he let him come in.

"You've cut your hair. I wouldn't have known you if I, well, didn't know you. Come on in." Owen explained briefly about him and Stephen deciding to split up and meet in Missoula after they dropped off the four children.

"Wait here, Owen. I have something for you." Father Flynn left Owen briefly. He came back a few minutes later with an envelope containing some cash. "Take this, Owen. It will get you started somewhere else. I suggest you leave the area immediately. I remind you about our agreement. Do not divulge information about your involvement with transporting children—or me. Can I count on you to keep your word?"

Owen looked at the money, then at Father Flynn. "You bet, Father. I'm out of here." Father Flynn watched Owen walk down the sidewalk. He knew that there was no way Owen could keep a secret, especially one of that magnitude. Father Flynn made a call.

Owen decided to leave in the morning. He went to bed looking forward to his last good night's sleep in the familiar, comfortable, bumpy bed. Shortly after midnight, he heard a knock on the door. He looked out the window to see if a sheriff's car was in sight.

"Who's there?"

"I have a message from Father Flynn." Owen thought a moment about the envelope of money Father had given him. Maybe the messenger had additional gifts. When Owen opened the door, the man stepped inside and told Owen to dress and put together a bag for a short trip. Owen did not question the man, and he dressed quickly. The two men left Owen's place in a dark car. Owen, indeed, received an additional gift from Father Flynn. Owen disappeared from Montana before law enforcement could find him.

54

PREPARING FOR THE CONCERT

Mrs. Clark was getting the choir ready for the first major concert. She had two students stay after class to sing a solo part; Julie was one of the two. As a freshman, Julie did not expect to try out for a solo, let alone compete with a junior. Both girls sang through the music together. Mrs. Clark said she would have them sing it in class the next day. That night while Julie milked Smokey, she sang the entire song several times. She sang to the rabbits, the chickens, and the pigs. She sang the solo part several times to the stars. The next day in class, Mrs. Clark asked Julie to sing the solo while the choir sang the background parts. She faced Mrs. Clark with her back to the class. She was nervous. Then she let herself imagine that she was outside looking at the stars. Only the animals could hear her. When the solo part arrived, Julie sang to her beloved animals with a clear, strong, melodious voice. She let herself feel the wonder the shepherds felt for Jesus as the lyrics described. When the song ended, the class was quiet. Then they all erupted into applause. Mrs. Clark was thrilled. Julie's voice was clear, moving from a steady pitch into a soft vibrato, then soft to loud gently and effectively. She seemed as surprised as everyone else that she sang the song confidently.

"Julie, that was wonderful! Deanna, are you ready to try this solo?" Mr. Clark asked.

"No, are you kidding? Give it to Julie. I couldn't do that well. Nice job, Julie!" Deanna grabbed Julie's hand when Julie returned to her chair in the soprano section. Deanna was popular and beautiful. Julie could not believe she had been so friendly and supportive toward her in front of everyone. Deanna was mostly motivated by not wanting to look bad or not getting the solo after hearing Julie.

Julie blushed. She wished that she had heard herself sing, but she was lost in her imaginary world and missed it. From that day on, Julie experienced more interaction with students. Her shyness remained, but her confidence in her ability to sing began to grow. Mrs. Clark had her practice another song entitled "Ave Maria" by Bach-Gounod. Julie met with Mrs. Clark during lunch to practice with the understanding that if she were ready, Julie would sing the solo for the concert. Julie practiced the music every morning and evening while she did her chores. In addition to being excited about singing, Julie loved to spend time with Mrs. Clark. She wanted to be just like her, a music teacher, when she grew up. She missed Darlene a great deal. Mrs. Clark was filling a little of the empty space that losing Darlene had created.

Darlene was busy preparing for motherhood, cleaning and recleaning their little mill row house and enjoying the freedom from fear and pain living at home had provided her over the years. She and Dick were excited about the baby. They were enjoying loving one another and beginning a life together. Darlene had not been home since the wedding. Dewey had stopped by a few times, and he and Darlene had brief visits. One time, Darlene talked bluntly about her mother.

"Dad, Mother can be nice, but she can be scary. She whispers frightening things to us, and she listens outside our doors and outside when we do chores. She wants us afraid of her. I stood up to her and she beat me anyway."

"But now that someone is there, she won't do it. The girls will be safe," he offered Darlene, hoping that their grandma would be able to change the fear factor.

"Dad, she has beaten us for years and you were there, right? Living in the same house? She threatened to hurt Helen if I didn't do what she said or if I told anyone. She kicked us, bit us, pulled our hair. She cut us with knives, burned us on the stove and with cigarettes, and then made up lies about accidents we had. Dad, you believed her. You never took us aside and asked us what happened." Darlene began to cry softly.

Dewey said as he put his arm around her, "I'll watch. I'll take the girls out and talk to them. I'll gain their trust and I won't let her hurt them. I promise."

"What I'm going to say is hard, Dad, but here it goes: I think she wants to kill one of us."

"No! She wouldn't do that. She—"

Darlene cut him off. "Dad, she has used those words with both Julie and me. 'I'm going to kill you!' Over and over. If she wasn't thinking about it, why would she keep saying it? I got out, but I'm still afraid. Right now I'm afraid that she's standing outside the door listening to us." Darlene jumped up and ripped open the door.

"She's at the store and I have the car. But I'll walk around the house if you want me to," Dewey offered. He was shocked to see how Darlene reacted. She was afraid of Betty even in her home.

"The fear is ingrained in my head. She was always listening in or watching us when we were doing our chores or homework or even sleeping. I used to wake up and see her walking at the end of my bed, looking in my coat pockets or clothing. I pretended to be asleep, but I was scared. Sometimes she'd touch me or whisper something weird in my ear like, 'I know you're awake' in an eerie voice. Or she'd say, 'I could kill you, you know,' but I would not show her I was awake." Darlene stood up and hugged her dad. "Julie is in danger. It may be when you are gone on a trip to Spokane for instruments or in the middle of the night or when she's doing the chores. Mother will push her down the well or 'accidentally' shoot her. She has an ache to break her, even though Julie does what Mother tells her to do." Darlene lit up a cigarette. Dewey was getting ready to go back to the store.

"Don't tell her what I said, Dad. I don't want her coming over here when I'm alone. I'm afraid of what she'll do—and what I might have to do to protect myself. You've got to watch her all the time—and watch the girls. Having Grandma there is great, but you know that mother hates her. Grandma could be in danger, too." Darlene put her arms around her dad. He held her briefly. "Will you come see me again? I hope I haven't upset you too much."

"Of course I will. Take care of yourself. Come out and see us and bring Dick. The girls miss you. Based on what you've told me, they probably need to talk to you." Dewey thought about what Darlene had said as he drove back to the store. He parked in back of the store; he took out a piece of paper and a pencil and wrote, "Look, listen, learn." He put it in the visor. The three *L*'s, he said to himself. Maybe Darlene was exaggerating. Maybe she wasn't.

Dewey reviewed the past successes he had experienced since Darlene's wedding. He had talked his mother into moving to Libby. She wanted to be with the girls, and she liked the idea that she would be useful and helpful. It had not taken long for the girls to make Grandma feel welcome. She was helpful, loving, and kind to the children, certainly a welcomed change from their usual life. Dewey had always felt close to his mother, and he was especially glad to have her there after learning how hard Betty had been on the girls. Having a stable, caring person with his daughters seemed like the answer to his prayers. Dewey had also gained Betty's help at the store, which was good for him and especially good for her. He had much to be thankful for. He had Dr. Willis's information from Warm Springs Hospital regarding their requirements for admission and what a mental health evaluation entailed. Betty had calmed down, the girls seemed settled, and Dewey hoped that Betty would not need special care. He wanted to give Betty time to change. *Dr. Willis had said I could just take her directly to Warm Springs if I had to.* His heart ached with the weight of this decision.

Julie had prepared a roast beef dinner after school, getting the roast, potatoes, carrots, and onions in the oven to cook while she and Helen completed their chores. Grandma Julia helped by setting the table and making the gravy once the roast was done. Julie could tell that Dad and Mom seemed to have had a good day at work because they were talking nicely to one another. That morning in choir class, Mrs. Clark had told Julie that she had prepared well for the "Ave Maria" solo and that she was on the program for the concert. Julie thanked her as she tried not to cry due to her excitement. She wanted her family to attend the concert, and she hoped that they would let her participate. She and her grandma had talked about how she could get them to go to the concert. It was only a week away. Julie decided to invite her family all at once at dinner the night before the concert. When dinner was about half over that night, Julie interrupted the silence.

"Tomorrow night is the school concert. I'm in the choir and I need to go for my grade." No one said anything. "I would really like for all of you to come to the concert if you would."

Grandma was the first to speak up. "That would be lovely, dear. I would love to go."

Dewey added, "We could do that."

Helen softly commented, "I would like to go, too. Julie's been practicing the songs when we do chores, and I'd like to hear the choir sing them."

Betty looked around the table. "Yes, let's go." The tension that had built up with Julie's first comment ended with Betty's simple answer. The atmosphere seemed to ease like air softly released from a balloon. Silence reigned again as dinner resumed. Julie kept her eyes down so she would not meet her mother's gaze. She had no idea what her mother was thinking and was very pleased that she said she would go. Julie did not want any additional information—no silent negative stab from disapproving eyes.

That night just before bed, Julie went to her grandma's room and knocked quietly. Julia welcomed her into her room. Julie asked if she could sleep with her just for that night. She said that she was nervous about the concert and thought that she would sleep better if she could sleep with her. Julia smiled and said that she certainly could sleep with her. Julie did not want her mother coming into her room and watching her sleep. She worried that her mother might do something to cause her to miss school or the concert, and she thought sleeping with Grandma would keep her safe from anything Betty might do. Julie slipped into bed and cuddled up to Julia. Both slept well.

About midnight, Betty was surprised when she entered Julie's bedroom and found only Helen asleep there. She looked around the living room, and decided that Julie must be in Julia's room. She hesitated outside Julia's door, pondering whether to open it. Her nocturnal walks had kept her from going into Julia's room up to that time. Betty's hand rested on the doorknob, and then she softly turned it. The knob turned in her hand, but when she applied pressure to open the door, it did not move. She pushed harder. Julia had wedged a knife blade into the doorframe, preventing anyone from entering her room. Betty had a strong need to whisper to Julie, but that prevented her from doing so. Should she wake them up by banging on the door? A voice in her head told her to wait. Wait. Another time. She could whisper to Helen, but if Helen woke up, Helen would reach up and hug her or not hear her at all. She craved creating fear, and Helen was too young to know the chill and terror Betty wanted to instill in her. She stood outside the door for a long time, then gave up and went back to bed.

Julia heard the turn of the knob and the soft pushing against the door. Every night she pushed the blade of her knife into the doorframe so no one would enter her room while she slept. If someone knocked, she could easily remove the blade and open the door. That night and that attempted intrusion reinforced for her the need to lock out an intruder. If Julie had not been sleeping there beside her, she would have called out loudly, waking Dewey. Next time she would make noise and wake everyone. She seemed to know there would be a next time. She had been waiting for a first time since she moved into Darlene's room.

Julie had completed her chores and her last major practice for her animal audience before the concert. She was on the school bus when her mother poured herself a cup of coffee. Betty's nocturnal walks often contributed to her sleeping late. She was still eager to leave the house behind and work at the store. Julia set out breakfast for Betty, poured herself a cup of coffee, and sat with her.

"Did you sleep well?" Julia smiled at Betty as she kept her own attitude pleasant.

"I've had better nights. I may not make it to that concert tonight if I don't feel good after work. You all could go without me. Helen can stay with me if I don't go." She took her coffee with her to get ready, leaving the breakfast plate behind. Of course, she would get it later. She loved to eat and Julia was a good cook. Julia knew she would be back and left the plate for her. When Dewey came into the kitchen, Julia told him how much she and Helen were looking forward to the concert.

"Helen wants to go so badly. She is excited to see Julie perform. Betty said she wasn't feeling well and might not go this evening. She thought she might keep Helen at home with her. Do you think you might make sure that Helen gets to go with us? Betty would be sleeping anyway." Julia was not going to leave that to a last-minute decision on Dewey's part.

"Of course we'll take Helen. I think Betty will want to go, too. I'll talk her into it. With a bunch of the band kids playing our rented instruments, I had planned on going anyway. Julie just makes it even more important for us to be there. Don't worry. Helen's going to be there." Dewey would not argue with Betty. He would let her stay home if she wanted to, but he would make sure Helen went with him. He was happy that Julia was there to help him keep his children safe. He had confidence that Betty was getting better, and getting her out with others might help. She was already a different person since she went back to working at the store. As soon as he and Betty went off to work, Julia called Eric and Darlene and invited them to the concert. Julia settled into a soft chair with a cup of tea, pleased with herself for speaking up for Helen. She would have to stay home if Betty kept Helen home. She decided that neither of the girls would be alone with their mother as long as she could be there with them.

55

THE CONCERT

The choir wore blue robes with gold collars. At least seventy students walked on stage and took their places on the risers. Julie was among them with the sopranos on the second row. During the third song, Julie moved between two front-row students and stood near the microphone. Dewey looked at Julia and then Betty, wondering if they knew she had a solo. He gave his full attention to the choir and his soloist daughter. The song swelled, and then the solo came. Julie was not in the auditorium in her mind. She moved to the barn and again sang to the animals, sweetly, purely, and confidently. She did not appear to be nervous, and she did not make a mistake. Even though it was a religious song, the audience clapped enthusiastically. Although others may not have thought much about a freshman soloist, Dewey was proud of his daughter. He was amazed at her composure. He was also amazed when he looked at Betty and saw her tears.

The choir performed two more songs, and then Julie came to the microphone to sing "Ave Maria." She looked out at the audience and saw her family watching her. She smiled. Then her mind placed her in the barn where she could see the animals, the only warm, loving, caring, safe harbor of her love. She sang the song with the maximum fullness her still immature voice could provide, using vibrato and pure tone intermittently to sing the tribute to the Virgin Mary. The piano swelled up and down, up and down in the background as she gave the audience a prayerful experience that surprised and pleased them. The highest notes rang out on pitch and unstrained. The audience rewarded Julie with applause. When she realized the song was over and people were applauding, she returned to her place on the risers and wondered what she had sounded like to them since she missed hearing herself sing. From the reaction of both the audience and the choir, she assumed she had done all right.

The band played several selections, and then a social gathering with punch and cookies followed the concert. Several people told Julie and her family members how much they enjoyed her solos. Darlene and Dick surprised Julie and they all hugged each other. Eric jumped in, lifted Julie up in the air, and twirled her around.

"What a voice! That's my sister!" Eric kissed her cheek and congratulated her on her performance. Helen put her arms around Julie's body, hanging on proudly and lovingly to her sister. Dewey told her that he knew she could sing and that she really did a great job. Betty was enjoying everyone's comments about Julie, taking their words personally, as though she were the one who sang. Betty told Julie that she had done well, and Julie hugged her mother and cried.

"Thank you, Mom. I love you." Betty embraced her sincerely, and Dewey joined the two. When Julia hugged her, Julie cried. "I'm so glad you're here, Grandma. And Darlene and Dick—and Eric! Thank you all for coming!" Betty had moved on to the refreshment table, and she missed an opportunity to become jealous as a result.

"Hey, you better get a cookie before they're all gone!" Dewey guided the rest of the family toward the refreshment table. The family should have had someone film them enjoying the evening together. They were usually so busy moving through their daily lives of stress that they seldom had moments when they embraced one another. Julie had brought them there, and they came and contributed their own happiness and love, however brief.

When Julie returned her choir robe to the music room, she saw Mrs. Clark with her student roster checking off the robes as they were placed back on the rack. Julie hung up her robe, and then she hugged Mrs. Clark. Through tears, Julie thanked her for the opportunity to perform the solos. Mrs. Clark smiled and hugged her closely. "You did a wonderful job, and I wouldn't have had you solo if you weren't capable of handling it! Nicely done—and no tears." Julie wanted to respond, but she knew she would cry even more if she tried to tell her how she felt. She decided to wait until she had her composure and Mrs. Clark was alone. She would tell her how much she meant to her. Someday Julie wanted to be a teacher because Mrs. Clark inspired her. As Julie turned to leave the music room, Dan came in to hang up his robe.

"Julie, you did a nice job!" Dan held her at the door, seeking her face with his hand. He put his hand on her chin, lifting her face. "Is everything okay? Why the tears?" Dan lifted Julie's chin up and kissed her forehead lightly. "You are my special friend, you know."

"I'm fine," Julie answered with a big smile on her face. "Really. I'm just happy. You are special to me, too, Dan. See you tomorrow in school." She hugged him, and Dan kissed her cheek. Julie gave him another smile and then ran out to join her family. When she saw them waiting for her, her mother looked different to her. She was shorter and weaker looking. Julie had grown taller. Lifting hay bales had made Julie stronger. The success of the concert gave her more confidence than she had ever felt before. Dan had declared his friendship. She sensed a beginning of separation from her mother's control. She was stronger and determined to survive.

That night about midnight, Betty decided she needed to whisper to Julie. She had to keep her frightened, and after such a successful evening, Betty wanted to reinforce her own power over her. When she entered the bedroom, she bent down near Julie's ear. At the first few hushed words, Julie sat up and said loudly, "What do you want, Mother? Are you having trouble sleeping?" Julie said it loudly, waking Helen.

Betty was confused. Julie had never reacted like that. "Just checking on you."

"I'm fine, Mother. I appreciate your checking on me, but you need your sleep." Julie got up and walked across the living room to her parents' bedroom. "Dad, Mother is having trouble sleeping." She woke him from a sound sleep. He sat up.

"What's going on?" he said.

"Mother is having trouble sleeping. This isn't the first time. Tonight she came into my room again and whispered to me. She may be dreaming or sleepwalking, I don't know, but you need to help her stay in bed at night," Julie explained strongly, kindly, and clearly as Betty stood there in wonder.

"Are you feeling all right, Betty?" he asked.

"I'm fine!" Her answer was edgy, ready to be angry.

"Great! I hope you can get back to sleep." Julie hugged her, smiled at her, and then kissed her cheek. "I'm going to try to get some sleep. And, Mom, please quit waking us up at night by whispering to us. We try to pretend we don't hear you, but both Helen and I wake up. Sometimes it's scary; other times, well, it's just hard to get back to sleep. And the weird things you say to us, like, 'I'm watching you' or 'I'll hurt you' or even 'I'm going to kill you'—well, both Helen and I wish you would stop that. We love you and we know you must be sleepwalking. Dad, we could use your help here. Maybe if you lock the bedroom door from the inside, Mom will just go back to bed when she starts sleepwalking. We're going to lock our door so we can sleep. Good night!" Julie kissed her mother and dad and went back to bed. Betty was confused. Why wasn't Julie afraid of her? How could she tell Dewey that she had been whispering to her and Helen at night?

Dewey, wide awake at that point, told Betty to get into bed and to stay in bed. "You need your sleep. We'll talk tomorrow. And I mean it—stay in bed. Leave the girls alone." Betty went to the bathroom and stayed there for about ten minutes. She went to the girls' room again, and when she tried the doorknob, it turned in her hand, but the door would not open. Julie, following Julia's example, had put a knife blade in the doorframe, blocking the door shut.

"Go back to bed, Mother!" Julie's voice carried across the house, and Dewey heard her. He yelled at Betty to come to bed.

When Betty and Dewey were back in their bedroom, Dewey was angry. "What the hell are you doing? The girls need their sleep. You need to get in bed and stay there! Do I have to sit up and watch you all night to get you to stop this?" Betty looked down. She went to bed and curled up into the fetal position with her back to Dewey. She stayed in that position for most of the night, but she did not get up until morning.

Julie had made a personal commitment to do something about her home life. That night she took a major step toward lessening her mother's hold over her by finally letting someone else know about her mother's actions. She knew that she would face her mother's retaliation, but she would expose whatever her mother did to her dad and to her grandma. She thought about telling Mrs. Clark. Her own silence had kept her in fearful bondage. If her mother were to kill her, she wanted others to know about her mother's actions so they might save Helen from her violence. She would stand up to her mother openly and even kindly. Hadn't she offered "sleepwalking" as an alternative? Didn't she kiss her mother good night? Julie climbed into bed and noticed her sister was already asleep. She gave her sleeping sister a hug and a kiss and felt herself smiling in the night behind her secured door. Julie and Helen slept well, undisturbed for the rest of the night.

Betty came into the kitchen late as the girls were already finishing breakfast and packing their lunches. She poured coffee and said to Julie, "You may think you got away with something last night." Julie looked at her and waited for her to say more. Dewey was waiting just outside the kitchen, listening to Betty. "You better not lock your bedroom door again or I'll take it off the hinges and you won't have a door. And if you say one more word to your dad, you'll be so very sorry."

"Will you kill me, Mother? Are you going to threaten me again? You have told me that so many times—or Helen, are you going to kill her or hurt her if I say anything? Mother, you have to stop this. I love you. I really don't know why after all the hitting and biting and beatings, but I do love you. But I'm not going to pretend anymore. I will tell Dad everything every time you hurt us or even threaten us." Julie was calm and confident on the outside, but inside she was frightened. This could go badly, she thought, as her mother picked up a carving knife.

"You better stop defying me or I will take care of you in ways you may not like, you little bitch!" Her body language was strong, vengeful, and frightening, and Helen yelled, "Don't, Mama!"

When Dewey walked into the kitchen, he saw Betty, knife in hand, stalking toward Julie. He recalled Darlene's comment about Betty wanting to kill Julie. What more proof did he need to finally understand that his children were in grave danger in that house? Betty put the knife down when Dewey walked into the room. "Get out to the bus, girls. Just get on the bus."

Before running out the door, Julie knocked on her grandma's door loudly and yelled, "We're off to school!" Then more urgently, "Dad needs your help *now*, Grandma!" The girls ran out the door, and Julia came right out to join the two adults in the kitchen. As the girls ran to the bus stop, they held hands, with Julie propelling Helen as fast as her little sister could go and not fall. The bus had not arrived yet, nor had the other children. They looked at each other, locking eyes. The questions between them were many. Will their mother kill their dad? Will Dad take the knife away? Will Grandma get there in time to witness a bad thing? Will Mother kill them both? Major changes were happening in their lives, and they were both too young to manage the changes on their own. They had to count on their dad and their grandma to make things better with their mother. The bus still had not come. They were earlier than usual getting out of the house.

"Helen, tell the driver to wait for me. If he won't wait, I'll walk to school. You get on and go. Don't worry. I have to see what's happening." Helen stood alone at the bus stop watching Julie run to the house. She saw her climbing up on the snow and looking into the kitchen window. She saw the bus coming down the hill. Julie left the window and ran to the bus. The neighbor kids were also running, and the driver was usually patient. Julie jumped on the bus. Exhausted from her run, Julie seemed to collapse into the seat next to Helen. When she gathered her breath and could form words again, she told Helen, "It's okay. They're sitting at the table. It's okay." Helen let her tears absorb into her mittens as she leaned into Julie for the ride to school. Julie was hopeful. She had sung well, her family had supported her by going to the concert, and she stood up to her mother for the first time in front of her dad. It was going to be a good day at school.

Julie noticed more of the students saying hi to her and smiling her way since the concert. The choir students were the most obvious "hi" sayers, and several students added "nice job" and "way to go" when passing her in the hall. She felt better about coming to school than ever before. She always liked being in school, even if she felt invisible, because the school had a special attraction for her. She felt safe from the fear of pain at home, and she felt warm. Even the bus was warmer than her house in the fall and winter.

She would not be able to tell how many hours and days her family spent chopping wood for the fireplace, the central heater for the whole house. Her dad had built a wood box beside the fireplace that had doors in the house and doors outside. When the wood box was crammed full, less warm air escaped to the outside. The girls knew that a wood box jammed tight was in their best interest in keeping the house warm for everyone.

After Darlene moved away, Julie had more wood to stack than ever before. She did it faithfully, missing school often just to fill the wood box and chop kindling. She hated to miss school. There was always work to do at home, and when her parents kept her home, she missed class instruction that was necessary to do a quality job on her schoolwork. Her grades were not representative of her abilities because teachers did not know her situation and thought that she was just not interested in school or she would attend regularly. She did not have the courage to tell them and simply gave the office the "needed at home" notes her mother wrote to excuse her absences. Julie made a commitment to herself to get her dad to help her in school more often.

Since the concert, even her teachers noticed that Julie seemed happier. She smiled more than before and answered questions more often and more clearly. Julie noticed that even some boys who had not noticed her before were talking to her as though they knew her well and liked her. She enjoyed the change, and she tried hard to look and smell good every day. She worked harder on her homework than ever before, checking her work several times before deciding she had finished each assignment. By having her work done well, she was showing her teachers that she was learning and that she cared very much about her work.

At lunch, she ate her sandwich with Kelly, and then the two girls would go to the Blue Bear just to walk a couple of blocks and get out of school. The girls did not ride around at noon, but they watched the other older students drive up and down Main Street, cruising the drag, showing off their cars, and having cigarettes before they went to afternoon classes. Julie and Kelly were going to split a Baby Ruth. They waited at the candy counter for quite a while before someone came to wait on them. Doc, the owner, finally came over, lifted the counter of the triangular space, closed the counter top behind him, and took several kids' orders for candy. Kelly was getting worried about getting back to school on time.

"What do you girls want today?" Doc asked them nicely.

"A Baby Ruth," Kelly noted, "and really quick, please, 'cause we're going to be late!"

"I'm sorry, girls. Today was really busy. I guess I need more help."

Julie did not know why she said it, but it came out strong and confident. "I could help you."

Doc looked at her and said, "Have you ever done any kind of work before?"

"Of course. I work all the time. I could come just at noon and work the candy counter for you. If you hire me, I could eat my lunch from home quickly, and be here to wait on everyone until I need to go back to school." Kelly looked at Julie in amazement. Who was the shy girlfriend so boldly asking for a job?

"Hey, let's give it a try. I'll give you lunch here. See you tomorrow."

Kelly and Julie looked at one another, laughed in amazement, and ran off to school. Julie had accepted a job or a chance to get a job. She had asked to help, and the owner had said yes! Then reality started crowding into her brain. What would her parents say about it? Maybe she would not have to tell them. But if they kept her home from school, she would not be able to work. She might lose her job and seem unreliable. She had to talk to her dad. If he said it was okay, her mother might go along with it. Since her mother had been working, she was easing up on Julie and Helen. After the scene that morning, though, who knew what her mother might say. If her dad said yes, and the job worked out for her, she would have a reason to attend school every day. They were both strong on meeting responsibilities, especially consistent work habits. If she missed school less often, her grades would get better, and maybe—Julie wanted to be like her music teacher and go to college. She wanted to be a teacher. That goal seemed almost possible.

Kelly could not stop talking on the bus going home from school. Julie could not get out of her fearful inward tunnel of thought to be part of the conversation. Kelly reassured her that her dad would understand and let her take the job. She told her to just ask him. Her advice seemed simple. Don't make a big thing of it.

"If you get too excited, you could ruin your chances. Just act like it's no big deal and that you're helping out by not having to pack your lunch at home." Kelly tried to encourage Julie, and her advice seemed to make sense. Julie knew that if she really wanted something, her mother would not let her have it. She had to seem like it was just a way to help out at home by taking less food out of the family groceries without taking time away from home. Simple. Why was she so afraid to ask?

Julie made a meatloaf, mashed potatoes, gravy, and corn for dinner with pie for dessert. Grandma peeled the potatoes and helped Helen set the table. Her dad ate without comment, and her mother, who ate about half the potatoes before Julie could get the food to the table, continued eating intensely during dinner. The usual quiet settled in as each one turned to plates of food and steady consumption of consecutive bites. When dinner was almost over, Julie went for it.

"I heard that there was a lunchtime job at the Blue Bear, so I asked Doc about it. He said he'd give me a chance at it tomorrow. It's just working at the candy counter. I'd get my lunch free. Could help out on our groceries a little and give me some job experience. What do you think? Should I try it?" Her practiced speech came out just right. She was so nervous that she really didn't actually hear every word that she'd said. But there it was—out there—and the reaction was continued silence. Then her dad spoke up.

"How long is your lunch time?"

"About forty-five minutes. But I'd only be working about thirty minutes. Time to get there and time to get back to school maybe leaves only five minutes." She told herself to quit talking. More silence. Mother said nothing.

"Sounds okay to me," her dad said. "You say you start tomorrow?"

"He said he'd give me a chance to try it tomorrow. If it works out, I could get it. If not, well, I don't mind trying." Again Julie reminded herself to stop talking.

"Okay with me. Betty?" Betty was working on her third helping of meatloaf. It was impossible to eat the meatloaf in advance because Julie took it out of the oven and placed it directly on the table.

Without much thought toward the topic and focused attention on her food, Betty said, "Okay," and she kept on eating.

Julie said a low key "thank you" and left the table to get the pie for dessert. Grandma got up to help her, and they hugged each other in the kitchen. Julie wanted to dance! Her heart was beating fast, and she had the greatest urge to sing out joyfully. Grandma put her fingers to her lips, warning Julie to keep quiet. Julie nodded and gave her attention to the pie. She kept under control, returned with the pie, and made sure to cut a larger piece than usual for her mother, keeping a low emotional level. She was anxiously awaiting cleanup and her family leaving the table. She was bursting to get a moment to herself to let off her pent-up emotions.

Grandma Julia did not participate in the conversation about the job. She watched Julie intently and noted the parental reactions to her request. She helped Julie with cleanup. When both Dewey and Betty were out in the living room, she gave Julie another hug. Helen joined in as well, but they all stayed very quiet. They did not want to call attention to the amazing thing that had happened because they all knew it could end in a moment if Betty decided to say no.

After dishes were done, Julie went out to the barn and told her animal friends about her job. Smokey mooed; her dog, Dusty, jumped up and down and enjoyed her petting him; and Julie let out the song she had been holding in since dinner. Her chores were done and she had been able to shout out loud and sing about her new job. It was time to go in quietly and do her homework. As she left the barn, she saw her mother coming out of the house and walking toward the barn. Julie was grateful that her mother had not heard her singing and talking to the animals.

When the two met on the path, Betty was the first to speak. "What's this job you were talking about?" Julie could feel her hopes for the job slipping away from her. What could she do to keep her mother from taking her joy away?

"Mom, I just want to be like you and help out a little. I know it isn't much, but it's a start. Both you and Dad work. I'd just like to try it to see if I can even get this job. I know I won't have free time to be with friends during lunch—I'd miss that, but..." Julie reminded herself to stop talking. She gave her mother two things to think about: being like her, and losing out on time with friends. Both points scored well.

"Whatever you want me to do is fine, Mom. I'm nervous about it anyway," Julie said as she put her arms around her. It dawned on her that as she hugged her mother, she was now taller than her mother. Her mother outweighed her by at least 150 pounds, but Julie was definitely taller. Somehow, Julie had been able to express herself in a way that sounded like she really didn't mind if her mom told her she could not take the job. Betty had thought about not letting her do it, but the one thought of Julie not having free time scored the best with Betty. She did not want her involved with the high school students who drove up and down Main Street, making their circle by the store, screeching their tires right where they turned around each time they would "drag the gut"—the description the teenagers used to describe their journey from one end of town to the other.

"You can do the job. I just want you to do your best tomorrow. It is a small job, but maybe it will turn into a bigger job next summer." Betty was encouraging her.

Fear drained from Julie. Her body relaxed and blood began flowing freely again. The two of them walked to the house as her mother continued giving her advice on how to act and what to do as she tried out for the job. Julie thanked her mother and went to her bedroom to do her homework. She collapsed on her bed for a few minutes in disbelief that she was actually able to do something she wanted to do. She put on the classical music her dad had given her from the record shop—the ones that didn't sell. Julie could block out the sounds of conversation and television from the other room. "Pachelbel's Canon" led Julie through her Latin assignment, and then her English composition followed with Brahms softly keeping out other sounds.

Helen was involved in various activities: playing with two favorite dolls and coloring took most of her time. She fell asleep long before Julie finished her homework. When Julie completed her last assignment, she reviewed her work. She slept a deep and happy sleep. She still barred her door with the blade in the doorframe even though things had gone well with her mother.

The next morning, Julie was up earlier than usual, completed her chores, and awakened Helen early to take care of the separator and help with the other chores. Helen was ready to help and excited for Julie, so there was no argument about the early start. Julie had some time to take a bath and wash her hair after chores. She knew the animals' odors sometimes accompanied her to school, and she just had to make sure that did not happen that day. Her long hair dried as she helped her grandma prepare breakfast. Grandma had just about everything ready when Julie came into the kitchen. Julie took her towel to the fireplace and flung her hair forward, working the heat into the hair to dry it. Her hair fell in soft waves when left to dry on its own. After some help from the fire, she brushed her hair and left it falling freely down her back. She held it back with a simple ribbon that matched her sweater. Her figure was showing as the sweater formed around her breasts. She often slouched to hide her new arrivals—but not that day. She stood up tall and straight. It was a very good day. If she were hired at lunchtime, it would be a great day!

56

JULIE'S NEW JOB

Julie's morning at school went well, but her concentration was focused on lunchtime. When the lunch bell rang, she darted quickly into the bathroom and ran a comb through her long, wavy hair. She ran off to the Blue Bear. Doc met her by the candy counter.

"Okay, here's the change box. You can make change, right?" Doc asked her. Julie nodded yes. "You'll find ten dollars worth of change in here. Be sure to keep the box protected so no one can reach in and take the money. Kids will do that. I've had it happen to me. A few kids will try to reach over the counter and take a candy bar. You need to be watchful."

Julie lifted the counter to get inside the triangular area. She set the change box behind her, out of reach of anyone, but she would have to turn her back to use it.

"That won't work." Doc told her. "When your back is turned, kids can take candy and you won't see them. Just set it here with the lid shut in between transactions, and keep an eye out. Most kids will have the exact change anyway. These candies are five cents. These are ten cents. The licorice sticks and lollypops are five cents. That's it. Any questions?" He asked, and then, when Julie just looked at him somewhat dazed, he walked away. "I'll help out today. Don't worry; just do your best. If anyone gets rude, you tell them to leave—or call out to me. You don't have to serve them."

Julie had a few minutes to look at where the candy was located. She had been there many times as a customer and already knew where to find most items. All five-cent candy was on one side, and the ten-cent candy was on the other. She could do it. Kids were coming in.

"I want a Big Hunk," her first customer said.

"Five cents, please," she said, holding onto the bar until she gave her the nickel. Doc was watching and couldn't help smiling.

"Two Joys with nuts!" Julie grabbed two Almond Joys and took two nickels in exchange. She kept up with the customers and watched her change box like a hawk. The crowd did not get too bad because she was there all the time, unlike in the past when the kids had to wait for someone to come over to the candy counter. When the lunch break was almost over, Doc handed her a hamburger and fries. She would have about five minutes to eat. He took over at the candy counter, and she sat on a nearby stool to eat her lunch. She wrapped some fries in a napkin and put them in her pocket to eat on the way back to school.

"Nice job today, Julie." Doc was glad to get the help, and he told her to get to school and not be late. "I'll see you tomorrow!" She left the Blue Bear, and she looked back to see him waving good-bye to her.

"I have a job! I have a job!" she said to herself as she hurried to get to school. She liked selling candy and watching the change box, even when there were several customers at a time. It was exciting, very busy, and fun for her.

Julie kept her enthusiasm under control at home, and the newness of the job gave way to the daily experience of gaining more confidence and handling the job well. Doc was glad he hired her. At the end of the month he gave her an envelope.

"Here's your paycheck," Doc said. "If you don't mind, I'll keep the envelope and reuse it next month." Julie looked at the check. She had worked a total of twelve days that month and there was a check for six dollars. She looked at Doc with a surprised expression. "What's wrong?"

"I didn't know that I would get this. I thought I was paid lunch. I mean, do you really want to pay me?" she asked, almost ready to cry.

"Of course I want to pay you. You help out more than you know. With you taking care of that corner, I can run the business. Lunch is a busy time. You earned this, kid. Now take it."

"I need to ask you a favor." Julie looked down at her shoes.

"What is it? If I can do the favor, I will."

"Could you not tell anyone I get paid? I mean, not anyone? If my mother finds out, I won't get to keep it. She thinks I get my lunch for working here and she was okay with that. But if she finds out I get money, she will take it—all of it. Could you do that? Just not tell anyone?" She looked up at him with tears already falling.

"What would your mother want...? Okay, uh, okay. It's our secret. No pay, just lunch. What are you going to do with it? I need you to cash the check."

"I think I'll put it in the bank. I want to go to college, and this, well...it's a start, right?"

Doc looked at the skinny young girl and couldn't decide if he should laugh at her for thinking the six dollars she held was a beginning of a college fund, or if he should encourage her. When he looked at her, he just didn't see a potential college student.

"College, huh? Do you have a bank account?"

"No, I don't. Are they hard to get?" The girl was serious. She wanted to bank it, save it, and go to college. He did not think for a moment that she would ever get to college, but she could save money.

"I'll get the paperwork for you to open a savings account. Sign the back of your check, and you can open it with that six dollars. I'll have it for you when you come to work tomorrow." He gave her a pen from his shirt pocket, and she signed her name on the back of the check.

"Thank you very much for helping me, Doc. I really appreciate it. Oh, and if you decide that lunch is all you want to pay, I'm okay with that. I've always been okay with that." Julie ran off to school with a strong feeling of self-worth. He smiled at her and shook his head. She really was content to trade her time for a lunch. He thought about how much she helped him and felt bad that he was only giving her fifty cents a day. That's what he paid beginning waitresses per hour, and Julie was only working for about half that time. The pay was fair, and he was happy to have found an honest student to help out. He was still confused about her mother, though. Why should she fear that her mother would take her money? He agreed to the secret, and maybe in time he would find out more about Julie's family. For the time being, he was happy to be able to run the café at lunchtime without the headache of the candy corner.

Doc went to the First National Bank just down the street after the lunch trade had slacked off. He knew the teller who waited on him and asked him for the forms to set up a savings account. He noted that he was helping an employee open a savings account. The teller explained that if the employee was a minor, a parent or guardian needed to sign as well. Doc left with the paperwork and thought about who might be able to sign on Julie's behalf that would keep her secret. The next day Doc explained the forms, and Julie said she had someone in mind who would sign for her and not tell her parents. She thanked Doc for his help. When she went back to school, she thought about what she would do to keep the secret. She planned to use her grandma as the adult signer. She also decided not to tell her grandma because she didn't want her to tell anyone. If she didn't know, she couldn't tell. That night before Julie went to bed, she practiced her grandma's signature. The next day, she filled out the forms at school, signed her grandma's name, and at lunchtime, gave the forms to Doc. That afternoon he delivered the forms and the six dollars to the bank. Her account was set up that day, and the bank people had not seen her so they would not be telling anyone of the minor transaction. She used the Blue Bear's address for her monthly statements. The following month she worked twenty days and deposited ten dollars. Julie used her math skills to project her potential savings by the time she completed high school. She made her own deposits by way of the night deposit box. She would find a way to become a teacher, and she knew that job would only be a small part of what she needed. It was the beginning, however. It was the hope she held on to because it lifted her from the heartaches and fears she sometimes experienced at home.

The first time the tall, good-looking senior ordered a Hershey Bar he teased Julie and tried to take the bar without paying. Instead of arguing with him, she called out to Doc, "Hey, Doc, put a Hershey on this guy's lunch tab!" Doc nodded and gave her an okay sign with one hand, and he pointed at Paul and shook his head and said, "No." She smiled widely at the boy and said, "There you go. Doc's got it!" She turned to another customer while Paul stood there, taking up space at the small, crowded counter. He was surprised at her response since he had hoped to fluster her and tease her. She continued to wait on others, ignoring him in a polite way. He went back to his table with three other guys who were watching him and laughing at him. Julie could tell that some sort of bet had taken place, and evidently, the senior had lost the wager.

At the table the boys huddled together, laughing, getting serious, and then looking over at Julie from time to time. Paul had a plan to get a date with Julie, and he made a bet with the other boys that he would score by the third date. Julie's handling of the candy transaction interrupted his plan temporarily. He didn't like to look bad. She not only didn't let him have the candy, she yelled out to Doc who made sure to charge him, and then she ignored him. He was committed now. Girls just didn't turn him down. Once he had them in his car, he had them. Period. He would get her. He just had to work out the details. Before he left the Blue Bear with his friends, for a moment he looked over at her as she continued waiting on other kids. She glanced up and saw him watching her. She flashed him a smile and went back to her work. He told the others to go on back to school. He planned to walk with Julie. When it came time for her to eat, Julie perched up on a stool at the counter and began eating her lunch. Paul came back in and sat on the stool next to her. Doc kept an eye on them from a distance.

"Why did you tell Doc on me? Can't a guy have a *piece* of candy now and then?" He said it, knowing his remark using "piece" would be taken poorly. He didn't know that Julie did not understand his reference.

"You have to pay for candy. You took it and didn't pay." Julie was uncomfortable with him. He was very cute, she thought—tall, big, strong, and scary. She had seen him in school but had never spoken to him.

"Well, I will pay. You could have let it go."

"Yes, and I could also lose my job." She looked at him, and then turned back to her lunch.

If he planned to take that one down, he would have to change his tactics. She had a point. She was wasting no time eating that hamburger. They both had to get to classes. His time was short.

"Okay. I didn't think of it that way. I'm sorry. Look, I was flirting with you, just trying to get your attention. Let me make it up to you. I'll walk you back to school and let's talk. I'm Paul. You've probably heard of me. I'm a senior. I play football." He was trying to charm her, but he wasn't sure if his approach was working. Julie was definitely not used to boys flirting with her. If the guy's idea of flirting was trying to steal a candy bar, she didn't want any part of him. He was older by three or four years, and he shaved. She wanted him to leave her alone. Julie finished her lunch, threw on her coat, and while Paul was paying his bill at the cash register, she ran out the door for school. He had assumed she would wait for him. Wasn't he just about the coolest guy in school? Doc took his time making change as he watched the interaction. Doc reminded him that he needed to pay for candy and not give the girls a hard time if he wanted to come there at noon. Paul was distracted, and between trying to see where Julie was and giving passive attention to Doc's lecture, he was not his usual cool self. Doc even dropped some coins on the floor to stall in giving Paul his change. Paul waited impatiently, and he bolted for the door when he had his change in his hand.

Julie had almost reached the school grounds when Paul left the Blue Bear. He called out to her, trying to get her to stop running. She looked over her shoulder as she opened the school door. She was relieved that he was unable to even get close to her, and she hurried to her locker and to class, hoping she would not run into him. She made it to her class on time, and even though she had the correct books with her, she still had on her coat. When she reached her desk, she collapsed quietly; gathered her book, notebook, and pen; and prepared to take copious notes from Mr. Keltner's blackboard full of information about world history.

On the bus going home, Julie told Kelly about Paul trying to take the candy and then wanting to walk her back to school. Kelly was amazed. "He's the most popular guy in school! He goes with really cool girls. What do you think of him? Are you going to date him?" Kelly could not believe Julie's good fortune to have Paul ask her to walk with him to school.

"He's good-looking, that's true. But, Kelly, he scares me. He tried to steal the candy bar, and he's—well—big! I'm more afraid of him." Then Julie added, "And besides. There's no way my folks would let me date anyone. Not at least until I'm sixteen. Maybe not then."

"Me, too. My folks won't let me date. But that's not a problem! No one's asked!" Both girls laughed, melting into their private conversation on the ride home.

Julie was glad that Grandma Julia had come to live with them. She loved having her help with the cooking and chores, but most of all, she felt that her grandma was the main reason she had not been hit or beaten for over two months. Mother seemed to enjoy going to work, and that helped both girls keep from being the targets of her anger or depression. Helen loved school with Mrs. Anderson as her teacher. Helen loved having Grandma live with them, too. Grandma found time to braid her hair and iron both girls' clothes. She also made them some basic items to wear: blouses, vests, and skirts that fit them just right. At times they seemed like a normal family. Getting lulled into a sense of calm and security was not necessarily good. Being caught off guard might mean more pain.

After dinner when Julie went out to finish the chores, Betty followed her. Once she was in the barn, Betty asked her who the boy was that was running after her at lunchtime. Julie was caught by surprise.

"What boy, Mom?" How did her mother know about the incident at lunch?

"That tall blond boy with the letter jacket on who was yelling your name and trying to get you to stop and wait for him."

"That boy tried to steal candy today, Mom. I told Doc, and he charged the candy to him and gave him a talking to about trying to pocket the candy. That boy was mad at me for turning him in." Betty looked at her with piercing eyes. She slapped Julie as hard as she could.

"You liar!" Betty hit her again, that time with her fist squarely in Julie's left eye. Julie fell back against Smokey, who moved when Julie's weight fell against her, and the cow's movements threw Julie off balance. Betty slammed her fist into Julie's nose. Julie tried to hold onto Smokey.

"Mom! Help me! I'm falling!" Julie lost her balance and fell under Smokey. "Help!" Smokey backed up, lifting her hoof up and putting it on Julie's arm. Julie used her other hand to move Smokey away from her and to the side before the whole weight of the cow could crush her arm.

"Mom! Ask Doc! He'll tell you. I was running away from the boy because I was afraid of him. Just ask Doc. Please." Julie had fallen in the stall and had cow manure on her hands, hair, and clothing. Betty grabbed her and pulled her up, only to push her farther into the darkness of the barn with punches, jabs, kicks, and another blow to her face.

"You can betch yer goddamned life I'll talk to Doc!" She left the barn. Julie was dazed by the beating and sat rubbing her arm. If Smokey had put full weight on that arm, it would have broken. She used the nearby shovel to help herself stand. She cleaned Smokey's stall and the rabbit cages, and she ran the large shovel through the chicken coop. They were all perched at that time of night, making it easier to clean under the roosts. When she went into the house, she headed first to the bathroom to assess the damage her mother had done to her face. She saw her bloody face, swelling eye, and manure streaked hands and clothing; even her hair had manure in it. She knew she needed a bath immediately. Grandma looked at her and hurried to her with outstretched arms.

"Watch out, Grandma. I have manure all over me." Tears had fallen freely in the barn while Julie completed her chores. When she saw how awful she looked, the tears began again.

"What happened to you, child?" Grandma helped her take off her coat. "Don't worry about me. I clean up just fine. Let's get these clothes off."

"Thank you, Grandma." Tears, feces, blood, and dirt streaked her face. She was a mess.

Betty said loudly, "She fell. I helped her up. She fell when she was doing chores. That's right, isn't it, Julie!" There was no question in the demanding tone of her voice what comment she expected from Julie.

"Mom helped me up." Julie didn't explain that her mother had caused her to fall and knocked her down, blackened her eye, bloodied her nose, and may have loosened some teeth. Julia knew that there was more there than either of them had said, but she was more focused at the moment on getting the wounds cleaned and the manure out of Julie's hair and off her body. She helped draw a bath for Julie, took her feces-covered coat, and told her to stay in the bathroom. Julia set the coat outside and returned to help Julie clean her wounds. Julie cried softly. Tears flowed easily. She had dared to believe that her mother was probably never going to hit her again. She hadn't been ready for her mother's attack. She had no time to protect herself through clever songs or quick thinking. No one was near for her to tell out loud or to witness her actions. She also had no makeup to cover her wounds and would have to go to school looking like she had been beaten. Well. She had been beaten. If she looked too bad, her mother would keep her home.

Grandma put a small partially frozen steak on her eye and nose to help reduce the swelling. Between applications of the steak, Julie soaked her hair in the bathtub, shampooing several times, and then draining the tub, cleaning it, and then drawing clean water for another bath without feces or blood. Grandma carefully prepared bandages for Julie's nose, and then she covered part of the broken blood vessels and bruises around her eye. In the meantime, Helen was trying to be as invisible as she could, coloring a picture in her room and waiting for Julie to finish her bath. She watched discreetly as her mother paced the living room. She could tell that her mother was not yet finished with her need to explode. She hoped her dad would get home before someone was hit again. She had a feeling that she was the next one since both Grandma and Julie were in the bathroom. Then she heard the car drive into the garage. She exhaled and waited for the door to open and her dad to come into the kitchen. Helen was glad that he was home, but she knew that he would believe that stupid story about Julie falling. How could she fall on her eye and nose? Even though Helen was only seven years old, she felt that her dad's lack of knowledge about her mother's treatment of her and her sisters was hard to believe. He had to know. She wondered how he would respond to the story. She was afraid to trust him because he did not make her feel safe.

Betty told Dewey that Julie had fallen while doing chores.

"Where is she?"

"In the bathroom with Julia. I helped her up, but she was pretty dirty from the fall."

"How did you happen to be in the barn right when she fell?" Dewey was suspicious.

"I don't know. I was checking on her like I always do."

Dewey knocked on the bathroom door. "Hey, what's going on in there? Can I help?" Julia opened the door about an inch with a bandage in her hand and told him to wait a few more minutes and they would be done. "I want to see her before you finish with that bandage." Grandma covered Julie with a towel and moved the bandage aside to show Dewey her eye and the left side of her face. Dewey was very angry. Calmly, he asked, "Did your mother do this to you?" Julie was quiet. Tears flowed again. "I need you to tell me in order to make this stop. Think about it." Dewey looked intently into his daughter's frightened eyes. He knew that a fall would not create multiple injuries.

"Mother, leave the bandage off for now. Let's ice it some more first." Dewey went to the kitchen and poured himself a cup of coffee. He saw Helen setting the table.

"Did you see Julie fall? What happened?" Dewey watched Helen as she continued rounding the table with the flatware.

"I didn't see her very much, but Grandma did. She took her to the bathroom right away." Helen looked at the table and the flatware, but not up at her father. He walked to her and lifted her chin upward so he could see her face.

"Tell me what you think happened to her." As Dewey waited for his daughter to answer him, Helen glanced toward her mother who was standing in the doorway.

"She'll be out soon, Daddy, and you will see for yourself." Helen answered him softly with tears in her own eyes running down her cheeks. Dewey saw the look of fear in Helen's eyes and prepared himself for the worst. Her expression told him that she was afraid to tell him and afraid of her mother.

Grandma came out of the bathroom first, then Julie. She was clean, holding the cold steak on her eye. Her dad came up to her and moved the steak aside to see the bruising and swelling forming there.

"Tell me how this happened. How did you come to fall? And tell me the truth. Exactly how did you fall and where did you fall—every detail." Dewey looked straight at her, holding her firmly with both of his hands as he guided her to the sofa. He made eye contact with her and nodded to her, encouraging her to tell him what had happened. Julie could not remember her dad ever asking for a detailed explanation after he had seen either her or Darlene following a beating. She decided to trust him, knowing the risk was great and that another beating might follow.

"I was milking Smokey, and Mom came out to the barn. I stood up and just about lost my balance." Julie paused and took a breath. "Mother asked me about a boy at the Blue Bear today who was running after me when we went back to school. I told her that he tried to steal candy today and that I turned him in. Doc made him pay. The boy was mad at me. I took off for school while Doc talked to him. He ran after me when Doc was done with him. Mom was angry and didn't believe me." Betty moved behind Dewey so Julie could see her. She was shaking her head, as if to say no. Dewey saw Julie looking at someone behind him. He blocked Julie's view with his head and moved closer to her. Julie continued, "She hit me in the face with her fist, causing me to fall in Smokey's stall. She hit me and kicked me several times, then she helped me up afterward or Smokey might have stepped on me. That's the truth." Dewey looked at her eye. He looked at Betty. He saw Helen who was hugging her grandma's waist.

"How many times did she hit you?" Dewey asked. "Your nose is possibly broken, your eye is going to look like you were in a boxing match, and your lip is swelling. Let me see your teeth." Dewey had Julie open her mouth. He could see blood along her gum line. "You'll be lucky if you keep your teeth on this side. Try not to work them over with your tongue. They may just heal and stay if you are careful with them. Now, how many times did she hit you? I see three areas damaged, so she hit you at least three times, right?" Julie nodded that she had. "And kicks, where did she kick you?" Julie moved her hand to her side, back, ribs, and then just shook her head and cried. Dewey held her for a few moments. He guided her back to Julia and indicated that she could bandage her nose. "She needs some ice on that off and on before bedtime. Can you do that, Mom?" Julia nodded that she would take care of her.

"Betty, we need to talk. Put on your coat." Dewey moved her toward the back door and out into the cold yard. While Betty was getting her coat, Dewey was taking a few deep breaths. He had to handle things calmly. He could feel his fists double up, but he knew that if he used violence on Betty, he was no better than she was. He had to handle it right.

When the two of them left the house, Julie, Julia, and Helen could not help their own curiosity and went to a window overlooking the yard, hoping to see whatever they could. There wasn't much to see. Dewey and Betty went into the barn and shut the door.

Dewey spoke first. "I told you that I would not have you beat my children. No more abuse." His voice was steady, thoughtful, but firm. "You doubled up your fist and hit that child several times to make that kind of damage! You knocked her down and kicked her."

"No! No. I just hit her once, and she was lying to me. That boy was sitting by her when she was eating, and he's probably her boy-friend. Do you want her pregnant like her sister? Do you?" Betty tried to defend her actions. "I'll prove it to you. I'm going to the Blue Bear and talk to this Doc and find out about this boy and Julie. I'll show you that she's lying!"

Dewey raised his hand. "Betty, I told you not to abuse my girls again. Whatever Julie did we can deal with together, and we don't have to hit her with our fists. No hitting. No fist beatings. No kicking. No, no, no!"

Dewey moved toward Betty, backing her toward Smokey's stall. Betty felt caged. "Let's go see Smokey." Dewey took Betty into the cow's stall area of the barn. "I don't know what I can do or say to make you stop the violence. I can tell you what is going through my mind right now. I'm wondering how you would like to fall down under Smokey. I'm wondering how you would like a black eye your-self. Do you think I could hit you just once and cause your nose to break, your eye to swell up, and your mouth to bleed? You're violent, and you're a liar." Dewey did not raise his voice, but his tone was strong. He sounded like he was thoughtfully and seriously contem-plating beating Betty.

Betty looked at him wide-eyed. He had never hit her. She had hit him, but he had never raised a hand and hit her. He grabbed her with his hands, one on each arm, and firmly held her.

"Look at me, Betty." She turned aside, but then decided she bet-ter cooperate. "Tomorrow I am turning in the forms to have you committed to the Warm Springs State Mental Hospital. I think that anyone who beats her children as you have done is a prime candi-date for an insane asylum. I've put this off too long and Julie's paid dearly for it."

"Oh, God, Dewey. No." She begged and sobbed, pleading with him to change his mind. "I swear that I will never do it again."

"I hope that is true. I have everything ready to go. I want to see a major change between you and the girls. A major change. You better decide that you want to get along and make this house a place where those kids feel safe. I want to see it happen beginning right now. Tonight! You quit terrorizing my children!"

Betty sobbed and made promises that she would change and that the girls would be safe. When they went back to the house, the girls and Julia could see that Betty had been crying. They did not expect to hear Betty's comments.

Dewey spoke to Julia loudly enough for the girls to hear him. "Mother, I want you to write down a description of Julie's wounds— the eye, nose, mouth—and also the whole mess you cleaned up, and what Julie told you about the cow. I'd like you to do it now while it's fresh on your mind." Betty knew that Dewey wanted her statement in case he needed it for some official purpose, perhaps a sheriff's report.

"I'm sorry, girls, that I have been making you afraid of me and being so strict with you. I'm going to stop doing that. I really am. I don't know why I do it, but I know that I won't do it anymore. Really. I'm not going to hit you anymore. Julia, please don't write anything too bad. I know I can change." With that, she turned and went to the bedroom. Before she could leave the room, both girls went to her and put their arms around her. They all cried together, and then Betty went into her room alone. Dewey watched the girls embrace their mother and wondered how they could love someone who beat them and threatened to kill them.

Before lunchtime the next day, Betty stopped in at the Blue Bear and talked with Doc. She asked him about the boy who was running after Julie. Doc explained that the boy tried to steal some candy and that Julie had told him about it. "When I saw him try to talk to her, I could tell from her actions that she wanted no part of him. I purposely detained him so she could get a head start to school. She ran all the way, and he tried to catch up. I watched right here out the window. But he didn't come close. He was upset because she told me that he tried to steal the candy, and I think she was afraid of him."

Betty was quiet. Doc continued, "She's doing a good job. It helps to have her cover the candy counter. She's good at making change and keeping the kids from taking the candy. I used to get blindsided all the time with kids taking stuff when I wasn't looking. I'm glad to have her work here."

"Thank you. I'm glad she doesn't have time to get into trouble." Betty left the Blue Bear and went back to work at the store. Julie had told her the truth, and she had beaten her. For a moment, Betty felt bad about hitting her. Just for a moment. It had been some time since she had used physical force, and she had to admit that it had felt good. The release—the feel of her fist on flesh. She would try to avoid doing it, but she felt stronger that day for having done it. She also had to get Julie under control again after Julie told Dewey about her whispering, and then about her last abuse. Then Dewey threatened her with being committed for her violence. The more she thought about the previous night and her hitting Julie, the more she began to see how important it was to protect herself. Julie was telling on her. How could she regain control of her? She decided that she had no regrets. Betty was convinced that Julie deserved her punishment. She would make Dewey see that Julie lied to her. Would Dewey talk to Doc himself? He might do that, and then Betty would be caught in the lie. Betty was confused. She had to think of a plan to keep Dewey from committing her. She decided to wait until she had a plan that would keep her out of an institution and still get Julie under control. Maybe it was time for Julie to get sick.

When Julie arrived at work, Doc noticed that she had a bandage on her forehead and one on her nose. The closer he came, the more obvious it was that Julie had been hurt badly. She had combed her hair over part of the eye bandage, but the wounded, discolored skin was bruised and still swollen. She had trouble getting her arm out of her coat sleeve.

"What happened to you? Who hit you, Julie?" he asked.

"I fell."

"If Paul did this to you, I'll never let him in the place again! I'm calling the cops!"

"No. Paul didn't do it. I fell."

"Someone hit your eye and your nose. Paul seems like the likely candidate. We'll talk after lunch." Doc left her at the candy counter and went to cook hamburgers at the grill.

Julie sold candy quickly and efficiently, even though one eye was not seeing clearly. Her arm was also hurt from the fall in the barn. Very few kids seemed to notice her bandages. They had their minds on candy and getting back to school. Time moved by quickly, and Julie was ready to eat her lunch. Doc brought her lunch and sat by her. Her lip was also swollen, making chewing difficult.

"What happened?" He waited. Julie sat quietly, unable to eat the burger.

"Let me get you something else." Doc took the hamburger away and brought her some soup with crackers and cheese. Between bites, Julie tried to explain the fall in the barn. Doc was adamant that a fall would not blacken an eye or break a nose. "I'll go along with the fall, but first someone hit you to cause the fall. Who did this to you? Did your dad hit you?" Just then two sheriff's deputies came in for lunch. They took a seat in a booth across from the counter. Julie watched them, her eyes following them to their booth, and then continued to see them look at the menus. Doc noticed her intent interest in the deputies.

"Julie, you need to tell me who hit you, or I'm going to have the sheriff look into this. I'm still thinking Paul had something to do with this. These two deputies are here right now. Let's talk to them."

"Please don't talk to them." Julie was almost crying.

"Okay, okay, okay. Look, if you tell me the truth, it's our secret. I won't tell anyone else. Now tell me."

"If I tell you and you tell anyone, my life could end. You're asking me to risk my life here." Her mouth was so sore that she could not speak clearly. Julie's tears were rolling down her cheeks. Her pain and fear were deep and real. How could someone so young fear for her life? He could see that she believed it. He could see that she was terrified.

"Come to my office in the back room." Doc picked up her soup bowl and led her to his office.

Julie went to Doc's office. She sat on a small padded chair and he sat at his desk. She ate the soup and crackers.

"What's this all about? What happened to you? You have my word that I won't tell." Both paused in silence.

"Yesterday my mother saw me run to school, and she saw Paul running after me yelling my name. She thought he was, I don't know, trying to be my boyfriend, or that I was his girlfriend. Anyway, I told her he tried to steal some candy and I told you, and that he got mad. He was chasing me because he was mad at me." She took a breath. "Honestly, he asked to walk back to school with me, but I didn't want to do that, so I ran. I didn't tell her that part. I just said I was afraid of him and took off running."

"Okay, your mother came in here this morning and asked me why you were running to school."

"Oh, no! What did you tell her?" Doc could see intense fear in her face and hear it in her voice. She trembled as she leaned forward, her hand on the desk.

"I told her that you caught a boy stealing candy and told me. He got mad about it. That's about it. She asked if he was your boyfriend. I said that I didn't think you had a boyfriend. I had never seen you with any boy. But, tell me. Who hit you?"

Julie was silent and seemed to be searching for her voice.

"It was your father, wasn't it? He did this, didn't he?" Julie denied it vehemently. "Then who? Your mother did this? Your mother hit you!" Doc said it in a way that indicated his own lack of belief that her mother did it.

Julie looked as though Doc had ripped a mask from her face.

"Has this happened before? Your mother hitting you?"

More silence. Then Julie said, "She does that sometimes. She loses it and just lets go."

"Julie, nobody should have to live like this."

"My grandma lives with us now, so it doesn't happen as much. My sister and I stay around her a lot when Mom is home. It's not as bad as it was. Also, Mom works now at the store and that keeps her busy. She has other things to think about, and we're not alone with her."

"If you had a chance to live somewhere safe where you didn't have to worry about being hit or beaten, would you go there?"

Julie looked at Doc questioningly. "I could never leave my sister. We'll make it. We're going to make it. Besides, Mom can't seem to help what she does. I love her. I just wish I didn't make her so angry." She wondered what Doc meant about being somewhere safe. What place was he describing? She had a place to go where she could escape her fears of pain and even dying: her imagination. That would have to do until she became eighteen.

Doc called the principal and told him that Julie would be a few minutes late returning to school because he had her do some extra work and that he would not do that in the future. Julie went back to school, wondering if her mother was watching her today as she had the day before. Would she ask why she was late going back to school? What was in store for her when she went home? Doc wrote her a note to take with her to school.

Julie took the note to the office and the secretary gave her a pass to class. She had never shared information about her abuse with anyone before. She felt a sense of fear and a sense of relief. The thought that her mother might kill her was never far from her mind. At least now someone might ask some questions about who the killer was. And then, just maybe, Helen would not die also.

57

THE CALL

Doc was upset. He cleaned the grill to keep himself occupied and cooked up the hamburgers as the orders came in. Lunch orders slacked off about 2:00 p.m., and he had some time to process what he and Julie had discussed. She was safe in school. He had noticed a small card pinned to the bulletin board at his church. Although he had read it a few times while waiting in the church foyer for services, he never thought he would need the information. He told Sarah that he had to run an errand, and he went to the church to find that card.

The message on the card stated, "No one should have to live with abuse. No one." There was a phone number. Doc wrote down the phone number on his order pad and returned to the Blue Bear. He went to his office and made the call.

"Hello, I'm calling about an abuse situation. I saw your card in our church. What do you do when you find an abusive situation?"

"Could I have your name, please?"

"I'm not sure I want to give it yet. I just heard of a bad case of abuse, and I thought I'd try to find a way to help."

"Hang up the phone and call back from a pay phone."

Doc hung up the phone. He went to a pay phone at a nearby service station. He placed the call and deposited coins as the operator directed.

"Hello, I just talked to someone a few minutes ago about—"

"Is law enforcement involved? Police or sheriff's offices?"

"No. I thought about that. The child said that if she told any-one she would be killed. That's probably an exaggeration, but she's scared and she believes it. This is a small town. People tend to look away when things like this come up. I thought that if the sheriff's office did get involved and went to talk to the family, the girl—oh, she has a sister she's afraid would also get hurt or killed—anyway, if the sheriff left them there, and the abuser lives right there, well, it could turn bad for them. The sheriff or deputy might not believe the girl."

"Do you know who is doing the abusing?"

"Yes. And I believe the girl. It's her mother. She was here this morning checking on the girl's story about an incident yesterday in my business. I believe the girl is telling the truth and that she is in harm's way at her home. She has a black eye and a broken nose and other damage."

"We have helped several children. We do an investigation of each situation to be sure serious, life-threatening abuse is taking place. No one, except the reporter—you, in this case—even knows we conduct the investigation. Then we help them. We have funding that helps them go to college or trade school. We also teach them not to be victims or to feel guilty. Children can be made to believe that it's their fault when their abusers victimize them physically and emo-tionally. We've seen severe burns that seared the skin, broken bones, amputations—you name it."

"You come here and investigate, right?"

"Right. If it isn't serious, no one ever knows we were involved, except you, the reporter."

"You said you help them. What do you do for them?"

"Each case is handled individually. Believe me, we provide them with a safe life where they can get up each day knowing that no one will harm them."

"Okay. My name is Derrick Ames. I live in Libby, Montana. I run a business called the Blue Bear on Main Street here in Libby. People call me Doc like in the Archie comics."

"Someone will contact you in a few days. He will identify himself to you in some way, and you will know that person is the investigator. Do not ask anyone questions. You might give us away. Do not call this number again. Never call it from your home or business." The person hung up the phone.

Doc and his family attended Mass as usual that Sunday. Doc liked the quiet before church. He could think about the past week, look for ways to improve his life, and get ready for the next week. He loved his wife and children, and he was happy to have his own business that was successful enough to pay the rent and to provide for his family. His children were good students, and he loved being a father. During Mass, his mind wondered to Julie's situation. He sat by his children and could not imagine hitting them the way Julie had been beaten. He hoped that he was making the right move in getting help for her. He had to stay anonymous. Who knows what her mother might do if she found out he was trying to get help for her children.

The sermon was excellent due to a visiting priest. Doc was not one to complain about sermons, but Father O'Malley's sermons tended to get long winded at times. The visiting priest was eloquent. After Mass, as the people were filing out and shaking hands with the visiting priest, Doc made a point of commenting on the excellent sermon as he shook his hand.

"Thank you, Father Flynn. I enjoyed your sermon this morning."

"Ah, you stayed awake then," he said as he smiled and shook Doc's hand. "What's your name?"

"Derrick Ames. Just call me Doc." Doc smiled and said that he really listened and that he usually tried to stay awake as he laughed with the priest.

"Well then, Doc, Father O'Malley said that a couple of the men in the parish might give me a hand this afternoon, say one o'clock. Could you stop by the parish? I promise it won't take long."

"Of course, Father. Shall I bring any tools or anything?"

"Ah, yes. If you could bring your toolbox, it could come in handy."

"Shall I bring my sons to help?"

"No, just you. I have already asked for the help I need from others. Just come alone." Father smiled, and then moved down the line of churchgoers, shaking hands and greeting them with comments and smiles.

After lunch Doc loaded his toolbox and drove to the parish. There were no cars, other than one he assumed belonged to the visiting priest, parked by the parish house. He must be the first one to arrive, he thought. Doc took his toolbox out of the back of the pickup and went to the door. Father greeted him and invited him in.

"Have a seat, Doc. Can I get you a cup of coffee? I'm getting one for myself."

"I'll have one with some milk if you got it."

Father returned with the coffee. "Well now, Doc, tell me about this child that you called us about on Thursday." Doc just about spilled his coffee. The priest was the investigator.

Father Flynn took notes while Doc gave him Julie's name and description, her parents' names, the name of their business, their home address, and how he came to know about the abuse. He made sure to tell him about the little sister and Julie's comment about both girls being hurt or killed if her mother found out that she told anyone. He also told him about the older sister who married before school started. He knew of rumors that she was pregnant. Father asked him a few questions about the town, where people gathered for coffee, and if Julie's parents participated in any organizations. Doc did not know the family well. He had met Dewey and liked him. Doc commented that Dewey visited with various business owners and was well liked in the community. He noted that he really had not met Betty face-to-face until she came in asking about Julie the week before. He had heard that Betty was sick a lot.

Father cautioned Doc to keep their visit confidential. He told him that their operation was a godsend to the children that they saved, but it was an illegal operation that was not sanctioned by the church or the government. A few private citizens got together and decided to do what they could for abused children. What they had been doing could be credited with saving hundreds of lives. However, it could all come crashing down if anyone exposed the operation. Father pointed out that if Doc said nothing, he also protected himself. He would not want exposure. He just wanted to help a child. Right? Exposing the children's underground railway to safety would only keep future children from being helped. Doc agreed that he would keep the whole situation a secret. He swore he would not even tell his wife. Father Flynn thanked Doc and then sent him out the door, praising him for his technical expertise with the hinges on the garage door. Bringing the toolbox was Father Flynn's ingenious way of providing Doc with a reason to be there if anyone saw him. It was reasonable to believe a parishioner would fix some hinges at the parish house.

58

QUESTIONS

The investigation began quietly. Several people helped who had no idea what the overall goal was. They gave information about families and friends to trusted people, and in a matter of a few days, Father Flynn was convinced that Julie and Helen were in serious danger. Dressed in a plaid shirt and work pants, Father Flynn went to the Bowman home while the girls were at school and the parents were at the store. He introduced himself to Julia and said he was a friend of the family. He brought her some rolls from the bakery to get her to let him in. She wasn't about to let him in until he asked her if she could give him any information about child abuse. She looked at him soberly. He took out his identification that verified him as a pastor.

"Someone believes that the children who live here may be in danger. Do I have the right house?"

Julia let him in. She offered him coffee and a chair at the kitchen table.

"I am told that the children are fortunate to have you living here, and that your very presence protects them from harm most of the time."

Julia looked at him and then at her teaspoon. She quietly stirred her coffee and said nothing.

"To protect the children, please say nothing of my visit with you. I think you know that if Betty found out she would do great damage to these children, and maybe even to you."

When the pastor said Betty's name, Julia broke the silence. "I have done what I can. Last week's incident was not expected. I was in the house. I should have gone out to the barn, but I didn't see it coming. Usually I can see it coming and intervene." Julia took out her handkerchief to dry her eyes.

"Do you believe in your heart that the children are safe from her abuse?"

"When I'm here, I can make a difference."

"Be honest. Could you really stop her if she decided to use a weapon? Look at the guns over there." He pointed to the gun cabinet with several rifles and a few handguns. "Could you really stop her? Would she use one of those?" Father Flynn pointed to the guns. He took a deep breath and continued in a very serious tone. "Do you think she would kill her children?"

Julia looked at the gun cabinet, and then she looked at the pastor. "When she gets in a rage, she could do anything."

"Could she kill them or you?"

Julia thought, swallowed hard, and then said quietly, "She could kill us all." Julia shook her head and cried. Father Flynn gently put a hand on her shoulder.

"Trust me, Julia. Never speak of my being here. Never share our conversation with anyone. I believe that you will feel safer yourself if you never tell anyone we met or that I was even here." Father Flynn put his arms around her and she sobbed in his arms. He left her there in her sadness. Telling someone the truth about Betty's violence was frightening to her, but still Julia felt better having told the priest. She feared for her own life, as well as the lives of the girls. She felt that the stranger had a plan that might help them. Maybe he would see to it that Betty was hospitalized where she could get help and no longer abuse her children.

She watched him drive away and silently prayed for her grandchildren's safety.

Paul was not about to give up on his quest to date Julie. No one turned him down, and he hated looking bad in front of his friends.

He had confidence that once he had a chance to talk to her she would fall all over him like the other girls did. He watched for her after choir so he could meet her in the hall. When she passed him, she was talking with Kelly. Kelly looked over and saw Paul trying to move in by Julie. Before she could do more than slightly nudge Julie, Paul spoke up.

"Hi, Julie. What class do you have next?" Then he saw her bandaged nose and eye. "What happened to you?"

"My next class is English, and I fell." Julie walked along with Kelly while Paul tried to look as though he were with Julie. English class for her was up the stairs. Paul's next class was on the main floor. When they reached the stairs, Paul said that he would see her at the Blue Bear at noon. Julie and Kelly walked up the stairs.

"He really wants to see you. What are you going to do?" Kelly was concerned because she knew that Julie could not date and would not sneak around and do it anyway. The popular boy could hurt Julie by saying things about her.

"He'll get interested in someone else by tomorrow. I can't date him or even sit with him at the Blue Bear. If my folks came by...you know I just can't take a chance."

"Maybe I can help you," Kelly offered. "I'll sit with you while you eat lunch, and we'll walk back to school together. Okay?"

"Thank you, Kelly. Let's do that." Julie was glad to have Kelly as her friend. Paul would not want to look bad in front of Kelly.

59

OBSERVATION AND
CONFERENCE

Mrs. Clark noticed the patrol car passing by her house several times. The students noticed it also. Every time students entered and left, the car seemed to be hovering nearby. One of the students said that it looked like someone in the car was taking notes.

"Maybe someone's parents are checking up on one of us just to make sure we are at practice," one of the students said to another within hearing of Mrs. Clark. The students told her that they saw the sheriff's car and wondered if she knew why it was out there. Mrs. Clark seemed intent on practice and kept the students involved in singing. When she held practices, she wanted to accomplish something. She was a taskmaster, but she also had some snacks for them, and the students really enjoyed being at her apartment.

The next day at school during choir practice, the superintendent walked in with his clipboard and took a seat as though he were conducting an observation for evaluation. Mrs. Clark saw him and tried to do her best to get the students seated and ready to sing. For the observation, she wondered why he was sitting so he could see the students more than watching her. She moved through her lesson, and the students sang several numbers. Mr. Cole was looking at the students, but was more focused on the boys than the girls. He observed them watching Mrs. Clark. He had roughed out a seating chart of the choir and made check marks where the boys sat. As he watched intently, he seemed to be able to tell which boys were paying attention and were involved in the music, which ones were screwing around, and which ones were taking the class for an easy credit. As he watched the students, he began circling places on the chart and then noting the names of the boys seated in those spots. After several songs, the shuffle between songs, and the teacher's comments to various students, Mr. Cole had determined that four boys in particular seemed to have an intense look in their eyes as they focused on their teacher. Dan was one of those boys. When Mr. Cole left the class, he thanked Mrs. Clark and the students for their music, and he told her that he would meet with her in his office right after school or during her planning period today. She said that her planning period would be better for her.

Mr. Cole went to the counselor's office and visited with Mr. Van Meter. "Tell me what you know about these boys." Mr. Cole shared the names and took some notes as Mr. Van Meter talked.

"Jerry is a top student academically. He cooperates in class. His dad works for J. Neils and his mother doesn't work. Dan is new to us this year. He is adopted, part Indian, lives out of town about eight miles—that place with the extra car bodies toward Kalispell. He's quiet, plays basketball. Del is a quiet boy whose parents went to Libby schools. They've lived here for years. He does well in school or at least a B average. And Dick's family, another local family, has been in Libby for generations. Dad runs the hardware store; his mom helps out or stays at home. Average to above average grades. Anything else?"

"Yes, how do they get along with other students?"

"Let's see, Dick is outgoing and well liked. Del is funny, popular, and so is Jerry. Dan is a loner. Kids like him all right. Stays to himself a lot. I've heard that he runs home to stay in shape for sports or because he has no ride after basketball. He plays basketball this season. Below average grades, but improving. He's been getting a lot of help from Mrs. Clark. He's in choir and the coach mentioned the other day that he was glad Mrs. Clark was helping him stay eligible for basketball. What do these boys have in common, Carl?"

"Oh, nothing. I was just curious. I saw them all singing in choir and just wondered about them. Thank you, Jack." Mr. Cole had a strong idea of one student in particular that he wanted to shadow for a few days before his next meeting with the sheriff. He had his secretary get him a copy of Dan's schedule, and he visited with the coach about how he was doing in basketball.

"He's my most dedicated player right now. He's aggressive, never misses a practice, stays late to shoot. I couldn't ask for a better player." Coach Ross found praising Dan easy.

"What's his downside, Bill?"

"Two things. His temper when he's playing. He can get really aggressive. I need that at times, but when Dan gets too riled up, he can't seem to come down from his anger easily, and he gets himself in foul trouble. The other side of that—he scares the hell out of the other team, and that works well for us at times."

"Yes, I know this boy. He's fun to watch, I'll admit. He runs without tiring—great on a fast break. You said he has two things. What's the other thing that's a downside?"

"His grades. Especially his math grade. Although lately Mrs. Clark has been helping him. She's been tutoring him for several weeks."

"How's that been going?"

"He went for about a week, then he wanted to quit. In fact, he came to me and wanted to talk to me about it. He doesn't talk much. I was busy at the time, but I told him to stick with Mrs. Clark and get that math grade up so he could play. Mr. Green pushed him to keep up the tutoring also. For some reason he didn't want to do the tutoring, even though he had improved his grade from failing to a C. Then I guess he decided to buckle down and study. He continued tutoring with Mrs. Clark, and, well, he meets with her at least two or three times a week."

"Thanks, coach. Good luck with the weekend schedule. Arlee is always a tough game." Carl Cole was surprised at what he had learned in one morning about the potential situation. He decided not to wait a week to meet with the sheriff. He had his secretary set up a meeting that afternoon.

When Mrs. Clark came in for the conference during her prep period, Carl Cole had a few questions for her. He had set up his questions to allow her to elaborate in areas where she had confidence, and then he would see what he could get from her about Dan.

Mrs. Clark was nervous about having a conference with Mr. Cole. Usually the principal did the evaluations. She was concerned about why he might be evaluating her. Mr. Cole's secretary welcomed her and alerted Mr. Cole that she had arrived.

"Send her in, please." Mrs. Clark went in and sat down. "I know everyone calls you Mrs. Clark, but I was wondering if you mind if I address you as Sandra."

"That would be fine, sir. I always have the students call me Mrs. Clark to make sure they know I am not one of them."

"I'm glad to hear that, and I agree that is a very good thing to do. While we are talking about students, do you find that any of your students act in an inappropriate manner? I ask because I have had new teachers worry about students getting too familiar with them in a personal way, and the teachers don't quite know what to do about it." Mr. Cole expressed himself in a gentle, concerned way.

"Well, I guess my students want to get along with me. I have lots of enjoyable times with them. Really, I can't think of any students who ever act inappropriately. They may act up in class and talk when they are supposed to sing, for example. I haven't had any flirting-type behavior. Being married helps me, I think. They all know that my husband is in the service."

"Let's get to the lesson. I enjoyed the selection of music I heard today, Sandra. How do you decide which songs you use for any given time of year?"

"I have learned many musical arrangements in my training, but I try to match up what I have learned with what I think will work best with my students. For example, I normally would not use the 'Ave Maria' for a high school group. When I realized I had a student with the voice to pull it off, I went for it, and it worked out well. Did you attend the concert?"

"Yes, I did. Who sang that solo? I recall her being a freshman, and I admired her composure. I don't think I could have done that myself, even if I could sing." Mr. Cole laughed softly.

"Julie Bowman. She has a clear, strong voice. I was surprised when I first had her audition for that song. I really didn't think I would be using it, even though I love the song. She pulled it off in practice, as well as in the concert. I think we'll be hearing her often. She loves to sing, and it has increased her self-confidence."

"How do you set up your practice schedule for after-school groups, and what are the student requirements for attending after-hours practices?"

"There just isn't enough time for all the groups to practice during the school day. We have solos, trios, quartets, an octet, and three other ensembles. I also have several students taking piano lessons. I set up a schedule that accommodates the students and their parents as much as possible."

"Let's pick one group. The boys' quartet, for example. Do these boys have sports practices and quartet practice?" He was getting to his student of interest as nonchalantly as he could.

"Two of the boys have both basketball and quartet. I schedule their practice around the basketball schedule."

"Who are the two boys?"

"One is Jerry Owens, and the other is Dan Eagle."

"Are they both able to keep up their grades with the load of both sports and music? Are they doing well in their academic classes?"

"I think Jerry is an honor roll student. Dan has had grade problems, but I have tutored him in math to help him keep his grades up."

"When and where do you tutor him?"

"Usually on Wednesdays right after practice at my apartment. Sometimes right after school in my office."

"Is that helping his grades?"

"The coach asked me to keep helping him so he wouldn't have to worry about Dan's eligibility. Mr. Greene is happy with the improvement also."

"Well, thank you, Sandra. I plan to give my notes to Mr. Erickson. He can consider my comments when he does your evaluation. I appreciate your interest in the music program. You seem to care very much for your students." With that comment, he held the door for Mrs. Clark as she was on her way out.

When Mrs. Clark was leaving the office, Sheriff Burns was walking in. Carl Cole thanked Mrs. Clark again, and then made a point of introducing her to the sheriff. "You two have probably already met, but Sheriff, this is Mrs. Sandra Clark, our music teacher. Mrs. Clark, this is Sheriff Marty Burns."

"No, I don't believe we have formally met, but I have heard a great deal about you, ma'am. Your music program is well known around town."

Mrs. Clark smiled her warm, friendly smile. "Thank you, Sheriff. It's a pleasure to meet you. I've been reading about you in the papers. Please excuse me. I have a class in a few minutes." She left to get ready for her next class.

"That was timed well, Carl." The sheriff said quietly as the two men went into Carl's office and shut the door.

"Yes, it was. I found out some things today, and I thought it best to tell you so both of us can have a productive week. What I have learned may not pan out, but then again, it might."

"Good. What did you find out?"

Carl told him about observing the music class and spotting the young men he thought showed the most interest in Mrs. Clark. He shared the counselor's information on four boys of interest, and that one of the four boys got tutored two or three times a week.

"Mrs. Clark tutors this boy on Wednesday nights after practice. He's quiet, adopted, stays to himself, dedicates himself to basketball. He's a loner and would be easy to target. He tried to quit working with her, but two teachers pushed him into sticking it out. I think he could be our boy, or—I hate to say this—but one of our boys, if this is true." The sheriff was interested and wanted to see Dan.

"Come over to the gym if you can about four thirty today and we'll see him at practice. We can watch a little and not pull him out or anything. I just want you to be able to recognize him if you see him at her house."

"I know him. I've seen him play. But I want to get a closer look and maybe talk to him if it works out. I'll come over. Let's take our time on this so we get it right. I would hate to have some unidentified accuser ruin a person's life. And use us to do it."

"You got that right!"

"However, I would also hate to see students taken advantage of by not checking this out. You never think these things happen in your town or your school. Let's hope we find some answers and that we take care of this the right way." The sheriff was committed to resolving the issue, and he appreciated the superintendent's investigative work.

60

THE THIRD LETTER

Carl Cole monitored Mrs. Clark's classes, all grades in both buildings during that week, looking for other students who might need help. The sheriff not only continued monitoring Mrs. Clark's apartment, but he had narrowed down Dan's tutoring time to Wednesday evenings when he was there alone with her. Mrs. Clark noticed the additional observations and the sheriff's attention being more than usual. She thought that meeting him at the office had piqued his interest in her, and he might be trying to get to know her, yet he was too shy to step forward, or he was married.

When she opened the plain envelope with no return address, she read the contents slowly. She put the letter on the table, poured herself a Coke, and then sat down. She read it again. Some passages caught her attention: "You are being watched by your supervisor and the sheriff's department…dirty little secret is out…sexually preying on innocent children." She looked out the window and saw the sheriff's car passing by again. The words were clear. Someone knew. The superintendent never observed teachers. The principal did that. She thought about his questions during their conference. He asked about Dan. He asked about other students, but he definitely asked about Dan. She needed time to relocate. The note indicated that she had a month. But if the superintendent and the sheriff already knew, they could have her arrested that night.

She turned back to the letter. "If you are still teaching and living in Libby in thirty days, I'll send the story to the *Western News*." She decided to pack everything she could in her car, leave the rest behind, and leave on Saturday. That would give her two days to change appointments, cancel future lessons, and pack her few belongings. She could be out of Libby by Saturday afternoon. She could say there was an illness in the family. Who would be ill? Fortunately, she was from Wisconsin, so no one really knew her family or her personal situation. Her husband was in the service. *I can say that he had an extended leave due to a medical reason. That's it! He was injured in the line of duty.* She began creating a story of his life-threatening injuries and his need to go to the Mayo Clinic. Being the dutiful wife taking care of her husband was the best excuse she could use, and people would accept it as a reason to leave suddenly and, of course, not come back. People might even feel sorry for her. Her emotional concerns subsided as she regained her confidence and direction.

There was a lot to do. She had to resign formally in a well-worded letter to the superintendent. That might prompt him to have her arrested. She would resign by mail. She could mail the letter to the school on Saturday. That would work. No one could know prior to her leaving town. She couldn't tell anyone, not even Dan. Especially not Dan. She spent the next hour preparing her letter of resignation. She wrote it several times before she decided to keep it as short as possible. *My husband was injured. He's being sent to the Mayo Clinic for medical reasons. I have to move there immediately to care for him. I'm sorry to leave without notice. Mrs. Wilson can substitute for me. Oh, yes. I'll miss the kids.* That was the content, but getting the words to fit together professionally took time. She made a late trip to the grocery store and picked up some empty boxes to pack her dishes, glasses, and other breakable items. There was a stack of newspapers near the boxes, which she also put in her car. Before she went to sleep, she had packed two boxes. She had a plan, and she needed to sleep.

At school the next day she canceled her after-school activities and weekend practices. Dan asked her after class, with a questioning expression, what was going on.

"Nothing, Dan. I just have to be away for a couple of days." He went on to class. He was all booked up with basketball, but he knew that he would not be getting a ride home after the out-of-town game.

He did not want to be with her anyway since she had other "interests," but the rides helped him out on cold nights. He would plan ahead on that with his dad.

To avoid as much attention as possible, Mrs. Clark put items in her car after dark, watching for any traffic or students, and avoiding as much attention to herself as possible. She was particularly watching for the sheriff's car. His car went by twice, but she was in the apartment both times. She packed her trunk full first, and then she began putting items into the backseat. She had no furniture of her own, so her main items were her clothing, sheets and blankets, dishes, flatware, bathroom items, and music. Lots of music. It boxed up easily. What about the piano? She arranged in another letter for the Bowman Music Store to pick up the rented piano. With her backseat full to the windows, all she had to do was throw in her blanket, pillow, sheets, and ukulele in the morning and drive out of town.

She tried to sleep. Her mind kept working, recalling the superintendent's visits to her classes, meeting the sheriff in the office, and hearing about both of those men attending practice. Dan had told her about it. Dan had said that the sheriff talked to him, told him how much he enjoyed the games with Dan's running and rebounding. He had even mentioned his getting his math grades up and taking advantage of tutoring. He even asked Dan if he was happy and if he was adjusting well to Libby after moving last summer, along with other personal questions about how his tutoring was going and if he was getting along with his teachers—naming Mrs. Clark specifically. The sheriff's car had driven by her apartment every night several times each night for the past week. About midnight, she dressed in her traveling outfit and threw the last items in the car. She drove by the post office and mailed her letter of resignation, other letters that terminated her resident requirements, and the transfer of her mail to her parents' home address. She used residential streets, staying away from main streets until she reached the edge of town. When she reached Highway 2 near mill row, she drove out of town toward Kalispell. There was no reason to stay and every reason to go. The risk of exposure and losing her teaching certificate became real to her for the first time. She loved teaching and sharing music with children. Her behavior could have taken that all away—and it still might. She would change, she told herself. Dan was not her first young lover, and he wasn't even the only one in Libby. When she came to Libby, she had told herself that she would not pursue boys. That was the second time she had come close to being discovered. She turned on the radio, sang along with some rock 'n' roll tunes, and watched for deer and other animals on the highway as she headed east toward her new life.

The deputy assigned to keep track of Mrs. Clark notified Sheriff Burns that she had driven out of town at 12:45 a.m. In spite of the late hour, Sheriff Burns checked her apartment. She had moved out. He called Carl Cole.

"Hello."

"Sorry to bother you at this late hour, but I thought you would like to know that your music teacher just left town."

"She left? Moved?"

"Yes, I just checked her apartment. Cleaned out. She's gone. My deputy said she mailed some letters before she drove out of town. I assume one of those letters is addressed to you."

"This is sudden."

"It may be sudden, but it's damn helpful. Looks like she was guilty."

"Yes. In some ways it's very helpful. We avoid a lot of problems with students and parents. Can you just see what we might have had to deal with? Parents sue over this type of thing. Hell, I'd sue if some woman sexually abused my son. But all that aside, I have to find a music teacher to cover for the rest of the year."

"Go back to sleep. You can solve that Monday."

"Thanks for the call. I appreciate knowing. Let's wait for the letter, if there is one Monday, and see what she has to say. Stop by, if you want to, after ten when we get our mail and help me sort through the letters."

"Okay. I'll do that. Good night, Carl."

When they ended the phone call, both men thought in different directions about the consequences of the teacher leaving town. Carl was thinking about getting a replacement teacher. Sheriff Burns considered the crime and the victim or victims. What impact had her molestation had on the boy? Were there other victims and how many? Usually by the time a person was caught in that kind of crime, there had been many victims. That type of abuse could have a lifetime effect on a child's self-esteem, confidence, and ability to socialize. Unfortunately, some of the abused carried the crime inside and made it part of their own lives by abusing others. Sheriff Burns believed that most abused people learned what not to do and went on to live appropriately, raising their children up right. Some did. Some did not.

At school on Monday, Carl asked his secretary to call the buildings to see if there were any teachers needing substitutes that day. He wanted a list of the teachers who were out that day for whatever reason. She gave him the list and Mrs. Clark's name was there. He drove to the post office and asked at the window if he could pick up the school's mail. Although that was a bit unusual, the postal clerk gave him the large box of mail, the typical way the mail arrived at the central office before being sorted into the building piles. When he returned to his office, he and his secretary sorted through the mail and found the letter from Mrs. Clark. He took the letter into his office and opened it privately.

"Dear Mr. Cole, I regret having to leave my position so suddenly, but I just learned that my husband has been badly injured in the line of duty, and I need to be at his side. Please consider this my resignation from my teaching position effective immediately. I have enjoyed my students and fellow teachers and staff. My best regards to everyone. Sincerely, Mrs. Clark."

Carl called the state department of education office in Helena. "Please connect me with certification. Thank you. Yes, I am in need of a music teacher immediately to finish out the school year. I called your office because I thought you might have information about recently certified teachers in our state." Carl was rewarded with the name of a newly certified teacher who graduated from Concordia early with a music teaching degree and was living in Cut Bank. Within the hour, he had contacted Phyllis Jonas for an interview set for that afternoon at 3:30 p.m. She sounded excited on the phone. He had decided that, unless she had a record for theft, murder, or sexual abuse, she was going to be Libby's new music teacher. His next call was to Sheriff Burns, confirming the arrival of a letter indicating that Mrs. Clark had left town for good. Carl reviewed Mrs. Clark's letter again, especially the sentence about "enjoying my students." She had indeed enjoyed some of her students. May God help them, he thought, as he filed her letter in the back of his bottom drawer so it would not be discovered unless he wanted it for some future legal reason.

Carl called his secretary into his office, where he quietly told her that Mrs. Clark was not coming back and that he did not want that to become common knowledge until he decided to provide that news himself. In the meantime, he told her to prepare some interview questions specifically for a music position before noon.

"Check out your interview questions file and put together about ten questions I can ask a potential candidate. I have someone coming this afternoon that may be able to fill in for the rest of the school year. Music is a hard position to fill, so don't make the questions too hard. We need this one now."

"Yes, sir, I can take care of that. Do you want anyone else to sit in on the interview? A board member? Parent? Teacher?" She was covering her bases on a short time line.

"Ask Mrs. Church to come in after school. The interview is at three thirty. Just tell her that I want to see her in my office right after school. Don't say anything about the interview. Also, see if Darryl Wood can come. I like having a board member for interviews. Again, just ask him to come over at three fifteen today, and I'll fill him in myself. As far as anyone is concerned, Mrs. Clark is sick today. No further information. We're going to call this 'sick leave' due to illness.

But that's not anyone's business but mine right now. And if I hear that any news got out that didn't come from me, I'll—"

"My lips are sealed, sir. I look forward to hearing the story myself, sir. I will not say a word." She left the office and made the contacts as directed. Both Mrs. Church and Mr. Wood agreed to meet with Mr. Cole after school.

Phyllis Jonas arrived in Libby about 2:30 p.m. and drove through town, looking at the main street and the businesses on Highway 2. She also drove by the schools. She had been to Libby several times as a student at Cut Bank High School. She had attended several sporting events, and she loved the mountains. Libby was beautiful. Cut Bank had a different beauty: flat plains with a distant view of the Rocky Mountains many miles to the west in Glacier National Park. She arrived at the high school at 3:00 p.m. One last look in her mirror told her that her blond curly hair looked great and her minimal amount of makeup accented an attractive, youthful, and energetic face. She felt a bit nervous but confident. She knew it could be hard to find a teacher to finish the year. But they could have a substitute who could do it. She wore a light blue tailored suit and a white blouse with black conservative heels. She practiced saying her name and smiling into the mirror. Enough! She was ready.

Mr. Cole's secretary met Miss Jonas at the front door and escorted her to the superintendent's office. Carl introduced her to Darryl Wood, a board member, and Mrs. Church, the freshmen and sophomore English teacher. Within moments, Carl began asking questions, and Miss Jonas answered each question to the best of her ability. Less than thirty minutes passed before the interview ended and Mr. Cole was asking her when she could begin.

"If I can find a place to stay for a few days, I could begin tomorrow. I packed with that in mind. I may seem very eager, sir, but I want this position, and I am ready to give it my best."

"I'll find a place for you for the rest of the week if you can really start tomorrow." Carl was amazed at his luck.

"Good. Could you take me to the former teacher's classroom? I would like to review her plans, see what she has been doing this year so I can come up with lessons for this week." Carl asked his secretary to round up a key to the music room and office, and he escorted Phyllis Jonas to her classroom.

He gave her a tour of the school along the way. Very few people noticed the tour since school had been out for over forty minutes. Phyllis Jonas was thrilled and had difficulty containing her joy. She was delighted when the superintendent had finished showing her around the music room, the practice rooms, and the one practice room designated as the music office. It had a piano crammed into it. She loved it. He left her there and said he would be back when he had word of a place she could stay for the next few nights.

Finally, she could relax, take several deep breaths, and really take in what had occurred that day. She had an interview, she was hired, she was getting ready to prepare for the next school day, and she was ecstatic! Mrs. Clark was fairly organized, and Phyllis was able to find the yearly lesson plan book and the list of all of the private lessons, ensembles, solos, and piano students preparing for the music festivals. She could tell that she was going to be extremely busy attempting to fill the entire schedule of rehearsals and lessons, and she was excited to give it her best effort. The choral selections were familiar to her, and the elementary lessons seemed organized and ready to present. Mrs. Clark had the added incentive of Mr. Cole's observations and interest that had prompted her to get her lessons organized during the previous week.

Mr. Cole held a brief staff meeting the following morning. He announced that Mrs. Clark had left unexpectedly due to her husband's health issues and that she would not be returning. He introduced Phyllis Jonas as Mrs. Clark's replacement, and he encouraged the staff to assist her in settling into the program in any way possible. He requested that questions be directed to him as necessary after the meeting, and then he dismissed everyone to get on with their busy day. Several teachers made their way to Phyllis Jonas and introduced themselves. The room cleared quickly as staff prepared to start the day. Students began flooding into school. Fifteen minutes later, the bell rang, the halls were clear, and classrooms were buzzing with a range of activities. Each teacher read the prepared statement to the first period classes: "Mrs. Clark has returned to her home in Wisconsin because her husband was injured in the line of duty and needs her there. Miss Jonas is taking her place for the remainder of the year. Please give your best assistance and welcome her to Libby High School."

The news of Mrs. Clark's departure caused the most unrest in the high school choir class. When Miss Jonas introduced herself, she could see the emotional reactions of the students due to the loss of their beloved teacher. Many of those students had spent time in private lessons and rehearsals preparing for the music festivals and several concerts during the year. Some of the girls were in tears. Miss Jonas let them ask her any questions, and she tried to answer them as well as she could.

"How did you know she was leaving? Did you take her job away from her?" a weeping girl asked in a soft, but accusatory way.

"I regret to say that I have never met Mrs. Clark. I can tell that she has done a great job with all of her students. When she found out that her husband was badly injured, she just had to be there for him because she loves him and he needs her. Mr. Cole contacted the state certification office looking for a music teacher, and they told him about me. I know you are all unhappy, and I know that I cannot take Mrs. Clark's place in your hearts. But you and I know that she would want you all to do well in the upcoming festivals. She was very proud of you all. I hope that we can work together and complete the work you and she started this year." Phyllis watched their body language. An idea hit her. She had nothing to lose, and it might work to lessen their heartbreak.

"Let's get going on our festival stuff, and when we complete our work, we can make a recording of everything and send it to her. She will love to hear all of your solos and ensembles, and of course the choirs and all their songs. We can do that!" It worked. They bought it. They started getting out their music. "Pick a song you especially like from the festival music and let me hear you sing it."

Miss Jonas took them forward, and they went with her and gave her their hearts and their devotion. Within the week, no one mentioned Mrs. Clark. There were many other areas in their lives, and they did not want to dwell on the loss of the music teacher. Phyllis had a built-in piano lesson schedule to augment her income. Not only did she receive her wage as a teacher and a stipend for festivals and concerts, she also took over the piano lessons of sixteen students who paid for private lessons. She kept the rate the same and enjoyed the extra income.

One day after choir, Dan asked her if she knew anything about math. Dan had been earning a solid C on his own after getting tutoring from Mrs. Clark.

"I'm sorry...Dan is it? I'm sorry, Dan. Although I liked math, I don't really feel competent to tutor anyone. Also, right now I'm pretty busy learning Mrs. Clark's job, with all the outside lessons and all. Can you get your math teacher to work with you?" Dan nodded, gave her a shy grin, and almost gave the impression that he was flirting with her.

"Are you sure you don't have time?" Dan moved close to her, causing her to step away from him. She picked up a handful of music and held it between them.

"I'm very sure, Dan. Check with your math teacher. He can either help you or find someone who can." She sensed his inappropriate interest, and she made sure that she did not feed into it. In college, one of her teachers had talked to the class about students who become attracted to their teachers, and the lesson was clear. Never get involved. Even though they seem mature, they are students. The teachers who get involved risk everything, including their teaching certificates. Without exception, a teacher-student intimate relationship was always the teacher's fault and often led to jail time. She had experienced students' crush-type attention when she was student teaching. She recognized Dan's body language, tone, eye contact, and his total demeanor. She shut him down without hope and redirected him to another professional way of getting math assistance.

Dan had hardened himself against trusting Mrs. Clark. He knew that she had used him, along with at least one other student. Her sudden departure, however, sent him off kilter. Why hadn't she told him she was leaving? When he saw her last, after she canceled their "lesson," she said she had to leave town for the weekend. She knew then that she was not coming back. His decision to use her and no longer trust her was a good one for him. He had seen her less often, and he knew that she had stepped up her time with Joey. His need for sexual gratification caused him to flirt with Miss Jonas. He hoped that she hadn't noticed his obvious flirting. He was embarrassed as he thought back on his own behavior when asking for math assistance. He knew that he would not go down that road again. He had a chance to be free of Mrs. Clark and any possible negative connection with her. Although he embarrassed himself with Miss Jonas, he felt relieved that she did not respond to his unspoken invitation. His commitment to sports was where he intended his focus to go, full time. He would stay in choir for the easy grade, but his heart was directed toward basketball and track. He also thought he could befriend Joey. Having a friend can help when someone has messed with your body and your mind. He could do that for Joey. Being a friend to Joey had a mutual result for both of them. Joey wouldn't feel as deserted, and Dan could play the big brother role that he wished he had known growing up.

As he walked to the gym, he saw Joey.

"Want to shoot some hoops?" Dan's invitation has an interesting effect on Joey. Joey looked at Dan with a blank stare at first. Then his face brightened up. He stood up, walked toward Dan, and made a minimal, but happy comment.

"Yeah, okay." The two boys went into the gym and shot baskets for the rest of their lunch break. Dan gave Joey a couple of pointers on shooting without taking the fun out of the game. Joey was delighted to get the coaching, even though he ended up losing at "horse" about six times before the lunch bell rang.

"See you tomorrow? I might beat you again!"

"You bet. I'll be here!" Joey's body language was positive as he ran off to class. Somehow spending time with Joey made Dan feel better. It was the right thing to do. Dan had not had the feeling of doing the right thing for a long time.

61

THE PLAN

Every day that Julie and her sister stayed in their home was another day their lives were at risk. Father Flynn had to get them out. The plan was in place. Doc dropped off his two sons at school, passed by the high school office, and stopped in to ask the secretary if she had a sports schedule he could have. When she turned to get one for him, he quietly slipped the note onto the counter and left the office. Several people came and went from the office before the secretary became aware of the note. When she discovered the note, she had a student take a pass to Julie to come to the office. Julie read the note.

"To the Attendance Office: Please excuse Julie from school at 11:00 a.m. Have her pick up her sister Helen from Mrs. Anderson's room and walk to their parents' store. We have business to attend to, but did not want them out of school all day. Thank you, Julia Bowman (grandmother)."

The secretary saw that the time was already 9:30 a.m. She prepared a pass and gave it to Julie, advising her to keep track of the time so she could leave as her pass indicated. She also called the elementary school and let the principal know that Julie would be picking up her sister at about 11:00 a.m. She moved on with her day.

Julie checked out of the high school office at 10:45 a.m. and picked up her sister by showing Mrs. Anderson her pass from the high school. The two sisters, bundled up in their secondhand coats, boots, mittens, and caps, walked out of the school.

Doc was watching for the girls, and he signaled Father Flynn when the girls were getting close. Father Flynn was waiting in his car between the Blue Bear and the Dome Theater. Doc went out to the sidewalk and met the girls.

"Girls, this is your ride. Meet Father Flynn. He's taking you to your family. I made you both lunch! Climb in!" Doc continued talking about milkshakes and hamburgers. He handed the girls the food. "Don't worry! This is going to be fun!" Father Flynn drove out of town in his black car with the dark windows. The girls were enjoying the food. They particularly enjoyed the milkshakes, not knowing the drinks were laced with a sleep-inducing substance. Julie wondered why their parents had the man pick them up. When she'd asked Doc where they were going, he only repeated that they were going to have fun. She trusted Doc. Even though she had not felt comfortable going with the old man in his big car, she had gotten in the car and took Helen with her.

The girls had finished only part of their food when they could no longer stay awake. Helen's milkshake fell from her hand, and when Julie reached for it, she knew that something was wrong. She could hardly move her own hand, let alone catch Helen's milkshake container. The last thing she remembered before she lost consciousness was crossing over the river on the Kootenai Bridge. Within an hour, Father Flynn was helping the pilot carry the girls to the small plane. The girls did not wake up during the loading process, not even when they were belted into their seats. There were pillows placed carefully around their heads to support them comfortably during the flight. Both the pilot and Father Flynn knew the dangers of cutting off their air supply if their heads flopped uncontrollably during turbulence. Both girls were packed safely for their long flight. The men placed ear protectors on the girls to buffer the sound of the plane's engine. Somewhere over Canada, Julie dreamed of flying. She worked hard to open her eyes and briefly wondered where she was. She saw Helen to her right and blue sky to her left. She could not hold her eyes open, but she was able to find Helen's hand near hers. She put her hand on Helen's as she surrendered to sleep.

Betty had not spied on Julie that day. A customer was in the store asking questions and considering the rental of a piano. The rental would help their income over time. They did not have a piano on site, but she had received a letter from Mrs. Clark about returning her piano. She thought that Dewey could pick up her piano and have it delivered right away. Betty was busy throughout the day. She did not want to take the phone calls from Julia, but she reluctantly took the call at about 4:30 p.m. Betty changed her attention from her work to Julia's comments when Julia told her that the girls had not arrived home on the bus.

"Did anyone call from school today?" Betty asked.

"No one called. I was here all day within the sound of the phone, and no one called. Maybe they missed the bus. I thought that either you or Dewey could check at school for them. It's just too cold for them to walk."

"They missed the bus! I'll talk to Dewey. We'll take it from here." Betty was angry. She grimaced, trying to control herself. She went to the back of the store and told Dewey that the girls had missed the bus. Dewey could see her anger swelling up.

"I'll go get them." He didn't give her time to respond. He grabbed his coat, gloves, and hat, and he was in the car before he had his coat on completely. She had to stay to take care of the store and she had no ride. It was too far and too cold for her to walk the length of Main Street to the school. He did not want her to be the first to find the girls for fear of her reacting violently toward them.

Dewey drove past the high school, watching for Julie and Helen, and then to the elementary school. When he went inside, he asked about Helen at the office and said that she had missed the bus. The principal told him that Helen had left earlier in the day. She walked with Dewey to Mrs. Anderson's room to see if Helen might be there. Mrs. Anderson had already gone home for the day, and no one was in her classroom. The principal called her from the front office phone. Mrs. Anderson told her that Julie had picked up Helen from her classroom about 11:00 a.m. She sent them to the office to check out of school. The principal relayed the information to Dewey.

He worked his mouth, biting his lip a bit to keep from letting his anger take over his reason. He watched the women make calls to find information about the girls. They seemed concerned, but not as concerned as Dewey would have liked to see. Every moment without knowing where the girls were frightened him.

"Mr. Bowman, Julie checked out at about 10:45 a.m. She came here, she picked up Helen, and the two girls left together intending to go to your place of business."

"My mother is at home and said that they missed the bus."

"I believe it was a grandmother who wrote the note excusing the girls."

"No, she didn't. May I please use your phone to call her?" Dewey did not wait for permission. He grabbed the phone and told the operator the number quickly and that it was a very important, quick call. He waited for the call to go through. They had a ten-party line. The operator interrupted a call and asked the two parties if they could give up the line for a few minutes for another important, but brief call. They agreed. Any one of the ten members of the party line could listen in and verify if the call was really important. The call went through, and at least one other person was listening in on the call.

"Mom, are the girls at home yet?"

"No, Dewey. They aren't here," Julia answered.

"Did you write a note excusing them from school?"

"No, I wouldn't do that. Not unless you asked me to write one. No."

"Stay by the phone, Mother. I'll check in with you when I find them. In the meantime, if they show up, call Eric and tell him to call me."

Dewey hung up the phone. He shook his head. "My girls are missing. I'm going to look for them. If they come back to school, please call my home and tell Julia. She is their grandmother, and she did not write any note excusing the girls. I will check in with her." Dewey hurried out the door but then doubled back. He needed their help, and he had been abrupt. "Thank you for your help. I'm sorry. I'm just worried about my girls."

The secretary and the principal were worried. "We understand, Mr. Bowman." The principal put on her coat and followed Dewey out the door. "Cynthia, I'm going to drive around and see if I can find the girls. Mr. Bowman, I will look everywhere I can think of. Please notify the sheriff's office right away." She drove every street in town and the surrounding area for an hour looking for the girls. Three times she drove Highway 2 as far as the Bowman home just in case they had decided to walk home.

Dewey went from the school directly to the sheriff's office and talked to Sheriff Burns. He had Dewey make a list of Julie's and Helen's friends. Dewey did not know which students were friends of Julie's in high school, but he knew several students from the music program. He listed their names as contacts just in case they might know why Julie was not on the bus. Teachers, administrators, the bus driver, students, neighbors, and people with businesses on Main Street were listed, with Doc among them. Dewey called Eric and asked him if he had seen the girls. He asked Eric to help him make calls to anyone who might know where the girls were. Eric was frantic.

"Of course, Dad. Come to my house. It's central to everything in town, and we can work from there. I'm taking off work right now."

Dewey told the sheriff about Julie's job at the Blue Bear. The sheriff decided to talk with Doc in person. Dewey drove almost to the store to tell Betty that their two daughters were missing, but he drove by the ballpark first just to see if anyone was there. He saw some boys playing stickball and asked them if they had seen his daughters. They knew who the girls were, but they said that they had not seen them. He walked over to three kids who were playing in a pile of vermiculite. They were jumping in it, throwing it up in the air, and falling in it, having a great time. They had not seen the girls either, and they agreed to call the sheriff's office if they did see the girls. The mention of "the sheriff" caught their attention for a few minutes, but then they returned to their pile of dust and insulation pellets. Dewey decided to talk to Doc at the Blue Bear before he went to the store. He did not want to face Betty without some knowledge of the girls. He had no idea what her reaction would be. She had yelled out her anger with him many times over the years, blaming him for her loss of health due to having the last two children. Darlene had told him that she was afraid that Betty would kill Julie. He almost feared that she would be relieved that the girls were lost. He couldn't think about that. His own heart was aching within his chest. If he couldn't find his girls, he thought he might have a heart attack. In the back of his mind, he feared that Betty might have had something to do with their disappearance.

Sheriff Burns sat at the counter and Doc offered him a cup of coffee. Both men, coffee in hand, settled into a booth.

"Tell me what you know about Julie Bowman. She and her sister Helen are missing."

"No kidding. You got to find them. Julie's been working for me since shortly after school started. Does a good job. Seems honest, and I felt I made a good hire. Maybe I'll put her on as a waitress this summer. Nice kid."

"Did she work for you today?"

"No, she didn't. She stopped by and said that she had to meet her folks and couldn't work today."

"Was she alone?"

"No. She had her little sister with her."

"Where did they go from here?"

"They went off that way. I didn't pay a lot of attention. I assumed they were going to their dad's store at the end of Main Street. Julie said she had to meet her folks."

"Is there anything I should know about the girls? Her family? Anything that might help me find these two girls?"

"Julie's mother was in here the other day asking about her. That was the first time I met her. Her dad has stopped in for coffee several times. He makes it a point to get to know other business people.

Seems like a good man. Oh, and the kids in music really like him from what I hear."

"What did the mother want?"

"The mother—you mean Julie's mother?" Doc was hesitant. How much should he tell about his interview with the mother?

"Let's see. Her mother had seen a boy running after Julie during lunch earlier in the week. She asked me about why Julie was running to school. I told her that Julie had caught a boy taking candy and she turned him in to me. The kid was just messing around—maybe even flirting with Julie. You know how boys are—just harmless flirting. I think she ran to school so she wouldn't have to talk with the boy. She's a quiet girl. The mother asked if the boy was her boyfriend. I told her that I didn't think Julie had a boyfriend." Doc was saying too much. Sometimes the truth was more information than anyone needed to know.

"How did her mother act? Worried? Angry? What?" Sheriff Burns asked.

"Closer to angry than any other thing. Julie came to work later that day with some bandages on her face and a sore arm. Somebody had hurt her."

"Did she say who had hurt her?"

"I asked her if the boy had hurt her; you know, the one she turned in for taking candy. She said no. She didn't want to talk about it, so I left her to her work." Doc knew that the banged-up condition of Julie's face was going to be revealed by her teachers at school. He needed his story to be consistent with theirs.

"What's the boy's name?" The sheriff was taking notes in detail now.

"Paul. I'm not sure of his last name. He's a good kid. Plays football. I think he was flirting with her and it didn't go well. I don't think he hit her, though. Julie is quiet. I don't see her with boys. She and her girlfriend used to come in now and then for candy. They walk together, but neither of them comes in with boys. Now that she's working here, I can say that she doesn't have any boy eating lunch with her or walking her to school. Kelly has eaten with her and walked to school with her. But, hey, they're freshmen. Give 'em a couple of years and then see the boys chase 'em!"

"What's the girlfriend's name?"

"Kelly Holland. Dad's a rancher out on Market Road." Sheriff Burns recalled the name from his investigation of the child found buried near the Holland ranch. He knew Tom to be helpful in that case, and he counted on that help again in finding out information about the Bowman girls.

"Thank you for the coffee, Doc. I may need to talk to you again. In the meantime, if you hear anything that could help us find these two girls, please call me right away. I won't kid you. I'm worried about them and the sooner we find them, the better."

"I sure will, Marty. I'll keep my eyes and ears open. Sometimes I hear a lot in this place." The men shook hands, and the sheriff left the café on his way to the Bowman Music Store. Doc watched him get into his car and drive away. He reviewed what he had told the sheriff. At first his focus was on protecting Julie from harm. He could see how taking the girls out of their home might be the only way to keep them safe. As he thought about it, he wondered to himself why the girls should have to start a new life in a new place when they were the innocent ones. Why hadn't a resolution focused on getting the abuser out of the house? He rinsed out the two coffee cups, wiped down the counter, and began preparing condiments. When he glanced toward the door, he saw Dewey Bowman enter. He walked to meet Dewey at the front of the store.

"I heard that you are looking for your girls, Dewey. Any word yet on where they might be?" Doc had reached out his hand to shake Dewey's hand. Dewey responded, but his heart was not in his handshake. He looked sick and frightened. Doc helped steady him and guided him to a seat.

"Doc, I appreciate your talking to Sheriff Burns. I just talked to him outside. Based on what he said, you might have been the last one to see the girls. No one else along Main Street seems to remember seeing them. Do you have any idea where they went from here?"

Of course, Doc knew where they went from there. He knew exactly where they went. At least he knew who took them out of town. When he looked at the pain in Dewey's face, he wondered if Dewey could see through his facial expression of sympathy to the fear he was experiencing.

"Dewey, I just have no idea where they went. I thought they were going to your store."

Dewey had come in with a slim thread of hope and found nothing to cling to. He rose to leave, but rested his hands on the front counter to steady himself. Doc thought he might collapse right there and offered him a seat again in a nearby booth. Dewey shook his head and put his hand up to his face. "No. Thank you. I have to find my daughters. If anything comes to mind, anything at all, please call my home and tell my mother, Julia. Or call my son, Eric. Here's the numbers. Time is crucial right now. We have to find them." He left the café and went back to the store.

Doc was beginning to understand a larger picture of Julie's home situation. Her father loved her very much, and his losing two daughters was tearing him apart. Doc had played a role in creating that pain, and he was having second thoughts about the whole situation. Two girls were taken from their home due to abuse that could have taken their lives. The abusing mother stayed home, free of any repercussions. The father had a broken heart. Who knew how the girls would take to their new surroundings and having to start all over in a strange place?

Betty was waiting to hear how the girls had missed the bus and were playing at some friend's house. When Dewey came into the store, Betty was quick to jump in. "I'll bet those girls are playing at some friend's house—one of Julie's friends. Maybe at that boy's house—you know, the one who was chasing her." Dewey had not said anything. He let her finish her tirade of blaming Julie. "Well, where are they? Any idea?"

"Betty, I've been to school, to the sheriff's office, to every store on Main Street, and to the Blue Bear to talk to Doc. From what I can tell, no one has seen the girls since they left school at eleven today." It was Betty's turn to be quiet, but only briefly. She had the vacant look that Dewey had seen many times. He didn't know that a soft voice within her head was telling her that Darlene had the girls hidden in her closet. When the voice stopped talking to her, she returned to her conversation with Dewey.

"Are they at Darlene's house? Eric's?"

"I called Eric and Darlene and asked them about the girls. Nothing yet. Let's lock up the store and check every place we can, starting with Eric's because it is close by. We need to get everyone looking as soon as we can." Betty grabbed her coat and handbag, and Dewey locked the door behind them as they went out to search everywhere they could. Betty whispered to herself loudly enough for Dewey to hear her say that Darlene had them hidden in her house. He knew that she was upset, but he did not want to talk about her accusations toward Darlene.

On the way up Main Street and on to Eric's house, Dewey observed each building from the car, asking himself if the girls would go in there or in there. Betty rocked rhythmically in her seat, working a piece of her coat between her fingers. At Eric's house, Darlene had been making calls in the neighborhood, but he had no positive information about the girls. Dewey seemed lost, but he was committed to looking for his girls even if it meant a door-to-door search. Eric had Darlene get anyone she could to search the area around the Bowman home for the two girls and to help him organize a search for the missing girls. She agreed to become involved in a search of the town. When Darlene began to leave the house, Betty flew at her angrily and demanded to know where she had hidden the girls.

"I have no idea where they are, Mother. I'm as worried as all of you are."

"You have them! Look at her house! They are probably sitting in a closet playing while we are here worried sick!" Betty appeared to be looking for someone or something to hold. Family members in the room looked at her as though she were some curiosity and then turned back to Eric as he began penciling off portions of the Libby map he found in the phone book.

"I'll get Tom Holland to check the area around Dewey's home. I'll take this section, from Railroad Street to the hospital. If anyone you talk to will help you cover the area, take them up on it. The sooner we get this town covered, the better chance we have of finding the girls. Dewey, take this section—right down Main Street again. You know these people, and get them to help us. They need to look in their stores—anywhere a child could crawl, hide, or fall—anywhere a child could be. Darlene, take the mill area—all of mill row and in both directions from there clear out past the pole yard."

Eric had called four neighbors, and he gave each of them another section of town. Libby was a small town, but a door-to-door search made it seem much larger. Betty did not seem coherent.

"Dad, take Betty with you. She's not going to be able to stay here. She'll want to keep busy." Eric couldn't leave her in his house, not the way she was acting. He could not send her out alone as part of the search team. "Any news, call Julia. She's at home and ready to take any calls. We can all check in with her, but keep calls short. Remember, everywhere you check get any help you can to look for the girls." Everyone left to search for the girls.

Betty sat in the car while Dewey went into each business. It seemed with every stop he made, he found people ready to help with the search. In less than an hour, over two hundred people were searching for the girls every place in town and along Highway 2 and Market Road, all the way to the Bowman place and beyond. Julia sat near the phone, answered many calls, took notes, and heard a hundred times or more the phrase "not here" from every caller. Julia had asked the operator to keep the line open as much as possible because their girls were missing. Julia explained to her that the family was doing a door-to-door search for two children. Between calls on her switchboard, the operator made calls asking people to search their own homes and yards for the two girls.

By 7:30 p.m., just about everyone had completed the search of their areas, and the relatives returned to Eric's house. The sky was dark and clear; the air was cold. The girls were out there somewhere, and a sense of hopelessness settled into Eric's house as the main search team came together with no children found or even sighted. There was nothing to do but go home.

Julia, Betty, and Dewey had little to say to one another. Julia was quiet and thought about the interview with the priest. Dewey wanted desperately to blame Betty, but he knew that she was at the store at the time the girls disappeared.

Eric had kept involved in the search process all day. Now that each person was going to his or her own home, he had time to check out a plan of his own. That Kootenai River Road might hold the key to his missing sisters.

62

ERIC'S SEARCH FOR HIS SISTERS

Eric drove across the bridge and down the river road with a vengeance. He looked for any side roads, took them, and looked for a black Ford coupe. If that bastard took his sisters to keep him from researching Zonolite, he was going to find him—and maybe also find his sisters. After five side roads, Eric found the Ford sitting by a small trailer. The lights were out. Eric parked, walked all around the trailer, and knocked on the door. A light came on.

A woman in a robe answered the door. "Is the owner of this Ford out here home? He lives here, right?"

"Who are you?" She turned on the porch light to see Eric better.

"He knows me. Is he here?"

"You lookin' for me?" The tall man moved the woman out of the way. "What do you want with me?"

"I want my sisters back. Now! I want you to stay out of my house." Eric was livid.

"I don't know nothin' 'bout your sisters. Nothin'! Hell, I didn't know you had sisters." The man pushed Eric off the porch. "Get outa here before I shoot your ass!" He aimed a shotgun at Eric and loaded a cartridge in the chamber.

"Are my sisters in there?" Eric yelled to the woman who stood looking at him from the doorway.

"No. We're the only ones here. Really." The woman looked angrily at the man. "Put that thing away. We don't want any dead bodies around here." She walked back in the house.

"Get outa here. Now!" The man's voice was as frightening as his gun and his size.

Eric scrambled to his feet and backed up to his car. He got in and drove off. He tried to read the mailbox on the way out, but it was too dark to see anything. When he hit the river road, he took off like a maniac just in case the guy came after him. Eric fastened his lap belt, which he had probably never used before. It was a long way down to the river if that creep decided to run him off the road. He didn't believe his sisters were there, but at least he finally saw the face of his intruder—and he knew where he lived. All he could think about were his two precious sisters being somewhere with strangers. God help them.

Before Eric reached the bridge, lights from a fast-moving car approached from the rear, moved beside him on the left, and tried to force him off the road and over the embankment. Eric tried to push back and hold onto the narrowing space. The Ford backed off briefly, then bashed Eric's car several times, sending it over the embankment. Eric's car went down at least a hundred feet of smooth rock wall, met head on with a pile of rocks, flipped over into the river, and was upside down in the water. The car, moving with the swift, strong current, rolled again, leaving Eric upright about fifteen feet from the rocky, forested bank. He unfastened his seat belt, rolled down the window, and dragged his battered body out of the window. He left the car before it filled completely with the frigid water.

Eric struggled to keep his head above water as he was pulled rapidly downstream by the current. He gradually made it to the rocky bank. Getting out of the river was a challenge, but he finally grabbed onto a fallen tree. He gave in to exhaustion and lost consciousness. He did not awaken when he was wrapped in a bear hide and dragged away from the river.

63

SHERIFF INTERVIEWS BETTY, DEWEY, AND JULIA

The knock at the door was the sheriff. Dewey invited him in. After Dewey let him look in the girls' bedroom, the sheriff sat down with the three adults in the living room.

"I know this is hard for you folks. I know about the search party and the house-to-house effort, Dewey. Good job on that. People respond quickly to the relatives and friends of the family."

"Eric organized that and Darlene helped," Dewey responded. "He had us out there. Julia, my mother—Mom, this is Sheriff Marty Burns—my mother stayed by the phone and everyone called in to her any news they had. You really did a great job, Mother." Dewey complimented his mother sincerely. She cried again, her face reflecting the anguish she was feeling. She showed the sheriff the list of everyone who called in, the times, and everyone she called with times.

The sheriff waited for silence then asked the question that would cause more heartache. "Dewey, Betty, I need clothing from both girls. I'm organizing a team of dogs to search for them. We're going to start right now in town where the girls were last seen, and then, well, we're going to search in some other places."

"My God. Oh, my God." Dewey was fighting tears that forced their way out. "Okay, I'll get some. You want clothing they have worn recently, right?" Dewey asked. "Mother?"

"I'll get some clothing." Julia went to the bedroom.

"That'd be good. I also want their pillowcases. Get those items for me so we can search more thoroughly." Marty thought his request had gone over well.

"Does this mean you think they are dead?" Betty asked. When she looked at the sheriff, he gazed back into her hollow, tearless eyes.

"No, ma'am, not necessarily. Their smell helps the dogs follow them wherever they went." Marty Burns was transfixed by the look in Betty's eyes. He took the clothing and pillowcases to the second car in the driveway, and the deputies drove away to begin the search with the dogs.

When the sheriff returned to the house, he had more questions to ask. "Betty, when I talked with Doc at the Blue Bear today he said that you had been in earlier this week checking on Julie. Can you tell me about that?" Betty was rocking rhythmically again, straining to listen to something or someone, but it was not the sheriff. She held a cushion from the couch and worked the edge of it constantly between her fingers.

"Betty. Can you hear me?" Sheriff Burns moved toward her and touched her shoulder. She looked up at him in a daze, as though seeing him for the first time.

"Can you tell me about Tuesday when you checked on Julie at the Blue Bear? Why did you do that?" Marty was calm, yet he was concerned about Betty's lack of focus. He also knew that people vary in their reactions to crises. Betty was obviously reacting differently from the typical mother, but who was he to judge?

"Yes. I went in to find out about Julie. The day before I saw her running to school after she worked at the Blue Bear. She works there at lunch selling candy. Anyway, I saw her running from a boy. I wanted to find out what that was about. Doc said that she caught a boy stealing candy and told on him. Doc said she ran off to school so she wouldn't have to talk to the boy."

"Did you ask Julie about what you saw?"

"I did. I asked her the same day I saw her."

"What did she tell you?"

"Same thing. She said she caught the boy taking candy and told Doc. The boy got mad, and she was afraid of him so she ran off to school."

"Did you believe her?"

"Well, yes."

"Then why did you talk to Doc about it?"

"Well, I just wanted to be sure she wasn't lying to me. Kids can do that, you know."

"Several people have told me that Julie had bandages on her face. Do you know anything about that, Betty?"

"Bandages?" Betty looked around the room, making eye contact with Dewey. He did not respond to her look, but waited for her response.

"Yes, bandages. Doc and some of her teachers said that she had bandages on her face and that her arm was also injured. One of her teachers said that she had trouble walking and could not participate in gym class. What caused Julie's injuries?"

"She fell in the barn. Julie has chores and when she was out there—must have been Tuesday—she fell into the cow's stall."

"Did you witness the fall?"

"Yes, I was there. I helped her up."

"I need to know more about this situation. Julie may have run away if she felt unsafe. Did any of you, or anyone else you know, hurt this child? I'm asking all of you. What happened to her?" The tone in Marty's voice was firm and demanding.

"Who put the bandage on her?"

"I did," Julia spoke up softly. "I cleaned her up and bandaged her face."

"All right, Julia. I want you to tell me what happened to Julie, what she told you happened, how she fell, everything you know about this accident." His stress on the word "accident" gave a hint of doubt about the correctness of that word.

"Julie called to me as she came in the back door. She had manure in her hair, on her clothing—everywhere, even her face. She told me at first that she fell in the stall. I took her into the bathroom and

I started cleaning her up and I could see that she had been hurt along her eyebrow, her cheek, and her mouth. I used a half-frozen steak to keep the swelling down. I had her hold that while I cleaned her up. She took a bath to get the worst off. I cleaned her hair some more. It took three shampoos and rinses. Then I cleaned the tub and started all over again. This time we got everything clean, and I began putting on some ointment and bandaging her face. Dewey came to the door and wanted to see her face before I bandaged it. I showed him. She also had scrapes and bruises on her body from the fall." Julia wanted to look at Betty, but she did not take her eyes away from the sheriff. Betty had stood up during Julia's explanation, and she walked back and forth behind her while she spoke.

Betty interrupted. "She fell in the cow's stall. She hit her head on the stall. The cow almost stepped on her arm. I pulled her out of the way and brought her into the house."

"Thank you, Betty." Sheriff Burns turned to Dewey. "Dewey, tell me what happened. What did Julie's wounds look like?"

Dewey looked at Betty. He looked at his mother. "I saw Julie's face before Julia bandaged it. It looked like she had been hit hard in the face at least three times." Betty looked at Dewey as though she had been hit. She became much more agitated and picked up a doily from the back of the chair, working the threads between her fingers even harder than before while focusing her gaze on the threads.

"What do you mean, 'hard'?"

"It looked like she had been slugged with a fist three times or more. Skin was broken on her brow and cheekbone, and her lip was bleeding. Her face was swelling even though Mother had put that steak on it. She looked beaten. When she came out of the bathroom, she had trouble walking, and her arm was bothering her. She was supporting it with her other arm. She was in a lot of pain." Betty was looking at Dewey from her new position, almost behind the sheriff, shaking her head and looking at him in a menacing way.

"Did she tell you what happened to her?"

"Yes, she did."

"Betty, would you please sit down." The sheriff's directive had the wording of a question but the tone of an order.

"I'll just stand, if you don't mind."

"I do mind. Sit down. Right here." Sheriff Burns had her sit next to him on the sofa. She continued to work the threads as she sat uncomfortably near the sheriff.

Betty was feeling several emotions. She was angry because both Julia and Dewey told their information in a way that pointed to her as the one who had beaten Julie. She was afraid of discovery and being blamed for the beating, which she had done, and because of that, for Julie's disappearance. She was trying desperately to control Dewey and Julia as she had been able to do in the past through looks and bodily actions, including shaking her head and staring at them in menacing ways. With the sheriff there, her strategies were not working. Underlying every emotion she was experiencing was the fear of confinement in an institution. Dewey had said he would make that happen. In that moment, she feared that the sheriff would take away her freedom. If not right then, it would happen soon. Betty went within herself, dialoguing quietly. She listened carefully to her inner dialogue. *You'll be all right. Stay calm. You can defend yourself soon.*

"Dewey, tell me what Julie told you about her injuries." As the sheriff listened and took notes, Betty stood up and walked behind the couch again. Marty did not have her sit down because she seemed calmer than before. Her hands were not intent upon the threads of the couch cushion as they had been. Dewey retold Julie's rendition of how she had received the damage to her face and body. Dewey told the sheriff that Betty had hit her, knocked her down, helped her up, and then left her in the barn. Julie had finished her chores before coming in the house. Julia saw her and helped clean her up.

Betty was only a few steps from the gun cabinet. *If I am quick, I can open the door and grab the gun.* Her inner conversation was evaluating her situation. She could open it and grab the .45 revolver before any of the three other people in the room could reach her. She could shoot them and run. *If I can just get out, I can take the car, and drive away.* Her mind created another idea. She could fake illness, leave the room to vomit or faint, and then escape through a window. She knew that she was too big to get through a window or to run. Her mind raced wildly, and it would not let her body rest. She feared that the sheriff was going to take her away.

Sheriff Burns stood up and walked near Betty. "It's okay, Betty. I know this is very hard for you with the girls missing and all. Just relax. I'll be through here soon and you can go to bed." He guided Betty to a chair, not the one right by him, and then stood beside her. "Dewey, did Julie say why her mother hit her?"

"She said her mother did not believe her when she told her why she had been running from the boy."

"Betty, did you discipline your daughter for lying to you about the boy? Did you think he was her boyfriend?" The sheriff's demeanor was calm.

"Yes. I thought she was lying. When Doc said the same thing about the boy getting caught stealing, I thought he might be covering up for her. I still think she was lying."

"I appreciate your truthfulness. Parents have a right to discipline their kids. If you thought she was lying, then I can see how you might need to discipline her. Tell me, what chores does Julie have here at home, Betty?"

"She helps cook, does the outside chores. Takes care of Helen."

"Julia, what work do you see Julie do here at home?"

"Oh, my! Julie cooks breakfast and dinner. I'm glad I'm here to help her out. Every day she cooks. She tends to all the animals, milks the cow, feeds and waters the over thirty rabbits, fifty chickens, collects eggs, separates milk, churns butter, and—oh yes—cleans everything...all that manure. She works hard, that girl. Up at five in the morning every day. She also cleans the house and does the laundry. I help her all I can. She cans food, bakes—she takes Helen with her, keeps her safe. I don't know how she does it all. And she sings! She soloed in the concert. I'm so proud of her." Julia was ebullient in her praise of Julie. "She's practically Helen's mother, she's so protective of her—" Julia stopped short.

"I think I'm getting a picture here of what might have happened." The sheriff waited for the three adults to focus on him. "Julie works hard and gets beaten from time to time. Disciplined, I'll say for the moment. She doesn't want to be beaten anymore, so she figures out that with her cooking skills and her experience in taking care of farm animals, she can get work somewhere else, someplace where she won't have to worry about being beaten. She runs away. She can't leave Helen because she's like a mother to Helen, and she wouldn't want Helen to get beaten as she had been."

"I just don't think she would run away," Dewey offered. "She is so responsible."

"Dewey, how badly was she beaten?"

"Bad. Very bad."

"Was she ever beaten before?" "Yes." Dewey nodded and then held his head. "Yes, she was. I shoulda known."

Betty moved closer to the gun cabinet.

"Betty, how often did you beat your children?" The sheriff stood up and took a new position in front of her with about six feet between them.

"Only when they needed discipline. You said it yourself. Sometimes kids need discipline."

"Dewey, how often did you discipline your children?"

Before Dewey could answer, Betty jumped in. "He never did anything to discipline the girls. He left it all to me. He left everything to me—the cooking, the garden, the animals—everything to me while he messed around at the store. Our daughter Darlene married at sixteen, pregnant! Because he didn't do his job as a father and make the girls mind! He's the one responsible for this whole mess!" Betty was angry, strong-willed again, and she was defending herself. "I've been sick! Sick because of his children. I wasn't supposed to have any more after Darlene, but no, he couldn't leave me alone! I almost died with both of them! Ask Julia! She saved my life after Julie was born. Tell him! Julia!"

"That is true. I helped in Julie's birth. It was a hard birth and both of them almost died. I was grateful to be able to help and afraid that I would lose them both." That was the first time Betty acknowl-edged that Julia had helped her and saved her life.

"Let's calm down. Dewey, I think Julie could have run away and taken Helen with her. There's a chance they just caught a ride, but more than likely someone she knew gave them a ride out of town. We'll work the dogs and see if that leads to anything, but in the meantime, we need to get some missing-persons signs out and the newspapers working for us.

"Betty, discipline and beating are not the same thing. From what I hear—and Dewey, tell me if I'm wrong—Betty beat this child. Right?"

"Yes, Sheriff, she did." Betty looked at Dewey with a shocked expression on her face.

"Julia, you cleaned her up. She was badly beaten, right?"

"She was, Sheriff."

By then Betty was just about at the gun cabinet. She had her handle on the door when the sheriff was looking at Julia. Betty had the gun in her hand when the sheriff turned toward her and realized that she was armed, aiming the gun at him.

"Betty, you don't want to do this. You have two girls out there that need you. Don't make a big mistake here by shooting someone."

Betty turned the gun away from the sheriff to a new position: the barrel was on her temple. The sheriff rushed her and knocked her to the floor. The gun went off under Betty. The sheriff held his forceful position on top of Betty, trying not to allow her to move the gun out from under her. Both the sheriff and Betty were still struggling when the gun went off again. Betty struggled less, and then stopped moving. Betty had the gun under her large body. The sheriff feared turning her over while she held the gun. If she had the strength, she might shoot again. He could not risk turn-ing her over to take the gun away from her. The first bullet went into the floor under Betty. The second bullet went into Betty's stomach.

The sheriff saw blood oozing from under her body.

"Push the gun out from under you! Now!"

"I'll kill you first. Get off me! I'm bleeding!" Betty forced the words out, rapidly losing strength. Blood oozed out from under her body, soaking the carpet.

"Push the gun out so I can help you! I'm staying right here until I see the gun without your hand on it!"

"If I let go, you'll kill me!" Betty was weakening, but frightened.

"If you don't let go, you'll kill yourself! You shot yourself with your own gun and you're bleeding. My gun's holstered. See my hands?" He waved his hands near her face to show he did not hold a gun. "Push the gun out!"

Betty was silent. Her body went limp. The sheriff stayed on top of her and told Dewey to call for an ambulance.

After Dewey made the call, he bent down by Betty and talked softly to her. "Betty, let go of the gun. You're hurt and you could bleed to death if you don't let me help you. Just push the gun out to the side so the sheriff and I can help you up." Betty turned her face toward Dewey. He could see blood coming out of her mouth. Her eyes were glazed over and she appeared unconscious.

"Julia, get some towels so when we roll her over we can put them on her wound."

The sheriff began to roll Betty, ready to take the gun. "Dewey, watch for the gun and help make sure it isn't pointed in a way that can hurt anyone." As Betty began to roll over, she still had a grip on the gun handle and a finger on the trigger. She slowly moved the gun from under her large body. Dewey and the sheriff moved simultaneously toward her and the gun. She tried to raise it, aiming it awkwardly toward Dewey, and she tried to fire. He reached out, grabbed the hot barrel as Betty sent a bullet racing past him, grazing his shoulder on its way.

Betty lost consciousness, as well as the grip on the gun. The sheriff took the gun, guarding the handle to protect the fingerprints. Three witnesses should be enough, but hard evidence might be necessary down the road. He was cautious and thorough.

Julia placed the towels on Betty's large wound in her intestines. She had lost a lot of blood. Julia was again trying to save Betty's life. After she placed the towels on Betty's stomach, she and Dewey applied pressure to help stem the bleeding. The ambulance arrived and the attendants took over tending to Betty. One of the attendants cleaned and bandaged Dewey's shoulder wound. Unfortunately for Dewey, the wound itself was less painful than the realization that his wife had tried to kill him. The wound would heal, but the knowledge that Betty intentionally shot him would live with him the rest of his life.

Julia stayed at home in case someone called with news of the girls. Dewey went to the hospital in the ambulance with Betty. Dewey reviewed the day's events. What good could he find in a day when his two daughters disappeared? His son and his neighbors, his daughter and her husband, and his mother had done all they could to find his two daughters, missing since eleven that morning. Hundreds of townspeople helped provide information about the girls—at least, where they were not. And his wife shot him and herself. He evaluated the shooting of the two of them as a good thing, strangely enough. It took that extreme measure to wake him up to his wife's serious illness. Her behavior was not normal and had not been for years. He knew she had mistreated his girls, but he didn't know the extent of that abuse because he didn't want to deal with Betty. He stayed at work late, ignored his family, and let the whole situation get out of hand. He wanted to die. Just die. But he couldn't. He had to find his girls, and then he had to take care of them, as they deserved. No excuses. He had to take care of Betty, too. He had to make sure she had the help she needed to get well. She was sick and needed to get help for her mind. He loved her. She did not want to go to a hospital for mental illness, and he didn't want to take her there. But she obviously needed that kind of help. The four-mile drive made him resolve to change their lives for the better. He was ready to commit to that change.

The ambulance arrived at the hospital in a flurry of noise. Betty was unloaded and given blood transfusions. She breathed on her own for a few minutes. The shot of adrenaline helped for a brief time. In the emergency room, Dewey stayed with Betty. She was on a gurney in a small curtained space. He held her limp hand. He kissed her hand. She turned her head, searching with her almost vacant eyes for whoever was there. When she saw him, she said in a labored manner, "I did it wrong. Dewey. Tell the girls I love them. Find them." Her voice trailed off.

"Betty, do you know where they are? Please, if you know anything, tell me now."

Betty looked into his eyes. "Do you think I had something to do…" She gasped for breath, and then said, "I don't know where they are. I didn't…I'm so sorry." She opened her eyes wide, gasped, and lost consciousness. The emergency staff revived her as her heart, once stopped, started again. Hospital staff moved her to isolation and hooked her up to various machines. Dewey stayed with her.

Marty Burns had called Eric to let him know of the shooting, but Eric didn't answer his phone. He called Darlene, and she and Dick came to the hospital. Darlene witnessed Betty's loss of consciousness, followed by a shock, and then unconsciousness again. She and Dick stood by Dewey, supporting him while Betty was moved to the ICU. Dewey attempted to hold his emotions, but the open arms of his daughter surrounding him melted his demeanor. As the two embraced, a new relationship began between them.

"I'm feeling lost. Thank you for being here. I—"

"It's okay, Dad."

"No, Darlene, you being here—you're a fine daughter. I couldn't ask for better. My girls. My baby girls. This is all my fault." Dewey broke down in Darlene's arms. After a few moments, Darlene guided him to a chair.

Dick and Darlene stepped into the ICU area watching Betty's machines react as she lay in a coma.

"I have to see her." Darlene went to her mother's side.

"Why do you want to see her like this? She may die any moment." Dick did not want to look at Betty.

"When I remember the way she was, I brace for her to hit me. I see her angry, and I feel her wanting to hurt us. I don't want to remember her as she was. I want to know for sure if and when she is dead and that she can never hurt anyone again. That she can't hurt my sisters, my baby, my family—anyone." Darlene looked at her mother. She touched her face. "Someday I'm going to forgive you, Mother. It's just too hard right now." She lifted the sheet up to her mother's chin, hoping that someone soon would pull it over her head indicating the end of her mother's suffering. She walked to her father and sat beside him, her hand on his shoulder.

The emergency doctor gave Darlene a sedative for Dewey. "This may help him sleep tonight. Only one. Be sure he only takes one."

"Thank you, Doctor."

The family regrouped at Dewey's house. They were all glad that Julia would be there with him through the night. Shortly after arriving home, Darlene gave Dewey one pill. He took it, and within a few minutes, he became sleepy. Dick helped him into bed.

Julia had a pot of coffee ready for anyone who might show up. The three of them gathered around the kitchen table. Dick asked Julia if she had heard from Eric. "No, I haven't, and I've been near the phone." Julia described for Darlene and Dick what had happened at the house and how Betty had accidentally shot herself and Dewey. It looked to her like Betty intended to shoot Dewey, but she did not think they needed to hear any deeper tale of violence regarding Betty that night or any night, especially from her. When Dick and Darlene had learned all they wanted to know and the coffee was gone, they quietly checked on their Dad. They regrouped briefly to discuss the missing girls. The sheriff had assured them that he would call if he found the girls, and so they decided to go home. The search of the town had been widespread and thorough but without success. Maybe the dogs would find something—a clue or a new direction. The family went home leaving Julia in charge. They were all exhausted emotionally and ready to give it up for the night.

When Darlene and Dick went into their home, Dick asked her to call Eric. "It's unusual that he wouldn't have been at the hospital or at Dad's tonight."

Darlene called, but Eric didn't answer his phone. She tried his work number, but there was no answer there either. "Shall we drive over to his house? If his car is there, we'll know he's all right." Darlene was worried and wanted to know he was all right as well as fill him in on the shooting incident herself. The two of them drove by his house, but his car was not there.

"I'll check in the morning. He's probably looking for the girls somewhere and will tell us all about it tomorrow."

Two days later, Betty was moved to a nursing home. She was in a coma, and Dr. Seifert recommended that she be allowed visitors, even though she could not hear or see anyone. He felt that the wounds would heal in the nursing home as well as they would in the hospital. He did not expect her to be able to go home for at least a week or two. *The Western News* had time to print a story about Betty's "accidental" shooting. The missing girls were going to be a major story with an obvious connection to Betty. Because of the missing girls, many people were involved in the search for the girls, and they would want to show their concern to Dewey and the family for Betty's serious condition. It was not just a group of nosey, curious neighbors. Those people were shaken up by the loss of the children, and then shaken again due to the shooting.

Eric's car got caught up on some large rocks along the north bank of the Kootenai River. Sheriff Burns shook his head in disbelief when he traced the license plate to Eric Bowman. "How much can one family take?" Eric was not at home and not at work. He was missing. The sheriff delivered the news to Dewey at his home. Dewey was on his way to see Betty when the sheriff's car arrived. All Dewey could think about was Julie and Helen. Had they been found?

Julia watched from the window. She couldn't hear the men, but she saw the sheriff supporting Dewey. She hurried out of the house.

"Sheriff, what news do you have?" Julia asked, yet afraid of what he was going to say.

"Eric's missing. His car was found wedged in some rocks in the Kootenai this morning. We haven't found Eric. Have either of you heard from him? He was not in the car—may have been swept downstream. A crew is searching for him now."

64

DELIVERY

The small aircraft landed on a private runway in a field near Saskatoon, Saskatchewan. It had made two stops for fuel, and the girls had slept through both of them. After the landing, both girls were awake and able to get out of the plane. They did not recognize the area, and neither of them had ever been in a plane. One thing that kept them from panicking: they had each other. They held hands and waited for someone to tell them something about why they were in a strange place getting off an airplane.

The pilot helped them disembark and smiled at them. "I'm glad you girls finally woke up back there. I was getting lonely!" He was hoping to put them at ease, but neither girl smiled.

"Where are we?" Julie watched the pilot, wondering if he would tell them.

"You're in Canada. Safe."

"Safe from what?"

"Listen to me, girls. You won't have to worry about being beaten ever again. No one's going to hurt you here. That's all I can say right now, so just relax and enjoy your new life."

The three of them walked toward a large building, which served as a hangar for several local plane owners. At the hangar, a car was waiting for them. Julie thought about running, but in what direction? And how would Helen keep up? The pilot had said that no one would hurt them. She had to hope that was true. Julie kept Helen near her at all times and she tried to learn more about her surroundings. Maybe her dad was involved in some way. Maybe he wanted her there. The car took the three of them to a large ranch a few miles from the airstrip. Julie tried to memorize the landscape, looking for any landmarks, hoping to get her bearings and find her way to somewhere. All she could see for miles was flat, harvested farmland.

The girls and the pilot went into a big two-story house and were shown into a large room furnished beautifully. Julie and Helen sat very closely together on a soft, comfortable sofa. Someone brought drinks. The girls were thirsty but feared drinking anything. The milk-shakes Doc gave them had taught them a lesson. Both girls looked at the details of the room. Julie was especially interested in the exits. Four doors opened onto the room. A stairway was in view through one of the open-arch doorways. Through the entryway, a strong older man wheeled an elderly lady into the room. He wheeled her in front of the girls, and then he stepped to the side as if waiting for the lady to tell him what to do.

"Welcome to my home, girls. You're Julie and you're Helen, right?" The girls nodded politely. "I want you to feel welcome here because this is not only my home, but it is your home now. In time you will get used to it. I'll show you around a bit. Come with me." Her helper pushed her chair and the lady gave the girls a tour of her home. The rooms were large, well appointed, and very clean. After they saw the rooms on the main floor, they went to the second floor. The lady used a special lift that took her up the stairs. The metal box that worked on pulleys fascinated the girls, taking the chair and the lady vertically to the top of the stairs. They met her on the second floor for the rest of the tour. She showed the girls her room and then their rooms. Each room had its own bathroom.

"I would like Helen to stay in the same room as I do, if you wouldn't mind." Julie was polite, but she did not intend to take no for an answer.

"I understand. However, I believe in time that Helen will want to have her own room. Right now, everything is so new to you both. It is fine for you to share this room." She invited Julie to look in the drawers. Julie saw several items of clothing. "Those are nightgowns for you, Julie. We'll bring in Helen's pajamas and tomorrow's clothing so she can dress in here. Right now, let's go to the dining room and have dinner. Then I will give you both some time together in your room."

The girls were hungry, and the food they were given tasted excellent. Julie had decided that they needed to eat. If those people really wanted to harm them, they would do so. At the moment, her sister needed to eat and so did she. She ate each food after she saw Mrs. Meister eat it, hoping it would not make her pass out. Helen was not as reserved. During dinner, Mrs. Meister introduced herself to the girls more personally, telling the girls about her family and where they lived.

"Girls, people who knew you in your hometown felt that your lives were in danger. That is why you are here. If there comes a time when that is not the case, you may return to your home. Right now, though, I ask you to give me your word that you will not run away. We live way out of town, and it is very cold in this country. I don't want either of you to hurt yourselves or one another. Julie, you would not want Helen to catch a cold or to get sick from being out in the cold, and Helen, you wouldn't want that to happen to Julie. Will you both promise me that you will not run away?"

"Why can't we see our dad? He would never hurt us."

"It seems, from what little I know about your family, that he could not protect you."

"Well, he was trying to. He was getting better," Helen offered.

"Julie, I see serious bruises on your face. They seem to be healing. Did your father protect you from those wounds?" Both girls were silent. Helen looked sadly at Julie. She could see that Mrs. Meister was right. Even that very week their mother had beaten Julie. Julie looked intently at Mrs. Meister, searching for some sign of meanness. There was none. Mrs. Meister had asked the question gently and with concern.

Julie responded resolutely, "We promise that we won't run away, for a while. If we decide to leave, we will tell you first."

Mrs. Meister smiled. "That's good! Now, let's finish eating dinner and then have dessert!" The girls could not believe their eyes when they tasted the well-prepared beef dinner and the wonderful cake and ice cream they were served.

"Mrs. Meister, will you promise not to drug our food? That's what happened to us in Libby before we ended up on an airplane." Julie was blunt, but she wanted Mrs. Meister to know that she was aware that she and her sister had been taken against their will and without their knowledge.

"I promise! If I change my mind, I will tell you first!" Mrs. Meister winked. The girls smiled. They had no control, and Mrs. Meister seemed nice. She entertained the girls with stories of her youth, the area, her family, and her friends. By the time the girls went to their room for the night, they did not intend to run away. Mrs. Meister accompanied them upstairs again through her special lift. She showed them the room in more detail—how to use the large tub and shower, where the special robes were for wearing after their baths— and before she left the room she made sure that Helen had clothing for the night and the next day.

"I can't tell you how happy I am that you both are here with me. I love children. Always have. You are welcome here as long as you want to stay. If you feel like you would want to assist me from time to time, I would be grateful for your help. The gentleman who works for me me is nice, but he is not as friendly or as delightful a companion as you girls will be. I would love to take you with me places—to church, shopping—and if you would join me, I know that I would get out more often."

Both girls agreed that they would love to help her. Both girls liked her, and additionally, Julie thought that going with her shopping and to church would help them get to know the area to find a way to go home.

"We rise at six thirty to prepare for breakfast, and your tutors arrive at eight sharp! School is important, you know. Good night, girls. God bless you for coming into my life. Oh, here's the lever to lock the door." To Julie, that sounded like permission to lock themselves in the room, and she felt safer because of it.

Taking care of their hunger and being in a warm, lovely room with their own bathroom had lifted the girls' spirits. The girls investigated their surroundings and found the room to be the most wonderful place they had ever seen. Julie began filling the bath. She wondered if the well had enough water to fill such a large tub. To the girls, the tub was as big as a small swimming pool. They took off their clothing and slipped into the water, feeling its warmth, inhaling the steam, and enjoying some bubbles Julie had discovered in the form of small glass-like balls in a beautiful dish on the tub's ledge. The girls washed their hair, played in the water, added more hot water, and rinsed off with a handheld showerhead on a short hose. Julie made sure to rinse Helen's hair and to get all the soap off her body. After Helen climbed out, Julie rinsed herself well, and then she rinsed out the tub. Both girls dressed in the nightgowns Mrs. Meister had left for them, and they put on the warm flannel robes. They climbed up on the large, extra-wide bed.

"What would we be doing right now if we were home?" Julie asked Helen.

"We'd still be doing our chores. You'd be cleaning pens, and I'd be cleaning the separator."

"You know, before that, when we got home from school, we'd get dinner started. You'd quietly set the table." Julie emphasized quietly. "We'd do some laundry or clean a room."

"Yes, Julie, and we would have to be very quiet so we didn't wake Mother."

"Grandma would help me get dinner ready, and then you and I would do most of the chores. Then we'd eat, then we'd finish chores, and *then* we'd do homework. That's not quite what we are doing today, is it? Add to that, we had to fear Mother getting angry and hurting us for some unknown reason. She'd start talking to herself and answering herself, then *wham!*"

"Who is the someone who said we needed help? Grandma?" Helen had mixed feelings about "being saved" from her family. So did Julie.

"It could have been Grandma or Eric. What if Darlene was the one? Or even Dad?" Not many people knew of their situation. They hadn't told anyone. Wait. Julie had told Doc. Whoever it was, the person had intended no harm. "Helen, I think we should give this place a chance. When we go to sleep tonight, the door will be locked and we will be safe from Mother for the first time ever. We don't have to leave the room to go to the bathroom. We get breakfast made for us. No cooking, no milking, no feeding animals. We are on a vacation! Mrs. Meister is a nice lady. Let's try to be happy here. If things change, they change. We are just going to have to see what happens next and stick together. Okay?" Julie had figured out the good side of the situation.

"I miss Grandma and Dad." Helen was close to tears.

"One thing is for sure. They are able to take care of themselves. They will be okay whether we are with them or not. Right? I miss them, too."

"I'm okay if you're okay. I love you," Helen said softly. The two girls embraced and climbed under the covers between the softest sheets they had ever felt.

Just before they fell asleep, Helen whispered, "What if they do something bad to us in the night?"

The same thoughts had crossed Julie's mind as well. Julie put her arm around Helen. "If anyone tries to harm us, we will stick together and fight them like two angry bears!" Julie tickled Helen and growled like a silly bear. They both laughed and settled into the comfortable bed. After Helen fell asleep, Julie let herself surrender to the soft pillow for a deep sleep, filled with dreams both good and bad.

Mrs. Meister had her own concerns. She was happy to get two girls that were self- sufficient. Julie could take care of Helen. Her role was not only to protect them and keep them hidden from their abuser, but also to teach them about abuse as soon as she could. The next day, after a couple of hours of tutoring, she planned to take them shopping and to her spa for hair trims and other grooming assists. By the next evening, she had to begin the abuse lessons.

They might try to run away. The sooner they understood how abuse controls them and affects them, even at a distance from the pain, the sooner they could settle in with her without confusion. She had known abuse first hand; she was committed to making those girls' lives better.

65

DOC AND SECOND THOUGHTS

When Doc learned that Julie's mother was in a coma and that Dewey's son Eric was missing, he called the church. Father O'Malley failed to answer after several rings. Doc assumed that the elderly priest had been napping. Doc was ready to drive to the parish house if he didn't answer. Doc was determined to find the visiting priest who investigated Julie's abusive situation and have her and her sister returned to the family. There would be no need for those children to start over with some strange family if their mother died. There was no need for Dewey to lose his daughters and his son. Doc felt like he had kidnapped the girls himself. He'd drugged them and put them in the car, for Christ's sake! He wrote the note to get them out of school. He had to get them back if Betty didn't get well as the doctor expected. It didn't matter that Father Flynn had orchestrated it. Doc had carried out a major role in a kidnapping. That had a life sentence consequence in Deer Lodge. Dewey was a broken man. Doc had to fix it. He was the only one who could change what had happened.

Doc gave up waiting for Father O'Malley to answer the phone. He went to the church. He had to find that card with the number he had called that started the whole mess. He searched the many notices, cards, and decorations on the boards in the foyer of the church. At first he missed it. There it was, behind the edge of the border. He took the card for the second time, hoping to undo what he could and get the children back home with their dad. He went to the parish house. Father O'Malley took his time getting to the door.

Doc greeted him, asked about his health, and told him that he had just called.

"Good to know. I was unable to get to the phone before the ringing stopped. Care for a cup?"

"No, thank you, Father. I have a question for you. When you were gone last month, who was the priest who covered for you? Father Flynn, I believe?"

"Yes, Father Tim Flynn from Missoula. He's retired, but he helps out at St. Patrick's in Missoula, and he covers for us out in the parishes so we can take vacations or whatever."

"Do you have his address? I'm going to be in Missoula, and I wanted to stop in and see him. We had a talk when he was here, and I found him to be a delightful man. He did a great job on the homily here in Libby while you were gone."

"He fishes, you know."

"Oh, yes, yes. He knows some great places to catch fish."

"I'll go look it up. St. Patrick's will do it, though. Just a minute." Father took his time and finally returned with an address. "Be sure to call him first. He has all sorts of projects going with kids and the men of the parish, and then he's out a lot covering for the parish priests."

Doc had stood up as Father returned, hoping to make a speedy exit. Father loved to visit, and getting away could be tricky.

"Thank you, Father. I'm off to the café. Stop in when you can, and I'll buy you a cup of coffee. You need to get out now and then. Make it for lunch and I'll take care of that, too."

"Now don't rush off, Doc." Father walked him to the door and reluctantly let him out.

"Thanks again, Father. Take care of yourself. See you Sunday."

When Doc returned to the Blue Bear, he pitched in with the girls and helped get through the busy part of lunch. Once the crowd had diminished, he retreated to his office to make that long distance call—not to the number on the card regarding abuse, but to St. Patrick's Parish House where Father Flynn lived. When a woman answered "St. Patrick's Parish," Doc asked if Father Flynn was available. "He's been out to Drummond, covering for Father Wagner.

He'll be back for his meeting with his teen group tomorrow at five o'clock in the afternoon. He may or may not be back late tonight—can't say. If you want to make an appointment to see him, call him tomorrow morning after ten. He should be here then. He always likes to get his day organized before ten, so he'll be here for your call. What's your name?"

"Thank you, ma'am. I'll call him tomorrow." Doc wanted things settled as soon as possible. He decided that a three- or four-hour drive to Missoula was in order. He went back to the café and organized the next day with extra help as he did when he had to be away for a day. He planned to leave at 6:30 a.m. so he could meet with Father Flynn before he left his home.

66

ERIC BOWMAN

When Eric awoke, he wondered where he was. His arms were tightly wrapped at his sides. A dark, hairy bear hide surrounded his whole body. As he looked up, he saw the sky through a hole in the—teepee? Yes, he was in a teepee. The hide did not wrap him so tightly that he couldn't move, but it was warm, very warm, and he was aware that he was wearing no clothing. He worked one arm free and began unwrapping himself from the hide.

The teepee was large with a metal stove in the center, radiating heat. Eric saw his clothes on a rack near the stove. Someone had removed them and placed them on the rack. He put on his clothes and stepped out of the teepee. A Native American man and woman were cleaning fish.

"Good morning." Eric walked toward them.

"You have had a long rest after a river ride. How are you feeling?" The man cupped his hand on Eric's shoulder. "Do you remember your journey in your car down the rocks?"

"Not really. I remember my car flying off the road and water— cold water. That's about it."

"You have been sleeping for two days. You talked in your sleep about your sisters many times. I feared they were in the car with you and then lost in the river." The soft spoken elderly man handed Eric a cup of coffee. "Sugar?"

"Yes. Thank you. My sisters are missing. I was looking for them, but no, they were not with me in the car. You saved my life. That cold water could have killed me, but you wrapped me up and took me in. How can I repay you?"

"Defend our fishing rights. And stay out of the cold river when driving!" He laughed. "It scares the fish." The friendly Indian shook Eric's hand. "Call me friend."

Eric laughed with him. "How far am I from Libby, friend?"

"Not far. Maybe three miles."

"I can walk that."

"Have some food with us, and then you can easily make it to town. Please don't bring anyone back here. You may come again, but we don't want nosey people here."

"I won't bring anyone here." Eric ate the fish, bread, and an apple. He felt safe and comfortable with his new friend, and if his sisters weren't missing, he could stay there indefinitely. "Thank you for my life."

Eric walked for at least two miles before he reached Highway 37. A pickup gave him a ride to the sheriff's office. The sheriff was both relieved and grateful to see Eric. He was relieved that Eric was alive and grateful to give Dewey some good news.

67

SASKATOON

The girls were up, dressed in the clothing Mrs. Meister had given them, and they had their bed made when someone knocked on the door. A young woman told them that breakfast was ready and to come down as soon as they were dressed. The girls checked their hair one more time, and then quietly walked down the curved stairway. Mrs. Meister was already at a small table in a room off the kitchen drinking from a cup. The room was a glassed-in area with a view of snowy trees, some birdhouses, and the open fields.

"Good morning, girls."

"Good morning, Mrs. Meister."

"Please, take a seat. Julie over here and Helen over here." She wondered if Helen would separate from Julie yet. She did as directed. "How was your sleep last night?"

"It was good!" Helen was cheerful and direct. Julie smiled along with Helen and agreed that she had also slept well.

A young woman brought in breakfast on a cart from the kitchen. She placed a bowl of fresh fruit in front of Mrs. Meister, who took a portion and then passed the dish to Julie. Julie took two spoonfuls and passed it over to Helen. When the three had finished their fruit, Mrs. Meister took another dish from the cart. Bacon and toast were next. The third dish held scrambled eggs. The girls demonstrated good appetites and reasonable, though not polished, manners. They used their napkins and chewed with their mouths shut, but they tended to take a little more on their forks than they should.

Mrs. Meister would work on that, but not on that day. The girls had enough to do for their first day. Manners critiquing could wait.

"Tell me, Helen, what are you studying in school? What does your teacher have you do?"

"We are learning letters and numbers, and we listen to stories and color. Oh, we have a music class. We play a thing like a horn or sometimes we sing songs." She took a deep breath. For Helen, that was a long speech. She was doing what she thought Julie wanted—giving the situation a chance.

"What do you like the best about school?"

"I like it all. I love my teacher. Julie had her, too. She's nice."

"Julie, what are you studying in school? You're in high school, right?"

"Yes. I'm in ninth grade. I have classes in English, math, history, science, typing, music, and gym. Each class is close to an hour, and that's the whole day."

"Do you like school?"

"I love school. The one thing I don't like is being absent! Sometimes I have to stay home and work, and then I get behind. It's hard to catch up."

"What's your favorite class?"

"Music. It's choir. I love to sing."

"Julie sings all by herself in concerts. She's good. We saw her do it," Helen said proudly.

"My, you must have a talent for music. Do you play an instrument?"

"We have a piano. I haven't had lessons, but I like to play it anyway, just by hearing the notes."

"Would you like to take piano lessons?"

"Yes, I would love to. My dad let me take three lessons, but then said I could learn on my own. Having only three lessons doesn't do much." Julie looked down at her spoon.

"Well, girls, I told you that your tutors are coming at eight. Both of the tutors are very good. One has been an elementary teacher for several years. Her name is Miss Jane. Helen, you will love her. Julie, your tutor is Mrs. Pierson. Her main field is humanities—English and social studies. She is also a whiz at algebra and geometry. When you get to calculus, we will find additional help. When you are finished eating, go brush your teeth and get ready to do your best. Today will be a short learning day because at ten we will be going to the city for some shopping!"

Julie thought about her plan. *Get along, make this work, and if it doesn't, cooperating will get us the information we need to find our way home.* Both girls excused themselves and thanked Mrs. Meister for breakfast. They carried their dishes to the kitchen. Mrs. Meister smiled and thanked them. She did not expect them to carry their dishes and even try to wash them. She was pleased to see that they were actively willing to help her. They went upstairs and huddled together in Julie's room behind the closed, locked door.

"You did great, Helen, really great! I didn't know you could carry on a conversation like that!"

"You said to make it work, and I'm going to do my best. I loved breakfast! What was the yellow stuff that tasted so sweet?"

"I think it was pineapple, but I'm not sure. I've never had it before. Now let's do our best with the tutors so they tell Mrs. Meister that we paid attention and that we have some brains!" Both girls brushed their teeth, washed their hands, combed their hair, and then went back downstairs. They sat together for a few minutes until their tutors came.

"I wonder what Mother and Dad are doing? I don't think Mother will miss us, but I think Dad might. I know Grandma misses us." Helen looked at her hands, twisting her fingers together.

"We can't think about that. We need to do our best to get along and learn all we can. I will take care of you. I will always take care of you. Crying will just make your eyes red and won't change a thing. Remember how tough Darlene was? Well, we have to be tough and nice at the same time. Come here." Julie put Helen on her lap and hugged her. "Let's squeeze each other until it hurts!" Helen laughed. They hugged and took one last look in the mirror. "Let's show Mrs. Meister what we can do!" Julie took Helen's hand, and they each went to work with their tutors.

Each tutor worked for two hours with her student. When they had completed their introductory lessons and initial testing, the tutors assured Mrs. Meister that the girls were cooperative and intelligent. They both looked forward to returning the next day for full four-hour sessions. Mrs. Meister had the girls get their coats and hats on and help her out the door to the car. Her assistant loaded her wheelchair after she climbed carefully into the car with Julie's assistance. Julie thought about how easy it would be to leave Mrs. Meister since she was unable to walk. Her legs were very thin, and she was light to hold as Julie helped her into the car. Julie was not proud of herself for that thought, but she was a survivor, and she would not stay there if either her sister or she were in danger.

The girls had never been on a shopping trip like this one with Mrs. Meister. She started with lingerie. Julie was fitted for bras. "You have to have a bra that fits right. The rest of your clothes look better with a good foundation." Mrs. Meister bought several bras in three colors. She bought silk slips and a warmer cotton slip for Julie and several slips for Helen. Tights were new to the girls, who had only worn brown cotton stockings with garter belts. The girls loved the tights. Panties, of course, and some thermal underwear completed that part of their wardrobes. From there, the girls tried on sweaters, skirts, dresses, coats, and even trousers. Mrs. Meister selected several items for each of them and said she would surprise them at home with what she bought.

The girls were amazed. They had not really experienced buying new clothing. Darlene's wedding dress had been new, and the fabric for their dresses had been new, but Grandma had made them. They had their dreams of ordering from catalogs, but they never ordered anything. The shopping trip was exciting. The next part of the trip, the visit to the spa, was even more beyond the girls' experience. Mrs. Meister joined the girls in a hot tub to soak for fifteen minutes. After that experience, with bubbles popping in the hot water, both girls had manicures and pedicures. They had their hair cut and styled. And they had massages. Following the spa experience, Mrs. Meister had a special turkey dinner for the girls at home. She filled them with mashed potatoes and carrots, turkey and salad, and then topped it all off with apple pie. Those were foods they were familiar with. She wanted them to feel at home.

After dinner she began her teaching process with them. She eased into the topic and encouraged Julie to explain to her what her life was like with her mother. At first Julie was reluctant. Mrs. Meister assuaged her concerns by telling her that no one was with them and that she would not tell anyone anything that the girls did not want told. She also said that telling about the harms Julie had experienced would help heal the wounds that were stored in her heart. Mrs. Meister told the girls that she had also been abused as a child. She was beaten and burned for what seemed like no valid reason. "I've been there, girls, and I understand much of what you have experienced because it happened to me."

Julie began by telling Mrs. Meister that she did not understand what made her mother hate her so much that she would want to kill her. She described the attacks her mother made for no apparent reason. As she described her mother's behavior of isolating herself, secretly eating sweets, striking her with whatever was at hand, biting the girls, and carrying on conversations with the air around her, Mrs. Meister began to understand.

"I believe that your mother is ill. She doesn't hate you—either of you. She is mentally ill and may be unable to keep from doing evil things. That doesn't lessen the pain, but it does mean that it is not your fault in any way that you are the object of beatings. You need to tell yourself that—both of you—many times a day. It is not my fault." Both girls repeated the sentence with her at her request. "I saw the scars on your back when we were at the spa, Julie. You did not deserve any of those scars. There are ways to discipline children, and beating them with belts or whips is not a good thing to do. Your mother being mentally ill does not make her innocent of the crimes she has perpetrated against you both. But it can help you learn to accept the fact that none of the abuse you received was your fault. You did not deserve this."

Julie told of her mother hiding and scaring them, lingering out-side their bedroom door, listening to them, and secretly watching them do chores. She told how her mother ate from the pans on the stove before dinner and then said she couldn't understand why she weighed so much since she ate so little at the table during dinner. Helen told about being afraid for Darlene and Julie, and that she knew she was going to get worse than slapping and spanking soon. Both children were burned and bitten to teach them lessons.

Mrs. Meister asked what their father did to prevent the abuse. Both girls admitted that he wasn't home very much. He didn't see their mother actually abuse them, but he must have seen the scars and the marks.

"It is hard to accept, but your father is part of the problem. As your father, it is his job to keep you safe. He should have been home more and known what was going on. He made the choice to stay away, and his daughters faced fear every day and, at times, horrible pain. He did not act on your behalf, so he is guilty of neglecting you and not defending you. He did not make the abuse stop. Maybe he was unhappy. Maybe he didn't know how to stop it. Your scars tell me, Julie, that he could have learned about your beatings if he took the time to be with you girls.

"As you face learning to live with what has happened to you, and as you get over feeling fear and the unjust feeling of deserving to be hit, you will have to forgive both parents for what they have done and what they have not done. You'll have to let go of your anger, your feelings of not being loved, and forgive them."

Both girls were crying. Mrs. Meister was close to tears. "You also do not owe them anything. You have a chance right here and now to take your lives in a different direction. Either your mother or your father could walk up to the door and say, 'You need to come home. We are your parents and we want you home.' You can say yes and go with them. Or you can say I won't be beaten anymore. I won't do all the chores and cooking. I won't miss out on my education. I want to make a success of my life and I can do that here."

Both girls looked at her as though her words were frightening. "But they're our parents. We have to go with them." Julie looked confused.

"Being a parent does not give a person the right to threaten to kill their children. It does not give them the right to make their children live in fear. Being a person—and both of you are individual persons—does give you the right to a life without fear and abuse. Unlike many abused children, you have a chance to change your abusive situation. Julie, a week ago when your mother beat you, did you want to just roll up in a ball and die? Being beaten makes a person feel unloved and alone. It takes away your dignity. You had to lie to others so they wouldn't know your family secret, didn't you? Think about how you felt then. And now, think about never having to feel that way again. Think about Helen never having to go through what you have gone through."

Mrs. Meister had hit home on some of her points. She had to let up now. The girls needed time to think about what she had said. They also needed to set aside their grief of losing their parents if they were to get any sleep.

"Enough! If you want to talk to me, just let me know. Right now, let's talk about our day." She diverted their attention to the spa and to the shopping trip. They visited a bit. Helen loved her clear nail polish. Both girls loved their hairstyles. Mrs. Meister brought out the clothing she had purchased for them, and they were eased out of their sorrow and into a happier state of mind. She wanted them to stay with her. The girls were sweet, kind, gentle, and damaged. She saw herself in Julie, and she never wanted Helen to experience what either she or Julie had felt. She was committed to keeping them with her, away from their abusive family, and to helping them rise above their abusive experiences.

Both girls were astonished at the gifts of clothing. They held up items, smelled them, and felt the softness of sweaters and the smoothness of silk. They could not believe their good fortune in having such a beautiful place to live, delicious foods to eat, and private tutors they liked, and now they had new clothing unlike anything they had ever worn before.

68

DOC SEEKS FATHER FLYNN

Doc was up early and out of town before 6:30 a.m. to reach Missoula by 10:00 a.m. He was convinced that the priest would get the girls back once the father knew that the girls would more than likely never have to fear their abusive mother anymore. The news of Betty Bowman's near-fatal accident was all over town, passed from person to person. In fact, it was all over the country. Father Flynn was well aware of Betty's gunshot wound. Accidental death was predicted as part of the whisper. Attempted suicide was also part of the news. Dewey's wound compounded the gossip, adding the spice that maybe he shot her and she shot back in self-defense. However convoluted the story had become, everyone knew that Betty's condition was critical and Dewey was injured. Doc did not think that Father Flynn could know yet, and he wanted to tell him without sharing the details of his own involvement with the telephone operator who could listen in on any call she chose.

As Doc pulled up to the parish house, a flick of a curtain indicated that someone had seen him approach. Father Flynn had given instructions to the parish housekeeper to tell the gentleman who was coming up the walk that he was not available. No details. Just unavailable.

Doc did not take the information well. "When do you think he will be available?" he asked the housekeeper.

"I really can't say, sir. I have no other information. He sometimes gets delayed when he covers for the parishes. He might be unavailable for the day or even several days. Please write your name here and your phone number, and I will have him call you."

Doc took the pencil and wrote his name and number. "I'm from out of town, so I hope to see him before I leave for home. I'll check back after lunch." Doc was upset. He should have called from home, but he didn't want to be told to stay home or that there was nothing to be done on the phone. He felt that he could convince the priest to get the children if he talked to him in person.

Father Flynn received the name and number from the house-keeper and thanked her for sending the man on his way. Father Flynn was one of the first people aware of Mrs. Bowman's serious injuries. He knew when she was brought to the hospital. He knew that Doc was going to ask him to return the children to their father. Part of the process of taking the children from abusive situations was to educate the children about abuse so they could learn to live a life free from abuse. He also had confidence in the woman who had the children. But she had to have time to be with them before he would consider taking the children back to their family. The family had a lesson to learn also. Children are sacred gifts to a family, not slaves to work for them or punching bags to relieve their anger. The physical abuse was obvious, and the neglect was prevalent. Someone allowed it for years. Someone neglected his children by his absence and his lack of action. Time without his children teaches a father more effec-tively than rewarding him too quickly.

Father called a fellow priest in Outlook, Montana. "I need to get away for a few days. Could you handle a guest? And would you like to take Sunday off?" Father packed up quickly and headed for the Highline, the northern highway and rail line across Montana near the Canadian border. This trip would bring him within a few miles of North Dakota and a long way from Missoula. He thought that would be far enough away to keep Doc off his trail and give Mrs. Meister time with the girls. He instructed his housekeeper to tell any-one looking for him that he had been called away to a parish near Billings. In the history of white lies, he thought he could justify his description of his destination. Billings was at least east of Missoula and near Outlook by a few hundred miles, give or take a few.

The housekeeper turned Doc away after lunch and suggested he come back about 3:00 p.m. That would give Father Flynn a huge lead if, indeed, Doc decided to follow him. At 3:00 p.m. Doc learned that Father Flynn had agreed to help a parish near Billings and would be back in about a week. He didn't have a phone number, but he might call in to check for messages in a few days. "He was here when I came this morning, wasn't he?"

"Sir, I just clean up the place. He did not appear to be here. I knocked at his door. I have your name and number, and I'll give it to him when he checks in for messages. That's the best I can do, sir." Doc left behind some gravel when he spun out of the parking area. He had no choice but to wait for the priest to return from Billings. He could drive there, but the Billings area could mean a quarter of the state and lots of towns. He resigned himself to the wait and drove back to Libby and the Blue Bear. He had a business to run.

Later in the week Doc learned that Betty's vital signs were improving, but she was still in a coma. He worried about Dewey and hoped when he finally saw Father Flynn he could help alleviate Dewey's sadness about Betty's injuries by helping to return his daughters. The whole town was curious about and supportive of Dewey, and many casseroles, pies, and other dishes appeared on his porch each day. Most did not know Betty very well, but everyone helped with the search for the girls. People wanted to show their support for the family that had a very sick mother, two lost girls and a missing son.

69

DEWEY AND ERIC

Dewey was devastated when he learned that Eric had wrecked his car in the Kootenai River. The river was deep and swift, full of rock formations that were seldom visible from the surface. When the sheriff's car pulled up at the store, Dewey feared bad news was coming—either about the girls or Eric. He couldn't get out the door fast enough when he saw Eric getting out of the car.

Tears came freely as he held Eric close. "Son! You're all right!"

"I'm lucky, Dad. Just lucky." Eric shook hands with Sheriff Burns. "Thank you for the ride, Sheriff."

"Dewey, I've nothing new on the girls. We know where they aren't—and that's nowhere in or around town. We think the girls might have run away, but we just don't know for sure. We'll keep looking 'til we find them." Sheriff Burns reached out to Dewey.

Dewey shook the sheriff's hand. "Thanks for bringing my son to me." Dewey couldn't stop the tears. Eric took him into the store, and the sheriff drove away.

Eric told Dewey about his attempt to find the girls through the person who had been breaking into his house over the past month. Dewey followed with an update on Betty—still in a coma, but moved to a care facility. Finding the girls was their biggest challenge and goal, and they decided that Eric should stay for a few days with Dewey and Julia.

"We'll bar the doors and take turns guarding the place at night," Dewey explained. "If someone decides to find you and throw you in the river again, they'll have to get by both of us—and a couple of rifles." Dewey and Eric locked up the store for the day. They had adequate topics to discuss and Dewey decided that business could take a backseat to his family. Dewey had a chance to protect Eric. He could not take a chance on losing any more family members, and he vowed to do all he was capable of doing to keep Eric safe. Eric planned to return to work at the Zonolite Mining Company even though he was sure that the man who ran him off the road and into the Kootenai River had a direct connection to the mining operation. He planned to keep out of trouble while he learned all he could about the company, the products, and the many people who were connected to the company. Time—all in good time.

70

SASKATOON VISITORS

J ulie and Helen had agreed to change their names to protect their hiding place in case anyone noticed two new girls with the same names as the missing girls from Montana. Julie became "Angela" and Helen became "June." Using their middle names made it easier for the girls to remember.

A full week had passed. Tutoring was fun for the girls. The tutors engaged the girls in their studies, creating an enjoyable learning experience. Both girls were also involved in piano lessons. With two pianos in the house, they could practice anytime they wanted, and even at the same time. Here were two girls who both knew hard work, very few amenities, almost no loving adult attention, and serious abuse. They now experienced luxurious surroundings, stylish clothing, attention from a doting adult who only wanted the best for them, and a total absence of violence in their lives. They were making excellent progress in their studies, moving at their individual rates, and covering a wider array of topics and assignments, more than a public school could provide an individual student. Julie had not milked one cow, cleaned one chicken coop, or scraped out one barnyard stall. Helen had not hidden from her mother or anyone since she'd arrived at their new home. Mrs. Meister's evening lessons about abuse were beginning to become ingrained in the girls. As painful as it was for them to accept, they began to realize that their father was also responsible for their abuse. They loved him, but he did not protect them. He had not spent time with them. Even when he used to take Darlene and Julie with him on his business routes to service jukeboxes, he drove them to Sandpoint and left them with their grandmother. When his route was completed, he would pick them up and go home. There were a few stops along the way, but generally, there was very little quality time between father and daughters.

Two weeks had passed when Mrs. Meister received a call from Montana. It took two minutes for the operator to connect Father Flynn to her phone. "Mrs. Meister. This is Father Flynn. I'm checking on the girls and you. How are you doing with the girls?"

"They are a blessing to me, Father. I hope you have only called to check on them and not to move them anywhere."

"The day they left Libby, there was an accident. Their mother received a very serious gunshot wound. Self-inflicted. It was an accident, but still. She has been in a coma since the accident."

"Do you want me to tell them that?"

"No. Not yet. There is the distinct possibility that she may pass away. She's critical, but she has improved minimally. Her recovery is going to take a long time. The abuser is out of the home. I want to wait and see how this works out. In the meantime, it is a possibility that they may be returned home."

"Father, you know that serious abuse like Julie experienced was not just her mother's doing. Her father let it happen for years. He's guilty of neglect. Serious neglect. And the amount of work she did was more than an adult man would do. My God, Father. You can't put them back. He let it happen for years. There's the older sister. Look at what her life was like. He had all of her life to turn things around. He can't just have it all back and continue the life he offered these girls. They are thriving here."

"You've bonded with them, I see. Of course, that's what I wanted."

"Father, you have to do the right thing by these girls. Their lives have never been better than here with me. Don't take them away. Please. I don't think I could bear it." Father was silent for a moment.

"I have a local man wanting me to get the girls home. He sees the father broken up, and he feels like he is responsible. He might threaten to expose our whole operation."

"Can he do that?"

"Well, he could certainly make a lot of trouble. I'd have to retire to some exotic place like Deer Lodge State Prison, taking a bunch of nice people down with me. Not my choice. I prefer an exotic place like Missoula without daily restrictions for any of us. I have an idea. You won't like it, but I think it will work. In two weeks, you'll have had the girls for one month. I'm going to talk to the girls' father. I'm going to tell him that his daughters are safe and why they were taken. I'm going to arrange a meeting with the father and the girls. Then, I'm going to separate them and let the girls think about where they want to be: with their father or with you. That gives you two more weeks to work your magic and continue to educate the girls so they don't end up back in an abusive situation again. Of course, the mother may pass away, and we'll have that to deal with as well. It will also give you time to brace yourself for a choice you might not like."

She was silent.

"Are you still there?"

"Yes," she said. "I'm here. I'm thinking."

"This should keep us from losing the program. Kids don't always know what they want, but either way, they will not have their lives taken from them. I'm going to have him see them at your place. He may feel like you can do better by them and want them to stay with you. But he may want to take them right then. It's a risk. I expect the man who helped me take the girls will want to go to the sheriff soon and confess his part in the operation. If he does, we lose the program, and we face the legal consequences that go with kidnapping."

"I love them. They have won me over. The last thing I want to do is lose them. But it looks like you have thought about this and have made up your mind. Am I right?"

"You can count on a call from me to let you know for sure when I'll be bringing Dewey to see his daughters. Don't tell the girls until I contact you. Who knows what might happen between now and the end of two more weeks. When I talk to him, he may not mind them staying as things stand. I doubt that, but it's possible. Signing off."

"Good bye, Father." Mrs. Meister had to make sure that the next two weeks were the best the girls ever had. If they stayed, she would love it. If they decided to leave, she would want to see them again, and she wanted to be sure that they did not forget her. If their father took them, she had to keep a door open with him so she could see the girls again.

Father Flynn made a call to Doc. He called the Blue Bear, and a girl answered. He asked her to take a message for Doc. "Write this down and be sure he gets it. Promise? Here goes. 'I know you are concerned, and I am in the process of taking care of it.' Got that? Is he at the café?"

"Yes. He's in the back room."

"Take him the message right now. I'll hold. He might want to talk with me." The girl took the message to Doc. He rushed out to the phone.

"This is Doc."

"Good. Sorry I missed you. I'm taking care of this. It'll take some time, so don't blow it. In a couple of weeks it will be over. Until then, keep yourself protected and stay out of it. No side trips to Dewey."

"Thanks. I understand." Doc hung up the phone and shook his head in relief. He muttered, "Thank God," and he went back to his office. Doc looked at the phone number in front of him. Moments before that call, he had planned to call Dewey and tell him he was going to try to get the girls back. He had not been sure how to word his conversation. He felt better after Father's call. He could wait. He certainly couldn't find the girls on his own. Waiting was the right thing to do.

Dewey was waiting, too. Eric remained on the farm after his shifts at Zonolite, and he cared for the animals while Dewey worked at the store. Dewey visited Betty before he opened the store and at the end of the workday. Most evenings he took Julia with him to visit Betty again, waiting for the moment when she would come out of the coma. The sheriff knew his schedule and talked to him a few times a week to update him on nothing, because there was no new information to tell. The sheriff also sent patrol cars to monitor Eric several times a day. Eric saw Dewey daily after work, and the two of them took turns sleeping and watching for any signs of trouble.

One day an old priest walked into Betty's room at the convalescent home while Dewey was there. He offered to pray for Betty.

"I'm Father Tim Flynn, helping out Father O'Malley for a few days. I've heard your story from many concerned parishioners, and I would like to pray with you for the return of your girls, and, of course, for Betty's health to return." Father sat down by Dewey and patted his shoulder gently and kindly.

"Thank you, Father. I guess I can use every prayer I can get these days. I'm not Catholic, you know. But maybe you are the one with just the prayer this family needs." Dewey knelt by Betty's bed. Father Flynn knelt with him and prayed for each member of Dewey's family.

When the prayer was done, both men sat down on chairs again.

"How is it you seem to know my whole family, Father?"

"This whole community is praying for your family, talking about all that's happened these last few weeks. I only know a little, but I know enough to recognize a man who could use an extra prayer." Father explained gently. "I guess I can say that everyone seems to know your business these days. There's very little privacy in a small town."

"I have to say that people have been real caring, Father. This whole thing, losing my girls especially, is hard to take." Dewey choked up and sobbed.

"I've heard that they might have run away. Why would they do that, Dewey?"

"My wife's a sick woman. I should have spent more time at home taking care of my girls, but I spent my time on the business. I found out she was beating them." Dewey paused. "It's my fault if Julie ran away. I worked her too hard. She was afraid Betty'd hurt Helen, and she couldn't let that happen. If I ever get 'em back again, no one'll ever hit 'em again. Never!"

Father Flynn handed Dewey a cup of water. "I would like to help you, Dewey."

71

FACING THE FUTURE

A month of tutoring, piano lessons, well-balanced meals, and impeccable grooming had made a major difference in the two girls' lives. Voice lessons were added to the schedule, and Mrs. Meister enjoyed hearing both girls sing. Socially, Mrs. Meister took the girls to concerts, plays, and social gatherings where they met other children their ages. The spa experience became a weekly engagement. The girls had also taken on more responsibility for Mrs. Meister's exercise routine. They sat on the floor with her and helped her do the stretches she was supposed to do to strengthen her legs. She had given up ever being able to walk because the doctors had given up. Julie sat behind her and supported her back while Helen helped her one leg at a time. The three spent one hour each morning and over an hour each evening working on Mrs. Meister's legs. The girls walked her around the house with braces on her legs. Julie asked at the spa where people go to get help learning to walk. She learned the phrase "physical therapy" and talked Mrs. Meister into trying a therapist she thought would let the girls help with the process. She agreed, and a new plan of assistance was soon in place. All three of them were feeling that it was working and that her legs were gaining strength. After two weeks she could get herself into the car with minimal assistance.

The girls had talked out their feelings of abuse more openly during the past few weeks. They shared their experiences and fears, and they made the commitment to Mrs. Meister that they would never allow themselves to be abused or neglected again. She could do no more to get them ready for their father's visit but love them, hope for the best, and keep the dialogue going regarding abuse and how it destroys confidence and common sense. She spent time individually with the girls, helping them understand how important each girl was to the other one in helping them stay strong and not become abused again.

Mrs. Meister shared her personal story of becoming wheelchair bound. Her former husband had been drinking heavily one evening, much like any other evening. That night he insisted that Mrs. Meister accompany him to a bar for additional drinks. She had already been in bed for several hours when he came to her with his plan to party all night. She didn't want to go. He grabbed her arm, dragged her out of bed, and physically pushed her and slapped her. He threw her down the stairs. When he saw her crumpled body at the bottom of the stairs, he called for an ambulance. "He thought that I was dead. When the ambulance arrived, he told the emergency team that I had fallen down the stairs accidentally." In the hospital, she regained consciousness. It took her several months to get better. Her spine, however, was damaged badly. Her doctor did not think she would ever walk again.

"Girls, I was so afraid of my husband. He threatened to kill me if I told about his violence toward me." Helen and Julie were riveted by the story. "He had been mistreating me for years and had really trained me to do as he said no matter how badly he treated me."

Julie could not help but ask, "Where is he now?"

Mrs. Meister explained that someone, a priest named Father Flynn, had been a friend of hers when she was in college. They had kept in contact over the years through Christmas cards. "One day while I was trying to master using my wheelchair, I wrote him a letter. In my letter I told him about my husband trying to kill me. The mailman picked up the letter just as my husband was coming home. He didn't see my letter in the postman's hand, or it would have never been sent. He would have torn it up."

"Did Father Flynn help you?" Helen asked softly, with tears in her eyes.

Mrs. Meister smiled through her own tears. "Yes. Three days later he arrived at this very house. My husband answered the door. He welcomed Father Flynn and the two gentlemen that were with him; he invited them into the living room to see me. He didn't realize what was going to happen to him."

"What did happen?" Julie asked. Both girls were tense, eager for an answer.

"Well, at first Father Flynn and I visited briefly. He asked how I was and said how sorry he felt regarding my accident. Then he asked me how it happened. My husband answered him. 'My wife is pretty clumsy, you know,' Todd explained. He was well into a bottle of vodka. He said, 'She was in a hurry, running around like a nut case as usual, and fell down the stairs.' Todd laughed and shook his head as he talked. 'She won't be doing that again!' He laughed a cruel laugh. Father Flynn laughed with him briefly. The other two men just watched quietly, hands folded on their laps.

"Girls," Mrs. Meister said, "for the first time in our marriage, I saw my husband differently. Three other men were in the room, and one of them was my very good friend. Father Flynn then looked at me and said, 'Jane, you and I have been friends for over thirty years and in all that time, I don't believe you have ever lied to me. Have you?' He looked at me confidently when he finished.

"I told him, 'No, Father Tim, I have never lied to you.'" Mrs. Meister took a deep breath.

"What happened next?" Helen asked. Both Julie and Helen were focused totally on Mrs. Meister.

"Father Flynn then said to me, 'What is your version of how you came to be in that wheelchair?' My husband looked at Father and then at me. For the first time, I said clearly, for all four of them to hear, that my drunk husband had beat me and thought he had killed me when he threw me down the stairs."

Julie burst out, "I am so glad that you told the truth! But what did your husband do then?"

"He called me a liar and laughed. The two men with Father Flynn were Canadian police officers dressed in ordinary clothes. They took my husband into custody and the law ran its course. He is in prison."

Helen, overcome with the tenseness of the scene, rushed to Mrs. Meister and put her arms around her.

"Girls, we have talked so many times about how abuse can make us afraid to stand up for ourselves and do the right thing for our own lives. As you know, I did just as you did. I protected the person who controlled me and beat me—who almost killed me. You must be strong as you let go of this horrible nightmare that you have lived. You deserve to be free, to be treated as a person of value, not as a whipping post."

When Father Flynn knocked on the door, Mrs. Meister had her cook's helper greet him and bring him into the room alone. She called to the girls. When they came into the room, at first they did not recognize the priest. He said hello to the girls and shook their hands.

"Girls, we met in Libby over a month ago. I drove the two of you to an airplane. You were probably too excited about the big car and the food from Doc to notice me."

"The food was drugged." Julie backed up a step. "You drugged us."

"No, I didn't do that. But I know who did, and I was part of the plan to bring you to Mrs. Meister. Please sit down so I can tell you all about what I did and why I did it." Father Flynn explained how helpless children feel when they are being abused. He noted that some people ignore abuse because they don't know what to do, or they don't want to get involved for whatever reason. "I had you girls taken when your grandmother, Julia, told me that she feared your mother would kill you. Were you also afraid your mother would kill you?"

"Grandma had you take us away?"

"No. I asked her if she thought she could keep you safe from your mother. She said she could not. I saw the gun cabinet in your home. I asked her if she could stop your mother if she decided to use a gun. She said she couldn't. I asked her if she felt in danger herself. She admitted that she was afraid of your mother. But she did not know of this program to protect children. She did not send you away."

"Mother threatened to kill me. If I told anyone that she hurt me, she said she would kill Helen." Julie was showing that she had learned her lessons well. She spoke clearly about her abuse mostly because of Mrs. Meister's lessons.

"How did your father help protect you?" Father watched the girls. They looked at each other.

"He didn't help much until a few weeks before we left. He didn't seem to know mother was abusing us. He worked a lot and wasn't home when she did it."

Helen whispered to Julie. "Remember when Mama beat you last time?"

"Once he saw me right after a beating and took mother outside to the barn. I don't know what was said, but when they came back in, Mother said that she was sorry and that she wouldn't hit me again."

"Did you believe her?"

"No."

"I have some disturbing news to tell you about your mother. The sheriff came to your folk's house to talk to your parents. He wanted to get information that might help him find you girls. He needed some clothing with your scent on it so dogs could track you. He asked your mother questions, and she became real nervous. He asked if she ever used force or hit you girls. Well, she panicked, I guess, and she took a gun out of the gun cabinet. The sheriff tried to defend himself by running at her. She fell on top of the gun. She shot herself accidentally in the stomach. They took her to the hospital. She is in a nursing home in a coma, recovering from her wound."

"Mother's in a coma?" Julie said softly. Helen looked horrified, then cried. Julie held her and cried with her. Julie didn't think that her mother would use a gun to hurt another person, except, maybe, her. Julie had imagined her mother shooting her, hanging her, running over her with the tractor, stabbing her, and smothering her with a pillow. She had a similar dream a week ago that her mother found her and killed her.

"We were both afraid of her, but we loved her."

"Your dad has been worried about you, as you can imagine. One day you're there, and then you both disappear. The family had a door-to-door search trying to find you. Would you like to see your dad again?" Both girls said they wanted to see their dad. "If I brought him to this house, would you want to see him?" The girls became excited.

"Is he here? Did you bring him?"

"I'll go see if I can find him." Father Flynn went to the car and brought Dewey into the house. When the girls saw him, and he saw them, they came together lovingly, happily with tears flowing. Dewey broke down sobbing.

"I was afraid that I'd never see you two again. My God! I've hurt you so much. I didn't protect you. I left you in harm's way. I never deserved to see you again. Can you ever forgive me?" Dewey held his girls tightly, so grateful they were alive and unharmed. Father Flynn was fighting his own emotions. Mrs. Meister was also moved at their father's remorse. When the girls realized that Mrs. Meister had come into the room, they left their dad and ran to her.

"Mrs. Meister, come meet our dad! Dad, this is Mrs. Meister. She's wonderful, Dad!" Julie exclaimed as she rolled the wheelchair into the room. "She has really been kind to us. She makes us feel safe, really safe." Helen added her own affirmative comments, and she took Mrs. Meister's wheelchair and pushed her closer to her dad so he could shake her hand.

"Thank you for taking care of my children." Dewey was choked up.

"You are welcome here, Dewey. We have dinner planned and places for both of you to stay for the night. I want you to see how well your daughters are doing. You will be so proud of them."

"Thank you. I don't want to impose. We could just go now if that's possible. I want to get the girls home as soon as I can. And my son needs me."

"We have to wait, Dewey. The plane needs work, but only minor repair. It should be ready by tomorrow, late afternoon. In the meantime, you can visit with your girls and Mrs. Meister. I'll take you up on your offer, also, Jane, if I'm not too much trouble."

"We have plenty of room. I'll get some refreshments for us. Girls, why don't you show your father some of your schoolwork? Or play him one of your songs on the piano? Helen's just beginning the violin. She seems to have an aptitude for it." Mrs. Meister left the room and allowed herself to sob privately. She could see their love for him. How could they choose to stay with her, seeing their joy at his arrival?

After dinner, Father Flynn asked Dewey to talk with him privately. "Dewey, I know you were terribly upset when the girls came up missing. Based on our earlier conversation, do you understand why they were taken?"

"Yes. Things were bad. I never should have let it get so bad. I was preparing to have Betty take a mental examination at the Warm Springs Hospital. She didn't want to go, but I should have helped her long ago. She might be a good mother."

"How would you rate yourself as a father to your girls?" Dewey looked at the priest questioningly.

"Well, I didn't keep them safe, if that's what you mean. I'd rate bad on any scale."

"How about the time you spent with them? Did you take them places? Play games with them? Take them to church? What did you do with Julie when she was younger?"

"Not much. I had the machine route that took me out of town a lot. Then I set up and ran the business in town. That takes time. To tell the truth, Betty and I didn't get along after Julie was born. Betty was sick a lot. Darlene and Julie's grandmother took care of them most of the time."

"During the next twenty-four hours, as you watch your girls with Mrs. Meister, I want you to see how they act, how they play, how they talk. Before we leave tomorrow, I want you to tell me in detail what your girls are like. Based on what you are telling me, you may get to know them for the first time while you're here." Dewey thought it was an odd statement. He said he would do that.

Dinner was lively with conversation from Julie, Helen, Mrs. Meister, and Father Flynn. They all included Dewey, but he was not used to visiting at dinner. He enjoyed the interaction, yet did not know how to join in with ease. He could talk business with anyone on Main Street any day in Libby. He was uneasy within a personal setting. After dinner, the girls helped Mrs. Meister with her exercises. They explained to their dad how important the exercises were, and they showed him how each of them, working as a team, made the exercises useful and helpful for Mrs. Meister. They showed skill and confidence in the process, and Mrs. Meister shared that she just did not know what she would do without them. The comment was a compliment, yet Dewey sensed she had a message for him within her statement. He could see that she needed them, but she could hire anyone to do what they were doing. She would be fine without them.

The next day from breakfast through tutoring, Dewey watched the girls go through their routines, including their piano and vocal lessons. He watched their interactions with those around them, including him. They were vivacious, loving girls. At home, he recalled, they seldom spoke, and if they did, it was in a whisper for fear of disturbing their mother. He also noticed their clothing, their hair, and Julie seemed to have on a touch of makeup. He had never seen them look so well groomed, so neat, or so confident. Mrs. Meister had been very good to them. While Dewey observed, Father Flynn subtly coached him. Later in the afternoon, Mrs. Meister visited privately with Dewey.

"I've never been one to avoid the truth, Dewey. Hear me out before you say anything. The girls have told me everything about their abuse. When a woman treats her children like Betty treated Julie, in particular, and Helen, too, the man of the house has to know what is going on. The girls said you were seldom home, spending time on the route, then at the store. Instead of being there for them, you avoided home and neglected them by your absence." She took a deep breath.

"I did. I was wrong. My wife and I didn't get along. She started getting sick after Julie was born and never seemed to come out of it.

Look, I know you want to make sure that I take care of the girls this time. I will. I swear I will."

"What's going to be different? Tell me. What will Julie's day be like? Chores? School? Tell me."

"Well, of course she has the chores, and then she goes to school. She cooks and cleans. My mother helps out, too. She's got the garden in the spring and summer. The usual stuff farm kids do. What's wrong with that?"

"Julie said she stayed home from school to help out at times. Is that right?"

"Yes, she did. She stayed home when Helen was little and Betty wasn't well. And I've had her stay home to hunt, to cut wood, and do other chores. She's a good worker."

"Dewey, it seems like you think of her as a hired hand without the pay. You are overworking her. When she went through her schedule for me, I could see why she had to get up at four in the morning to do homework. Did you know that she wants to go to college?"

"She don't need college. It's a waste of time and money. I can help her start her own business when she's older, and she can work for herself. I've done it all my life and it worked for me."

"How is it working for you? Is your family important? Have you put them first? What can you say about your life? What is working for you?"

Dewey was silent.

"You can give your girls the best chance that they can have for success in their adult lives."

"How can I do that?"

"Leave them with me. You can see how happy they are. I will take care of them every day and every night. I don't have to leave them to go to work. I can send them to college. Dewey, I won't ask you for a cent for their care. Please. Put their interest first and let them stay with me."

Dewey stood up, looked at Mrs. Meister, and said nothing.

"I am sorry that your wife is in a coma. You must hope that she comes out of it as soon as possible, I am sure. But in the meantime, the girls can complete at least a semester of school. When Betty is better, you can think about this again. Leaving them for a few months while Betty recovers will help them get over their deeply engrained fears of living in your home. They were afraid to sleep at night. Give them this time to get over their fears and catch up their schoolwork. Julie is bright, but missing so many days in the past years has had its toll on what she has to know to graduate."

Dewey looked at Mrs. Meister. He slowly walked out of the room.

Mrs. Meister did not follow him. She rolled her chair into the kitchen to check on dinner. She and the girls worked on her exercises with great team spirit.

Father Flynn saw Dewey watching the exercises from a distance. The girls were happily involved with Mrs. Meister, interacting with her in a way children should act with their mother. They had never had a loving mother. Father left him with his own thoughts about seeing his beautiful daughters in a happy place.

About an hour later, Father told Mrs. Meister and Dewey that the plane would be ready by 6:30 p.m. Dewey told the girls to start getting themselves ready to go home. Father Flynn brought the group together into the living room. He was ready for his bold plan.

"Girls, tell me truthfully, would you rather stay here with Mrs. Meister or return to your home in Libby? Think before you say anything. Where would you rather be if you had the choice?" Julie and Helen looked at one another, then at their dad and Mrs. Meister.

"I would rather be here with Mrs. Meister." Julie spoke first. "I love you, Dad. But I can see my future here. I'm a very good student, and I can learn here every day and not miss school to chop wood or reroof the barn. I feel safe."

"But Libby is your home. Your grandmother is there, Darlene is there, and the rest of the family. That's where you belong." Dewey was surprised at Julie's clear expression of what she wanted. "I need you."

"Honestly, Dad, you don't need me. You spend your time at the store. At home I'm the housekeeper. I cook, clean, do the chores, and I'm fourteen years old. I don't have a life as a person, just a home servant with no pay. You could hire someone to do my work. You won't even notice Helen and me a week after we get home. I'm sorry if I hurt your feelings, but that really is how it is at home."

Julie addressed her next comment to Mrs. Meister. "Mrs. Meister, you have been wonderful to Helen and me. We both call you Mom when you don't hear us! We have never felt safe or loved until we came here. Thank you for everything you have done for us. You may not want us to stay, and we can understand that. If I did have a choice, I would stay here. I would want Helen to stay with me, too. She has a right to speak for herself, but I love her and have always protected her as well as I could. What do you want, Helen?"

"Dad, I love you. If I went back with you, I'd be the one who had to do all the work. You'd never be there. I want to stay with Julie if Mrs. Meister will keep us."

Father Flynn could see that Dewey was astounded. He had come there to take his daughters home, and they were telling him that they didn't want to go with him.

"We could visit sometime, maybe," Helen said.

"Dad, you could visit us. We could visit you," Julie offered.

"Daddy, would you let us stay? Would you?" Helen put her arms around his neck.

"I could make you girls come home. The law is on my side. Father, you took them from me illegally. They're mine." Julie and Helen looked at him in disbelief. He seemed to be standing up for them, but it did not feel right.

"Yes, I did. I took them to save their lives. If I had left them, Betty might have beaten them again—or worse, she might have killed one of them." Father Flynn defended his actions without guilt. "Julie has had at least six years of torture—fear of being beaten, then actually being beaten. Your daughter Darlene couldn't wait to get away from her life of fear and torture." Father was emotional and somewhat angry. "These girls have done no wrong to deserve the poor treatment they received from their mother. Now they see a better life. For their sake, for God's sake, give them a chance at a better life."

Dewey stood up and walked to the door. "Girls, if you're coming, do it now. That plane should be ready."

Helen made a slight move, and Julie moved behind her and put her arms around her. "We'll come visit, Dad. We'll see you in the summer. And we'll write."

"We'll write, and I'll draw you pictures. I love you, Dad!"

Dewey walked out the door. The girls ran after him to say their good-bye one more time. He had a glimmer of hope that they would go with him. They hugged him and kissed him. They both said they loved him, but he could see that they were not going to go with him. Their father, who had never uttered the words "I love you" to either girl, managed to say through his parting tears, "Me, too."

Dewey went from holding his daughters to Father Flynn. "They're my daughters. I don't want to lose them. But I can see that they are happy here. I need to take care of Betty now until she's strong again. I need to be there for Eric to keep him safe from God knows what. So I'll leave them here for a while. Since I know I can come visit them, and I can see that Mrs. Meister is more than just good to them—she's good *for* them—I'll let them stay for now. But eventually, they'll need to come home."

Father Flynn shook Dewey's hand. "That's okay. We'll all live with that for now. I'd appreciate it if you kept our arrangement confidential. There are a lot of kids alive right now that would have been, well, otherwise, without our help."

"I don't know that I approve of your methods. I'll keep it to myself, though. And thank you for taking care of my children—both of you. I know full well that things were wrong at my house. I have time to fix that now, and I will."

The girls watched their dad and the priest climb into the small plane and take off for Montana. They forgot to tell him to take care of their mother. Each girl knew he would help her and protect her as he had for years. He also had time to learn how to protect them when they went home. The girls hoped he would do just that because they loved him and they didn't want to live in fear again.

I Can't Breathe Sequel

H. M. Bowker's sequel, *I Can't Breathe! 2*, takes place in northwest Montana in the 1960s. Eric Bowman's undercover research of the Zonolite Mining Company leads him in two directions. One direction involves getting to know many relatives, friends, and victims of asbestos-related diseases. He learns about their stories, their hardships, and their personal issues with the mining company. The other direction takes him into the heart of the company and how it manages to maintain operations even though evidence is mounting regarding the hazards of asbestos and its many related products. The new owner, W. R. Grace Inc., could be a catalyst for positive changes—or not. Mrs. Meister's husband escapes from prison, and he negatively affects the lives of the entire Bowman family as well as Father Flynn. The shadow of corporate, physical, and sexual abuse continues to darken the miners and consumers of Zonolite ore products, the Bowman girls, and Dan Eagle. The Zonolite Mining Company, Betty, and Mrs. Clark are still involved in the story.

Readers may communicate with H. M. Bowker on the website titled icantbreathenovel.com. The author hopes to hear the personal stories from Libby residents and their families, as well as stories of abuse from readers anywhere. The website will also give more insight into characters, the setting, and the sequel. Although the novel is fictitious, a great deal of truth often comes to life through fiction.

www.ingramcontent.com/pod-product-compliance
Lightning Source LLC
Chambersburg PA
CBHW060759030726
47503CB00002B/309